WYCHWOOD

WYCHWOOD
Rose Shipley

Barrie & Jenkins
London

First published in 1989 by
Barrie & Jenkins Ltd, 289 Westbourne Grove,
London W11 2QA

This is a work of fiction.
Any resemblance to real persons, living or dead,
is purely coincidental.

British Library Cataloguing in Publication Data
Shipley, Rose, 1932–
Wychwood.
I. Title
823'.914 [F]

ISBN: 0–7126–2088–5

Printed and bound in Great Britain by
Richard Clay Ltd, Bungay, Suffolk

For my daughters,
with love

ACKNOWLEDGEMENTS

For the background details of the Boer War, I am indebted to contemporary accounts in *The Times* and also, in particular, to *To the Bitter End: A Photographic History of the Boer War 1899–1902*, Emmanoel Lee, Guild Publishing, London 1985, on p. 100 of which is quoted a letter to a Mr Raphael about the death of his son, which I have used as the model for the one on p. 356 of *Wychwood*.

Part 1

Dieppe, 1894

CHAPTER 1

'Please to smile, madame, for me? Not so the frown. And the little mademoiselle, please to keep still?' The photographer ran agitated fingers through sweat-drenched hair, dislodged his green velvet cap, swore eloquently, though fortunately in French, retrieved the offending cap and leant momentarily against the tripod for support, of a mental as well as physical kind.

The Dieppe afternoon was blisteringly hot. Sun blazed from the sea's flat surface and shimmered from the empty sands. Here, in the boxed-in privacy of the hotel garden, it was worse. Only Englishmen were mad enough to group voluntarily in the baking airlessness of early afternoon, when all civilised people were behind closed shutters, the more energetic indulging in lazy, or less lazy dalliance. There was a particularly agreeable laundry maid at the Metropole with whom he himself had spent many an afternoon siesta. He wiped his brow on the sleeve of his loose green shirt and swore again, though this time under his breath.

'Please, I beg of you, everyone be still or my picture is never finished.'

'You could have sketched us all twice over by now, Rose,' whispered Claire, 'in crayon, then in gouache.'

'And done a full-length portrait of Monsieur Grasshopper himself,' whispered Rose, straight-faced. 'His legs are lovely, no? So spindly and, how you say? *Elegant!*' Rose gave a wicked parody of Monsieur Leblanc's accent and Claire spluttered with suppressed glee.

'Sh!' warned Mrs Millard, her eyes swivelling sideways in reproof. 'And keep still! You heard what the gentleman said. Claire, stand straight and do not simper. Rose, your hat is crooked. Sara, take that rebellious look off your face at once. This is a family photograph, not an entry for the *Illustrated Police News*.'

'Yes, Mamma.'

'Charlotte, what are you doing? Stop wriggling so.'

'She wants to *go*, Mamma,' hissed Maudie out of the side of her mouth, her eyes fixed on the camera's evil eye. 'We've been standing here for half an hour.'

'That is no excuse,' replied Mrs Millard, her mouth stretched determinedly in a particularly angry-looking grin. 'Mind over matter, remember. Mind over matter.' She gave her furled silk parasol an impatient twitch, readjusted her white-gloved hands over the tortoiseshell handle and smiled sweetly ahead.

'I told you not to drink that lemonade,' whispered Maud anxiously. 'Can you wait?'

'I don't know,' wailed Charlotte, *sotto voce*, and crossed one silk-socked leg tight over the other. Her brown ringlets quivered with anxiety and her small top teeth bit hard into her lower lip.

'*Yes you do know*,' warned Mrs Millard, still managing to smile serenely at the camera. 'You will wait till we return to the hotel. And you will *stop writhing*.'

'Please, please, *mesdames*.' The photographer reappeared from under his cloth, his face damp red with perspiration.

'Like a stewed Victoria plum,' whispered Rose gleefully to Claire.

'Or one of Smelly Annie's raspberry moulds.'

'Ladies. All together, for one little moment.' His voice rose to the edge of hysteria. 'Please to *stand still!*'

For a startled moment, they obediently stood, frozen in unnatural immobility, five young girls in muslin dresses and pert straw hats, five maidens with English complexions and the freshness of innocent expectation about them, from the eldest in her cornflower blue flounces and hair newly 'up' to the fidgeting youngest in her knee socks, her pink silk sash and daisy-petal skirts.

'*Qu'elles sont gentilles*,' thought the photographer behind his exasperation. It was because they were so pretty that he had agreed to photograph them here, in the afternoon heat of the hotel garden, against a background of tea roses and geraniums. It had to be afternoon, for the light. One day, perhaps, someone would perfect a means of taking an acceptable photograph with artificial light, but until then the sun was essential if the likeness was to be recognisable. Sometimes, of course, a blur was preferable – the mayoress, for instance, was decidedly improved by a sepia haze – but these girls needed no veil. Mentally he kissed bunched fingers in appreciation and ducked back under his blanket. Yes indeed, he thought as he moved the lens a fraction to fix the group to his satisfaction, they are a veritable posy of wild flowers, fresh and sweet, with the dew of morning still upon them. But the mother – ah, she is a different bloom. Full-blown, luxurious, perfumed, *womanly* . . .

He studied her appreciatively through the eye of the camera, the bulb of rubber held ready in his hand. On a wicker chair in the centre of his group sat Rebecca Millard, full-bosomed, thick haired, a rope of pearls around her splendid neck and a serene expression on her dark-browed, fine-drawn face.

'*Mais qu'elle est formidable!*' breathed the photographer in admiration.

'Good God, man, get on with it!'

The photographer, startled, jerked the bulb in his hand and fixed for all time the expression of exasperated fury on the face of the only male in the group. Dark-haired, dark suited and correct, Mr Millard stood behind his wife, one hand on the back of her chair, his side-whiskered face mottled with heat and the constriction of a high starched collar, brows drawn together and mouth open in mid-oath.

Claire, on the other hand, was laughing, with a spontaneous naturalness which no amount of posing could have achieved. So was Rose, only in her case the laughter was concentrated in her eyes. Both girls looked outstandingly pretty, with the simplicity of unadorned youth. The third daughter, Sara, was staring with an expression of private absorption apparently at nothing in particular, while Maudie was looking anxiously at Charlotte, who wore an expression of mortification and misery which nevertheless did not detract from the sweetness of her five-year-old face.

'I said I couldn't wait,' she sobbed. 'I *said* . . . and my socks are all wet.'

'Never mind,' comforted Maudie. 'You come back to the hotel with me and Mademoiselle will find you clean ones. Then when we have had our rest, we will ask Mademoiselle to take us to see the Pierrot man and buy a little hokey-pokey ice-cream, shall we? Here.' She took a lace-edged if grubby handkerchief from her pocket and wiped charlotte's eyes. 'There. That is better. Now smile for Maudie?'

Obediently, behind her sniffing, Charlotte smiled.

'*Quelle horreur!*' cried Monsieur Leblanc, waving agitated arms and tearing his hair. '*Un accident!* The camera take the picture when I do not wish it. And now the little mademoiselle is *desolée* because my picture is ruined! No matter. I will take another. Please to gather yourselves and return to this place in half of an hour, yes?'

'No!' Mr Millard's patience, never in lavish supply, was at an end. 'We have stood here like a row of Aunt Sallys in the public garden with half the hotel peering at us through the shutters for nigh on an hour, while you bob in and out of that ridiculous curtained bird-cage of yours, for all the world like a circus clown!'

'*Clown!* What is "Clown"? I am artist, monsieur. I am *artiste photographique*. I tell you no one calls me, Yves Leblanc, "clown".'

11

'Well I do, and you are.' Mr Millard had not made his fortune by mealy-mouthed diplomacy or what he called 'fancy manners'. By his own reckoning he was a plain man, which meant, as his perceptive wife had once told him, that he felt licenced to speak his mind, lose his temper, or indulge in any such 'ill-bred' liberty whenever he chose. He chose now.

'I was told you were the best, or I'd not have hired you. Only the best is good enough for Herbert Millard. But if 'best' is you, then I'll pack my bags and get back home where a workman works for his pay or by God he's out on his ear.'

'Monsieur, you insult me! I demand satisfaction. I . . .'

'Come along, dear,' said Mrs Millard, taking her husband's arm and smiling serenely at Monsieur Leblanc. 'I am sure Monsieur Leblanc has taken an excellent photograph. You will send it to the hotel as soon as possible, monsieur, will you not? We are so grateful. But remember, monsieur, that we want your best mount and your best frame and we will, of course, recommend you highly to all our friends. And now, my dear, I think a little lemon tea is called for, in the shade. Goodbye, Monsieur Leblanc.' She gave him her sweetest smile and leant becomingly on her husband's arm, with a pressure and a warmth which instantly defeated him.

Herbert Millard had been married almost twenty years, and still could not quite believe his good fortune in having won Rebecca Stanhope for his wife. The daughter of a retired tea-broker who had made his fortune in the China trade, she had both beauty and wealth and, more important from Millard's viewpoint, she had the ability, as the only and long-awaited child of doting parents, to wheedle anything she wanted out of her elderly, widower father and, though he did not realise it, out of him. So when she wanted a tailor's assistant fifteen years older than herself for a husband, she got him – though only on the understanding that the assistant set up shop under his own name-board on the spot, with Rebecca's father's backing. It was what Herbert had dreamed of and he could not have asked for a better wife. He fulfilled his part of the bargain with alacrity, and Rebecca hers. His shop flourished and his wife was sweet, demure, obedient, loving. Moreover, she gave him five healthy daughters, though alas no sons. A pity. With the clothes they could have had from the shop, he could have dressed five sons like five toffs at cost price. But he loved his handful of daughters as he loved his wife, with indulgence and all the generosity his bank balance allowed.

That balance had been handsomely increased on her father's death and he had been able to expand and develop as he had hoped.

His own drive and determination had done the rest so that what had started as a simple tailor's shop in the Tottenham Court Road had become a large and flourishing Gentlemen's Outfitters in a respectable part of Town. Millard's of High Holborn was renowned for good quality at a good price. 'Nothing fancy, nothing cheap' was Herbert Millard's motto, but a solid profit margin on every item, from a simple hat band for a schoolboy's boater to a gentleman's Grosvenor overcoat in best quality cashmere cloth. Herbert Millard had doubled his wife's money in the first year of business and since opening his Schools department – boys' Buckingham suits, boys' Rugby suits, boys' Scarboro' and Dartmouth ditto, with Eton jackets, cricket, tennis and boating outfits, even cyclists' suits – had doubled it again, though the opening of the new branch in Regent Street had taken a hefty slice of capital and a heftier bank loan. A brief frown came and went again as he reviewed that particular gamble. But the new shop was a step up the social scale and a project dear to his heart. Besides, the firm was flourishing. Profits were good. Good enough to bring the family on a holiday to Dieppe anyway, and to do it in style: first-class from Victoria in the Dieppe express and rooms in a first-class hotel. As to the bank loan, he would pay that off soon enough, once the new shop was established.

'Lemon tea it is, dear. And afterwards, perhaps a stroll along the promenade, to hear the band?'

'Oh Papa, may we swim first?'

'Yes, please, Papa!'

'It is a lovely afternoon and I am so hot!'

'Please, please, Papa dear!'

The girls clamoured and twittered like a flock of little songbirds, except Sara who, as usual, stood a little apart. But she, too, said 'Please, Papa?'

'Oh, all right. I will order the bathing hut at the hotel. But only after your Mamma has had her lemon tea and a rest.'

'And nothing to eat or drink for you, remember,' warned Mrs Millard, brows drawn. 'Or there will be no swimming. You know the dangers of cramp.'

'But you may have ice-cream afterwards, if you are good,' smiled their father, any lingering irritation with the French photographer quite forgotten. He liked to see his daughters happy – and in their bathing costumes they made a charming sight, especially little Charlotte in that pretty pink and white striped flannel outfit Rebecca had bought her. It would be a pleasure to watch them playing in the water and here in Dieppe there was more freedom to enjoy

13

family bathing than there was at home. 'Now run along, all of you,' he said kindly, 'and find Mademoiselle.' He offered his arm with formal courtesy to his wife. 'Come, my dear. I will order tea to be sent to our room.'

Mrs Millard looked at him with a startled expression which softened to private understanding. 'Behave yourself, Herbert,' she murmured, with a straight face, but her eyes had mysteriously darkened and her voice held a timbre which put new vigour into his step.

Sara, lingering behind the others, turned her head and saw her mother smile. Then her father called out, 'Run along, Sara. Tell the others I will order the bathing hut for five o'clock.'

'Stay with Mademoiselle till then,' added her mother, 'and do not disturb us. I wish to rest.'

'I don't,' murmured her husband and Mrs Millard laughed.

'Why did she laugh?' puzzled Sara, straggling towards the hotel in the wake of her sisters. 'And why did papa say "I don't"? He always rests in the afternoon. He sits in the hotel lounge, with the other men, with the daily paper spread out in front of his face, and stays there till Mamma appears and makes him move.'

She glanced back over her shoulder for enlightenment, but her father was staring straight ahead of him now, with the 'do not disturb' expression which Sara knew meant preoccupation of a private kind, not to be broken in upon, and her mother looked as serenely untroubled as ever – and as unapproachable. Sara turned away before they should see her staring and quickened her steps.

The hotel faced the seafront, on a slight eminence, its garden sloping away to the south, parallel with the shore, but shielded from the constant procession of promenaders by a high and aromatic hedge. The path from the hotel rose garden, which had been chosen for their family portrait, led through parallel lawns, past a sun-bleached stone cupid (at which they were forbidden to look) perpetually urinating into a similarly sun-bleached urn of vaguely classical associations, and a rockery of more rock than plant; up three shallow, sandy steps to a terrace with, at the *Plage* end, metal tables and red and white striped umbrellas. In spite of the *garçon*'s constant efforts with the broom, the terrace was always dusted with a fine coating of sand. There was grit on the table tops and the sticky feel of salt on the wicker arms of the chairs. But the terrace was empty now, save for the far left-hand corner, nearest the beach.

This table was occupied by a pair of immaculate white flannel

14

legs, one crossed nonchalantly over the other, together with an open copy of yesterday's *Times* and a cloud of cigar smoke. Sara felt a quickening of excitement: it was Claire's Interesting Englishman. She slowed her steps and watched him surreptitiously as she ambled past the fountain, eyes obediently averted, and on towards the terrace.

Rose and Claire had reached the steps and as usual had their arms twined round each other's waists, heads close, and were whispering and giggling, apparently impervious equally to their surroundings and to Flannel Legs.

They look lovely, thought Sara, without envy. Like one of Alma Tadema's paintings. Rose had told her about Sir Lawrence Alma Tadema who had a house in St. John's Wood, not far from their own, but much grander, of course. His was like a palace, with verandahs and porches and a splendid garden with oleanders and a marble basin for the goldfish. He painted beautiful girls with flowers in their hair and flowing garments and sometimes no clothes at all! If Flannel Legs looks up and sees my sisters, thought Sara wistfully, he is sure to think they are as lovely as any painting. So far, however, the *Times* had not stirred though Claire and Rose were on the terrace now. I wish I was tall, with a bosom and a waist, sighed Sara. As it was, she was a flat-chested, gawky child with pale hair and anxious eyes and no inkling yet that she was to be the most beautiful of the five. Maudie has more bosom than I have, she thought, watching the fourth sister haul the fifth at a trot into the shade of the hotel hall.

Claire and Rose were loitering on the terrace, apparently adjusting Claire's hat pins, and Sara overtook them easily.

'Aren't you coming in?' she asked. 'You know Mamma said...'

'In a moment,' interrupted Claire. 'You go on ahead.' She added something Sara could not catch and Rose laughed. Feeling excluded, Sara turned and made her reluctant way into the hotel. Palms in brass pots were dotted about the parquet floor of the entrance hall, amid low tables and herds of rattan chairs with chenille-covered cushions and fringes everywhere. Illustrated journals of tattered antiquity littered the tables together with yellowing newspapers, many of which were at present held open in front of various red-nosed and perspiring versions of the Englishman abroad: some *en route* for Paris via Rouen or Pontoise; some on their way home again; some, like the Millards, merely enjoying the tranquil comforts of a fashionable watering place, but at the same time unwilling to lose touch with their interests – and their investments – at home. But intellectual concentration was hard work in the heat, especially on a stomach replete with good French food and even better wine, and through the silence could be heard the steady breathing of surreptitious sleep.

Behind the gilt and marble reception desk the hotel *concierge* also slept, upright in his chair, his black moustache rising and falling with gentle regularity over his half-open mouth. Unconsciously, Sara held her breath and began to tiptoe across the parquet.

Then she saw the footprints, small, damp prints the size of Charlotte's feet, and immediately above them, by some mischievous chance, a stern notice '*Défense d'entrer dans l'Hotel au pieds mouillés*' with, underneath, a quainter English version: 'It is forbidden to walk the sea-water into the hotel.'

A rare glee erupted inside her and she sped after her sisters to tell them. 'Maudie!' she cried, in a penetrating stage whisper that set the newspapers rustling. 'It says to walk the sea-water is forbidden – but not to walk the pee!'

Maudie stopped in her tracks and, still clutching Charlottes' hand, looked back over the somnolent hall to where a trail of damp prints marked their passage from sunlit doorway to where they stood. For a startled moment she looked at Sara with horrified eyes, then together they snorted with suppressed delight and scrambled for the stairs. 'Quick, before they see!' Sara seized Charlotte's other hand and all three scurried for the upper regions of the hotel and the safety of their own room where Mademoiselle would be waiting to chide and grumble and settle them down for their afternoon rest.

In the adjoining bedroom, Claire and Rose were supposedly resting too, though neither was in the least inclined to sleep. The room was large and dark and cool, with a solid wooden bed of regal proportions and a wardrobe large enough to live in. Both pieces were of black and venerable age, with ponderous carved grapes and assorted wooden foliage adorning every panel, and had obviously been designed to outlive many generations of hotel guests. There was a step for mounting the bed, a smothering ocean of feather quilts and a bolster of particularly unyielding rigidity. A marble-topped washstand with basin and jug was half-concealed behind a folding screen the panels of which were enlivened by layers of pasted illustrations from, apparently, the rejected journals of the hotel hall. But it was a comfortable room, smelling of *pot pourri*, and now, with the louvres closed, delightfully cool after the heat of the garden.

Claire sat at the dressing table in her white silk combinations, her stays, petticoats and dress tossed anyhow onto the bed and her new kid shoes discarded somewhere under the furniture. Overhead the fan slowly turned, shifting the warm air from one part of the room to another and gently rustling the pages of Rose's sketch pad.

Rose pushed the damp hair back from her forehead and concentrated hard on her drawing. Drawing was more than a mere ladylike accomplishment to her: it was at one and the same time a never-ending hunger and a feast; a refuge, benison, challenge and, at rare moments, triumph like none other she had known. When Rose was at her sketch pad she was drawn into another world where the small troubles and irritations of the real world played no part – she forgot everything except the beauty of shape and line, the density of colour, and the infinite variations of highlight and shade. Her only troubles were the obstinacy of pencil or paint brush, the blocking of the artist's channel from thought to paper, the terrible despair of failure.

But this afternoon her brow was unfurrowed, her dark eyes warm with private happiness. She was sketching Claire, seated at the dressing table, with her reflection looking back at her and the French sunlight slanting in through the slatted louvres to touch her bare shoulders with bars of gold. It was only an outline, in colour wash, but she would add detail and form to it later. Then Claire moved.

'Do you think he will still be there this evening?' she said dreamily, picking up a hairbrush and drawing it through her hair with long, lazy strokes. The tortoiseshell back was almost the exact colour of her hair, rich brown with tawny lights and streaks, heightened now by the sun in spite of her array of jaunty straw hats.

'Who?' said Rose, deliberately obtuse. Curled on the window seat, drawing pad on her knees, she continued to sketch without looking up.

'Who do you think, stupid! *Him* of course.'

'Oh, you mean Flannel Legs, your Interesting Englishman.' Rose concentrated in silence for a moment as she shaded the folds of drapery in the background of her picture, then said, 'No.'

'No what?' said Claire, taken aback. She looked over her shoulder at Rose and unconsciously made a perfect symmetry of line with her mirror image.

'No thank you?' suggested Rose, absent-mindedly. 'And don't move. I'm trying to draw you.'

'Not again,' Claire sighed, but only half complaining. She had suspected as much and had posed accordingly at the mirror with more than her usual studied grace. There was something satisfying about being sketched with such devotion. She knew the devotion

17

was to the art and not to herself, but it made no difference. Being drawn was so flattering, especially as Rose's pictures were good. 'But what did you mean by "no"?'

Rose laid aside her brush in exasperation. 'You said did I think he would be there. I said "No".'

'Why not?' Claire's face was at the same time indignant and anxious.

'Because I do not think about *your* Interesting Englishman at all. Remember the Rule? And *keep still*.'

Claire opened her mouth to speak, but changed her mind. The Rule was secret, solemn and sacred. Long established and of her own invention, it meant, briefly, that Claire, as eldest, had first choice in everything and to encroach on her ground was family treason. Claire was naturally attractive and self-confident: the arrival of four equally presentable sisters might have diminished that confidence in anyone less strong minded; or given rise to plain sibling jealousy. Claire had suffered neither fate. With each arrival she had merely consolidated her own position as eldest, demanding unquestioning admiration and obedience from each in turn.

The admiration was difficult to exact, especially as the girls grew older, but the obedience was simple. Claire had introduced the Rule. To reinforce it she had made each sister swear on the open Bible, and in secret, at an impressionable age. She knew that all four, even little Charlotte, regarded that oath as sacred, never to be mentioned to anyone, and certainly never to be broken. Now, Claire smiled with something of her mother's serenity and remained obediently, if impatiently, motionless until Rose executed a flamboyant signature and tossed the paper to her sister.

'There. How do you like yourself?'

Claire studied the picture for a moment before saying, with satisfaction, 'It is lovely, Rose. You are so clever.' Carefully she laid it aside before continuing, 'But I am glad you remembered the Rule. I mean to marry well and, as eldest, naturally I will marry first. Then I shall invite you all to stay and you may take your pick of my house guests. I will invite only the eligible young men, of course, and possibly a specially artistic one for you, Rose. I know Papa is "trade" but he is rich trade and with the new law about Death Duties the landed gentry will need trade to help them out. I heard Papa discussing it only the other day. Death Duties will cripple the large estates, he said. So the landed gentry will have to marry money to pay the bills. At least, I think that was the argument. So I see no reason why I should not have any husband I choose.'

'Even your Interesting Englishman?' Rose had retrieved her

18

sketch and was studying it, frowning. There was something about the composition that dissatisfied her and she was only half attending to Claire's daydreams.

'Why not, if I choose? In my place you would be just as interested, you know you would.'

'Why should I be interested, as you put it, in a boring, supercilious snob, who does nothing but sit on his white-flannelled behind all day and smoke? It is not even French tobacco, which might at least add a touch of daring, but he obviously hasn't the wit to think of that – only of how superior he is to everyone else in sight. Actually,' she hurried on as Claire spluttered a protest, 'he is probably the victim of some rare hereditary disease that will erupt with horrible virulence all over his silly face if he so much as looks at sunlight, which is why he wraps his head in newspaper all day and ... ow! stop it!'

Claire had walloped her, hard, with a cushion, and followed that up by two more feathered blows to the head before Rose was able to get a grip on the over-stuffed weapon and struggle for possession. That failing, she snatched up a pillow and went gleefully into the attack. Claire had started it, so fair was fair.

'How dare you...' panted Claire, between blows, 'You beastly ... disagreeable ... aggravating...'

'Girls!' The door opened behind them and Mademoiselle stood glaring reproof. 'Remember you are young ladies, not young *poissonières*!'

'Yes, Mademoiselle,' 'No, Mademoiselle,' chorused Claire and Rose, breathless and dishevelled, but bobbing identical curtseys.

'And remember your Mamma is sleeping. She does not wish to hear the *brouhaha*!'

'*Oui*, Mademoiselle.' The sweetness of their combined French, as usual, mollified Mademoiselle and, with a reiterated warning to, '*Taisez-vous*,' and, '*Restez tranquille*,' she left. Claire and Rose glared at each other in silence for a simmering minute, then exploded into glee, all hostility forgotten.

'But you really should not tease me,' warned Claire when she had brushed her hair smooth again and refreshed her skin with eau-de-Cologne.

'Why not?' Rose had long ago discovered that such teasing was her best weapon. If the Rule could not be broken, at least it could be compensated for and Rose had a wicked wit when she chose to use it. 'Surely you are not serious about Flannel Legs?'

'I might be – who knows? And I really do find him interesting.' Claire retrieved her petticoats from the bed and began to dress.

19

'You realise, of course,' said Rose pompously, 'that it will be no good at all unless he finds you interesting too and I suspect that we are all of us, in company with most of the human race, beneath His Loftiness's notice.'

'Why? Help me do up these horrible stays, Rose. You can see I can't manage alone. The hooks won't reach.'

'They would if you did not insist on having the things made two inches too small!' Both equally red in the face, Rose hauled at the strings while Claire manoeuvred the button hook until the last hook was fastened and the garment in place. Claire turned sideways to admire her figure in the dressing-table mirror. The new stays were really most flattering.

'Why are we "beneath his notice"?' she demanded, still studying herself in the mirror. 'I am attractive and so are you, Rose, in your way.'

'Thank you, dearest sister, for that unsolicited testimonial.'

'We are well dressed,' continued Claire, ignoring the sarcasm. 'Look how much Mamma paid for our summer outfits and from the best dressmaker in Knightsbridge. She makes gowns for the aristocracy. Mamma had it on the best authority or she would not have taken us there and this dress of mine was copied from an exclusive summer model designed for a *debutante*!'

'Really? How too, too enthralling.'

'You think it does not matter, but it does,' said Claire hotly. 'One day you will see. You think because you paint pictures you can dress like ... like some sort of gypsy if you choose, but it is just Not Done if you want to get on in society.'

'Which you do, of course?' said Rose solemnly.

'Of course! And I see no reason why we should not all get on equally well – even you, Rose. After all, we are educated. We can read and write and speak a little French and look at all those museums Mademoiselle has dragged us to see. We can even sew and play the piano ...'

'After a fashion.'

'... so what more could a man want?'

'Really, Claire, you are so naive.' Rose's patience was at an end. 'Come down to earth and be sensible, for pity's sake. There is still such a thing as class. No amount of Papa's money can buy background and breeding. Land, yes. A country house, yes. Even an estate in the Highlands, with shooting and fishing. But not a true-blue family tree. Flannel Legs and his like are not for us.'

'Why not? The best marriages are true partnerships in which one partner complements the other. So he shall provide the background, and I the money! After all, Papa is rich.'

'Rich maybe. But he is also too sensible to let you throw yourself blatantly at the first landed gentleman you see.'

'No.' Claire sounded thoughtful. 'That would not be the way to do it. But I am serious, Rose, nevertheless and I don't care what you say about class. I mean to marry someone of importance one day. I say! Do you think Flannel Legs is an Honourable?'

Disgusted, Rose returned silently to her drawing. After a moment Claire said, in a different voice, 'I know! We could go down onto the terrace and order lemonade!'

'Now?'

Claire nodded, her face bright with suppressed excitement.

'But Mamma said we were not to eat or drink anything if we want to swim. Besides, I am busy.' Rose turned back to her drawing pad with an air of dismissal, but Claire persisted.

'Please, Rose. You know I cannot go down alone and I do so want to do something exciting. Something the tiniest bit daring. We have been here almost a fortnight now and what have we done? Walked about the town admiring the architecture and the churches, strolled on the *Plage* in the evenings, looked at the shops, but always with Mademoiselle and the sisters, or with Mamma and Papa. We have been allowed to swim, admittedly, but never alone. And that dreary museum! We have not done anything really exciting since we came here and I do so want to ... want to ...'

'Meet a man?' supplied Rose innocently.

Claire blushed prettily into the mirror. 'It sounds so forward when you say it like that, Rose, but yes I suppose I do.'

'Then I shall certainly be in the way. If I come with you, you will speak to me and not to him and he, seeing us together, will have no excuse to speak to either of us. However, if you go down alone, you can look lost and helpless, trip and twist your ankle, faint at his feet, anything to raise the dormant chivalry in his manly breast. He will sweep you into his arms as Willoughby swept up Marianne, and before your fluttering eyelids open, his lips will ...'

'No!' Scarlet faced, Claire struggled to close Rose's mouth with her hands, but Rose twisted free and continued, in a voice of throbbing passion, '... crush down on yours with a deep and burning hunger which ...' But Claire had stopped her ears. 'Oh well,' said Rose, resuming her normal voice. 'I suppose I could take my sketchbook onto the terrace and draw that dreadful little fountain.'

21

CHAPTER 2

Edward Rivers had had a dull week. Had it not been that he had undertaken to travel with his cousin and Aunt Clementina would be angry if he arrived back at Wychwood without him, he would have left Harry to stew in his own juice – or whatever pickle he had got himself into this time – and would have sailed for home. As it was, Edward had given Aunt Clementina his word and Edward's word was the word of a gentleman, binding unto death. And death of an early kind was what Harry seemed intent on pursuing, thought Edward sourly as he tried to concentrate on the newspaper. Silly young fool.

Harry had behaved well enough in Venice, at the Palazzo d'Estarte, under Edward's mother's intimidating eye. He had talked solemnly of Renaissance architecture and the Venetian school, had admired Lady Portia's Canaletto with knowledgeable enthusiasm, and had even fed Amaretti biscuits to her horrid little dog. Harry had opened doors, tucked in chairs, offered his arm or his umbrella, escorted his hostess to innumerable evening concerts and afternoon teas, been unfailingly charming to her coven of black-clad dowager friends and received all her most barbed and caustic comments with unfailing good humour.

But he had hardly stepped into the gondola that was to take them on the first stage of their homeward journey before Harry's model behaviour disintegrated into shameless dissipation.

'Girls!' he cried, tossing his new straw boater into the air and failing to catch it again so that it bobbed, bottom upwards in the Grand Canal and had to be retrieved by the gondolier with a boathook. 'Lovely, naughty girls! Farewell to the Gorgon – begging your mother's pardon, of course, old chap, – and welcome women of a kindlier kind.'

'Sit down, idiot, or you will capsize the boat.'

'Nonsense. Gondolas never capsize. Sink maybe – glug glug – but capsize? Never. It's all a question of hydro something or other so no need to worry, old fruit. We'll reach the delectable Maria's in a brace of shakes.'

'We are going to the railway station,' reminded Edward.

'You may be, Edward, but I have a pressing appointment else-where. Though perhaps pressing is an indelicate way of putting it! I say, gondolier, can't you propel this old shoe a bit faster? God, Edward, how can you be so calm? Don't you feel the sap rising?'

'I wish you'd behave,' grumbled Edward, 'at least until we're out of sight. Mother might be watching.'

Harry turned round, making the boat lurch dangerously so that water slopped over the side and round their feet, in a torrent of protest from the gondolier. With an elaborate sweep of the hand he waved his dripping boater in the direction of the Palazzo d'Estarte. 'Farewell, Lady Gorgon. Farewell, Art and Culture and all things Improving. Farewell, solemn music. I am starved for wine, women and song. Not that your mother's cellar is not excellent, old chap ... but a glass of humble vino with the buxom Maria on my knee is far more to my taste. I say, gondolier, pull in at the next jetty, will you? Why don't you come too, Edward? Maria's a great girl, with plenty of delectable friends who would be happy to entertain you. You can take your pick – they're expensive, but clean and worth every lira.'

But such shared excursions were not Edward's style. 'I will see you at the station,' he said and added ominously, 'Remember I have the tickets.'

After that, there had been that dreadful woman in Florence, who had pursued them, screaming, to the train.

'She wants me to stay, that's all,' Harry had shrugged and blown her a kiss from the carriage window. It had been the same in Monte Carlo. And now Paris. You would think the fellow would learn sense, or at least caution, but not Harry. Jumped into trouble feet first, both eyes open and exulting. Remembering that disgraceful episode in Montmartre, Edward wrenched the page over too hard and tore it in the process.

'Damn.' It was so hot and tedious. He had already visited the *Musée*, the obligatory churches of St Remy and St Jacques, and had dutifully studied the more notable points of architectural inter-est in the town. He had even inspected the *marché au poisson,* one morning early, and on another occasion had walked the cliffs to Pourville, a pretty little bathing place some two and a half miles west of the town, under the mistaken impression that the Marquis of Salisbury had a house there. He had planned to rectify the mistake the next day by a walk to Puys, but had somehow lost interest. Sightseeing, whether educational or otherwise, had palled at an early stage of his tour and he felt restless and dissatisfied. Even sea-bathing had lost its attraction for him. He would give

23

anything to be on a horse, at Wychwood, on a tranquil summer evening, or going for a walk through the woods of home in the half light of dawn, his dog at his heels and his gun primed. The air would be cool on his cheek, his nostrils full of the familiar scents of dew-drenched grass, ripening corn, hedgerows and wood smoke from the cottages at Wychwood Bottom. Last year's leaves would crumble under his shoes as he trod softly, eyes alert, ears straining, as his dog's ears would be, into the expectant silence.

The foxes, his father wrote, were bad this year. Took thirteen hens from the home farm in one night and another seven from Dan Bird's place. The men had set traps all over the place for the red-brushed devil, but with no success. Then his father and Bird had sat up all night with shotguns behind the hen house, lying in wait for the vermin, and had picked off two. He wished he could have been there. That was the sort of shooting Edward liked – vermin shooting of a workaday kind. Not Harry's kind where the beaters threw up clouds of birds so that only a fool could miss. Not that Edward was not good at that too – and in demand at all the best shoots. The fact that he was 'eligible' increased his popularity, though so far he had managed to escape all matrimonial designs. As to entanglements of a less official nature, he had access to an excellent address in Town where everything was arranged with admirable discretion. Not like Harry who left behind him a string of damsels variously squealing, weeping, cursing, or pleading, according to their natures, wherever he went.

But this time Harry would have to behave. Before leaving him, Edward had removed from Harry's possession money, passport, and everything pawnable. He had taken Harry's luggage with his own and booked passage for them both on the cross-channel steamer. Aunt Clementina, Edward had threatened, would be Told All if Harry was not there, at the gangplank, by eight a.m. on Saturday. Left with only a few sous to his name, Harry had cheerfully agreed – and insisted on enjoying his last days of what he called 'freedom' in Paris before returning into bondage. But it was Friday already and no sign of the wretch.

Harry Price-Hill was rich, healthy, carefree, and, thought Edward with resignation in which there was more than a little envy, would no doubt be enjoying life to the last irresponsible minute before arriving on the quayside, cheerfully unrepentant, on the metaphorical stroke of midnight. Whereas Edward himself, cursed with a conscience and a well-developed sense of responsibility, would find every earnest minute hang heavy with boredom and a niggling anxiety. He was fond of Aunt Clementina and, against all sane

24

argument, fond of his cousin Harry.

'Silly young fool,' he muttered and tried to concentrate on the Stock Exchange page. But after only a few minutes he gave up all attempt to follow the intricacies of Canadian Railways or Rio Tinto Copper. The sun's glare was too bright for concentration, even with the sea breeze and the umbrella's shade. Perhaps he ought to go inside?

He was idly debating the relative attractions of an airless corner room, where at least he could strip down to his skin if he chose and read, and a more energetic sight-seeing trip to Puys, when a movement caught his eye. Someone was stirring inside the hotel and approaching this way. The waiter, perhaps, roused from his siesta and preparing to serve over-priced *citron pressé* to an over-heated clientele? Edward readjusted the newspaper to shield himself from attack. But the hushed twittering of girls' voices made him readjust it a moment later to allow him a glimpse of flowered hat and cornflower blue skirts, with straw hat and blue and white striped skirts, at a table near the steps into the garden. Blue-stripes had a sketch pad and watercolours which she was setting out upon the table while cornflower-blue watched her with unnatural attention. Then the brim of the flowered hat tilted slightly and he caught the full shaft of a pair of brown eyes, hastily averted. For some reason, the exchange unsettled him and when next he allowed his eyes to wander in the direction of the artist's table, he saw that cornflower-blue had readjusted her chair so that she sat in profile to him, her eyes apparently on the garden. It was an extraordinarily attractive profile.

Edward remembered seeing a family of English girls on the *Plage* earlier in the week, and he had run into the father in the entrance hall a couple of days ago. Trade, of course, but obviously prosperous trade. He had seen them again in the hotel dining room, though only through the open door, for he preferred to eat out in the town. There was a particularly good sea-food restaurant near the harbour with an excellent wine-list – that last Muscadet had been outstanding – whereas the hotel dining room was invariably crowded and hot, the service appalling. If for any reason Edward chose not to eat in the town, he ordered a tray in his room.

Now, however, he allowed his attention to wander from the interminable intricacies of the Dreyfus case and idly studied the pair. Stripes was blocked almost entirely from view by her sister, though he could see a slim hand holding a paint brush, and the tilted brim of a hat from under which rippled an untidy mass of reddish hair. Cornflower, in contrast, looked cool and serene, neat-

25

waisted, hair of the colour the French called *châtain* coiled off the nape of a slender and graceful neck, and that classic profile. With such a complexion, he found himself thinking, she should have had blue eyes, not brown. Then, as if feeling his own eyes on her cheek, she half turned to glance in his direction and he retreated hastily to Dreyfus. What would she think of him, staring in that ill-bred fashion? Only boredom could have made him so forget himself. He was getting like Harry. In a moment he would find himself rising from his chair, strolling across the terrace to their table, and offering to order them lemonade! Even sitting with them while they awaited its arrival, talking perhaps of stripes's painting or the view.

Damn Harry, he thought with irritation. Damn Dieppe. Damn this whole scheme of Aunt Clementina's which had sent him on a European tour with his cousin when he would far rather have stayed at home at Wychwood where everything was as it had always been and where he knew everyone and everyone knew him. 'Remember, Edward,' his father had taught him from an early age, 'no one is too lowly for you to speak to, and no one too high.' Yet all the same, one did not thrust one's company upon strangers uninvited, especially not female strangers and the daughters of Trade at that.

Irritably he folded his paper, pushed back his chair, and strode into the hotel.

'Oh well,' sighed Rose, straight-faced. 'There goes another ailing knight at arms, *alone and palely loitering.*'

'But he is not loitering,' said Claire crossly, looking over her shoulder as if to admire the sea-view but really to check the shadows of the hotel entrance. 'He has completely vanished.'

'Gone to look for a patch of withered sedge, no doubt, to wander by,' said Rose, dipping her brush into the colour wash she had mixed and sketching in the outline of a shadow. *'Where no birds sing.'*

But Claire, for once, ignored the challenge to cap quotations. Instead she said thoughtfully, 'But you must admit, Rose, that he looks interesting?'

'If by "interesting" you mean you know nothing at all about him and would like to, then I do agree. If, on the other hand, by "interesting" you mean to imply a poetic nature, a skeleton in the family cupboard, or an unrequited passion, like a worm i'the bud, eating away his soul, then I do not agree. His name, by the way, is Edward Rivers and he is a perfectly ordinary and respectable country gentleman from Suffolk.'

26

Claire's pretty mouth fell open in astonishment. 'Rose! How ever do you know that?'

'Papa was talking to him yesterday, in the hotel foyer,' said Rose airily, executing a delicate green patch of moss at the base of the forbidden fountain. 'Sara told me. You know what she is like.'

Claire knew all too well. Sara could be relied upon to collect all sorts of snippets of household conversation, not always of a wholly repeatable kind, and to relay them to her sisters, in private. It was best not to speculate how Sara acquired her gossip, but she was a solitary child and often in places where her sisters were not.

'What were they talking about, Rose?' A dreadful thought struck her. 'Papa was not giving him our Catalogue, was he?' Mr Millard never travelled without a sheaf of 'Millard's Outfitters' latest brochures somewhere about his person and lost no opportunity to distribute them to possible clients, at home or abroad.

'No. At least, I do not think so. Sara said they were discussing death duties.'

'How unromantic.'

'Even your Interesting Englishman is hardly like to discuss romance with Papa, is he?' teased Rose. 'Unless you think he was making an offer for your hand?' She struck a theatrical pose, back of hand against brow, and declaimed, 'Mr Millard, of Millard's renowned Outfitters, I love your eldest daughter to dis-trac-ti-on!'

'Stop it, Rose! He might hear.' Blushing, Claire tried to snatch Rose's sketch pad as the only sure weapon she knew of, but Rose had anticipated her and whipped the paper out of reach.

'"Dear Mr Millard," he pleaded, "I have loved your daughter from the moment I set eyes on her loveliness and am wasting away with the pain of unrequited passion. I weep, I sigh, I fade, I die ... Save me, Mr Millard. Save the life of a hapless lover. Give your daughter to me, tonight!"'

Claire, scarlet-faced with mortification and fury, all decorum forgotten, snatched up the jar of paint-water and threw it full in Rose's face.

Edward Rivers, standing at the reception desk in the hotel, waiting for the concierge to answer his bell, saw the exchange and grinned. He was suddenly reminded of his own sisters, in the family schoolroom long ago, before they married and became respectable matrons. Those Millard girls were delightfully unmatronly and, at the moment anyway, not at all respectable. The recollection somehow lifted his spirits. Ancient history could wait and the Gallic 'oppidum' at Puys would still be there tomorrow – or next year. After all, it was a hot afternoon. He would go bathing instead.

27

'Can you hear anything, dear?' asked Rebecca Millard, stirring lazily in the huge French bed. Herbert merely grunted in an accommodating sort of way and moved his arm further across her breast. But Rebecca was wide awake now, ears straining into the filtered sunlight of late afternoon. Surely she had heard something? Girls' voices, arguing?

The room was high ceilinged and large, its two shuttered windows overlooking the garden. The striped umbrellas of the terrace tables, like so many coloured cartwheels, were immediately beneath, with the geranium beds and the lawns beyond. In the morning and evening a steady drone of conversation drifted up from the terrace, but now, at siesta time, there should have been silence.

Rebecca reached a cautious hand towards the heavy oak commode beside the bed and felt about for her safety-pin watch. She did not want to disturb Herbert by moving any more than was necessary, but if it was approaching five she would have to wake him before the children arrived at the door to remind them of the bathing expedition. Her fingers had just found the oval disc of her watch when, unmistakably, she heard, 'Claire, you beast! You horrid, disagreeable...' then a squeal and the crash of breaking glass.

Rebecca shot upright in bed, forgetting for a moment that she was naked. Hastily she pulled up the counterpane to cover her breasts.

'Don't go,' said her husband, half-opening his eyes. 'Not yet.' But Rebecca was not listening to him, only to the sounds from below. A male voice now, French and polite, and a female, subdued, apologetic.

'What are they doing?' she demanded, swinging her legs over the side of the high bed and feeling for the steps, at the same time slipping her arms into the sleeves of a frilled and ribboned *peignoir*. Her hair hung loose to her waist and, arms raised, she bundled it impatiently back as she went to the window and made to open the shutters.

Herbert watching her thought, not for the first time, what a splendid figure of a woman she was. She had always been full-breasted, with ample hips and a waist he could span with his two hands. Childbirth had, if anything, improved her. 'What are who doing?' he asked lazily, admiring the curve of her body against the light from the louvres.

'Who? Your daughters of course! I distinctly heard them on the terrace where they have no business to be. What will people think? Bother those umbrellas,' she grumbled, peering through the half-

28

open shutters. 'And the sun is in my eyes. I can't make out who is down there, but I know I heard Rose's voice and Claire's too. They really are too bad. I distinctly remember ordering them to their rooms until . . .'

'Five o'clock?' supplied Herbert. He held out her watch in the palm of his hand. 'It is ten minutes past already.'

'Oh dear, so it is. But I will speak to them nevertheless. It is not ladylike. Not fitting. I will not tolerate such hoydenish . . .'

She was interrupted by a knock at the door and Mademoiselle's voice calling, '*Madame Millard, les enfants sont prets à baigner.*'

'*Un moment, s'il vous plait.*' Rebecca looked round in agitation for her chemise.

'Tell them to go on ahead,' mouthed her husband, enjoying her confusion.

'Mademoiselle, take the girls to the beach now, if they are ready. I will join you.'

'*Oui, madame. Tout de suite.*'

'I think I might swim myself, today,' said Herbert Millard, stretching luxuriously in the huge bed. 'But first, come here, wife and give me a kiss.'

'Hush!' warned Rebecca, one eye on the door. 'Mademoiselle will hear.'

'And if she does? Is it so shocking, when we are married? But she will not hear. Listen.'

For a moment there was silence, then a chatter of familiar voices from the terrace below.

'I said, come here,' repeated Herbert. When she turned instead to the dressing table, he added conversationally, 'Did you know that gown thing of yours is transparent?'

'It isn't!' She looked at him in horror, then, at the look in his eyes she blushed and laughed. 'All right, dear. But only for a moment. Remember you have booked the bathing hut and we have lost thirty minutes of it already.'

'Thirty minutes gone,' wailed Maudie. 'Why can't we swim?'

'You will await your Mamma,' said Mademoiselle. A plain-faced woman of twenty-five with an ambition to fulfil, she was unused to frivolity, even of a health-giving and invigorating kind, as sea-bathing was reputed to be.

'But we cannot all change together in the little bathing machine anyway,' pointed out Sara. 'It is sure to be wet and horrid, with sand on the floor, and there will be no room.'

'Please, Mademoiselle,' said Charlotte, looking up at her with

29

innocent blue eyes. 'Please take us? You have such a lovely bathing costume, much prettier than Claire's.'

Mademoiselle hesitated. Everyone knew she favoured little Charlotte with as much love as her calculating prune of a heart allowed. Monique Piton came of sturdy peasant stock. Orphaned early in life, she had been raised in a convent orphanage and had one ambition only – to amass the money she had always been without. With the convent's help, she embarked on a succession of respectable appointments in bourgeois families, leaving without compunction or regret the moment something better appeared. The Millards were her first English employers and would, she had calculated with shrewd French common sense, provide her with an *entrée* into the best circles. The best, in Mademoiselle's judgement, was assessed purely on economic grounds and she had not been disappointed. The Millards had money and paid well: something which did not always follow. Not that they were not stern masters, the pair of them, but Mademoiselle did not mind that. 'Work well and you will be paid well,' Monsieur had told her. 'Any trouble and you leave on the spot,' Madame had added. 'No notice, no references. Do you understand?' Monique Piton understood and far from resenting such bluntness, admired it. You knew where you were with employers like that, and the money was excellent. So were her own private prospects.

For Mademoiselle Piton intended one day to open a school of her own – an expensive school for the daughters of the best families. But first, she needed capital. She saved every sou of her salary and already had a sizeable nest-egg which she hoped to double with the Millards' help. What she had not anticipated, however, were any disagreeable stirrings of affection towards her charges. So when Charlotte looked up at her with childlike trust and pleaded, 'Please?' Mademoiselle was momentarily at a loss.

'Perhaps it would be a good idea,' said Claire innocently, one eye on the *Plage* and the gathering promenaders. 'You take the younger ones first, before the heat goes from the sun. Then when Mamma and Papa arrive, Rose and I can take our turn?'

'Please, please!' The younger girls pestered Mademoiselle until, with hands over her ears, she relented. 'Very well. But you will do exactly as I say, *oui*?'

'*Oui*, Mademoiselle.'

Herding the younger ones in front of her, Mademoiselle mounted the steps of the wooden hut and the door closed behind her. The attendant gave the horse a sharp smack on the rump and the hut creaked into motion across the sands towards the water. There were more bathing huts dotted along the beach, some still empty on the high sands, some at the water's edge so that the occupants could step discreetly from the wooden privacy of their mobile changing room straight into the colder privacy of the sea.

Along the promenade, groups of men cheerfully trained eye-glasses and telescopes onto the bathers, who for their part seemed little concerned. Further along the beach men in bathing garments of black, or coloured stripes, many with the name of the Casino stamped across their backs, frolicked with ladies in knee-length sleeveless dresses and frilly pantaloons. Children with bunched skirts paddled in the shallows while older children rolled up trouser legs or tucked dresses into waistbands and waded knee deep into the sea. Squeals and splashes echoed the length of the *Plage* and on the flat expanse of sand which divided promenade from sea were dotted family groups with sun-umbrellas and sand-castles, tipped like jelly moulds out of miniature buckets to be flattened eventually by miniature spades or miniature feet. Ice-cream vendors threaded the crowds with others selling sweetmeats or lemonade and on the promenade near the sea wall was a pompommed Pierrot band.

'Shall we stroll a little?' suggested Claire, glancing over her shoulder at a group of Frenchmen in flannels and jaunty panama hats, sauntering slowly in their direction.

'If you like.' Rose was studying the sea and trying to imagine which wash would be the best to capture the particular glint of sun on water. 'I wish I had brought my paints with me.'

'Don't be so stuffy, Rose! You can paint at home. You ought to want to do other things here. It's so exciting to see men and women bathing together, not at all like at home, and some of the bathing costumes are so daring. Rose, you must walk with me. I can hardly walk alone, can I, and I do so want to see.'

'There is no need to walk at all,' retorted Rose. 'You could sit here in a deck chair and stare at the passers-by in comfort.'

'But they could not see me, could they? Besides, there is another band somewhere, I am sure, and Mademoiselle says there is a peep-show on the promenade. And we will not walk far. Merely to that flag-pole and back. Please?'

Harry Price-Hill alighted from the Paris train at Dieppe at precisely five twenty-three. It was a sweltering afternoon, but the dry heat from the station platform was tempered by a breeze which held a refreshing hint of sea. He stood a moment, taking his bearings. The engine, still snorting sooty fumes and coughing grit, quivered and steamed into silence, bumper to bumper with the end of the line.

31

Overhead the sun glared through the glass-and-metal-domed roof but the deeper vaults of the station were in shadow. Doors opened and slammed, porters shouted, children and dogs squealed. A trolley, loaded high with cabin trunks, wicker baskets and the assorted paraphernalia of children's sea-side entertainment narrowly missed his new hand-made brogues and he swore cheerfully under his breath.

But the crowds were thinning out, sucked into waiting carriages or the unknown streets. He knew the name of Edward's hotel, knew it was on the sea-front, but he had no intention of surrendering himself into Edward's custody until he had tasted freedom in the town. Thanks to that remarkable run of luck at the *Lapin Bleu* he still had a franc or two to his name and wasn't the sea bathing here reputed to be remarkably good? Far more interesting than at Brighton or Bournemouth where male and female were still ridiculously segregated. On French beaches men and women could enter the sea together and what an opportunity for a frolic that could be! Fifty centimes for a costume would be cheap at the price.

Harry swung his carpet bag from left hand to right and strode for the exit.

'Are you ready, dear?' Rebecca took a last look in the mirror, adjusted her hat a fraction of an inch and turned sideways to check the line of her neat-waisted summer coat and skirt. The wide silk revers were such a becoming shade of old rose and her new chiffon blouse with the Zouave front added the perfect touch of elegance. Satisfied, she leant gracefully on her furled lace parasol. Her figure was still remarkably good, she reflected smugly, for a matron of thirty-nine.

'In a moment.' Herbert retied his cravat, added the final touch of an opulent pearl pin, and offered his arm to his wife. 'There. I believe this new summer suit of mine sits remarkably well. Quality always shows.' He stopped thoughtfully. 'Quality shows through? No, not forceful enough. Millard's for Quality? I am thinking of taking space on a London omnibus when we get home. On the best City routes, of course and nothing vulgar. What do you think, dear?'

'I think ... oh, Herbert, you are so much cleverer than I am at that sort of thing. You must decide everything yourself. But I do think one thing...' She laid a gentle, gloved hand on his arm and smiled her sweetest smile. 'I think that you should forget about business for this afternoon and take me out.'

'You are quite right, quite right.' He glanced over his shoulder

32

into the mirror. 'We are a real pair of swells today, and no mistake. It would be a pity to keep the public waiting.'

'It would indeed. But it was the children I was thinking of,' said Rebecca primly. She did, however, take a last look into the mirror to admire her newest hat – a breathtaking confection of cream-coloured lace and ribbons – before moving gracefully for the door.

The promenade, as usual, was crowded when they stepped out of the hotel into the Rue Aguado and turned left in the direction of the Casino or *Etablissement de Bains*. To their right lay the estuary of the Arques and the harbour from which, as well as the steady trade in coal with England and timber with Norway and Sweden, two steamers plied daily from Newhaven, bringing the more selective English visitors to what had become a fashionable watering-place.

The *Plage*, or marine promenade, some two thirds of a mile long and very handsome, was much favoured by foreign and native visitors alike who delighted in strolling to and fro, admiring the constantly changing activity of *Plage* and sea. Some trained telescopes on the charms of costumed bathers, others watched pierrots, bought lemonade or ices, played ball. Or merely meandered at will through the ever-changing crowds, forgetful of politics, stock exchange or business anxiety and enjoying only the sun and sea and the happy relaxation of the young.

'Will you really swim today, Herbert?' asked his wife, one arm in his, the other tipping her parasol to shield her complexion from the sun. 'I know your doctor recommended it for relaxation and well-being, but you do not want to over-tire yourself.'

'Over-tire? What is tiring about a dip in the sea? Besides,' he added, looking at her mischievously, 'I feel quite sprightly today.'

'So I noticed,' she said, straight-faced, but she squeezed his arm with private meaning and set her head at a more jaunty angle. 'I wonder where the girls are?'

'With Mademoiselle, of course, at the bathing hut.' They both studied the row of bathing huts in the distance, trying to pick out their particular group, then gave up the attempt. There were some two hundred huts and the girls, as Herbert said, would be safe with Mademoiselle. Somewhere ahead of them a band was playing a Strauss waltz with a particularly French intonation and a great deal of what Herbert Millard called 'Oompah'.

'Oh dear,' said Rebecca, on a thought. 'I do hope those silly girls did not eat or drink anything this afternoon. I know for a fact that Sara has a *cache* of apricots in her room and as for Claire, you

33

know she loves to drink lemonade on the terrace at the slightest opportunity.'

'Do not worry, my love. That, after all, is what we pay Mademoiselle Whatsername to do for us and I will not allow a frown on my little Becky's face.'

Rebecca brightened with pleasure. 'You haven't called me Becky since our courting days.'

'Then I have been very remiss, my dear. And to make up, let us stroll a little together and enjoy ourselves as we used to do.'

But they had not walked half a dozen steps before Rebecca said, 'Have you noticed how mature Claire has become lately?'

'Mature? I would not have said so. Merely because a girl puts up her hair and wears a tighter corset does not make her automatically mature.'

'You know what I mean,' protested his wife. 'She looks womanly, somehow, and at the same time restless. As if . . . How soon do you think she ought to marry?'

'Marry?' Herbert stopped in his tracks. 'Good lord, woman. She is still a child.'

'No, Herbert. She is sixteen. In no time at all she will be completely grown-up.'

'When she is twenty-one will be time enough to talk of such things.' Herbert sounded brusque and dismissive, but Rebecca persisted.

'I know you think of all the girls as little children still, and I suspect you always will, but they must marry sometime, you know, and they are all of them attractive and will collect suitors soon enough.'

'Humph! I don't know why you say "must" marry. They may live with us in spinster comfort for as long as they choose.'

'But surely they will not choose?' Rebecca was astonished at the suggestion. 'Spinsters are regarded as failures, as you well know – unless possibly if they are caring for the aged or infirm and we, thank the good Lord, are neither. Our girls will surely want to marry, like any other normal girls of their age, and find husbands to cherish them. They will have offers enough, I'll warrant you, if the looks they attract already are anything to go by. I know I always wanted to marry . . .'

'Just because you were a dear, sweet, conventional young lady does not mean our girls must be the same. Why may they not continue to live at home, in luxury, with us? I will guard their welfare and cherish them, as I cherish you, my love. Do not trouble yourself for one instant on their account. As long as I am alive they will have all they could ever want, and more, by George!' He glared defiance at the world in general and thumped his silver-topped cane on the promenade to emphasise the point.

'I know, dear,' soothed Rebecca, alarmed by his heightened colour. 'You keep us all in great comfort and . . .'

'Will be provided for, Rebecca,' interrupted her husband. 'You need have no fear of that. If I die . . .'

'Herbert, don't! You know how it upsets and frightens me to hear you talk of such things. How could I ever manage without you?'

'If I die,' he repeated firmly, 'remember our girls are to live the lives they choose, married or single, it makes no difference to me as long as they are happy.'

'How could we ever be happy with you gone?' Her lips trembled and tears blurred her eyes.

'Now, now, Rebecca. Pull yourself together. I am still here, am I not? Then smile for me?' Obediently she did so. 'That is better. Now, we were talking of the children. My sister, as I have often told you, could have been a talented artist, but she found no encouragement from her father or from her husband. They both saw drawing as unwarranted idleness: an understandable viewpoint in a working-class home, where a woman's place is to work. But I saw my sister's pain, Rebecca, and her unhappiness and the unrelieved drudgery which brought her to an early grave and I vowed then that should I ever have daughters I would try to make their lives happier than hers had been.'

'And fulfilled . . .' murmured Rebecca.

'That too. One way or another. But there are other ways of fulfilment than by raising children. Mind you, I am not saying that that way is not the best for some women,' he added, seeing her face. 'Only that there are others. Rose is a talented artist as, with the smallest encouragement, my poor sister could have been. That pastel sketch Rose did of you the other day was lovely. It could have been my own little Becky looking out at me from the page.' He squeezed her arm and she smiled up at him.

'Rose may wish to study abroad,' continued Millard, elaborating his theme. 'Even have her own little studio one day. Nothing vulgar, of course. No nudes or anything. Flower pictures, portraits and suchlike. And by George if Rose wants a studio, she shall have one. And Sara is clever with words. Our daughters could be talented in so many fields. Then what a comfort they could be to us in old age. No, the more I think about it, the more I believe there is really no need for any of them to leave home.'

'No, dear.' Rebecca suspected ordinary male jealousy lay behind the expansive statement, but forebore to say so. 'Nevertheless,' she went on, 'I think Claire will want to marry, as I did. She is so very attractive and I have seen the way men look at her. Oh not in any immodest way,' she went on hastily, 'merely admiring – and I know she likes to be admired. Whatever you say, dear, I hope they all marry. Then think how many grand-children we will have.'

'Well ... I suppose that might be an advantage, if you say so, Becky.' He smiled indulgently and drew her hand further through his arm. 'Then one day, we will bring them all here to Dieppe. Hire a villa, perhaps, at Puys. I hear it is a very pretty little bathing-place with some fine furnished houses to let and if it is good enough for a Prime Minister, then it is good enough for Herbert Millard. We will take a whole row of bathing huts for a grand family party. When I have made our fortune.' A brief frown clouded his brow as he thought of that loan for the new premises, but vanished again at the sight of the first of the bathing huts and a gaggle of children in the shallows, splashing and squealing with delight. 'Maybe you're right, Becky. Marriage and grandchildren would be a fine aim for our girls and a pleasure for us in our old age. Now, our hut was number 57 if I remember rightly. And I shall certainly swim.'

'Remember, Sara, you are not to swim far.'

'Oui, Mademoiselle.'

'You mean no, silly.'

'No I don't, I mean ...'

'Quiet, girls, and do as I say.' Mademoiselle stood knee-deep in the shallows, her bathing costume of sleeveless, short-skirted dress and frilly drawers revealing a surprisingly good figure. The pretty mob-cap into which she had tucked her hair softened her usually severe expression and made her look suddenly young and pretty.

'Hold my hand, Mademoiselle,' cried Charlotte, jumping from one foot to the other on tiptoe to keep the cold water from rising higher. Her mob-cap was bigger than Mademoiselle's, her flannel bathing dress already soaked and clinging to her skinny figure.

Beside her Maudie shivered, knees together and arms crossed over her budding breasts. 'I'm cold, Mademoiselle. I want to go back.'

'Don't be silly, child. Sea-bathing is good for you and see how clever is Sara, she swims already. How can you hope to do the same or to grow strong if you do not try. Come here. Give your hand to me. See, we will all three dip under the water together. One, two, three ...'

'Oooh, Mademoiselle,' cried Charlotte delightedly when they came up a second later, streaming sea-water, 'Your dress is all silky, like skin. I can see your . . .'

'Hush! Charlotte,' said Maudie, teeth chattering as she tried to shake the water out of her eyes. 'Don't be rude.'

'But I can. I can see her bosoms!' Abruptly Maudie splashed her. Charlotte screamed, then splashed back while Mademoiselle tried at the same time to cover her breasts and to avoid the showers of water. Ignoring the hubbub, Sara continued to swim steadily to and fro, to and fro, her head held upright so that no water should touch her face, her thin arms and legs jerking in the prescribed actions of the breast stroke, like a skinny clockwork frog. Then a large striped beach ball plummeted smack into the water in the centre of the group.

'I say, I am most frightfully sorry,' said a cheerful male voice. Mademoiselle brushed the water out of her eyes with the back of one hand and saw a blond young man in a hired bathing costume wading towards them waist deep from not ten yards away. He grinned engagingly and said to Charlotte, the nearest to the ball, 'Would you be awfully decent, young lady, and throw the thing back to me?'

After that, no one quite knew how, a light-hearted water-game developed between Mademoiselle and the young man, with Charlotte and Maudie at first joining in and then somehow finding themselves on the steps of the bathing hut, towels around their shoulders, shivering and watching while Mademoiselle and the unknown blonde gentleman continued to throw the ball to each other with a great deal of laughter. The gentleman threw the ball higher and higher so that Mademoiselle had to stretch, then jump up almost out of the water, her clothes clinging tighter to her shapely figure.

'He is doing it on purpose,' whispered Charlotte gleefully, 'to make Mademoiselle *wobble*.'

'Don't be rude, Charlotte. It is very rude to . . . oh!' A worrying thought struck her. 'Where is Sara?'

'I don't know,' said Charlotte. 'You know what she is like. She always goes off somewhere. Jump higher, Mademoiselle!' But Maudie had ceased to listen. She stood on the steps of the bathing hut, scanning the stretch of sea between their hut and the next, growing rapidly more agitated. 'I don't see her anywhere. Mademoiselle!' she cried anxiously, 'Where is Sara?'

Mademoiselle clutched the ball to her dripping breast and looked around her. 'Sara? Where is she? Oh *mon Dieu!* Sara! *Sara!*'

37

CHAPTER 3

Sara liked swimming. She liked the freedom of her cotton bathing dress and long-legged knickers, gathered into frills above the knee. She liked the feel of the water, cold and clean against her skin; liked the rippling pressure of it as she pushed her praying hands forward as she had been taught, then turned them back to back and parted them; liked the kicking motion of her legs which reminded her of the baby frogs they had kept at home one spring. She liked the solitude, where no one worried her to hurry up, or pay attention. But most of all she liked the feeling of superiority swimming gave to her. Her sisters could not swim. Charlotte and Maudie were too timid and too young; Claire and Rose too self-conscious. All they did was giggle and pretend to splash each other and try not to get wet above the knees. But Sara had decided on the first day that she would swim and she had. They had hired a *guide-baigneuse* to start with and she had shown Sara how to do it. She had shown the others, too, but only Sara had learnt how.

Now, with the muffled sounds of the beach behind her, she swam carefully to and fro, following the line of the shore so as not to drift out too far. Together. Push. Out. And in. Together, push, out and in. Thin arms jerked, thin legs followed suit for as many as ten strokes at a time. Then she let her feet find the sandy bottom and rested, looking shorewards to the long line of the *Plage*, with the Rue Aguado beyond and the imposing fronts of the best hotels: the Royal, the Metropole, the *Hôtel des Etrangers* and the Grand. She could even see the town hall, the tall chimneys of the tobacco factory and the distant spire of a church.

The beach was thick with people and parasols and the uneven row of bathing huts indicated where the sea, too, was busy with bathers. By their own hut she could see the others playing their splashing games in the shallows. She could even see their lips move. There was Charlotte being rude again and Maudie reproving her as Maudie always did. From the day Charlotte was born Maudie had taken on responsibility for her proper upbringing, just as if she was Charlotte's mother instead of only her sister. Sara could not understand it. She had felt no such maternal feelings for Maudie when she was born – or for Charlotte either. Only a shameful jealousy which made her withdraw even more into her private world. 'Daydreaming' her mother called it. 'Inattention' was Mademoiselle's complaint. But Sara was not wilfully inattentive, merely preoccupied. She had her own ways of finding out what was going on in the world around her. She knew, for instance, that Mademoiselle was not as stern as she pretended. That when Monsieur Leblanc had asked to take her photograph one day, all by herself in his studio, Mademoiselle had said *'Peut-être'* as if she really meant 'yes'. Sara knew that Claire wanted Mr Rivers to speak to her although she pretended she didn't. She knew that Mr Rivers himself had inquired the times of omnibuses to Puys, then changed his mind. She liked to collect such snippets of information and save them up, so that she could take them out and examine them one by one, when the others were whispering together and she was excluded. They were her secret friends.

Watching her sisters splashing and squealing in the shallows, Sara noticed a blond young man with a beach ball in the sea beside them. Then she saw him, accidentally on purpose, throw the ball into the middle of the little group. Moving her hands in a gentle swimming motion, feet still safely on the sandy bottom, Sara watched with mounting indignation as Mademoiselle and the man proceeded to throw the ball to each other with much jumping and squealing while her sisters stood in the shallows and watched. They had obviously forgotten Sara completely. It was disgraceful. What would Mamma say if she could see Mademoiselle, playing in the sea with that man and both of them half-naked, when she ought to have been minding her charges? It would serve Mademoiselle right if . . . then Sara had her idea. She would swim about a little longer, where she could still reach the bottom, of course, then if Mademoiselle had still not noticed her, she would pretend to be drowning and call for help. That would show her.

Delighted with her scheme, she lifted her feet and kicked out, while her hands pushed forward and round. Soon she was swimming steadily to and fro and still Mademoiselle flirted with the unknown gentleman and ignored her. But Sara's arms were beginning to tire. I will swim ten more strokes, she decided, then I will shout . . .

But at the seventh stroke her arms and legs refused to co-ordinate and she decided to rest a little before continuing. She reached searching toes down for the comfort of the sandy bottom – and found nothing, only an emptiness, deep, hostile and cold . . .

She scrambled arms and legs in sudden panic, fighting to regain the surface, but already the sea-water was at her chin. She tipped her head back frantically to keep her chin above the surface, but her ears filled with water and she gulped an unexpected mouthful of bitter smacking sea. She forgot what the *baigneuse* had told her about floating, forgot how to tread water and rest, forgot her plan to catch out Mademoiselle, forgot everything in the panic of knowing that she was out of her depth. She could see everybody still playing and squealing and laughing not thirty yards away from her, and could hear nothing but the pounding fear in her own ears.

'Mademoiselle!' She opened her mouth to cry for help and instead swallowed sea-water, choking and foul. Her ears sang with strange sea-music, her chest fought against the weight of smothering water, her legs scrabbled desperately as she surfaced, coughed and gurgled, then sank again in a trail of bubbles and a sudden, smothering silence in which green shapes swirled slowly round her, and she was drawn inexorably down...

Edward Rivers was swimming lazily in hired bathing suit and cap at the farthest end of the Plage when he became aware of some kind of commotion at the bathing huts: shouting, a sudden surge or movement, more shouting. He trod water, searching the shore line until he found the epicentre of the disturbance – but when he did, he lost no time in thought. Head down, arms beating the water like the arms of a watermill, he sped towards the area of sea in front of hut 57.

'Whatever is happening?' asked Claire, looking around her in surprise. They had almost reached the bandstand after a slow meander which had involved much stopping to admire the view, arms round each other's waists and parasols prettily tipped at just the right angle. Both knew they made an attractive picture together and Rose was in no way discomposed to see that most male attention was directed first, and last, at Claire. Rose was not interested in men except as friends, whereas Claire searched every male face for a Heathcliffe, a d'Arcy, or, in her more daring moments, a Don Juan. She had had a happy half hour, catching compliments and ignoring them, in between admiring the ladies' costumes, the *théâtre de Guignol*, the Pierrots with their white baggy suits and black pompoms, and finally the band.

But it was the sudden shouting from a group of young men with telescopes that attracted her attention now, and together the girls tried to locate the source of the commotion. One man was shouting and pointing at the beach, two more had trained telescopes in the same direction, while a fourth and fifth were already running towards the bathing huts.

'*Au secours!*' '*Accident!*' '*Une beigneuse qui plonge!*'

'I think someone is drowning,' said Rose, white-faced, 'but I am not sure.'

'We will ask,' cried Claire eagerly and dragged Rose by the hand to the nearest telescope, an elaborate affair on a tripod. 'Please, monsieur, can you tell us what is happening?'

'Please to see for yourself, Mademoiselle.' He stood aside with a bow and Claire, on tiptoe, applied her eye to the instrument and followed the line of vision. A moment later she stepped back in alarm, her face ashen.

'What is it, Claire?' Rose pushed her aside, took one look, and said, 'Oh God!' They linked hands and ran as fast as their skirts would allow towards the row of bathing huts and hut number 57.

Herbert and Rebecca Millard had reached the first of the huts when they heard the shouting, then suddenly they were caught up in a throng of people, all hurrying towards the scene of whatever drama was in progress. 'Keep tight hold of my arm,' warned Herbert, trying to shield his wife from the buffeting of the crowd. 'We will be all right in a moment, when they have passed.'

'But what is it, Herbert? Why is everyone running? I thought I heard someone say "drowning".'

'I think ... I am not sure, but...' Mr Millard was struggling to keep his footing on the sandy ground, to protect his wife from the crowds and, at the same time, to see over the heads of the milling mass. Then, through a brief gap, he saw enough to send the blood from his cheeks and to set his heart pounding painfully hard against his ribs. 'My God. It seems to be a child – and in the vicinity of our hut.'

Rebecca clutched his arm as her strength left her and she swayed, but only for a moment. Then she was fighting her way forward like a mad creature, with elbows, nails and feet, while Herbert followed close at her back.

'Keep back. Keep back all of you. That is better. Give her air.' Harry Price-Hill stood, arms stretched wide, sea-water streaming from his black striped bathing costume and glinting on the blond hairs of his outspread arms and firm, muscular legs. His hair was plastered to his head, but still managed to glint like gold in the afternoon sunlight and his bronzed skin gleamed with youthful health and vigour. He was a handsome man and he knew it. At that moment he was also triumphant, though full happiness would not burst through until the child sat up and breathed again.

At the moment, she lay face downward on the beach, head turned sideways, a trickle of seawater running from her open mouth, her hair in pathetic tendrils, like seaweed against the sand, while Edward Rivers knelt beside her, his shoulders gleaming with water-drops as, firm hands spread, he forced her puny little rib cage down and up again, down and up, in the regular rhythm of breathing.

The crowd fell silent, waiting, every eye on that green-tinged, sodden little body. Mademoiselle stood, ashen-faced, impervious to the clinging revelations of her own bathing costume, clutching Charlotte by one hand, Maudie the other. She hardly turned her head when Claire and Rose arrived, as white-faced as Mademoiselle, to stand equally silent beside her. Claire had not even the spirit to say, 'It is him!' but only, like the rest, to watch and wait and to gabble over and over inside her head, 'Please God don't let her die.'

'Please God, don't let it be one of mine,' prayed Rebecca, over and over, as she ran. But she knew before she reached the knot of people on the shore by hut 57 that it was. She thrust her way through the crowd and into the centre, ignored Harry's warning and threw herself down on the sand.

'Sara! Sara!' She pushed at Edward and tried to gather the child in her arms. 'It is your Mamma, my love. Speak to me.'

'Please, Madam,' said Edward Rivers, with gentle authority. 'I am an experienced life-saver. Let me try to revive her in the best way possible.'

But Herbert, red-faced now and labouring each breath, had joined them. He pulled his wife away. 'Let ... the gentleman ... see ... to her. It is ... best.' He put his trembling arm around her shoulder and together they stood apart from the rest of the onlookers, in the charmed circle beside the prostrate child, while Harry continued to prevent further encroachment and Edward resumed his steady pumping, up and down, up and down, until, on a collective, indrawn breath, Sara's eyelids fluttered and she moaned.

With an answering moan, Rebecca slipped quietly to the sand in a dead faint.

After that, all was once more busy confusion. Someone fetched blankets, someone else sal volatile, and, when it was plain that *la petite* was not dead after all, the crowd began to disperse again, in twos and threes, to whatever amusements they had abandoned in the excitement of the rescue.

42

Mademoiselle, still white and silent as if expecting the executioner's axe to fall at every second, herded the two youngest girls into the bathing hut and dry clothes. Not knowing what to do for the best, Claire hovered between Sara and her mother, both wrapped in blankets and ensconced in the deck chairs someone had kindly provided, while Rose took charge of her father, whose colour and laboured breath continued to alarm her.

'I am perfectly all right, Rose,' he said testily when she suggested he sit down. 'It has been a shock, that is all. Just give me time to gather breath and don't fuss.'

'Perhaps a brandy, sir?' suggested the dark young man. 'It might be advisable for us all,' added the blond one cheerfully. 'Harry Price-Hill, by the way.' He held out his hand. 'And that is Edward Rivers who has the misfortune to be my cousin.'

'I believe we have already met, Mr Rivers.' Millard shook hands with them both, then said, 'I cannot thank you enough for what you have done for us. Just to think that Sara might have been ...' His voice faltered and he shook his head impatiently to clear his eyes. 'We owe you a great debt.'

'Nonsense,' said Harry. 'No debt at all. Young Sara was a bit too adventurous, that is all. Isn't that right, Sara?'

Sara, swathed to the chin in rugs, was sipping her reluctant way through a glass of warm sherry wine and water which a boy had fetched at the run from the Casino. She shivered and nodded, her eyes unnaturally large, her hair still plastered flat about her head.

'You'd best take her straight home,' said Edward briskly. 'We share the same hotel, I believe? The Metropole? I will send someone to find a *fiacre*.'

'We cannot thank you enough,' repeated Herbert. 'There is nothing I wouldn't do ... Tell me, is there any way I can show my gratitude? Any way at all?'

'Certainly not,' said Edward.

'Only glad we were on the spot and able to help,' added Harry cheerfully. 'Though I wouldn't say no to that brandy.'

'Then brandy it shall be. At the hotel. Ah, here is the *fiacre*.' A smart equipage had drawn up at the promenade above them, the dappled grey horse decked with scarlet rosettes and the cab-driver sporting a similar decoration is his grey top-hat. He jumped down smartly to open the door of the carriage. 'Claire, Rose, see to your mother. Mademoiselle, bring the little ones. Come along, Sara.' He bent to pick her up in his arms.

'No, dear,' cried Rebecca. 'She is too heavy for you.'

'Nonsense. Light as the proverbial feather, aren't you, my dear?'

43

Sara buried her head in his chest and wept, with misery and joy and relief and the comfort of being held safe and close against the familiar serge of her father's coat.

Later, in the hotel, when Sara and her mother had retired to their rooms, to the ministrations of the chambermaids and a light supper on a tray, Herbert Millard bought brandy for Edward Rivers and Harry Price-Hill – in moderate amounts for Edward and in immoderate amounts for his cousin. But Herbert was glad to do so, and to drink his daughter's rescuers' health and success.

'And if ever you gentlemen are in need of a new suit of clothes,' he said, later in the evening, 'just call in at Millards. We will be delighted to fit you out in the best cloth and the latest style, absolutely free of charge. Allow me to give you my card.' He felt in his breast pocket for his card case and presented one first to Edward, then to Harry. 'And if you would care to peruse it, I have a copy of our latest catalogue in my room. Let me fetch it and ...'

'No, no, that will not be necessary,' said Edward Rivers. 'Millards has the highest reputation, and we thank you for your most generous offer. The circumstances which brought us together were not perhaps, of the happiest, but we are delighted to have made your acquaintance, Mr Millard. Unfortunately, we leave for London on the morning packet, but we wish you and your family well.'

'London, eh? Then you must call in at our High Holborn branch and be measured at once. Tell the manager, Mr Blunt, that I sent you and that you are to have the very best service, the very best.'

'Thank you, sir. Most generous of you. Now if you will excuse us, it is growing late and we have to make an early start. Coming, Harry?'

'In a moment, old chap.' Harry was enjoying himself. It was not every day that he found himself a public hero. Admittedly Edward had turned up to share the glory, but Harry had reached the child first, and it was Harry who had carried her, lifeless, up the beach to lay at the buxom Mademoiselle's feet. Naturally, Mademoiselle had been terrified, but by now she would feel only relief and gratitude. As for Harry, now that the danger was over and the child apparently unharmed, he was revelling in the glory, the hospitality and the attention. Those Millard girls had been positively doting at dinner. Why Edward had wanted to eat out, Harry could not imagine, not when there was so much ready-made talent on the spot. Every time he had looked up from the table he had seen one or other of the lovely creatures looking at him from across the room. They were not his class, of course, but he liked that – at least they would not expect him to marry them – and their old man might be only a tradesman, but he was a generous old buffer – generous to a fault. Millard had sent champagne, claret, and a bottle of vintage port to their table and now it seemed Harry could have whatever more he chose.

'I'll just have one more glass of this excellent brandy if I may, Mr Millard, then I will join you, Edward.'

'Remember that the ship sails at eight,' warned Edward, frowning. Then, with a shrug, he took his farewell of Mr Millard and left.

But that was not the only appointment Harry had to keep. One more brandy would set him up nicely for a private rendezvous of a different, more intimate kind.

'Do you think we will ever see them again?' sighed Claire as she and Rose prepared for bed.

'Probably not. Unless of course they take up Papa's offer of a free suit of clothes,' said Rose calmly.

'He didn't!' Claire was as mortified as Rose had hoped for. 'You are inventing it.'

'No, I'm not. I heard Papa telling Mamma it was "the least he could do".'

Claire cringed at the mere idea. 'Perhaps he only talked of it and did not actually do it?'

'Rubbish. You know Papa. If he talks of doing something, he does it. Flannel Legs is probably leafing through the brochure at this very moment, selecting a new pair of Oxford bags, and Cousin Whatsit a boating outfit or a cycling suit.'

'Rose, you are a beast!' cried Claire, her cheeks burning. 'I hate you!'

'Whatever for? And don't be so snobbish. They did us a service – that is, if you call rescuing Sara a service, the little pest. I half suspect she staged the whole thing on purpose to be the centre of attention. But why should Papa not reciprocate if he wishes? It is only polite.'

Neatly she dodged the pillow Claire hurled at her, and said quickly, 'Which of them do you favour anyway? You had better tell me so that I know which of them I am allowed to look at. Though surely even you would not be unfaithful after loving Flannel Legs passionately for five whole days? Unless, of course, you plan to bag them both?'

Ignoring the sarcasm, Claire subsided gracefully onto her bed and lay back with a luxurious sigh, her skirts in careful disarray. 'Oh, I don't know which I favour. They are both so ... so manly, somehow. Of course, I really ought to be faithful to Mr Rivers I suppose, but then Mr Price-Hill looked so splendid wading out of the sea with Sara lifeless in his arms. He was just like a Greek God.'

'Nonsense. She was not lifeless for a start, and secondly, he had far too many clothes on.'

'But he was only wearing a bathing costume,' protested Claire.

'That is what I mean. Now if he had been naked...'

'Rose! You are dreadful.' Claire blushed scarlet. 'Whatever would Mamma say?'

'Not dreadful at all,' retorted Rose in a matter-of-fact voice. 'Merely practical. If I am to study art I must know about such things. Michelangelo's David in Florence, for instance, though of course his inspiration was from Donatello. Then the splendid group of figures in the classical Laocoon. Michelangelo saw the potential there, too. I am talking of the expressiveness of the naked figure – and don't look so prudish, Claire. The naked male form is, after all, a thing of beauty, just as the female's is.'

'But...' Still blushing, Claire looked down at her hands while her fingers twisted awkwardly in and out. 'Are you not embarrassed, Rose, even to think of such things, let alone look?'

'No. Why should I be? Men look at women.'

Claire was silent, marvelling at her sister's boldness. Or was it sheer bravado, deliberately designed to provoke? Claire was not sure – but she did know that she herself felt acutely uncomfortable and somehow ashamed at the thought of nudity, especially male nudity. She wanted a husband, of course, to admire and cherish her, but not a naked one. Determinedly Claire attempted to lift the discussion back to a more romantic and fully clothed level.

'You must admit, Rose, that they are both very brave. The way they swam to our sister's rescue was superb. And tonight, at dinner, Mr Rivers looked so handsome, in a dark sort of way. But then, so did Mr Price-Hill.'

'In a fair sort of way?' supplied Rose mischievously, her mouth full of hair pins. *'How happy should I be with either were t'other dear charmer away...'* she sang, through the pins. Then she freed the last looped coil of hair so that it tumbled to her waist in tangled waves of red-glinting chestnut brown. 'If you can't make up your mind which of them to admire the most, then for goodness sake have done with it and take neither – or both.'

'I might,' said Claire airily. 'Who knows?'

'So I may not have either of them, dear sister?'

'No. At least, not until I choose and then, I suppose, you can have the other.' She sounded reluctant to concede even that.

46

'Thank you, dearest sister, for your boundless generosity,' said Rose with exaggerated humility. 'As it happens, I intend to dedicate my life to my Art.' She posed, hand on brow, in an attitude of classical inspiration.

'Good,' said Claire briskly. 'I should hate us to come to blows about it. But we'd best renew the Rule just the same. It is months since we did and I should hate one of us to forget, especially you.'

Rose was suddenly sober, all play-acting forgotten. Originally Claire's way of maintaining precedence and defining individual rights to shared property, the Rule had evolved with age to include more complicated areas of activity. But it was one thing to swear to let Claire have first choice of ribbons or comfits, library books or sheet music; or to swear never to copy her hair style or play her best tunes on the pianoforte. It was quite another to apply the Rule to people. Suppose there came a day when they both wanted the same man, for instance, and it was no longer a light-hearted game. Then what would happen?

'I am not sure we ought to,' she said slowly. 'It seems wicked.'

'I don't see why,' said Claire. 'Whereas it would be wicked to take away my man if I wanted him. I am the eldest, remember, and you swore a solemn oath, *on the Bible.*'

'I am hardly likely to forget,' said Rose sourly. 'You have reminded me often enough. But if it is any consolation to you, I have no intention of "taking away your man" as you so delightfully put it. Always supposing you had a man.'

'You say that now,' said Claire fiercely, 'but how do you know how you will feel in two years' time?'

'I don't and neither do you. You will probably have forgotten them both by then anyway.'

'Then the Rule will not apply,' said Claire triumphantly, 'and it will not matter. So swear!'

'I wish to put on record that I do this unwillingly,' said Rose to the room at large.

'No crossing your fingers behind your back,' warned Claire.

Rose shrugged. 'Oh, what does it matter. I don't care for either of them anyway.'

Solemnly they linked thumbs in the secret ritual of childhood. 'Now wet, now dry, cross my heart and hope to die.' Then Rose intoned, threefold, 'I promise never to take your man. Till you have done with him,' she finished bitterly, and turned her back.

'You do not look well, dear,' said Rebecca with concern. She had left the children at last to settle down for the night and she herself

47

was in bed, propped on the high, lace-edged pillows and waiting for her husband to take his place beside her. 'I am really quite anxious about you, Herbert. I wish you had let me ask the doctor to take a look at you.'

'Don't fuss, woman.' Millard glared into the mirror as he removed his collar stud. Her solicitations were the more annoying because he knew she was right. Not about the doctor, damn fool of a fellow. He had come prancing in in his velvet collared jacket and white kid gloves, listened to Sara's chest, felt her forehead, looked down her throat and pronounced, 'No harm done. As well as can be expected in the circumstances. Sleep and rest. Sleep and rest.' Had accepted a glass of the hotel's best brandy, shaken his hand and presented his bill – an exorbitant one. But she was right about her husband. Millard acknowledged that he did not feel well.

He had felt odd ever since that moment on the promenade when he had realised what was happening and his heart had begun to beat all anyhow. It had calmed down since then, and the brandy had helped, but he still had a pain in his left arm and around his chest. From carrying little Sara, no doubt. But he had wanted to carry her. In some ways she was his favourite child – a quiet little thing, she seemed more vulnerable than the others, as if she lived in a private world of her own that was lonely and a little frightening. She made him feel protective and he had protected her, by George, as he would always do.

Slowly he unbuttoned his waistcoat and hung it, with his jacket, in the huge and heavily-ornamented *armoire*. The action brought on the pain again, sharper this time, and he stood motionless, one hand on the cupboard door, head bowed, waiting for it to ease.

'Are you sure you are all right, Herbert dear?' He was taking a long time undressing. He was usually so brisk and efficient. But then it had been an exhausting and a harrowing day, one way and another.

'Yes.' He spoke without turning round. 'A touch of indigestion, that is all. Go to sleep my dear, and stop worrying. At least Sara is safe and that is what matters.'

'Will you be long, dear?' she asked meekly, when he did not move.

'No. But I think I will just sit for a while in the chair and drink a glass of Perrier, to settle the stomach.'

'Very well, if you are sure.' Herbert was always so capable. Rebecca did not know how she would have managed without him on this dreadful day. Her husband had organised everything, had guarded and protected her from worry, had spread his masculine strength like a protective umbrella over his wife and daughters. And now the girls were all safely in bed, even poor little Sara, and so was she. Reassured, Rebecca turned on her side with a sigh of weary relief, closed her eyes, and slipped unexpectedly into sleep, to dream of death and danger and the slow encroachment of a hostile sea.

When she woke, anxious and sweat-drenched, some hours later, to the first dawn sounds of the waking town, the bed was still empty beside her. Startled, she reached out a questing hand, felt the cold space where her husband should have been, and sat bolt upright in bed, her heart pounding hard with fear. The half-light of early dawn filtered through the louvres in a colourless glow which painted the room in ghostly monochrome. In the chair beside the window she made out the white shape of his shirt, with the pale smudge of face above it and, as her eyes grew more accustomed to the gloom, the darker outline of his outstretched legs. He must have fallen asleep, still clothed, in the chair. Tenderness flooded through her, with exasperation and relief . . .

'Herbert?' When he did not answer, she swung her legs out of bed and went towards him. 'Herbert dear, you will catch cold sleeping there in the chair. Come to bed.' Gently she took his hand – and dropped it again with a gasp of horror. Then she screamed.

CHAPTER 4

The service in the Anglican church was short, poignant and final. Afterwards in cheerful sunshine they stood round the open grave in the churchyard while the chaplain read the final blessing – seven ladies in black crepe, from the youngest child to the widow herself, solicitously supported by the British Vice-Consul on one side and the doctor on the other. Also in concerned attendance were the hotel manager and a lawyer from the town, with a handful of sympathetic hotel guests.

Rebecca did not weep. Since that involuntary scream when she had realised her husband was dead, and the wild sobbing which had followed, she had maintained a white-faced, trembling composure which had stirred every chivalrous male breast to offer her support. The doctor, lawyer, vice-Consul, priest, had between them shouldered all the harrowing business of funeral arrangements, telegrams to London, documents for this and that. The hotel manager had summoned a discreet and competent dressmaker to measure the Millard ladies for mourning garments, and provided sustaining cordials for the grieving widow, and had set aside for the family's use a private salon where suitably light lunches and delicate suppers were served. Rebecca could not have been better looked after had Herbert been alive and she had submitted to every arrangement with grateful and unprotesting obedience.

The manager had appealed for discretion – 'We do not wish to discommode the other guests. So disturbing to the spirits to have a demise on the premises,' but they had, of course, found out. Servants when in possession of so dramatic a piece of news could not be expected to keep it to themselves – but as the news was, so to speak, unofficial, the family suffered little attack from the curious and the genuinely sympathetic were as discreet as the management could wish.

The London steamer left, apparently untroubled by any news of calamity, and the resort resumed its carefree life of pleasure, though, remembering the drama of the previous day when that *pauvre petite fille* had so nearly drowned, mothers and nannies alike kept a more watchful eye over their charges, and held them on a tighter rein.

Dressmakers came and went again, taking sheaths of measurements with them and the sample bolts of black silks and taffetas they had brought for Rebecca's approval, and arrangements were put in hand for the funeral. When Sara cried out in anguish, 'But we must take Papa home!' she was only saying what all of them felt.

'It is not possible, my child,' explained Mademoiselle, her eyes puffed up with crying and a nervousness still in her voice. She expected every minute to see Madame's composure snap and to receive the full fury of recrimination and blame. Mademoiselle, after all, should have watched Miss Sara and it was the shock of Sara's accident which had brought on Mr Millard's death. Everyone was saying so. Mademoiselle expected Madame at any moment to say the same and to dismiss her. 'There are so many difficulties,' she went on hesitantly. 'The permit. The money. And the ships do not like to carry . . .' Her voice faltered and she blew her nose loudly on a large white linen handkerchief.

'Papa will stay here, Sara,' said Rebecca, in the light, expressionless voice which had become habitual in the days since her husband's death. 'He was happy in Dieppe. As I was,' she added, in the emptiness of her thoughts, 'and will never be again.'

Now the small group stood in silence as the priest intoned, 'Dust unto dust, ashes to ashes,' and sprinkled the first handful of earth onto the coffin lid.

Rebecca stepped forward, reached out a slim, white hand and dropped a single rose into the pit. One by one, her daughters followed, scattering rose petals or carnations, and finally Mademoiselle, with a timid, 'You permit me, Madame?' added hers. Of the seven, only Madame Millard was dry-eyed.

Afterwards the management provided sherry wine and a light collation in a private room, all free of charge.

'People are very kind,' said Mrs Millard over and over, till the words became the burthen of the day.

Finally, when what guests there were had left, and the tables had been cleared of all trace of funeral meats, Claire ventured, for them all, 'What happens now, Mamma?'

But that morning a telegram had arrived from her late husband's lawyer, Simeon Proudfoot of Proudfoot, Proudfoot and Dodds, Chancery Lane, in answer to that of the French lawyer, sent on Rebecca's behalf. Remembering its contents, she answered Claire's question in three bleak words.

'We go home.'

Among the articles that went with them was a photograph in best sepia print, mounted on stiff card, gilt edged around the border and finished – a last-minute substitution for the planned light oak – by a gleaming ebony frame.

CHAPTER 5

The drawing room of the house in St. John's Wood was a large and comfortable room, its polished floor adorned with an expensive Chinese carpet and its heavy polished furniture capped with lace-edged mats of crisp and startling whiteness, apparently supporting every ornament money could buy. There were china statuettes on little tables, oriental vases, crystal dishes and lacquered bowls of pot pourri, and on the rosewood top of the grand piano a positive army of silver-framed photographs. Above the fireplace a large, gilt-framed mirror served to duplicate the room's splendour and in the fireplace itself an unnecessary but comforting fire of pine logs both warmed and scented the late summer air. Mrs Millard, in widow's weeds, sat on an over-stuffed sofa opposite the fire, her daughter Claire beside her; both looking particularly vulnerable and appealing. A piece of half-finished embroidery and a basket of coloured silks lay on a small table beside them. Rose, the second daughter, also in black, sat in an armchair a little to one side, with what looked like a small sketch-pad on her lap and a pencil in one hand. Simeon Proudfoot, casting his eye quickly over the sheltered comfort of the room and remembering what he had come to say, ran a finger quickly round the inside of his collar.

'I am so sorry, Mr Proudfoot, if the room is a little warm for you,' said Rebecca, 'but dear Herbert never stinted where our comfort was concerned. Would you like me to ring for the parlourmaid to open the window?'

'No, no, that will not be necessary,' said Mr Proudfoot hastily, for he knew that no amount of open windows could blow away the unpleasantness of what he had come to say. Let the dear lady enjoy her comfort while she may.

'Then perhaps you had better tell us what you came to tell us, Mr Proudfoot,' said Rebecca with a sad smile, but one in which Mr Proudfoot could detect no apprehension of what was to come. He swallowed, cleared his throat and made great play of taking a sheaf of papers from his leather bag and leafing through them.

'Do please use my bureau if it would make things easier for you,' suggested Rebecca. 'I know you are used to working at a great, leather-topped desk and it was very good of you to come to the house. I don't think I could have borne it if I had been required to visit that intimidating office of yours in Chancery Lane.'

'Certainly not, Mrs Millard. Out of the question.' But Mr Proud-foot accepted her offer and moved gratefully to the small mahogany bureau which stood against the far wall. He opened the flap, laid out his few papers and sat down, his back to the room.

'Well?' prompted Mrs Millard after a moment's silence.

Proudfoot took a deep breath, half turned towards them and said carefully, 'Mrs Millard, I must ask you to prepare yourself for an unpleasant shock.' There was an audible indrawing of breath from all three ladies before Rebecca said sharply, 'Mr Proudfoot, what-ever can you mean?'

Chivalry triumphed over cowardice and Proudfoot pushed back his chair, stood up and moved to stand with his back to the fire, hands clasped behind him and what he hoped was an expression of benign reassurance on his face. Three pairs of eyes were fixed on his and in them he read apprehension, astonishment, and the first hint of fear. He said carefully, 'There is money, of course. A little. To be honest, a very little. In fact,' he went on as no one spoke, 'and not to burden you with all the painful details, the best that your daughters can hope for, Mrs Millard, is marriage and, if I may be absolutely honest with you, the sooner the better.'

Mr Proudfoot rocked gently on his heels and lifted his coat flaps, hands still clasped behind him. A heavy gold watch-chain brightened the sombre regions of his waistcoat and his pin-striped trousers were immaculately pressed. 'But they are young ladies of remarkable beauty,' he added with elderly gallantry, 'a beauty, if I may be permitted to say so, rivalled only by their mother's. They will find many suitors...' He looked benignly over his half-moon glasses at the elegant, black-clad figure on the sofa and gave her a reassuring smile. Mrs Millard, in grief, brought out the chivalry in every man she met – and particularly in Proudfoot who, as her father's lawyer, had known her since she was a knee-high child.

Rebecca, however, ignored the compliment. Two red patches had appeared in the pallor of her cheeks and her eyes were suspiciously bright. 'But Herbert was going to make provision...'

'Was going to,' the lawyer soothed. 'And there you have it. You know his wishes. I know his wishes. Unfortunately, Mrs Millard, those wishes are not recorded on paper and "going to do" is not "did". I am afraid there are debts,' he went on gently, as to a delicate and sensitive child. 'Large debts. And those debtors have first claim, my dear. Until the claims are met there can be no division of spoils, if you will forgive the levity, and no spoils to divide.'

'What are these ... debts?' asked Rebecca in a small, tight voice. She had known that Herbert's estate would take time to put in order – or to 'wind up' as the lawyers put it. The shops alone would necessitate that, and then the complications of a death abroad had increased both the formalities and the delay. But Herbert had always cocooned her in comfort and the idea of poverty had never occurred to her. Or, she was sure, to him.

'The debts?' Mr Proudfoot looked at her with the same soothingly benign expression he would use, thought Rebecca, to announce debts of ten pounds or of ten thousand pounds. Her wits sharpened by fear and a new and growing anger, she listened closely as he went on, 'Various wholesalers, suppliers, nothing you need concern yourself about, my dear. The main one, of course, is the loan on the new premises which, as you know, are barely established as yet. Still in helpless infancy, you might say.' He smiled indulgently and Mrs Millard's anger increased. 'Your late husband had ambitious plans which no doubt would greatly have increased his profits, but alas, such things were not to be . . .' He paused, in respectful silence, before continuing briskly, 'However, when the business is sold – and the main branch, as we know, is a thriving and well-respected enterprise – and all debts paid, we should be able to find enough for a modest annuity for yourself, but your daughters. . . .'

'Must marry,' interrupted Rebecca. And as best they can, she added grimly under her breath. So much for the handsome settlements, so much for the penniless aristocracy queueing up for a rich wife from among her daughters. The girls would be lucky to find a tailor's assistant, as she had done. But the memory of Herbert's humble beginnings brought others in its train – her father's money, for instance, which had provided the dowry to set them on their way – a dowry which Herbert had planned for his daughters and which they could never have now, unless ... The blood of her adventurer-father stirred in her veins, together with the obstinate determination which had won her Herbert for a husband in spite of her father's objections. Herbert had started with little enough, but he had had the courage and the determination to achieve his aims and to keep his family in comfort. She owed it to his memory not to let Mr Proudfoot or anyone else destroy what her husband had worked so hard to achieve. It was not Herbert's fault that his wishes had not been recorded. Mr Proudfoot should have seen to it that they were. 'And must marry, I assume,' she finished coldly, 'without dowries?'

'I am afraid . . .'

'Quite,' interrupted Rebecca in a voice that forbade comment, while clear in her head rang Herbert's voice, saying 'If I die, remember the girls are to lead the lives they choose, married or single...' and now, it seemed, they were to be denied all choice. She glared at Mr Proudfoot with open hatred. How dare he decide their lives for them? How dare he dictate what they might and might not do? How dare he condemn Rebecca herself to a 'modest' annuity? Herbert would not have stood for it. And nor would she.

'You say the business must be sold, Mr Proudfoot,' she resumed, with deceptive sweetness, 'in order to pay the creditors. But is there any reason in law why I should not keep on the business and the new premises and operate them as my husband would have done, had he lived? I and my daughters are prepared to work, Mr Proudfoot...'

'Mamma!' cried Claire in horror. 'Whatever are you saying?'

'To work,' repeated Rebecca with a frown at Claire, 'as manager, cashier, accountant, clerk, whatever is necessary, Mr Proudfoot, and of course,' she added, suddenly submissive, eyelids demurely lowered, 'always supposing you would continue to give me, as you so generously gave my father, your expert guidance and advice?'

Rose regarded her mother with open amazement while Claire bit her lip and wrung her hands in appalled and tearful protest. 'Mamma, you can't,' she wailed, but her mother ignored her. Rebecca was focussing all her feminine batteries on Simeon Proudfoot and when he hesitated, she added softly, 'I am not destitute. I still have a little money of my own, from my dear father...'

Mr Proudfoot looked at her sharply, reminded of that occasion some twenty years ago when he had drawn up her marriage settlement to a fellow she insisted on having against all his and her father's advice and recognised the same obstinacy as he had seen then behind the heart-melting smile. Now, as then, the smile defeated him. After a startled moment, he readjusted his ideas, with his spectacles, shuffled his feet on the hearth-rug and said carefully, 'That is a new and interesting idea, Mrs Millard.'

'It is a dreadful idea!' cried Claire, hot tears of fury in her eyes. 'You cannot *work*, Mamma! Whatever will people say?'

'Wish her good luck, I should think,' commented Rose and was ignored. But even Rose found the idea disturbing. For herself, she didn't mind what she did as long as she still had time to draw and it would do Claire good to have to do something useful, but her mother had *never* worked.

When Rebecca said, 'Be quiet, Claire,' the new note of resolution silenced Rose also. 'I apologise, Mr Proudfoot,' went on Rebecca sweetly, 'for my daughters' unseemly interruptions. Do please continue.'

Proudfoot cleared his throat unnecessarily and did so. 'As you know, your husband left his estate entirely to you and your daughters. As your executor I had thought that an annuity would be the best, if not the only solution and had hoped to find sufficient outlay to allow you to live, if not in luxury, at least in a modicum of comfort, but...'

'But no dowries.'

'I am afraid not. Your husband's wishes, of course, were plain and, given the years of consolidation which he had expected, would no doubt have been most adequately fulfilled. As it is...'

'As it is, I would like, Mr Proudfoot, to carry out my husband's wishes.' Her voice was firm, her back straight, and with a sense of impending defeat Mr Proudfoot recognised the inflexible obstinacy behind her apparently diffident remark. 'Claire is sixteen,' she went on, her eyes holding his in a level gaze. 'I would like to be able to give her, as eldest, at least a half of what her father had planned for her by the time she is twenty-one. Is that possible?'

'Mr Blunt is an excellent manager,' said Mr Proudfoot warily, 'but he cannot achieve miracles. And there is the question of the debt.'

'But if the business flourishes, as I intend to ensure that it does, there will be profits. You must tell the creditors so, Mr Proudfoot. Tell them their money is safe with Millards and that the interest will continue to be paid.'

'But what will you and your daughters live on? How will you pay your servants? Keep up your house? I really would advise you, in your own best interests my dear Mrs Millard, to consider selling.'

'No.' Rebecca had made up her mind and no amount of Mr Proudfoot's protectiveness or chivalry would change it. But to take the hurt look from his eyes she went on sweetly, 'That is, of course, with your considered advice, Mr Proudfoot. There is something called a limited liability company, I believe, and I wonder if we might ... but you know so much more about such things than I do. The important thing is that I would like to keep on Herbert's newest premises and carry out his wishes as best I can, for his sake. You do see that, Mr Proudfoot? Mr Blunt, I am sure, will be as generous as you have always been with your experience and worldly wisdom and I shall rely on you both, heavily.'

Rebecca was shamelessly using her femininity to enlist his

sympathy, but she did so without sacrificing the strength and determination which showed now in every line of her elegant figure, from the set of her black-veiled head to the dignity of her crepe-covered paramatta gown and the polished perfection of her black kid buttoned boots. Even her jet earrings reflected a subtle blend of dignified sorrow, dogged determination and touching femininity. A widow's grief, a mother's fierce protectiveness, and a lovely woman's courage made an unbeatable combination and Simeon Proudfoot, for all his wisdom, was defeated.

'If that is what you wish, Mrs Millard,' he said, blushing like a schoolboy under the warmth of her soft brown eyes. He adjusted his collar which had suddenly become uncommonly tight, swallowed, then made for the bureau and the comparative protection of his papers. He sat down and drew the folder towards him. 'I will just run my eye over the figures once more...'

With the dignified grace of the victor, Rebecca rose and moved to the bell-pull. 'I will send for tea, Mr Proudfoot, if you permit me. And perhaps a glass of madeira? We have all had a distressing time and we have a long morning's work ahead of us.'

'Thank you, Mrs Millard. Refreshment would be most welcome.' The maid came and went again. Rebecca resumed her seat. Mr Proudfoot took up an inkless pen and scratched absent-mindedly at the desk flap of the bureau before recollecting where he was. Hastily he attempted to obliterate the scratch with the ball of his thumb, while he shuffled the papers yet again, then as the silence stretched behind him, he turned in his chair and said, 'While we await refreshment, Mrs Millard, is there any particular information you would like me to give you?'

Rebecca Millard was, for a moment, at a loss. She stood up, hesitated, then crossed the room to stand beside him. Then, as she looked down at the folder of papers on the open flap of her bureau and recognised the pattern of Mr Proudfoot's still visible scratchings, confidence flooded back to her and, with it, inspiration.

'Perhaps the figures for last year's advertising?' she began. 'I believe that Herbert planned to advertise on a London omnibus for the winter season. Nothing vulgar, of course – Thank you, Mr Proudfoot,' this as the lawyer pulled up a chair and offered it. 'He talked, as I recall, of a message such as "Millard's for Quality" – but only on the best routes.'

'Hmmm,' said Mr Proudfoot thoughtfully. Without his volition, his hand took up the pen and resumed its scratchings while his eyes rested admiringly on the comely figure beside him.

'And I wondered,' continued Rebecca softly, glancing briefly at the desk-top, 'whether in the new premises, in honour of my dear husband, we might perhaps open a Mourning department?'

For under the nib of Mr Proudfoot's inkless pen had emerged a perfect replica of Rebecca's black-veiled cap.

Part 2

London, 1897

CHAPTER 1

On that gusty May morning of 1897, the shop was particularly busy. No one intended to be outshone in the matter of what was both correct and elegant attire for the Queen's Diamond Jubilee celebrations and half London was vying with the other half for precedence in sartorial splendour. Gloves must be immaculate, hats stylish, collars crisp, cravats elegant or debonair and, of course, where the ladies were concerned, all such considerations were multiplied a hundred times. But, apart from the eminently discreet Mourning department, the premises of Millard and Blunt in Regent Street catered principally for gentlemen – and today there were too many.

Claire Millard pushed the damp hair from her forehead with the back of one hand and a pout of annoyance while with the other she unclipped the metal cannister from the overhead wires and tipped out its contents onto the desk. 'Item, one gent's dress shirt, 4s 11d, item, $\frac{1}{2}$ dozen stiff collars ..., item, one pair best kid gloves...' Impatiently she checked the total, counted out the change from the open cash box, let the coins run through her fingers neatly into the cannister, and snapped on the lid. She reached up, clipped the cannister in place and pulled the lever which sent it skimming across the overhead wires to the assistant in the shirts department. She hardly had time to spike the shop's half of the receipt before a sharp 'ping' announced the arrival of another cannister and she reached up, opened, counted, replaced in the dreary sequence that had become automatic over the two years she had been required to work at Millards.

Millard and Blunt's to be correct. Claire had not followed the intricacies of Mr Proudfoot's financial jugglings, with the ins and outs of transforming what had been a private family firm into a public limited company. Nor had she bothered to try, though her mother had summoned both Claire and Rose to listen to the lawyer's explanations. For on that dreadful day two and a half years ago the chrysalis of their known world had burst open and they had emerged, not gaudy butterflies, but plain, work-a-day moths.

'And clothes moths at that,' Rose had said, with melodramatic

63

relish. 'The kind Smelly Annie crushes to messy powder between finger and thumb.' Smelly Annie was still with them, out of pure and dogged loyalty, for Mrs Millard had explained that she could afford no more than a scullery maid's wages. But parlourmaid, butler and nanny had all gone, with the old house in St. John's Wood and the old, comfortable life.

Claire had fought briefly against the move from careless elegance to the sort of respectability that hung on only by the fingertips and fought again, more fiercely, against her mother's decision that Claire should take over the running of the diminished household so that Mrs Millard herself could devote her energies to the shop. Rose was to work in Millard's and Claire, too, when required to do so. The idea appalled her even more than the idea of her mother going out to work and she resisted both with all her strength. But she might have known it would be no good. Claire was obstinate, but her mother was more so, and though Claire might be head of the sisterhood, Rebecca was head of the house. The shop was doing well, they still held a controlling share in it, and though dividends were small as yet, one day they would improve. It behoved them all to work and save, till the family coffers were once more brimming.

Claire had raged and pleaded, had declared she would never find a husband once they had 'stooped to trade', that her hands would roughen, her skin coarsen, her complexion fade to a bilious yellow, she even claimed her lovely hair would fade and fall. 'And when I am a plain, bald, middle-aged spinster, then perhaps you will be sorry!'

Rebecca had stared her into silence before saying only, 'You will start tomorrow.' She did, however, make one concession. On the days when Claire was required to work in the shop, she confined her to the cashier's office where, if not entirely out of sight, she was perched so high above the body of the shop, behind a mahogany and glass partition, that at least the Beau Monde could not easily see her fall from grace. And Claire discovered, when her pique allowed her to look about her, that she was ideally positioned to look down upon the shoppers, 'Like a look-out in a crow's nest,' said Rose. Claire said haughtily, 'Or God.'

But then Rose did not seem to mind their changed circumstances as much as Claire did. Claire felt her father's death had ruined her life and whereas she was truly sorry he was dead, a small, secret part of her felt resentful and angry that he should have chosen to die when he did – and before providing proper dowries. She hated being 'in straitened circumstances', hated working in the shop, hated all the niggling household economies that had been forced upon them – though she enjoyed the satisfaction of making one shilling do the work of two and found she was surprisingly good at it – and vowed to marry money at the first opportunity.

'It will be difficult enough to find the kind of husband I want with no dowry to offer,' she told Rose, with a mixture of fury and despair, 'And downright impossible if I am required to parade my poverty by marketing in the streets with the kitchenmaids and working as a common shop assistant. How can Mamma expect it of me?'

Rose was more philosophical. If they were poor, then that was that. Poor people worked. Besides, it might be quite interesting.

But Rebecca knew her daughters' talents and Rose, who was quite prepared to work at the counter, selling boaters to schoolboys or dashing silk cravats to their elder brothers, was allowed to do neither. She was ordered into the inner office, with not even a bird's eye view of the outside world, to set her artistic imagination to work on everything graphic, from eye-catching price tickets for the garments in the window, to tiny pen-and-ink sketches for newspaper insertions or the Spring Catalogue.

On that particular May morning she was chewing her pen over a design for the ornamental lettering of their new advertisement on the London omnibus. Something large and easily readable, even for the illiterates of whom there were many in the London streets and not all without money to spend. It was a far cry from the water-colour sketches of river scenes and seascapes, the pen-and-ink portraits of her sisters, or the careful copies of Old Masters, but it was still drawing of a kind. So Rose, whose father had once promised her Florence and the riches of Renaissance Italy, drew meticulous sketches of Eton Jackets and tweed knickerbocker suits in miniature during the day and in the evening, in what spare time remained, she continued to sketch her sisters, to paint vases of cornflowers and sweet williams, or merely the view from the small front window of their small terraced house off the Brompton Road. At least, Mrs Millard had pointed out, it was a respectable area and within walking distance of the shop.

'Don't you *mind*?' demanded Claire fiercely.

But after the first rueful shrug Rose had said, cheerfully enough, '*Farewell happy fields where joy forever dwells. Hail horrors, hail Infernal world, and thou, profoundest Hell, Receive thy new possessor.*'

'Profoundest Hell' is right, thought Claire morosely as she emptied yet another cash canister, checked, re-filled and despatched it on its way. She was idly watching its swaying progress down the overhead wires towards Handkerchiefs, Ties and Cravats when her eye was caught by a figure in the throng near Boys' School Outfits. Among the mothers and schoolboys this figure stood out, being head and shoulders above the rest and with an air of supreme self-confidence which set him immediately apart. With a quickening of the blood Claire studied him until she was sure, then she unhooked the receiver from the black and gold telephone beside her and wound furiously on the handle.

'Yes? What is it this time?' Rose sounded exasperated and decidedly cross.

'Is Mamma there?'

'No she is not and . . .'

'Where is she? Quick, Rose. It's *urgent*!' The man was standing still now, looking around him as if searching for someone.

'I don't know where she is. What is the matter with you, Claire? Has someone tried to pass a forged half a crown?'

'Of course not! I said *urgent*! Oh, for pity's sake, Rose, where is she?' The man had spotted whoever he had been looking for and was making his way towards a group at the Schools counter – a woman in grey with her back towards Claire and a young girl beside her. A boy stood on her other side, trying on a cricket cap. As she watched, the man came up behind the woman and . . . no, it was impossible. If he really had done what she thought he had, the woman would have spun round and hit him. As it was, she barely turned her head and he began to speak to the little girl. Claire must have been mistaken. But where was Mamma?

'Where is she?' repeated Rose with infuriating calm. 'Goodness knows. Why?'

'Because I want her to go down and catch him before he gets away.'

'Catch who? Don't tell me there is a pickpocket in the shop! How exciting.'

Claire could not tell from her voice whether Rose was being serious or sarcastic, but she had not the time to find out. 'It's Harry Price-Hill, you idiot. Down there in the shop. I'm sure of it!'

There was a small pause of surprise, then Rose said, in a different voice, 'What is he doing? He's surely not ordering a suit after all this time?'

But Claire was too excited to catch the reference. 'No. He is in the Schools section. He was looking for someone, but I think he's found them. A governess, I think, with a boy and a girl. The boy is choosing a hat. Quick, Rose! Find Mamma before it's too late. It's our only chance, Rose, don't you see?'

'No, I do not. And I'm busy, so stop pestering me and . . .'

'Then if Mamma is nowhere to be found,' said Claire, making her decision, 'I must go myself.' She put her mouth close to the telephone mouthpiece and deliberately shouted, 'Come here, Rose, to the cash room. Now!'

'Ouch, you pig! That hurt. Just for that, I won't come. The cash room is your job anyway, not mine, and I can't get this wretched 'M' to . . .'

'You must. I'm not letting this chance slip through my fingers for you or for anyone and I can't leave the cash-room unattended so come, Rose, and hurry, before it's too late.'

She hung up the telephone receiver before Rose could reply and stripped off her cotton overall and sleeve-guards in almost the same movement. Thank the Lord she had put on her sprigged muslin today in spite of Mamma's disapproval. What was the good of keeping it 'for best' when there never was any 'best' to speak of? Besides, the journey to and from the shop was the only occasion on which Claire had the opportunity to display herself in her true colours, and she made certain that inside the office her precious finery was protected both from office dust and from unworthy eyes – in particular Mr Blunt's. Mr Blunt, balding and bespectacled, and forty years old if he was a day, might be Rebecca Millard's new business partner, but he was still only a shop manager and her father's shop manager at that. Mr Blunt might have scrimped and saved and invested till he could afford to buy into the company, but that did not give him the right to look at Claire like a hungry dog eyeing a particularly succulent bone.

'He is disgusting,' Claire complained to her mother on an occasion when he had spoken to her and she, according to her Mamma, had been 'unnecessarily rude'.

'He is a respectable bachelor,' her mother had said in stern reproof. 'And, moreover, one who owns a considerable number of shares in our company. You could do a great deal worse for yourself, young lady.'

But Claire meant to do a great deal better, and the arrival of Harry Price-Hill in the Regent Street shop offered the longed-for opportunity.

Swiftly Claire tossed aside the voluminous cotton overall and sleeves, kicked off her office pumps and found her little kid shoes, smoothed out the creases in her dress, adjusted hair, then bonnet, slipped on clean kid gloves (her last, precious pair) and snatched up the pretty frilled parasol which completed her toilet. She was standing impatiently in the doorway, small foot tapping, and trying to watch both the shop and the back stairs at the same time when Rose at last appeared. Two cash canisters jangled unheeded above the desk and a third was already skimming its upward way.

'That is from Schools,' warned Claire. 'Leave it till last – and don't hurry! Give me time to get round to the front of the shop before he leaves.'

Before Rose could answer, Claire was away, scurrying down the back stairs, her parasol in one hand, her bunched skirts in the other. Out through the staff entrance into the rear alley, past the dustcart and the heaps of refuse from the neighbouring hotel kitchen, round the corner into the side alley, down the alley at a run, then a momentary pause on the corner to draw breath, compose her face and her dress, and finally, open parasol at just the right angle, to walk briskly towards the doorway of Millard and Blunt's – and collide, head-on with a gentleman coming out.

It could not have been better timed. Oh blessed Fate! thought Claire as she dropped her parasol. And thrice blessed, she added gleefully as it bowled neatly into the road and under the wheel of a passing carriage. Why had she ever called Fate unkind? But he was speaking.

'I really am most frightfully sorry, madam. Please accept my most heartfelt apologies.'

The same voice, the same manners, and when she looked up into his face, the same handsome, concerned expression. Nevertheless, she indulged in a calculated moment's maidenly confusion and dismay before allowing recognition to break through.

'But isn't it...? Aren't you ...? I do believe we met, sir, some three years ago, abroad. You did our family a great service. Mr Price-Hill, is it not?' And she looked at him with her most appealingly innocent expression.

'By Jove! I do believe you're right. What confounded good luck – Bad luck, I should say, for your parasol, but confounded good luck for me. Miss Millard, I believe? Miss Claire Millard, if memory serves me aright, and, if you will excuse the liberty, more beautiful than ever. I say though, Miss Millard, I was most frightfully sorry about your father. I trust you received our condolences? My cousin Edward wrote for both of us, from Wychwood.'

'Oh, yes. Thank you. It was most kind.' Claire, unknown to her mother and after what she considered a decent interval, had purloined the black-edged card from her mother's writing desk and had kept it secretly in her own, as a reminder of possibilities glimpsed and as a boost for ambition. 'Wychwood, Wintlesham, Suffolk' had been the address, with the signature 'Edward Rivers.'

And here was his cousin now, standing almost chest to breast. The thought brought the colour most becomingly to her cheeks and when someone pushed past them out of the shop and he took her arm, saying 'We seem to be in the way here,' she leant against him trustingly and let him draw her a little aside.

'I say, Miss Millard,' he went on, steering her to a spot of pavement out of the main stream. 'I am most awfully glad to meet you again. And how is that talented sister of yours? Still drawing?'

Over his shoulder Claire could see one of Rose's tickets on a tailor's dummy in Millard's window. 'Oh, yes,' she said solemnly. 'Rose still sketches every day.'

'And the aquatic one? Young Sara? No more mishaps, I trust?'

'Oh no. None since you so gallantly rescued her.'

'Nonsense. Nothing gallant about it, Miss Millard,' but he looked pleased nonetheless. 'Fine young gal. Do tell her I was inquiring after her, and give her my best wishes.'

'I will.' Claire was searching anxiously for some other topic of conversation when she saw Harry Price-Hill draw the gold watch from his waistcoat pocket, consult it, and drop it neatly back. Any minute now he would send his regards to her mother and take his leave. Panic threatened as she searched her mind for some delaying tactic. But she had forgotten that parasol.

'I have an appointment in an hour's time, Miss Millard, but before then there is ample time for you to accompany me to Madame Rossini's so that I may buy you a parasol to replace your own poor mangled one.'

'Oh no,' protested Claire, as hope flooded through her. 'I could not possibly allow such a thing. It was an accident, after all.'

'Nonsense. My fault entirely. I insist upon replacing it.'

'But perhaps it could be mended,' she faltered, praying he would not take her at her word. They both turned to study the broken parasol, which still lay where the carriage wheel had crushed it, but even as they looked, an urchin darted out from nowhere, snatched it up, and disappeared again as swiftly as he had come.

'That settles the matter,' said Harry cheerfully. 'You have no choice but to accept.'

'I am not at all sure I ought to come with you,' hesitated Claire, weighing up decorum against opportunity. 'My Mamma...' She could have kicked herself as soon as she spoke for Mr Price-Hill mistook her meaning.

'Oh dear, I was forgetting. You were busy on some errand, no doubt, of family business and I have detained you.'

'No, no. At least ... I was only going to pass on a message to the manager, from Mamma, but it can wait.' She did not want Mr Price-Hill to think that she ran errands, or to know that any of them actually worked in the shop, but she could think of no other story on the spur of the moment. Fortunately, Mr Price-Hill seemed satisfied.

'Good. That is settled then. Allow me, Miss Millard,' and he offered his arm, with all the courtesy and charm she had dreamt of. 'Madame Rossini's is only five minutes' walk away.'

The five minutes passed all too soon, and they arrived at a small, discreet and obviously expensive shop off Bond Street, in whose velvet-draped window reposed one exquisite hat. Inside, deep carpets cushioned their tread, gilt-framed mirrors dazzled from every wall and the only merchandise in sight consisted of two more hats and a pair of carefully arranged gloves. But when Mr Price-Hill explained their requirements Madame whisked a succession of breath-taking parasols from discreet concealment, opening them, furling them, twirling them, and all the time prancing to and fro like a spirited and restless mannequin with nothing but disdain for her clients. She was a small, dark, intense woman of sinuous grace and uncertain years who managed somehow to make Claire feel gawky and ill at ease. Harry, on the other hand, reclining on a gold brocade sofa, arms spread wide and legs outstretched, was obviously enjoying himself, for all the world as if he were in a box at the theatre. When Madame executed a particularly intricate twirl with a lace bedecked parasol of canary silk, he actually clapped and cried 'Bravo!' But it had early become plain to Claire that Madame knew Harry Price-Hill well.

'Enough, woman,' he said now. 'The parasol is for Miss Millard, not for you. Let her have a chance to try them for herself.' So, after the first uncertainty, Claire strolled and posed with a succession of delightfully pretty parasols before a succession of flattering mirrors and an even more flattering admirer.

'Charming!' 'Perfect!' 'Delightful!' Harry Price-Hill was as attentive as even Claire could have wished and when the choice was finally made to their mutual satisfaction, she would have been entirely happy were it not for Madame's contemptuous eyes and the fact that only five minutes remained of Harry's company. For had he not mentioned an appointment?

It was Madame Rossini herself who saved her. 'You will be watching the Procession from your own drawing-room, monsieur?' she said, when he requested that she add the sum to his account. 'An address on the royal route is much to be envied, monsieur. Many families have already made hundreds of guineas hiring out a

70

mere window, and if one possesses a balcony or a drawing room with a bay, la! what a fortune could be made.'

'I will tell the Mater you said so,' said Harry cheerfully, 'Though I fear our own windows will be too full of inquisitive relations to leave room for any fee-paying voyeurs.'

Nevertheless they were half way back to Millards before Claire found the courage to speak and then only when Harry Price-Hill himself gave her the opening.

'Edward and I really were most awfully sorry about your father. Such a generous old buffer, if you will pardon the expression. A pleasure to meet him. And a tragedy for you all to lose him so abruptly, with no warning. So if there is ever anything we can do for you, Miss Millard, or for your family...'

'There is one small thing,' said Claire in the desperate knowledge that it was do or die. 'My mother and my sisters would dearly like to see the Jubilee procession, but we do not relish the crush of the public street. Mamma has made inquiries, but all the best windows are already taken. So if by any chance you were to hear of anything suitable...'

'Is that all?' Harry laughed. 'Nothing easier. As Madame Chapeau said, our place has windows and to spare, and right on the procession route. Here. I will give you my card.' He stopped, reached inside his waistcoat, and produced a gold card case from which he took an elegantly tooled piece of pasteboard. He turned it over and wrote quickly on the back. 'Best come early, so as not to miss the fun. And in case I am not around when you arrive, just show them my card.'

But they had reached the doorway of Millards and Harry Price-Hill drew out his watch again to check the time. 'Sorry. I must dash. An urgent appointment I'm afraid. But delighted to have met you. *Au revoir*, Miss Millard. *A bientot*.' Then, with a bow, he was gone.

Keeping her excitement decorously in check, Claire watched till his tall, square-shouldered elegance merged into the crowds at the curve of the street. Only then did she look down at the card in her hand. 'The Honourable Harry Price-Hill,' read Claire with awe. So *he* is the Honourable, not Mr Rivers. With a silent whoop of triumph, she looped her skirts and sped back up the side ally towards the rear of the shop and the staff entrance.

CHAPTER 2

For the next three weeks, Claire lived on a cloud of elation. She had made contact. She had gained an introduction into Society. She, among all the sisters, had her toe in the door and she was determined that that door would open wide to welcome her inside. Her one concern now was how to make the best impression with her limited resources.

Fortunately, Rebecca Millard was entirely on her side. She had shelved the idea of marriage for her daughters until, business troubles safely past, they could begin to look for profit. But that time was approaching and Claire had done well. Had Rebecca herself been on the premises when Mr Price-Hill arrived, she could not have done better.

'The invitation was for how many?' asked Mrs Millard, swiftly calculating the cost of a brougham in which to travel the distance from Knightsbridge to Piccadilly.

'Harry did not say,' said Claire with daring. She had taken to referring, nonchalantly, to 'Harry' as her excitement grew, as if by pretending to that intimacy she might actually achieve it. Rose, of course, was not deceived, Charlotte merely imitated her and was ordered by Maudie not to be rude, while Maudie herself ignored any reference to Mr Price-Hill, or changed the subject. Only Sara displayed a most satisfying mixture of envy and awe.

'Harry obviously expects me,' Claire went on, preening, 'and he asked particularly after Rose. Sara too,' she conceded, 'and of course you must come with us, Mamma.'

'There is no reason why we should not all go,' said Rose. 'After all, he knows how many there are of us and if he was foolhardy enough to issue the invitation, then he must accept the consequences.'

'I don't want to go to Mr Price-Hill's house,' declared Maud, 'and neither does Charlotte.'

'Yes, I do!' cried Charlotte indignantly and Sara added, 'Please, Mamma? Let me go too?' Ever since she had opened her eyes on that beach in Dieppe and seen him standing over her with the sun in his hair and water sparkling all over him like a frosted Prince from fairyland, she had loved Mr Price-Hill with a secret, hopeless fervour known only to her diary, for she would rather die than confess it to a living soul. He was much older than she was, of course, and in a different social sphere, but he had rescued her from drowning, which surely meant there was a special bond between them now, a bond that transcended all differences and would last for ever? 'Please, Mamma?' she pleaded again.

But in the end it was decided that only Rose, Claire and Mrs Millard should take up Mr Price-Hill's offer, while the others went with Annie and the children from next door, to a stand in Trafalgar Square. Sara was angry and fretful, declaring it was not fair and that she had as much right as anyone to go to Harry's house, but it did her no good.

'We cannot afford new clothes for everyone,' said Rebecca. 'It is better to make a good impression with two, than a bad with five. Besides, now the introduction has been made, I expect we will see Mr Price-Hill again.'

So Sara stored away her grievance and was required to make the best of it, while Claire bubbled with hope and excitement and the heady fare of dreams.

'Suppose he asks us to stay to dinner, Rose?' she sighed, languishing at the very thought. 'Or has taken tickets for a theatre? I would dearly love to hear Patti before she leaves London and it really is *the* entertainment of the season. It is her very last appearance after the Jubilee procession and *everybody* will be there. Oh, Rose, suppose he asks me to go with him? And then to supper afterwards? An intimate theatre supper, at some discreet and wildly expensive restaurant. Then later, perhaps, he will invite me to the country ... I suppose you will have to come too, or it would not be proper.'

'Thank you very much,' said Rose drily, without lifting her eyes from her sketch pad. They were in the front parlour of the house in Knightsbridge, a small, well-proportioned room but crowded with over-stuffed chairs, little tables, house plants, china ornaments and bric-a-brac, even a clutch of dusty ostrich feathers in a vase. A paper cascade concealed the empty grate while heavy lace curtains concealed the street.

It was a mild evening in early June, the birds vociferous in the lilac tree and a scent of roses in the air. From somewhere in the distance came the cheerful sound of a barrel organ and from closer at hand, the gentle clip-clop of horse's hooves on cobbles and a chattering of children's voices, playing.

Mamma was in the basement kitchen supervising Annie's preparations for dinner, and the others were somewhere upstairs. Maud

73

would be overseeing Charlotte's lessons and Sara no doubt writing her interminable diary instead of tackling the family mending which she should have finished weeks ago. But in the front parlour there was peace. Claire was busily unpicking stitches in a length of mauve material which had once been a tea gown of her mother's while Rose, in the window seat, sketched her sister's portrait, as a change from Eton collars and Gentlemen's serge suits.

'Remember you are not to mention the shop,' said Claire, suddenly fierce. 'We have nothing to do with it and certainly do not work there.'

'Oh?' Rose raised an eyebrow. 'How extraordinary. You mean we are to tell lies?'

'No, of course not!' snapped Claire. 'Merely . . . evasions. It is no good pretending we are not daughters of trade, because he knows that we are – but he does not know we are poor. And will not – unless you let the secret out. We are shareholders in an excellent investment – that is the line. Millard and Blunt's was up one percent on the Stock Exchange yesterday, I heard Blunt tell Mamma, and that, apparently, is good. Just remember, Rose.' She swung round suddenly in her chair and glared a warning at her sister. 'I am still the eldest. This is *my* opportunity and I am not going to let you or anyone else spoil it. If you do, I swear I'll kill you!'

'Claire the Ripper,' said Rose coolly. 'Just remember murder is against the law and you'll be hanged. Anyway, if you frown like that you will ruin your own chances with no help from me. One look at you and he will be out of the door before you can say Jack Robinson and running for his life.'

Claire was momentarily taken aback, but instead of resorting to missiles as she would once have done, she said, with new urgency, 'Please, Rose, promise you will help me? I do so want to make him like me. It is my only chance to be accepted, don't you see? I cannot bear the thought of this,' and she waved her hand despairingly to encompass the room, 'for evermore.'

'But you are only going to watch the procession, Claire,' said Rose, exasperated. 'Come down to earth. You can hardly expect the man to propose to you over the opera glasses and the smoked salmon. He will probably be far too busy watching his friends in the Life Guards or the Household Cavalry, or gawping with everyone else at the Borneo headhunters even to notice your existence! It is not as if you were invited to *dinner*.'

'Not yet,' said Claire, undeterred. 'But . . . oh, Rose, suppose he does?' Then her face set in determination. 'He will. One day.'

But even to Rose she could not voice the full extent of her hopes –

that Harry Price-Hill would be so captivated by her that he would sweep her up in a whirlwind romance which would end in a cloud of orange blossom, at the alter. This time next year, she thought with awe, I could be *married*. I wonder what title belongs to the wife of an Honourable?

The morning of the great day dawned overcast and dull. Obviously the heavens had not been informed of Queen Victoria's Diamond Jubilee procession or, if they had, were displaying lamentable lack of patriotism.

'Of course it will clear up,' said Mrs Millard briskly. 'Stop moaning and hurry. I ordered the brougham for eight o'clock.'

The three younger girls, scrubbed and brushed to Sunday splendour, had been dispatched half an hour ago to join the neighbour's children next door, from whence, eventually, they would catch an omnibus, but such transport was, of course, out of the question for Mrs Millard's party.

She had had much heart-searching about the time they should arrive in Stratton Street. The crowds, of course, would be dreadful, and the road traffic worse. People from outside London had been travelling up to Town throughout the night and by dawn hundreds were already occupying coveted positions all along the route. The whole city buzzed like an excited beehive and even from inside the house they could hear the unaccustomed noise of tramping feet, distant drums and trumpets, and the steady clamour of the gathering, expectant crowds. The moment London Bridge was closed to traffic at midnight, apparently, scores of people had rushed in to secure a good vantage point, quite content to settle down with their newspaper picnic parcels on their newspaper mats and spend the whole night there. Many other streets were to be closed to traffic this morning and whereas the driver of the brougham, naturally, would know which these were, it would not do to set off too late, find their access barred and be forced into a long and costly detour. On the other hand, too early and they risked being thought ill-mannered and ill-bred.

But already the streets of Knightsbridge were seething with people bound for the Palace gardens, Hyde Park Corner, Constitution Hill or places beyond, and any minute now the troops whose job it was to line the route would be marching to take up their positions. The unaccustomed crowds and the general air of excitement filled even Rebecca's breast with anxiety to be on their way before it was too late. The distance was not far, of course, and they had no need to worry about finding a suitable vantage point, but they had no way

75

of telling how long the journey would take them through such unusually crowded streets. She had decided, after much tormented thought, that to arrive by half past eight would be both prudent and acceptable, but now, as the noise outside swelled and the hands of the clock moved with infuriating slowness towards the hour she began to doubt her own wisdom. Suppose the brougham was late? Or did not come at all?

In consequence, they were all three ready and waiting in the hall a good five minutes too soon. Mrs Millard was elegantly correct in widow's black. Claire wore her new mauve gown, which even the sharpest eyes would not have recognised as an old garment remade, with cream lace and ribbons and a mauve bonnet decorated with cream silk flowers. She had drawn her corset in an extra inch at the waist and carried the cream silk parasol that Mr Price-Hill had bought her. Today her cheeks needed no pinching to give them colour and, when appealed to, Rose conceded that her sister looked remarkably pretty. Rose herself wore a blue pre-widowhood dress of her mother's, which suited her well enough, and carried a sketch pad.

'Surely you are not going to draw?' cried Claire, aghast.

'Of course. It is a perfect opportunity. I might even sell my sketches,' she added, straight-faced. 'If I am quick, I could spread them on the pavement in Trafalgar Square before the crowds disperse.'

'Rose! You *wouldn't*!' Too late, she realised she was being teased and turned on her sister in fury. 'Why do you never take anything seriously? I have such hopes of today and I know you are going to spoil everything!' She stamped her foot in rage. 'This is *my* day, remember! What I say, goes, so you had best not forget it.' She nipped Rose's arm with darting venom.

'Ow! You beast!'

'Girls, girls,' frowned Rebecca. 'How do you expect me to hear the carriage wheels through your unseemly squabbling?'

They rode towards Hyde Park Corner in silence – at first from annoyance, then, as their driver made necessary detours to avoid the more densely crowded streets, from gathering excitement and awe. For even the side streets were thronged with people, most of them in their Sunday best and many carrying covered baskets of provisions – it promised to be a long day – and every building had been tricked out in some sort of holiday attire. Bunting and patriotic streamers, flags, greenery, coloured lanterns: every householder, shopkeeper and office worker, it seemed, had thrown heart, soul and pocket into adorning the Queen's city for the Queen's Diamond

76

Jubilee. St James's Street, the cabbie told them, from the depth of his superior knowledge, was much the best though he readily admitted a partiality, the club gentlemen there being among his best clients. But to the three Millard ladies in the brougham every new adornment was a subject of wonder and amazement and as for the people, they had never seen so many crammed so tightly together, not even on the gangway of the cross-channel steamer. The grass under the trees of Green Park was coloured thick with them, as if a thousand many-coloured flowers had sprung up overnight, and the ranks of wooden stands were already full and dazzling with the splendour of the assembled ladies' toilettes.

As they approached Hyde Park Corner, they saw the pavements there were lined twelve deep with sightseers, many of them overflowing into the roadway. Mounted police and more on foot struggled to keep the crowds in their proper place, while other, more daring spectators had already scaled the roof of St George's Hospital and the nearest houseroofs in Grosvenor Place. Some enterprising adventurers even perched on the arch at the top of Constitution Hill. The doorway of St George's flashed with the white starched caps and aprons of assembled nurses and everywhere was colour, noise and gaiety. It was not the common generality of public exuberance, however, that claimed Claire's attention. Her eyes were fixed on the stately mansions, decked in arrogant splendour in honour of their Queen, and her expression was that of a child who had been given her heart's delight, twice over.

'Oh Mamma,' she breathed, 'I do believe we have *arrived*.'

As if in confirmation, the cabbie turned his head, jerked an expressive thumb and said nonchalantly, 'Lord Rothschild's place.'

For a moment Claire's assumed sophistication fell away and she stared, open-mouthed, as the brougham bowled past the awesome edifice. Its front was studded with trophies of flags, like arrogant jewels of red, white and blue. The spectator-seats rising above the courtyard were draped with red striped canvas and topped by a regal canopy of the same material, while festoons of pink and white flowers, strung between red and white poles, completed the splendid effect. Even the railings had been concealed under red and white painted boards and in the face of such reckless expense even Rebecca Millard's careful composure cracked. 'Well...' she breathed in admiration, while Rose made frantic efforts to capture at least the outline in her sketch-book before they were carried past.

Then they were in Piccadilly and were once again struck wordless by the vista opening before them.

The length of the avenue, from Hyde Park Corner to St James's

Street, stretched a succession of Venetian masts, supporting, on the Green Park side, festoons of evergreen and artificial flowers with red and blue glass lamps, which here and there spanned the street from one side to the other. Smaller, old buildings and newer mansions alike were decked in crimson for the occasion, many with touches of dark or lighter blue, their balconies studded with flags or draped with patriotic colours. Claire found herself hoping that Harry's house was one of the larger ones, preferably with a balcony and heraldic crest, but even a small one would do. 'Mamma,' she said again, but in a voice which imbued the simple word with all the excited pride and hope and social expectation which had fuelled her dreams since that triumphant meeting with Harry Price-Hill. Mrs Millard laid a gloved hand briefly on her daughter's, in a way which both commended and warned, as if to say, 'You have done well so far, but there is a long way yet to go.'

Claire, already in her mind's eye sweeping up some elegant stairway on Mr Price-Hill's arm, disregarded the warning and accepted only the praise. For here was Devonshire House, at its gated entrance tiers of seats, draped in crimson, and in gold lettering, the loyal emblem 'V.R. 1837, 1897,' and she, Claire Millard, had single-handedly engineered an invitation to one of the Duke's nearest neighbours. She was smiling in serene anticipation as the cabbie flicked the reins and the carriage turned the corner into Stratton Street. A moment later the vehicle pulled up at the entrance to the Price-Hill mansion. They had indeed arrived.

'There,' said Claire with quiet triumph. 'Did I not tell you we would have a perfect view?'

The house was certainly well placed and on the Piccadilly side its decorations were spectacular. The entire wall had been hung with drapery representing leaves and this novel background had been festooned with swathes of gold-edged crimson and mauve velvet, topped, lest anyone should fail to catch the imperial message, by a splendid gold crown.

As they stepped from the brougham to the pavement, the high skirl of bagpipes came suddenly over the park from the direction of the Palace. The 1st Battalion the King's Own Scottish Borderers was marching to take up guard position on Constitution Hill. All over the City similar bands of troops, uniforms impeccable, buckles, belts and buttons gleaming, moved to take up similar positions along the route and the air was suddenly filled with the thud of marching feet and the insistent throb of regimental drums.

Half-past eight, thought Rebecca with satisfaction. She could not have timed it better. 'Do you have the card, Claire?'

After a moment's agitated searching in her drawstring bag, Claire produced the precious scrap of pasteboard and, taking a deep breath, her mother rang the bell. They waited in breath-held silence while in the street behind them people shouted and cheered, dogs barked, and in the distance the bagpipes triumphantly played, as if to herald their arrival. They heard footsteps approaching. A manservant in awesome livery opened the door. Rebecca explained their visit and handed him the card.

With a curt bow, he requested them imperiously to 'Follow me' and led the way across the marble hall towards the stairs. In silence, under an intimidating chandelier, they mounted the gracious sweep of white and gold to the first landing – a long gallery, richly carpeted, and lined with portraits in gilded frames. Through a half open door Claire glimpsed a window framed by long velvet curtains, looped back with tasselled ropes, and the trees of the Park beyond. A row of Chippendale chairs in the window stood waiting for their occupants and there were gilt-rimmed china coffee cups on a mahogany side-table. From the invisible body of the room came the steady hum of conversation.

The time has come, thought Claire, her heart thudding faster, her excitement almost unbearable. Any minute now and Harry Price-Hill will step forward, hand outstretched, to welcome me. She was preparing the special smile she had practised before her mirror for weeks when she realised with surprise that they had not arrived after all. The man-servant was leading them on, up a second, narrower stairway to a darker, narrower passage, with linoleum on the floor and no pictures. But of course. He was taking them to some discreet disrobing room, where they might leave their wraps and give the last touches to their hair. When they were ready, he would usher them downstairs again, to that elegant drawing-room.

He stopped at a door half-way along the passage. He opened it and stepped aside for them to enter.

'In here,' he said, with an expression which reminded Claire uncomfortably of Madame Rossini's disdainful stare. Stepping past him into the room, the first glance told them there were no mirrors at which to powder one's nose or adjust one's hat. No dressing table with powder puff, tortoise-shell backed brushes or stoppered bottles of eau-de-Cologne. No day-bed for discarded wraps. Only linoleum on the floor, a rag rug by an empty grate, a deal table, scrubbed but ink-stained, a sagging Ottoman with a faded patchwork quilt. There was a blackboard on an easel in one corner and an abacus, broken. It was the family schoolroom.

After the first stifled gasp of dismay, they stood in silence, not

79

looking at each other, ashamed, as the door closed firmly behind them.

Rose was the first to recover. After the first disconcerted moment, she shrugged her shoulders, said 'Oh well . . .' and went to investigate the wooden bench which served as a window seat.

'At least we have a splendid view,' she remarked with equanimity. She took out her sketch pad and crayons and prepared to draw.

No one answered. Mrs Millard was too affronted and too angry to speak. Claire, after the first shock and outrage, was similarly speechless, but with a choking, all-consuming shame. Shame that Mr Price-Hill should think her unworthy of the drawing room, that a mere servant should despise them, that she had dressed for the orchestra stalls and been sent to the gallery, that she had been mortified in front of her mother and her sister; shame for her shattered dreams and her empty hopes. Her cheeks flamed while her eyes stung with tears of rage and humiliation. She turned her back so that her companions should not see.

But Rebecca Millard had recovered dignity. Her bosom still high with outrage, she said, with ominous calm, 'As we are here, we had best enjoy what small benefits there are. What can you see from the window Rose?'

'Almost the whole of Piccadilly,' said Rose with satisfaction, 'with a splendid view of the park. In fact, it couldn't be better. Come and see. And this bench is really quite comfortable.'

Claire, listening to them, flushed afresh with mortification. It was all her fault. She had boasted of her triumph, had brought them here with such hopes. She had promised them Society and a drawing room of elegant companionship – and found only an empty school-room with holes in the linoleum and not even a pleated paper in the empty grate. But it was not her fault. It was a mistake, that was all. And at least they were here, she reminded herself fiercely, here in the Honourable Harry's own house, and the day was not yet over. She composed her face, joined them at the window and said, in almost her normal voice, 'The servant has made a mistake. When Harry comes, all will be well.'

But Harry did not come.

They heard sounds enough from below – footsteps on the stairs, the opening and closing of doors, the chink of glasses and fine china, and, whenever a door opened, a gust of lively conversation and laughter. Later, the insidious aroma of fresh coffee wound up to tantalise their emptiness and when it was joined by the smell of hot scones and newly toasted muffins, Rose groaned aloud.

'Why did we not think to bring a picnic, like those sensible people down there?' she moaned, indicating the crowds across the road, under the trees of the park, many with open picnic hampers beside them. 'I declare I'm hungry enough to eat that blue-jacket's horse!'

Because, thought Claire with bitterness, we expected to be fed. As it was, they must endure until someone appeared to liberate them, or until the Procession was over and they might make their humiliated escape. So she sat uneasily on the wooden bench, ignoring hunger, defying shame and regarding the street below with determined interest while her mind went over and over the appalling snub they had suffered and her ears strained for sounds of approaching feet. None came.

In Piccadilly wheeled traffic had stopped and the troops who were to keep the route were taking up position to the encouraging cheers of the spectators. With splendid disdain, Rebecca Millard took out her opera glasses and, her back unbending, trained them on the street below. Claire feigned similar interest, though the prospect had lost all colour and excitement for her. The street might just as well have been in dreary monochrome and the spectators mute. Of the three, only Rose found genuine interest in the spectacle as the 1st Battalion Manchester Regiment marched past them eastward, followed by the 2nd Battalion Royal Irish Fusiliers who broke ranks, spread out and made a human fence on either side of the path along which the Royal Procession would pass. Their motionless, blue-uniformed figures added yet another layer to the already brilliant canvas till even Rose's artistic appetite was surfeited. For not only was every private mansion the length of Piccadilly decked in loyal finery, but the Junior Athenaeum and the Service Clubs too were openly competing with any and everyone in the matter of jubilee embellishments. There was enough imperial velvet and gold braiding on display in this one street, thought Rose, not to mention flags and crests and loyal emblems, to equip the casts of a dozen Gilbert and Sullivan operas. And the Procession had not even begun. Her sketch book was rapidly filling and she began to wish that she had brought a larger.

The three sat in silence, two communing with their own sombre thoughts, the third with her pencils, until, shortly after nine o'clock, a huge wave of cheering wafted towards them from the direction of the Palace.

'That will be Field-Marshal Lord Roberts,' said Mrs Millard, consulting the Order of Procession which she had carefully snipped from the previous day's *Times*. 'He is to lead out the Colonial troops who form the vanguard of the procession. It is apparently Canada first, then New South Wales and Victoria.'

81

'Really?' said Claire without interest. She had expected to watch the procession from a stylish drawing room, with Harry and his distinguished friends beside her, not from a dusty schoolroom, with only her mother and Rose. Inside her head the words drummed monotonously on, 'Why doesn't he *come*?'

'Pull yourself together, Claire,' said her mother sharply. 'Remember we came to enjoy the procession. I order you to enjoy it!'

'Yes, Mamma.' But her mother was right. If . . . *when* Harry did come, he must not find her deflated. A little reproachful, perhaps, but appealingly so, and quite in control of the situation. Enjoyment was much the most dignified course. And the most sophisticated. Resolutely Claire held out her hand for the programme.

'I wonder if we will see any natives?' speculated Rose idly, her head on one side as she held up a pencil to the window and squinted at it in order to measure the proportions of a mounted policeman against a tree. 'Aborigines, perhaps, or Maoris in tribal dress? If they have a tribal dress, that is, and don't just go about naked.'

Her mother and Claire ignored her, both being intent on memorising the order of carriages in the Royal procession, or as much of it as they could manage before the vanguard appeared.

Rose had covered several more sheets with sketches when a new cheer rose from the direction of Hyde Park Corner. A moment later the advance party of the Royal Horse Guards turned into Piccadilly, with Field-Marshal Lord Roberts himself on a superb grey charger, and following, in a glorious river of moving colour, the Canadian Hussars, the 2nd Canadian Dragoons and the superbly hatted Mounted Police. Gold braid dazzled, scarlet blazed, black leather shone like mirror glass, horses steamed and sparkled under flashing harness and glinting spurs. The stirring sound of massed horses' hooves on road metal and the jingling of massed harness vied with the wild cheering of the crowds, and the stirring beat of the military bands; the flashing of steel and gleaming flank with the flamboyance of the garlanded streets. And the sun triumphantly shone.

Somewhere beneath them, from the windows of that elegant, favoured drawing room, the Price-Hill party watched, as they did: but any sounds of voices or laughter that might have floated up to them were obliterated now by renewed cheering, the high skirl of approaching bagpipes and the thudding rhythm of the massed drums, until even Claire no longer listened for a footstep on the stair.

Then the State Landau of the Premier of Canada, drawn by four horses, each with its uniformed postillion, rolled in august grandeur beneath their window and for the next twenty minutes they watched a succession of splendidly accoutred men and horses trotting through the cheering crowds on a tidal wave of ceremonial splendour. Australian Lancers, their helmets bound with scarlet pugarees, escorted the carriage of the premier of New South Wales.

When a harmless-looking contingent in khaki appeared, Rose cried, 'There go the Borneo men! They are all headhunters, Annie says, and one of them has thirteen heads to his credit.'

'I wonder which one?' said Claire, with the first real interest of the morning, and leant forward the better to see.

Maoris of warlike aspect, Cypriote Zaptiehs in dark blue with scarlet fez and sash, Hausas from the Gold Coast, Chinese police from Hong Kong. The band of the London Scottish beat its rousing call in a skirl of triumphant pipes as regiment after regiment marched past in splendid symmetry – until even Claire managed to forget rebuff in the pleasure of watching such martial pageantry.

Then suddenly there was a pause. The final contingent of Canadian Mounted troops had ridden eastwards into the crowds at St James's Street and no others had arrived to take their place. The first procession was over and with the respite, humiliation, and hunger, returned.

'The Royal Party should be next,' said Rebecca calmly, after consulting the programme. 'Led by Captain Ames of the Life Guards, and a naval field battery of guns.' Her back was ramrod straight, her expression untroubled. She had not forgotten, and certainly not forgiven the snub, but no one should detect the fact from her demeanour. 'Next, the aides-de-camp and the equerries, then the carriages – sixteen of them – before the Queen herself.'

'Perhaps Her Imperial Majesty is taking coffee,' said Rose wistfully. 'Viennese coffee with whipped cream in delicious swirls on top and grated chocolate. And a slice of wickedly fattening cake. By Appointment.'

'Shut up!' said Claire, colouring. 'I don't want to think about it.'

'Petticoat tails,' went on Rose, 'Or even gingerbread. One of those gingerbread men Charlotte loves, with currants for eyes. And it doesn't have to be coffee. Cocoa would do. "Cadbury's cocoa makes strong men stronger." Or even tea.'

'Perhaps we ought to . . .' began Rebecca and stopped as they all three heard hurried footsteps on the stairs. Then the door burst open and an untidy young woman shot inside, to slither to an embarrassed halt as she saw their three startled faces.

'I say, I do apologise. I did not know anyone was up here.' She pushed the hair back from her face and said, with a disarming grin, 'I am Georgina Woodstock, by the way.'

Mrs Millard, summoning courtesy, made the necessary introductions.

'Mr Price-Hill invited us,' said Claire, with dignity. 'But he does not seem to be here.'

'Oh, he is here somewhere,' said Miss Woodstock cheerfully. 'But you know Harry. He's invited half London, including Boo Boo Tavistock's crowd and you know what they're like. A plague of locusts, Aunt Clem calls them, only locusts don't usually swig champagne by the bucketful. He's probably forgotten he asked you by now. I say, I didn't mean to be rude,' she added hastily. 'Just that Harry's probably squiffy. I'm afraid I don't always think enough before I speak. Aunt Clem's always telling me so. I just meant that ... oh never mind. I hope you are comfortable up here?'

She looked around the room with obvious pleasure. She was a tall girl, of the build called statuesque, with thick, pale hair, bundled unsuccessfully into a heavy chignon, and startling dark eyebrows that almost met across her small, straight nose. Her looks were certainly unusual, yet with a classical beauty of the kind, Rose said afterwards, to be found on Greek or Roman remains. But her friendliness was real enough.

'I have always liked this room,' she said now, smiling. 'It is so much more friendly than that imposing drawing room with its precious porcelain and crystal. I am always terrified of breaking something. Besides it's cram full of dowagers today, so that I can't get near the windows for love nor money and I *must* see Percy.'

Claire and Rose exchanged questioning glances, and Mrs Millard said politely, 'Your brother, Miss Woodstock?'

Georgina beamed her pleasure. 'My twin. He is a captain in the Guards and I do so want to see him ride past. He said he would be near the front, just after the naval guns. I hope I haven't missed him?' she finished anxiously.

'I don't think so.' Mrs Millard indicated the order of procession in her newspaper cutting. 'Nothing has passed since the Colonials.'

'Then that's all right. I am just in time. Percy will be in the next lot.' She had joined them at the window and was peering anxiously along the procession route towards Hyde Park Corner, when in the distance they heard the sudden joyous clamour of bells from St Paul's, a salvo of guns boomed out in answer from Hyde Park and a distant band launched into the national anthem. 'They're off!' said Georgina with cheerful disrespect. 'But no need to worry. We've a good ten minutes spare. There's Constitution Hill first, and we will hear the cheering long before they reach here. I say, watching all those people eating down there makes me hungry. Have you had coffee?'

Reluctantly they admitted they had not, and, when pressed, that they had had nothing since seven that morning.

'You poor creatures, you must be feeling positively faint,' cried Miss Woodstock. 'What is Harry thinking of? But then he is so busy, poor lamb, with the house full of visitors to be entertained, I suppose one should not complain. The party in the drawing room has already eaten everything in sight and as for drink, our dear Queen will live to be a hundred three times over if even half their loyal toasts are answered! But I will see what I can rustle up for us. I know I'm ravenous and you must be too.'

'Miss Woodstock,' protested Rebecca, 'there is really no need to . . .'

But Miss Woodstock had gone, on the same gust of cheerful energy that had blown her in.

'I hope she does not miss the procession,' said Claire. Whoever Georgina Woodstock might be, she was the only member of the household to show them any civility and Claire would not wish her to miss her brother's appearance on their account.

But she need not have worried. Georgina Woodstock reappeared after a scant seven minutes, bounding up the stairs two at a time by the sound of it, to arrive breathless but triumphant at the window, just as the first cheer reached them from Hyde Park.

'No bubbly I'm afraid,' she apologised. 'But Roberts has been persuaded to part with a couple of bottles of Dry-Royal and a game pie from the kitchen and I've told him to bring coffee, too. Are they in sight yet?' She peered eagerly out of the window. 'Yes . . . I think . . .' Another great wave of cheering surged towards them and she cried 'Hurray! Here comes Captain Ames. Doesn't he look splendid, all by himself with his sword upright and his breastplate gleaming? Like St George, expecting a dragon. And his escort of four troopers. They are from Percy's regiment, you know. Percy says their helmets are dreadfully hot, especially on a day like this. But it's all right for them, they're on horseback. Look at all those poor seamen. Fancy having to drag those guns all over London on a day like this.' Her next words were drowned in the lusty strains of the national anthem as the first of the military bands passed beneath their window and the first of the cavalry regiments approached, but everyone heard her squeal of excitement as she spotted her brother. 'Oh, look! There's Percy. Third from the left in the second row!'

The loving admiration on her face was touching to see as the troop of Life Guards rode into sight, their saddle-cloths, breeches,

85

gauntlets and helmet-plumes dazzling white against the scarlet of their regimental jackets and the black of their leather riding boots and gleaming mounts. Their silver breastplates flashed back the sunlight in a thousand stabbing stars, their helmet-plumes rose and fell in swaying unison, their horses trotted in perfect, high-stepping symmetry, impervious to the roar of cheering from the crowd. Dragoon guards followed, scarlet-plumed, and the 2nd Dragoons, their plumes black, their horses bay. The 6th Dragoon Guards, the Carabiniers, wore blue, with white plumes, and yet more squadrons followed, till the avenue seemed a blurr of moving blue and scarlet and white, of glittering cuirasses and helmets, flashing swords and nodding plumes, of prancing, richly caparisoned horses. The bands played, the crowds cheered, Dragoons gave place to blue-coated, busby-ed Hussars, then Lancers, also in blue, with pennons fluttering, but Miss Woodstock kept her eyes on her brother's upright, expressionless figure till the troop of Guards was lost in the crowds at St James's Street and a new troop took its place.

Georgina sighed her pleasure and turned smiling, apologetic eyes on her companions. 'Sorry,' she said, with a disarming laugh. 'Rude of me not to utter, but Percy always looks so splendid. Good seat, too, wouldn't you say? You don't have to agree with me, of course, probably looked no different from the next man to you, but ... I mean ... well, he is my only brother!'

Before anyone could comment on this charming partiality, there was a discreet knock on the door and a manservant entered carrying a linen-covered tray on which lay a silver-lidded dish and a pair of bottles in a silver-rimmed ice bucket. There were crystal glasses, bone china plates, and heavy silver, wrapped in starched linen napkins. A maidservant followed, similarly starched and bearing a tray of coffee cups and a steaming silver pot.

'Thank you, Roberts,' said Miss Woodstock, barely taking her eyes from the spectacle outside where aides-de-camp, equerries, gentlemen-in-waiting and military attaches were now flowing past in full ceremonial splendour. 'We will serve ourselves.'

Claire watched her from lowered eyes, with a mixture of awe and envy. Miss Woodstock was large and plain, no older than Claire herself and not nearly as well dressed in that shapeless Grecian thing she wore, even though it was pure silk, and as for those awful shoes ... Yet for all that she had an air of supreme self-confidence and unquestioning authority which Claire would have given her entire wardrobe to possess.

'Fizz?' said Georgina and poured them each a sparkling measure. Then she raised her glass to 'Her Majesty, God bless the old

86

dear,' and drained it in one draught. 'That's better,' she announced cheerfully, wiping her mouth with the back of her hand. 'I was dry as a mummy's tomb. Now, who's for pie?' Without waiting for an answer she handed them each a hefty slice on a delicate Sevres plate, then picked up her own slice in her fingers and bit into it with large white teeth and a healthy appetite. When she had refilled their glasses and helped herself to more pie – Claire dared not eat hers at more than nibbling speed lest her corsets burst open and Mrs Millard took similar care – Georgina, munching happily, resumed her place in the window and unashamedly looked over Rose's shoulder.

'I say, Miss Millard, that is really frightfully good.'

Rose, after the first satisfying bite, had returned to her sketch, a young guardsman on a prancing horse whose rear legs would not come right. 'Do you think so?' she said doubtfully. 'I can't get this wretched fetlock to behave as it ought.'

'Horses are notoriously difficult to draw, and to sculpt, too. I ought to know. I've tried often enough.'

'Really?' Rose looked at her with new interest. 'I have always wanted to meet a sculptress. Tell me, have you seen Donatello's Condottiere at Padua? Or Verrocchio's Colleoni and those splendid bronze horses on the basilica in Venice?'

'No,' sighed Georgina, 'but I would dearly love to do so. It is one of my dreams to travel in Italy.'

'And mine. To see real genius, face to face, must be an inspiration worth a hundred reproductions,' said Rose, remembering those dreams of her childhood, before her father died.

But before they could pursue the subject further, another roar from Hyde Park Corner announced the imminent approach of the Royal contingent while simultaneously, under their very window, a similar cheer hailed the Imperial Service troops, with their dark-bearded faces and flamboyant uniforms, Lieut-Colonel Maharajah Sir Partab Singh, in upright, turbanned glory, resplendent at their head. Now, in both directions, as far as the eye could see along the tree-lined, garlanded street, there stretched a moving pageant of kaleidoscopic brilliance, as troop after troop rode majestically past between the lines of motionless foot soldiers who kept the cheering crowds in place. Handkerchiefs waved above the crowds like flocks of demented butterflies, bells rang, trumpets sounded and finally the booming of cannon from Buckingham Palace announced the Queen's own coach had started on its way. This time even Claire could look on the pageant unfolding under her window with breathless and unqualified delight. What if Harry Price-Hill had forgotten her? She was not the only one, if Miss Woodstock was to be believed, and when memory returned, he would no doubt appear. Meanwhile, Miss Woodstock was as welcoming, and as knowledgeable, as anyone could wish and the coffee was superb. Stomach comforted and pride soothed, Claire turned her happy attention to the first of the glittering carriages in the Royal parade.

'Good Lord!' cried Georgina. 'They have put the Papal Nuncio and the Chinese Emperor's chappie in the same landau. At least if it gets too hot, they can share a fan!' That set the tone of her comments as the dazzling carriages passed, their occupants resplendent in every kind of ceremonial uniform, medals and orders flashing, their escorts immaculate, their high-stepping, bedizened horses faultless.

The first five carriages, landaus and pairs, contained the foreign envoys, of no more than passing interest to the watchers in the schoolroom, but once the Royal carriages began it was a different matter. And Georgina was invaluable. She seemed to know everyone without recourse to Mrs Millard's list.

'There are the Battenberg children,' she cried as the eighth carriage passed. 'That's little Princess Ena in white, the happy-faced one who is bowing to right and left as if she really enjoys it. And there is the Princess of Connaught – what a fright she looks in that tiara – and Schleswig-Holstein . . . and there's old Buffy! I bet he's roasting under all that ermine. And Lotty looking disapproving as ever. My stars! Look at the Duchess of Teck's dress! I wonder what our dear Queen thinks of that one? But aren't the horses superb?'

The twelfth carriage was drawn by four magnificent Hanoverian horses ridden by postilions in scarlet liveries embroidered in gold, and contained, Claire noted with awe, three princesses and a duchess. But then so did they all. Princes, princesses, duchesses, dukes – a Grand Duke in the thirteenth – and three Grand Duchesses in the next. Claire's head was spinning now with titles, her eyes dazzled by jewelled tiaras and necklaces, medals and decorations and orders of every kind, gold epaulettes and brilliant silks and mile after mile of gold braid, while the bands played, the sun blazed down and the cheering continued unabated. Sparkling fairytale carriages with sparkling Royal passengers continued to roll past as if to a perpetual Cinderella's ball and with Georgina Woodstock beside them to give that knowledgeable and disrespectful commentary, Claire shed the last remnant of the morning's shame and gave herself up to pleasure. She was one of the inner circle, one of the favoured few who ate off delicate china with a crested fork from the family silver, and who knew Princesses intimately, by nickname.

'I say,' said Georgina, when the sixteenth carriage had passed and there was an expectant pause before the Parade of Princes which would precede the jewel of the procession, the State carriage of the Queen, 'you must be the family Harry met in Dieppe. With the little girl who nearly drowned. Am I right?'

But any reply was prevented by renewed cheering from below as the Colonial Escort rode into view, at the head of the Escort of Forty Princes: princes old and young, English and foreign, their uniforms dazzling in their magnificence and variety, their orders multifarious and awesome – Egypt, Siam, Persia, Schaumberg Lippe, Anhalt, Russia, Luxemburg – riding three abreast in princely majesty, their horses as magnificently caparisoned as themselves. The cheers by now were deafening, but the party in the schoolroom watched in sudden silence, too awed even to speak, as the Queen's own carriage came into view and approached on a tidal wave of tumultuous fervour to pass beneath their very window. The state carriage, golden in the steady sunlight, was drawn by eight cream-coloured horses with harness as beautiful as themselves, high-stepping with the graceful arrogance of perfect breeding, postillions on their backs and red-coated footmen at their sides, and accompanied on horseback by the Prince of Wales in scarlet Field Marshal's uniform, and the Dukes of Connaught and Cambridge. And inside, a white-haired old lady in a black dress, Victoria, Queen of England, Empress of India, Defender of the Faith.

The Queen, small and plump and, in spite of her years, looking in no way fatigued by the demands of the day, turned her head graciously this way, then that, acknowledging the plaudits of the crowd with a smile and a bow of the head. Like Mrs Millard, Her Majesty was in widow's black, but the royal gown was silk and thick with steel and silver embroidery, the black lace bonnet glittering with diamonds. A wreath of white acacia blossom and an aigrette of more diamonds completed the royal toilet, with a parasol of frilled white lace. It was the outfit Mrs Millard had anticipated and recommended to her dowager customers. Accordingly, she was well pleased, but Claire beside her was less so. The Princess of Wales who, with Princess Christian, accompanied the Queen, wore a dress in the same mauve shade as Claire's, but trimmed with lace and spangles, and her mauve bonnet bore a wreath, not of contrasting, but of matching flowers. Much more elegant, thought Claire, whose own cream flowers seemed suddenly vulgar. I will remember that.

But the state carriage was moving on towards St James's Street and the service in St Paul's. The Royal Standard followed and the field officers' escort of Life Guards, then the street was once more full of horses as equerries, Royal Irish Constabulary, and finally the Royal Horse Guards brought up the rear. Almost 47,000 troops of all ranks and regiments had taken part in the procession, whether as guards of honour or in lining the streets, and it seemed to the spectators in the nursery that a good 46,000 of them had passed beneath their window.

Now the Procession was over. Nevertheless, they continued to stare out of the window long after the last guardsman was out of sight, hoping for some diversion to prolong the pleasure and postpone the necessity of leaving, while in the street the crowds began to stir, pack up their belongings and prepare to move on to whatever entertainment next awaited them.

Only Rose seemed impervious. She was working busily at that pencil sketch of a solitary horseman. Then, with a flourish, she sketched in a scribbled initial, tore the sheet from the pad, and handed it to Georgina. 'For you. A poor likeness, I know, but the best I can do.'

'But it's lovely!' cried Georgina with genuine pleasure. 'Percy will be most flattered – and there is a likeness, whatever you say. You must tell me how long you have been studying art and the teachers you have had. I am at the Royal College, but it took me two years to persuade Papa to let me go and then only in the afternoons. The modelling classes are fairly mediocre, but I don't tell Papa that or he might withdraw permission! Sculpture is my field, you see. And I do not draw half as well as you. Let me see what else you have done.' She sat down beside Rose who began to turn the pages of her sketch book and soon the two of them were deep in a discussion of perspective and the efficacy or otherwise of foreshortening.

Claire and Mrs Millard exchanged questioning glances. Then the latter moved resolutely for the coffee tray with a murmured, 'If I may? More coffee, Claire?' She took up the crested silver pot and poured. There was no saying what friendship might develop between Miss Woodstock and Rose, and Rebecca was prepared to drink a sea of coffee, if necessary, to keep them together.

But there was a sudden flurry of voices, moving feet and opening doors from below, then hurried steps on the stairs and the door burst open.

'There you are, Georgie! I might have known it! I must say I call it pretty mean of you to sneak off and ... oh.' Harry Price-Hill's expression moved rapidly from astonishment, to consternation, to red-faced embarrassment and the patent wish to be somewhere else.

'Oh Lord,' he said and would have fled had not manners got the better of him. Instead, after only a moment's hesitation, he advanced into the room with outstretched hand and a determined smile.

'Mrs Millard, isn't it? So glad you could come.'

Rebecca Millard kept her own hands firmly clasped across her well upholstered bosom. 'We came,' she said coldly, 'on your express invitation. I had thought it customary for a host to greet his guests. Obviously I was mistaken.'

'Mamma,' cried Claire, blushing with embarrassment. 'It does not matter.'

'Nonsense. Manners always matter.' Now that she had that charming Miss Woodstock on her side, Mrs Millard was prepared to stand by her principles and she fixed Harry Price-Hill with a look so stern 'that it practically speared me to the wall,' as he reported later, in the safety of his club. 'As if I had committed all seven deadly sins and she was on door-duty at the Heavenly gates.' However, he stood his ground.

'I really am most frightfully sorry, Mrs Millard,' he said. 'The house is positively bursting at the seams today as you can see and . . .'

'Harry!' An imperious voice called up the stair-well from the floor below. 'How much longer are you going to stand there dithering?'

'Sorry,' said Harry again, grinning ruefully at Claire, then at Rose. 'Have to go. Oh. Almost forgot. The Mater wants you too, Georgie. Sent me to find you. Wants you to help the old biddies into their coats and point them in the right direction for home.' He made for the door, turned, said 'Hope you enjoyed the procession anyway,' then he was gone.

'Drat!' said Georgina, with feeling. 'I'll have to go. But don't leave, please. I will come back and see you out myself. And don't worry about Harry. He's scatterbrained, that's all. He means no harm. The "convenience", by the way, is through that door, in Nanny's old room.' Then she was gone.

Dry-Royal, coffee and the morning's constriction made her solicitude particularly welcome.

'What a charming, thoughtful girl,' said Mrs Millard, adjusting her hat before Nanny's mirror. It was beneath her dignity to comment on Mr Price-Hill's conduct.

'A pity she is so plain,' said Claire smugly, admiring her own reflection. She had removed the offending flowers and concealed them in her draw-string bag: the result, as she had hoped, was definitely more elegant. Moreover, the 'fizz' and Georgina's

91

company had quite restored her confidence. As for Harry, he had come to find them after all, just as she had said he would. (The fact that it had been Georgina he was searching for she discarded as irrelevant.) And the house really had been frightfully full, just as he said. He obviously hadn't had a minute of his own, poor man. She wondered, hope restored, if he would be there in the hall to see them out?

But when Georgina Woodstock eventually returned to escort them down the stairs and out into the street where a brougham had been expressly summoned for their use, the house was quiet and there was no one in sight.

'They've all gone on to the Tavistocks',' explained Georgina, 'to continue the party. I don't expect they will be back till the small hours, if then.'

'Please thank Mr Price-Hill on our behalf for his kind hospitality,' said Mrs Millard, with a dignity worthy of the Queen herself.

'Tell him we enjoyed it greatly,' said Claire, with her sweetest smile. 'And that we are so sorry to have missed him.'

Rose merely said, 'Goodbye, Georgina, and thank you.'

To Mrs Millard's and Claire's astonishment, Georgina leant forward and kissed Rose on the cheek.

'Goodbye, Rose. *A bientot.*'

'And what exactly did she mean by that?' demanded Claire the moment they were in the brougham. Rose merely turned to wave to the Woodstock girl and did not answer.

'Don't be vulgar, Claire,' reproved her mother. 'And wave Miss Woodstock goodbye.' She raised her gloved hand in farewell and, glowering, Claire followed suit.

But Claire did not easily give up and later, after hours of relentless questioning, she achieved her end, as she had meant to do from the start, though they were both in bed and the lamps out before Rose at last capitulated.

'Oh? Did I not tell you?' she said and yawned with aggravating thoroughness before adding, 'She has invited me to visit her studio, tomorrow.'

Claire, of course, was furious. It should have been *her* day, her triumph, her invitation – though the invitation she had dreamt of was of quite a different kind. Georgina Woodstock might be rich and well-connected, but she was a girl, and a great, clumsy girl at that, with a plain face and plainer manners. And whoever heard of anyone wanting to be a sculptress? It could only be because she despaired of catching a husband, and no wonder. Who could imagine that Amazon as a blushing bride?

Yet at the same time, Miss Woodstock had a studio, and sometimes artistic people could be quite romantic. Look at Mr Rossetti, for instance, or Alma Tadema. But no one like that could possibly visit the Woodstock girl's studio and a lot of artists were dirty and poor. If Rose wanted to consort with such unsavoury people then she was welcome. Nevertheless, as eldest, Claire should have been consulted and invited too. It was her right. Only the thought that through Rose and the Woodstock girl she might one day meet the Honourable Harry again, or someone equally well-connected, kept Claire from screaming her frustration aloud. That, and a growing sense of dignity, caught, like measles, from the day's procession. So, instead of attacking Rose with pillow, tooth and claw, she said piously, 'Remember you don't have a holiday every day. You are working tomorrow, in Millards.'

'I have not forgotten, Claire dear,' said Rose in a voice of sweet deference which should have put Claire on her guard. As it was, she was quite unprepared for the *coup de grace*. 'I told Georgina all about the shop and she quite understands. I am to go in the evening, after Millards has closed.'

'Rose, you *didn't*!' Claire was almost speechless with horror and fury. 'Did you tell her I worked there too? And Mamma?'

'Of course. But she doesn't mind at all. She is a Liberated Woman. Besides, she has shares in Millards herself.'

Claire could have wept with despair, but it was too late now. Rose had torn away her carefully constructed veil of respectability and had betrayed them. But at least the Woodstock girl had not withdrawn her invitation.

'Just remember the Rule, that's all,' she said with venom. 'Because if you forget it, Rose, *you will be sorry*.'

CHAPTER 3

Georgina Woodstock's studio was functional, spartan and utterly charming. Above her father's coach-house in Kensington, it was approached through a courtyard and up an outside wooden stairway to what had been the hay loft and stable lads' quarters until the substitution of a motor car for the family carriage made such quarters obsolete.

The loft was empty now of hay, but the bare boards still held particles of dust and straw lodged in the cracks. The roof sloped to the floor on either side, but the inverted 'V' was high enough in the centre to accommodate the tallest visitor, in spite of the beams which spanned the space at regular intervals. A row of skylights filled the room with pale light and the end wall, of solid stone, had been newly whitewashed. An ottoman heaped with rugs and a couple of straw-bottomed chairs made up the furniture and from a shelf on the far wall a collection of assorted busts, many of them of children, stared with sightless clay eyes into the beamed and vaulted silence. The newest, unfinished head was on a modelling stand in the centre of the room and covered by a draped wet cloth. On a small table nearby were wires, pincers, callipers and assorted modelling tools, and on the floor a cloth-covered iron bin containing damp clay. There was even an oil stove and, behind a folding screen, a wash-stand with ewer and jug.

In spite of the city noises drifting up from the distant street – carriage wheels, costermongers' cries, a barrel organ – there was an air of tranquillity and harmony in the place which reminded Rose of a simple country church: she fell in love with it on sight.

'You could live here, Georgina,' she said, with envy. 'Here is everything anyone could possibly want. You are lucky to have such understanding parents.'

'Not understanding at all. They merely humour me and, I suspect, are glad to get me out of the way. And Daddy can afford it.' She whisked the cloth away from the clay model and studied the half-shaped lump with critical eyes. Here and there matchlike pieces of wood protruded from the 'skull'. Frowning, Georgina took a pair of callipers and measured between two of the matchsticks. 'I am not sure I have positioned the ears properly. They should be between two horizontal lines,' she said. 'The brows and the bottom of the nose. But then perhaps the nose is wrong? Certainly the cheeks are too hollow. I shall build them up.'

She peeled back the cloth from the iron tub and took out a small piece of clay which she began to work between her fingers. 'Build up, they told me, rather than cut down. Cutting down is for carvers. There is so much I don't know, Rose,' she sighed. 'I get so despondent.' When Rose made no comment, but stood watching her as she added a small, flattened clay disc to the bust's cheek, she went on, 'One day I shall travel to Italy and study at the feet of masters. London is full to the brim with artists in paint and canvas, but when it comes to sculptors there is Onslow Ford, of course, but the rest are few, mediocre, and for the most part worship at the altar of the Deadly Commonplace. We are limited to funeral urns and Niobes weeping over tombs.'

She stood back and stared critically at the clay lump, her head on one side. 'It is supposed to be Percy, but he cannot often sit for me so I work from memory. It's not easy and this wretched clay is either too wet and slippery or so dry it refuses to work at all.'

'I know how you feel,' sighed Rose. 'I spend all day drawing silly pictures for Millards' catalogues or writing out price tags and then when I do get any time of my own, nothing goes right. For instance, I am doing a water colour sketch of Claire – she is good to draw and she loves it, which helps – and I can't get the light right, whatever I do. I've held the wretched thing under the tap twice already.'

'Start again,' suggested Georgina. 'I've done that often enough. Poor, dear Percy here, for instance, has had half a dozen noses already, and none of them right. Fortunately, he doesn't mind, bless him. He is totally uncritical.'

'Unlike my sister,' frowned Rose, studying Georgina's clay head. 'She expects me to make her perfect every time. Why don't you try shortening the nose a little? Then maybe building up the chin? I don't know what Percy looks like, of course, but I think it might help the proportions.'

'Hmm . . . I think you may be right.' Georgina studied her efforts, head on one side, then took up a palette knife and began carefully to trim her brother's nose while Rose watched, as absorbed as Georgina was in the effect.

'Yes,' cried Georgina, standing back to admire the result. 'Why didn't I think of that? It has made all the difference.'

She wore a gown of a dull gold trimmed with lace, with fashionable leg-o-mutton sleeves and of impeccable cut, but topped by a clay-spattered canvas apron of voluminous proportions. Her careless disregard for fashion should have made her look unkempt. Instead, it gave her an air of stylish individuality which her dishevelled hair and serious expression merely emphasised. To Rose she looked what she was – a handsome, liberated young woman of enviable independence.

'You were too close to it,' said Rose, 'as I am to my painting, and sometimes it takes an outsider's eye to spot the obvious. You must do the same for me one day. There is no one at home to make the right sort of comment.'

'I know what you mean. "It's lovely, darling," if they like it and "I'm sure it will be lovely when it's finished, darling," if they don't.'

They laughed in perfect understanding, then Georgina said seriously, 'I intend to work in marble one day. If ever I am good enough.'

'You will be, Georgina, if you work and work and let no one deflect you. That is the important thing.'

'Yes, but sometimes, when I've had a bad day and everything has gone wrong, I wonder if perhaps ... oh, Rose, do you ever lose confidence in yourself?'

'Frequently. For instance, when I have mixed a perfect wash of delicate twilight green and it comes out on the page like boiled cabbage. Or when I sketch a perfect church spire and find it out-Pisas the leaning tower.'

'I'm so glad,' cried Georgina, laughing. 'Because I *know* your work is good.'

'And so is yours,' countered Rose, then added seriously, 'But I think your children's heads are best. They have a freshness and an innocence which is enhanced by your unspoilt approach. The adult heads look merely ... amateur.'

'I know,' said Georgina humbly and quite without resentment. ' "Unskilled" would be more apt than "unspoilt". But some of the child heads are good. It was when I actually sold one that Daddy agreed to give me this,' and she waved her hand to encompass the bare studio with its cool north light and its one oil stove.

But in July the sun's heat kept the edge from the air and filled it instead with the warm scent of clay and linseed oil and old, tired wood. 'I want you to use this place whenever you choose, Rose,' she went on. 'You are the first friend I ever had who really understands and I want to share everything with you. Come and go when you please, whether I am here or not. I want it to be your artistic home, as it is mine. We might even hire a model one day and work

96

from life. I have always wanted to attempt a full sized figure and there is no better way to practise. Oh, we will work so well together, you with your pictures, I with my clay. I hang the key on a hook above the lintel, by the way, when I'm not here. Just let yourself in whenever you feel the need, day or night. It doesn't matter when, so long as it is for Art.'

Rose was overwhelmed. Her father had promised her a studio of her own, though his ideas encompassed only pictures of flowers in vases and perhaps a series of crayon drawings of her sisters. He would certainly never have countenanced the hiring of a *model*. But with his death she had thought her studio lost to her for ever. Now Georgina Woodstock was offering her that dream afresh.

'I don't know what to say . . .' she managed, her eyes bright with emotion.

'Say you will, of course. You will, won't you?' Georgina finished, suddenly anxious.

Rose looked at her with brimming eyes. 'Of course I will.' Impulsively, she kissed Georgina on the cheek. 'Though I don't deserve it.'

'Nonsense. You are the first person I've met who has given me an honest opinion and we will work so well together. I know it.' She added, suddenly grave, 'I make only one condition, Rose.'

'And what is that?'

'That you never touch my work.'

'Is that all?' Rose laughed with relief. 'I promise it shall be safe as the Holy Grail.'

'I would not have mentioned it,' went on Georgina with a look of mingled sadness and intensity, 'and I know that *you* would not, but one's friends are not always so sensitive. Once Harry came here after a party, when I was not here, and someone hacked a turnip grin into the head I was working on so that when I took off the cloth the next day, there it was, grinning at me like a Hallowe'en lantern, with a *carrot* for a nose.'

'How dreadful!' cried Rose with genuine horror. 'Whatever was he thinking of?'

'Oh it was not Harry,' said Georgina quickly, 'Although of course he said it was and took the blame. It was one of his drunken Philistine friends, I am sure of it. Harry was frightfully apologetic, said it was only a lark and all that, and no harm meant. All the same, I wish it hadn't happened.'

'I should think so!' cried Rose indignantly. 'I know how I would feel if someone painted a moustache on one of my paintings.'

'Unless it was a picture of Percy?' teased Georgina and they both

97

laughed. Percival Woodstock sported a splendidly glossy moustache of which Rose suspected he was inordinately proud.

'Nevertheless, whether it was Harry himself or not, he was quite right to apologise. It was his responsibility.'

'Rose, there is one more thing you had better know, in strictest confidence...' She looked down at her clay-streaked hands in momentary embarrassment, before saying in a rush, 'Harry and I are unofficially engaged. That is, our parents arranged it years ago – for property reasons, I think: our estates are next door to each other – and it is understood that we will marry one day when, as Aunt Clementina puts it "that young man can be brought to heel." I have loved Harry hopelessly since I was a child, even though I am not at all the type of woman he finds ... attractive. But I cannot help it and that's that. I just thought I had better warn you.'

'Oh...' said Rose awkwardly, remembering Georgina's too-cheery talk of Boo Boo Tavistock and "all that crowd". 'I did not know...' Poor Georgina, she thought with new compassion. If all I know of Harry Price-Hill is correct, she is right. She is not his type at all.

'No matter,' said Georgina briskly. 'Now that dark secret is safely out of the cupboard we'd best put it back again and forget it.'

'Of course,' said Rose quickly and added, teasing, 'Is there anything else I ought to know before I commit myself?'

'You already have – but if that nose is too short, Rose Millard, I may have to reconsider...' Grinning, Georgina took up a knife and began to scrape carefully at her model and Rose watched her in contented silence, while the summer evening shadows lengthened and the studio was barred with fading gold. Rose had positioned herself under the skylight furthest from the door so that she did not at first see their visitor, though she heard his voice and Georgina's cry of welcome.

'Percy! How lovely to see you!' Georgina tossed aside her palette knife and ran to embrace her brother with exuberant affection. 'I was hoping you would come today, Percy, as your nose will not behave.' She indicated the clay model with a pout of annoyance and Percy grinned.

'Give me any nose you like, Georgie, it's all the same to me.' He tossed his hat onto the ottoman and reached to loosen his collar stud. 'Phew, but it's close in here. Can you not open a window?' Then he saw Rose watching him and stopped. A slow flush of embarrassment spread over his face and he muttered hastily, 'I am sorry. I did not know you had a visitor.'

'I haven't,' said Georgina cheerfully. 'Only a friend. Come out of your corner, Rose, and be introduced.'

Smiling, Rose obeyed. In deference to the summer and the occasion, she had discarded the high-necked blouse and tight-hipped skirt which her mother usually required her to wear to Millards, and wore instead a loose-flowing garment of sea-green silk, bound under the breasts with a band of gold, and a green silk bandanna in her thick, red-tinted hair. She looked, to Percival Woodstock's wondering eyes, like a Roman maiden strayed from some sun-drenched villa in Pompeii and could not have presented a greater contrast to his own dove-grey correctness of morning suit and high-starched collar. His confusion was increased when she said, in a low voice rich with humour and a strong Scottish burr, *'As Tammie glow'rd, amaz'd and curious, The mirth and fun grew fast and furious.'*

'Don't tease him, Rose,' said Georgina, slipping her arm through Percival's and leaning affectionately against him. 'He is a dear boy and, moreover, my brother.' Then, with mock flamboyance, she added, 'My new friend, Rose Millard.'

'I am honoured,' murmured Percy and bowed with military courtesy, reminding Rose of his uniformed splendour of the previous day. But Percy Woodstock was handsome even out of uniform, tall and blond like his sister, with all the advantages of a military bearing – which made his shyness so unexpected and touching. They talked politely of the weather, the Jubilee procession and the progress of the Afghan war, before Rose excused herself and got up to go.

'No, stay!' ordered Georgina. 'At least until you can see if your suggestion was right.'

'Oh dear,' said Rose. 'Would it not be safer for me to leave now?'

'Certainly not, so sit down and behave,' ordered Georgina, laughing, and Rose obeyed.

Percy, on Georgina's orders, arranged himself on the ottoman, gloved hands folded over silver-topped cane and profile carefully turned to the light. It could have been mere coincidence that turned the young man's eyes in the direction of Rose's chair, but the result was unsettling. Now and again Rose caught scraps of desultory conversation from across the room, but whenever she looked up, she invariably found Percival watching her until she began to feel uneasy. Perhaps he wanted to be alone with his sister, to discuss family matters without the inhibiting presence of a stranger? When Georgina at last tossed aside her palette knife and said, 'That's enough for this evening,' Rose prepared to leave.

This time, Georgina let her go, though not before they had

99

exchanged promises to meet again very soon. Percival had leapt to his feet the moment Rose stood up and now he insisted on escorting her to the street where he summoned, and paid for, a cab. When she protested, he said, 'I insist. And so does Georgina. If you are truly her friend, you will accept.' Rose accepted. But when she turned to look back as the cabbie touched the horse into trotting motion, she saw Percival still watching her with an expression that made her decidedly uncomfortable. She vowed there and then to be independent both of cabs and escorts.

'A *bicycle!*' cried Claire in horror. 'Rose, you cannot. It is so unladylike, so vulgar, so ... so ...'

'Daring?' supplied Rose. The family was at dinner some days later in the small dining room at the back of the house. The heavy oak table was covered with a white damask cloth, a centrepiece of roses (picked by Sara from the garden) added a touch of grace, but the silver-plated cutlery and onion-patterned china seemed suddenly oppressively *bourgeois*, as did her mother's widow's weeds, her younger sisters' aproned neatness and most of all, Claire's sleek coiffure, her high-necked blouse and carefully corseted figure. Since the Jubilee procession, Claire had paid close attention to her wardrobe, snipping off lace here, adding braid there, and generally altering what had been a froth of feminine frills and ribbons into what she considered a more sophisticated style. Remembering Georgina Woodstock's casual disregard for appearance Rose was both amused and irritated by her sister's attempts at elegance and more so by her ruthless pursuit of respectability.

'But think of the time I will save,' she said, in a voice of sweet reason. 'And the money for cabs. Besides, Georgina has a bicycle and we intend to go bicycling together into the countryside. Bicycling is quite the thing, you know, among ladies of high society, though of course one must dress the part. I shall make over that old blue dress of mine into a bloomer suit,' she added, straightfaced. 'And perhaps Georgina's brother will lend me his woollen stockings. I will need a Norfolk jacket, of course, and a sailor hat and a good pair of sturdy shoes. Though I suppose I could adapt a pair of knickerbockers from Gent's Outfitting – at a discount, of course.'

'Mamma, tell her she mayn't,' cried Claire, appalled, while Charlotte clamoured to be allowed a ride on Rose's new bicycle when she got it, Maud told her it was far too dangerous and she would only fall off and get killed, and Sara's head turned from one to the other as she followed their arguments, to record later, in secret, in her diary.

100

Mrs Millard did not answer. Instead, with an impatient gesture, she waved their bickering aside. There was instant silence. Even eight-year-old Charlotte knew better than to interrupt when Mamma was 'thinking'. In silence, eyes lowered, they ate their way dutifully through 'summer' broth, mutton cutlets and the inevitable vanilla mould, while the marble clock ticked loudly on the mantelpiece beside the silver framed photograph of Herbert Millard, looking sombre and reproachful, and every sound of spoon or fork on china, of swallowing or chewing, was magnified into deafening embarrassment.

Upstairs, in her bedroom, Rebecca Millard sat straight-backed and thoughtful on the dressing-table stool. Her black taffeta gown and black lace cap were sombre enough, but the black ribbons which trimmed them and the black jet which was all the jewellery she chose to wear since her widowhood added an appealingly feminine touch. Though forty-two and mother of five daughters, Rebecca Millard was still a striking woman with a figure many women half her age might envy. It was not her own attractions, however, which occupied her as she stared into the dressing-table mirror. On the oak chest of drawers, reflected in the looking-glass and flanked by a pair of flowered china candlesticks, stood a photograph, in a chased silver frame, of her husband, a younger version of that in the dining-room, and it was to this photograph that she looked daily for guidance.

Three years of widowhood had not been easy. She missed Herbert every moment of the day and at night when she turned down the light her solitary bed was over-large and cold. She missed his dominance, his irritability, his gruff affection; she missed his stability, his solid circumstances, the reassurance of his presence as head of the household. And secretly, with a different ache of the body as well as the heart, she missed the comfort of his love. Throughout those three years of lonely struggle it had been the memory of their last afternoon together which had sustained her, a memory which she revived, deliberately, whenever despair or misery threatened to overcome her.

Now, staring at Herbert's likeness, at the starched wing collar and carefully combed moustache, she remembered that Dieppe afternoon with poignant affection. They had made love with the comfortable, satisfying pleasure of people who, from years of affectionate intimacy, were at ease in each other's company. Just to think of it brought a languorous glow of remembered joy, though that joy was tinged inevitably with sadness.

101

But it was a different memory that she called to her aid whenever the cares of business grew too burdensome, or when the children's needs obtruded, as they did now. It was the memory of Herbert saying, 'If I die, remember the girls are to live the lives *they* choose, married or single...' It was those words which had driven her to fight to keep on Millard's after Herbert's death, and to build it up as best she could in the way he would have done himself had he lived. He had wanted Rose to pursue her art, to go abroad to study, to have her own studio one day. And though he had not relished the thought of losing any of his daughters in marriage to another man, he had wanted to provide for them, and give them 'all they could ever want, and more, by George!' And by George, thought Rebecca, the best way she could pay tribute to her husband's memory was to carry out his wishes, to bring up his children, as she had always done, with firmness and rectitude, and to see that they achieved their ambitions.

Charlotte was only eight and happy enough. By the time she was of marriageable age, the business should be on a firm enough footing to provide more than adequately for her. And Charlotte would certainly want to marry. Of Maudie, Rebecca was not so sure. Since Herbert's death Maud had avoided male company and when it was forced upon her, became awkward and withdrawn to the point of surliness. It was a phase, no doubt, and one she would grow out of, with adolescence. Meanwhile she was contented enough at the little dame-school which the three youngest girls attended and later she could work in Millards, or help at home. As for Sara, she had taken her father's death hard. It had made her withdrawn, almost secretive...

Sara had a habit of watching people which was vaguely unsettling. She was still a little gawky for fourteen, but growing remarkably pretty, with her fair hair, hazel eyes and clear complexion. But Sara knew more than she ought to at her age, and was given to remarks which, while not actually impertinent, were what her teacher called 'too clever by half'. Rebecca suspected that her daughter already knew more than her teacher and that the teacher resented it. Sara wrote too much, too. She kept a diary which she locked away in a drawer when she was not writing in it endless pages of tiny script. Rebecca would dearly have liked to read that diary, but of course it was out of the question. Other people's letters and diaries were sacred. Even children's. But in many ways Sara, at fourteen, was less of a child than Rose or even Claire. Of all the five, Rebecca knew least about her middle daughter and, as yet, had little inkling of what Sara's hopes and ambitions were. Sara would have to be watched, and if necessary kept in check.

Rose was quite different. Rose lived for her art and was cheerfully open about it. Moreover, she had talent. Herbert had intended to encourage her and Rebecca had hoped to be able to do the same. Since Herbert's death, Rebecca had begun to fear that Rose's artistic career would be limited to the illustrated advertisements of Millard and Blunt's, but if Rose's friendship with the Woodstock girl continued it looked as if she might get her studio after all. Even, perhaps, her study tour abroad, and, if she played her cards right, without recourse to the family savings. It was an exciting prospect and one which Rebecca wholeheartedly approved.

As for Claire, it had become clear to Rebecca long ago that Claire's heart was set on marriage and, moreover, on a marriage which would lift her up the social scale. Once, that would have been eminently possible with the dowry Herbert talked of providing: now it would be difficult – and impossible if Claire's choice were limited to the dreary social round of that class of society to which their straitened circumstances had condemned them. Whist, bezique, tea and tinkling pianos, with bank clerks and tradesmen, worthy and respectable enough, but a step down rather than up the social ladder and not at all what Claire wanted or what Rebecca wanted for her. The Woodstock contact was a chance for Claire as well as for Rose and one that must be taken and exploited to the full. It would still be difficult, of course...

Difficult, but not impossible. Though it would take time. Shares would not be enough to offer. It would have to be a lump sum, and a large one. But the Woodstock brother sounded 'possible' and if Rose's friendship with the sister blossomed... Claire was an attractive girl who knew how to dress. Rebecca had noted her changing taste with approval, though that approval had not extended to what she saw as Claire's heartless snobbery where Mr Blunt was concerned. Mr Blunt was respectable, unmarried, and since his purchase of shares in the company, a senior partner, with his name above the shop. Marriage to Mr Blunt would be no shame – after all, Rebecca herself had married a shop assistant. It would consolidate the enterprise and, moreover, keep the shares firmly in the Millard family. Mr Blunt, she knew, was more than willing, but Claire would not begin to entertain the idea. She wanted more than an honest tradesman old enough to be her father. She wanted Class.

'And by George she shall have it!' The words sounded as clearly in Rebecca's head as if the photograph had spoken aloud. And Rose, of all things, wanted a bicycle. The two things might not, after all, be unconnected.

103

With deliberation, Rebecca reached up and unpinned her hair. It was the signal that her decision was taken. Rose could have her bicycle. But first, Rebecca had matters to discuss with Mr Proudfoot.

CHAPTER 4

The hedgerows in Rosary Lane stood knee-deep in blossom – harebells, yarrow, daisies, field poppies and a dozen different kinds of feathered grass. Branches grew so dense they almost met overhead, making a scented tunnel of the narrow country lane which dipped and rose again in a long, straight ribbon of sun-threaded dust.

'I hope we don't meet a hay wagon,' cried Rose, one hand holding her wide straw hat which, though secured with a trailing gauze scarf, was lifting alarmingly.

'Or Daddy's beastly motor-car!' Georgina laughed into the wind which funnelled warm on their cheeks as they gathered speed on the downhill run, to slow again into pedalling effort on the long, uphill ride.

'Phew, but this is hot work,' gasped Rose and shamelessly dismounted, tossed her bicycle onto the grass verge and collapsed beside it. Laughing, Georgina joined her and for a blissful few minutes they lay, breathless and panting, eyes closed, arms outspread, skirts like drifting blossom in the lush grass. For in spite of her threats, Rose had not adopted the bloomers, the thought of which had so horrified Claire – except for one, harem-style pair of "pyjamas", ballooning like an Ali Baba slave's in yellow cheesecloth she had dyed herself. But they were for her daily bicycle ride through the streets of London on her way to Georgina's studio, when the crowds and the carriages required that she concentrate on navigation rather than on protecting her skirts. Here, in the untroubled sunlight of a Suffolk lane, such sophistication was inappropriate and both Georgina and Rose wore the more conventional dress required by a country house weekend.

Since that first meeting at the Diamond Jubilee procession in June, the friendship between the two had quickly strengthened and consolidated to a relationship in which shared interests, shared ambition and mutual respect combined. Whether speaking or silent, as now, they were at ease in each other's company, with no need to impress, ingratiate or entertain. It was a mark of their particular friendship that there was no rivalry between them except in the sense that the success of one spurred on the other to greater effort: similarly, a mood of black despondency in one brought forth sympathy and encouragement from the other, and both suffered equally when their work failed to meet expectation. There was also, more importantly, no possessiveness on either side, so that when Rose was needed to prepare some new display for Millards, or to help with jam-making or some other seasonal domestic task, and stayed away from the studio for days at a time, Georgina made no comment. And when Georgina herself disappeared, sometimes for a week or more, to one or other of the dances and house parties of her particular social circuit, Rose missed her, but felt no sense of exclusion.

At first, Claire had nagged Rose persistently to elicit an invitation for them both to one of the envied 'week-ends'. Harry Price-Hill had proved an empty hope. In spite of Claire's careful thank-you note, they had heard nothing from him, 'Not even an apology,' as Rebecca pointed out and added, 'You are wasting your hopes *there*.' Rose's friendship with the Woodstock girl was altogether more promising, but so far Rose had remained impervious to all Claire's cajoling and all her threats. If Georgina wanted Rose's company, she would ask her. If Rose wanted to accept, she would. If not, not. Though she had the prudence not to reveal the number of invitations from Georgina which she had turned down, not from any sense of inadequacy or inverted snobbery, but merely because the idea bored her. Claire might lust after the butterfly brilliance of the social scene, but Rose found all the excitement and satisfaction she could wish for in the Kensington studio.

Once, Claire sought her out there, but after half an hour's silence in which the Woodstock girl worked away at a lump of clay and Rose ground different coloured pigments into fine powder, she left again for the livelier company of Millards' cash office where at least someone spoke to her.

'Rose is impossible,' she complained to her mother. 'She never sees an opportunity, or if she does, she refuses to take it.'

'I will speak to her,' said her mother, but after the first unsuccessful urging, Mrs Millard retreated into watchfulness and bided her time. But she had not spent an entire morning cajoling Mr Proudfoot into admitting that a dowry of quite reasonable proportions *might* be arranged within a year if required; had not, with that hope, released Rose from half her normal duties at Millards and excused Claire not only from the cash office, but also from the more onerous tasks of household management, to have them spend the summer at home like wilting wallflowers.

106

That particular decision had caused rumpus enough as it was. Sara, with astonishing impertinence, had declared she was not going to take Claire's place in the cash office, now or ever, and had finished, with defiance, 'I shall go to college. Papa said I could!' Mrs Millard, remembering those words of Herbert's at Dieppe, had punished the child for rudeness, but had agreed to allow her to continue at school. Millard's shares had been 'up $1\frac{1}{2}$' that morning and perhaps they could afford it.

Perhaps also Rose was right to resist any urging to angle for party invitations and instead to play the waiting game. After all, she had not known Miss Woodstock long. But at the same time, delicacy could be stretched too far and neither Claire nor Rose was getting any younger. Claire was nineteen – more than old enough to marry – and Mr Blunt the faithful still hovered hopefully in the wings. If an invitation did not come soon, it might well be advisable for Claire to take the bird in the hand, especially when the bush seemed increasingly unwilling to give up whatever superior birdlife it might hold.

But Rose was not altogether antisocial. When a crowd of Georgina's friends gathered at the studio, as they frequently did, Rose often joined in their impromptu revels, with wine, cheese, bread, and endless talk, Montmartre style. They discussed art, theatre, morality, Free Love, even, sometimes, politics. It was on these occasions that she displayed her acting ability, dredging up from her cornucopia of reading splendidly apt quotations, often drily disrespectful, and delivering them with a histrionic expertise which soon won her the reputation of being both a wit and a good dramatic actor.

But she always excused herself before the night-life revels began in earnest and made her way home. And, giving no reason, she steadfastly refused all invitations.

But towards the end of August, when they had known each other almost eight weeks, Georgina had begged Rose to join her for a long weekend in Suffolk. 'The company will be deadly, I warn you, Rose, but I can't get out of it. Daddy always expects me for his birthday and I really owe it to the old dear to turn up, at least once a year. So please come with me? The old place is very picturesque,' she added slyly. 'Real Constable country. You will find a visual banquet, I promise you – and I invite you, not to make up any silly numbers, but as a friend.'

Abruptly, Rose had given in and the pleasure and excitement she felt at the prospect made her suspect that there had, after all, been an element of false pride in her previous refusals.

Claire, of course, had been furious.

Rose had announced her news casually, just before the end of dinner. Mrs Millard, at the head of the table, had smiled with quick satisfaction, composed her face again, and said only, 'How kind of Miss Woodstock. Do please convey to her my very best wishes.'

Claire sent no such message. 'You absolute beast, Rose!' she said, with venom, when they were alone together in their room, preparing for bed. 'You might at least have got me invited too! All I ever get is deary suppers at the Proudfoots or at some tedious neighbour's house, with Mr Blunt popping up everywhere like a leering jack-in-the-box! After all, who was it got you the introduction to the Woodstock girl anyway? If it hadn't been for me, you would never have met her.'

'It is a private birthday party, Claire, not a charity ball. I wouldn't dream of asking if I could bring along a friend.'

'Friend! I like that. When have you ever been a friend to me? You're just a selfish, scheming *viper* and I know very well why you don't want me to go with you. You are afraid your precious Percival will fall in love with me and desert you!'

'How utterly ridiculous,' said Rose with genuine astonishment. 'Why on earth should you think that? And he is not "my" Percival. He is just a friend.'

'And I suppose that particular "friend" will be at the party, even if I am not?'

'Well of course he will, idiot. He is Georgina's brother!'

But Claire had refused to be pacified. 'Just remember that I am the eldest, that's all. *I* get married first, and *I* have first choice. Or had you forgotten the Rule?'

'You and your stupid Rule,' said Rose, losing patience. 'I thought you had grown out of all that nonsense years ago.'

'It is not a question of "growing out of" it,' said Claire with an intensity which raised Rose's eyebrow. 'And it would serve you right if I did take Percival Woodstock from under your supercilious nose. You don't want him anyway. You're just a bitch-in-the-manger!'

Rose doused the light and turned her back. She did not deign to reply.

But so far the weekend had produced neither Percival nor anyone else and she and Georgina had spent the afternoon happily together, bicycling in the country lanes around the Woodstock estate. Percival and the rest of the party were to arrive in the evening, in time for dinner.

Lying on her back under the hedgerow, her eyes shut against

108

the dappled sunlight, Rose thought ahead to the evening without apprehension. Percy was easy company, as long as they were in a crowd together. It was only if they found themselves alone that the awkward, tongue-tied silences arose – tongue-tied on Percival's part, awkward on hers, for she suspected he might say something embarrassing, given the slightest encouragement. If she broke the silence, with her usual light-hearted chat or telling wit, he would blush and swallow and hover so obviously on the brink of speech that Rose usually made some excuse to rush away. His devotion, if it was devotion, both touched and embarrassed her. He was a good-hearted, honest, noble-spirited young man and she would not hurt him for the world – even if he was a trifle dull, she added wickedly, in private. Though she would never say as much to Georgina who, she knew, adored her brother and who, she suspected, would be delighted to see a match between brother and friend.

The sunlight prickled her eyes with gentle warmth and she turned her head away, seeking the shade. Through half-opened lids she saw the gleaming stalk and fresh-glossed leaves of a buttercup close beside her head. There were daisies, threaded with sunlight, their white petals pink-tipped, their stamens pools of dusty gold, stitch-wort, celandines, shepherd's purse, and the speckled blue sprays of forget-me-nots, their tiny flowers perfect in cerulean miniature. There was a Renaissance painting with a foreground as rich in flowers, perfectly painted, as this patch of hedgerow. Idly she tried to remember which it was. Her hand spread lazily in the grass and she was aware of the touch of leaf and grass blade, the minute brushing of an ant's foot. The richness and beauty of the world filled her suddenly with an exuberance as invigorating as champagne. She snapped off a buttercup, rolled over, and held it quivering under Georgina's up-stretched chin, waiting for her to feel the reflected glow of the golden petals and studying her friend's tranquil face with an artist's close attention.

Dark lashes over closed eyes, dark brows almost meeting above a small, straight nose with the faintest spray of freckles on its bridge and on the line of cheekbone. Lips surprisingly full and rose-coloured without aid of lip balm, and hair the colour of dry tumbled straw, thick and long. Where the buttercup hung motionless, the skin of her throat was smooth and pale, pulse-quivering and tinged with gold. How dare Claire say Georgina Woodstock was plain? Not one of God's creatures was plain if you looked closely enough and certainly not Georgina. Hers was a strong face, but essentially feminine, even queenly. She would make a perfect model. For Boadicea perhaps, or Juno. Or one of those Roman maidens leaning

109

over white battlements in flowing robes that Tadema was so fond of painting.

'I will try her in crayon,' she thought idly, 'Or, better still, in oils. Full-length. For the Royal Academy.' Lost in her dream of future fame, she let the buttercup petal dip too close.

Georgina's eyes jerked open and she twisted her head away in protest, laughing. 'What are you doing, Rose?'

'Merely seeing whether you like butter.'

'And do I?'

'Of course. Doesn't everyone?' Rose tossed aside the crumpled flower and scrambled to her feet. 'Race you to the top of the hill!'

With a whoop of challenge, Georgina followed and side by side, scarves flying in the wind, they pedalled furiously up the incline and out into the sunlit openness of hayfield and standing corn. There were poppies in the corn and ox-eye daisies and on the far horizon, the motionless white plume of some farmhouse chimney's smoke.

'By the way, I didn't tell you,' called Georgina as they free-wheeled down the incline. 'We are all invited to Wychwood tomorrow, for tennis and tea.'

'*Wychwood*?' At the name from the past Rose swerved suddenly and almost lost her balance.

'Edward Rivers' place at Wintelsham. Why? Do you know it?'

'No, but I have heard the name.'

'From Harry I expect,' said Georgina easily. 'They are cousins, though you would never know it. Two people could not be more different.'

No, thought Rose, remembering. One was courteous, carefree and open, the other equally courteous, but supercilious and withdrawn. Oh well, let him be supercilious, she did not care. The weekend was Georgina's, not hers. It was only later, as she dressed for dinner with more than usual care, in deference to Georgina's father, that Rose remembered that scene on the Dieppe beach and Edward Rivers' strong, gentle hands on Sara's sea-drenched "corpse".

Wychwood was not what she expected, whatever that was. An imposing classical edifice, perhaps, on an eminence, in parkland, or a many-chimneyed, red-bricked and vaguely sinister Elizabethan manor house, oppressed by too much greenery, in a shadowed dell. Instead, it was neither, but a small, comfortable country house built less than a century ago. It was of pleasing proportions, with a porticoed entrance on the west side and on the south, french windows leading to a tennis lawn. There was a charming walled garden with a lily pond and peaches espaliered on the south-facing

110

wall, apricots, greengages, plums, and several kinds of apple as well as herbaceous borders ablaze with every colour of the rainbow. And beyond the garden and the home meadow were woods, sweeping east and south to enclose the property in a girdle of green leaf, thick and secret and alive with birdsong and the rustle of invisible woodland feet.

Rose was enchanted. And when she saw the stable block at the back of the house, with the old, abandoned brewery, the dovecote and the hay carts under the shadowed arch, she was doubly so. What a place to paint.

But of course the weekend was for tennis, not painting, and besides, she had left all her sketching equipment at Georgina's house. Nevertheless, it was with an artist's eye that she regarded the heavy front door which stood open, revealing a hatstand loaded with outer garments of an ancient and assorted kind, walking sticks, dog leads, umbrellas, a collection of wellington boots and a square of tiled floor. The inner door was closed, but through its glass panes Rose had the impression of oak panelling, flowers and carpeted quiet before a neat, black-and-white clothed maid appeared from the inner regions to welcome them.

'They are all on the tennis lawn, Miss Woodstock, and I was to tell you to go straight through.'

The maid disappeared again into the gloom beyond the grandfather clock which ticked steadily into the silence of the hall. From somewhere beyond one of the closed doors came the sound of girls' voices and laughter. Georgina led the way past heavy oak chest, brass dinner gong and banks of flowers to a panelled door with a painted china handle. 'In here,' she said and opened it.

Rose found herself in a sunlit drawing room whose french windows, shaded by a striped canvas awning, were open to the garden and the tennis lawn where a group of young people, including Harry Price-Hill and Percy Woodstock, were variously occupied in playing or urging each other on. As Rose watched, one of the men detached himself from the group and came towards them, hand outstretched.

'Georgina – and Miss Millard, I believe. Delighted you could come.' Edward Rivers was dressed for tennis in open-necked white shirt and white flannel trousers and looked very like when Rose had first seen him, on the terrace in Dieppe, though this time his expression, though still to her mind arrogant, was not so patently bored. In fact, he was looking at her with decided interest. Unaccountably confused, Rose murmured something appropriate and looked past his shoulder to the tennis lawn where she could see

111

Harry Price-Hill with a trio of giggling girls. Harry lifted a racquet and waved.

'Georgina mine,' he called with extravagant good humour, 'and the lovely Rose, at last. Well, come on, Georgie, now you're here. You and I will show these delightful young creatures how tennis ought to be played. How about it, Edward?'

'Perhaps you will do me the honour of partnering me, Miss Millard?' said Edward Rivers gravely.

'I doubt it will be any honour,' retorted Rose. 'I don't know how to play. But Georgina will show me, won't you?' For some reason she did not want Mr Rivers to teach her, to show her how to hold the racquet, to guide her arm.

'Five minutes,' agreed Georgina cheerfully, 'then you will be as good as any of us, Rose.'

'And we will have our game,' said Edward, handing her his racquet. The handle was warm where his hand had held it and Rose felt herself blush. But that was stupid. She mumbled her thanks and pushed past him into the garden, wishing she had never come. Georgina followed and Rose proceeded to try her hand at returning the ball which Georgina lobbed at her over the net, to groans from the others when she missed, or hit it wildly out, and extravagant cheers when she managed to return it. Then, to a countdown to the final second, Rose hit her last ball and the five minute period was declared over.

'I say,' said Percy Woodstock, blushing, 'you really did most awfully well, Rose. Will you do me the honour of . . .' but Edward Rivers interrupted.

'Now the lesson is over, Miss Millard, we have an engagement, remember? Against your sister, Woodstock, and my ass of a cousin.'

'Then later, perhaps?' managed Percy and Rose felt sorry enough for him to say, 'Yes.' Then Edward led her out onto the grass court, Harry took his place beside Georgina on the other side of the net and after a great show on Harry's part of measuring the net's height and testing his swing, they embarked on a light-hearted game which Harry and Georgina won without difficulty, as they did the ensuing five, to win the set 6–0.

'I am sorry,' said Rose stiffly, avoiding Edward's eye. She felt foolishly inadequate and out of place.

'Why?' he said. 'Because you did not win? When it is on your own admission the first game of tennis you ever played?'

'You did splendidly,' cried Harry, vaulting the tennis net and clasping her hand in both his. 'In fact, I vote we have a tournament, each one plays everyone else, till tea. What do you say?'

112

'Not me,' said Rose. 'I've had enough tennis for one day.'

'Nonsense. Everyone must take part. Isn't that right, Edward old chap?' Harry, in his tennis whites, his skin tanned golden by the sun, looked handsomer than ever and when Georgina said eagerly, 'I'll draw up the programme now,' Rose felt her heart twist with pain for her friend, especially when two of the visiting damsels linked arms with Harry, one on each side, and begged him to play with them first.

'Come, come, Miss Millard,' said a low voice in her ear. 'Surely you are not going to sulk because you did not win?'

'Of course not,' she snapped. 'I merely prefer not to waste my time – or anyone else's – by my own incompetence.'

'What high standards you must set yourself,' he said gravely, but his eyes were twinkling with private laughter and Rose could have stamped her foot with annoyance. Instead she said coldly, 'Of course,' and turned her back.

Nevertheless, remembering that arrogant accusation of sulking, she took her turn in the afternoon's tournament, batting the ball back as best she could with the little practice she had had and her hampering skirts, and tolerating with a determined smile the flirtatious banter and inane conversation, usually with the ebullient Harry at its centre, until at last she contrived to slip away unnoticed, and escape. The social obligations and the relentless jollity the occasion demanded were becoming wearisome and Rose wanted only to be alone, to drink in, in solitude, the particular beauty of Wychwood.

So, while the tennis party continued their cheerful frolicking, Rose walked alone in the woods which gave the house its name. Beech mast crunched underfoot and the cool greenery wove a shielding lace of shadow overhead. From behind her came the soft 'putt' of tennis ball on racquet and the laughing voices of the others, shouting encouragement or mockery. In the house beyond the tennis lawn maids would be setting out cucumber sandwiches and slivers of buttered white bread, with caraway seed cake and petticoat tails. If she listened hard, she would probably hear the chink of china tea-cup on china saucer as the heavy trays were carried by white-aproned, black-gowned servants across the banked grass to where the trestles had been set out in the leafy shade of the copper beech. The silver tea-kettle would dazzle in the sun.

It would be a good half hour before anyone missed her. Longer if she was lucky. She looked back over her shoulder to where the red stone block of Wychwood with its climbing roses and striped awnings glinted through the tangled trees – and walked on again,

113

faster now and with a new excitement in her step. Then she was in a glade of green shade at the heart of the wood's being, and stopped. Alder, hazel, beech, some slender and pliant, some stiff with ridged maturity – her eager eyes drank in the many-coloured intricacies of bark, the pin-point brilliance of the mosses which cushioned stone and fallen tree-branch, the larger splash of splendour from toad-stool, harebell, or wood anemone.

'Bliss,' she sighed and stretched her arms luxuriously wide. Then, with a swift movement of one hand, she loosed the pins which secured her hat and tossed her hair free. Next she kicked off her neat leather shoes, bought on her mother's insistence for the occasion, and curled her toes gratefully over the coolness of grass and tangled plants.

'Stuffed shirts. Pompous, prancing popinjays. Braggadocios. *Bores*!' She loosed her insults in a crescendo of silent laughter. Then, with a disregard for both propriety and her new muslin skirts (run up by her mother in forty-eight hours of brisk efficiency) ('I am not having you disgracing us with your Bohemian draperies, young lady! You will dress as is appropriate, out of courtesy to your hosts.'), Rose sprawled on the grass, skirts kicked up above arched knees, put her hands behind her head and looked up through the tangled leaves to the skies beyond. In literature, she thought, sky was always blue, but this sky was white – a vibrant glare behind the colourless darkness of massed leaves. Leaves were green, of course, but she would paint these ones with umber, or a mixture of cobalt blue and gamboge; and the tracery of branch and leaf would make a pattern of its own, unrelated. She must go to the galleries again and study the masters. Corot. Sisley. Then one day she would go to Florence, to the Uffizi – Mamma would not refuse her, surely? – then to Venice, to study Canaletto and his knack of painting water and sky...

Sky ... She gazed at the patterned blotch of white until the glare stung her eyes and she closed them...

The rustle of leaves, too close to her ear, woke her with an uncomfortable thud of the heart. Reluctantly she looked upwards, her eyes following the length of white flannelled legs to a white cotton shirt, open at the neck, and a dark shadowed face.

'Why did you run away?'

Rose shot upright, blushing with confusion, and pulled her skirts down quickly over her ankles while she cast about for her shoes until, to her increased embarrassment, she saw that he was holding them in his hands. 'How long have you been watching me?' she demanded, suddenly vulnerable and angry. Her skirts, she remembered, had been above her knees. 'It is not polite to creep up on someone unawares and intrude on their privacy.'

He looked down at her steadily from veiled eyes and she had a sudden wild suspicion that he was laughing at her though when he spoke it was in a cool, impersonal voice. 'Nor is it polite for a guest deliberately to avoid her host. As you have done since the moment you arrived.'

'You are mistaken,' said Rose, with as much hauteur as she could manage, shoeless. 'Circumstances have merely conspired to keep our paths apart.'

'Circumstances perhaps, but with considerable help from you, Miss Millard.' Irrelevantly, she saw that he had lost a shirt button and that his chest, where the collar opened, was shadowed with dark hair in which beads of perspiration glinted like dewdrops in an early morning web. The skin of his throat was reddened by the sun and she could see the pulse beat, hard and strong. 'Do not tell me again that I am mistaken,' he said softly, watching her with those unfathomable eyes. 'Ever since that first, disastrous game you have deliberately avoided me, though I acknowledge I am not the only one. I notice you are adept at avoiding poor Percy, too, or at least at contriving always to be in a crowd. But in my case I find it the more reprehensible since it is surely not my fault that you have never played tennis before. Besides, I believe we have already met – in circumstances unhappily not as fortuitous as these, but we have met, nonetheless. In Dieppe, four years ago? Or perhaps you have forgotten?'

'How could I possibly forget Flan...' She had been going to say 'Flannel Legs', but checked herself in time. Instead, she finished humbly, 'I remember. You did my family a great service and I am grateful.'

'But you are still annoyed with me? And the burden of gratitude is not one you carry lightly? Nor one I wish you to bear. So let us make a pact. The past, until this moment, is forgotten, the slate washed clean. We will start as strangers meeting. May I introduce myself, Miss Millard?' Silently he held out her shoes. Avoiding his eyes, she took them, slipped them on, and stood up. Then, remembering, she turned her back, twisted her loose-flowing hair into a hasty chignon and secured it, precariously, with a pin. Finally she turned round to face him and any further embarrassment he might inflict on her, armed with the memory of Claire's Interesting Englishman and at least a modicum of respectability.

He looked at her straightfaced and said, with solemn courtesy, 'Edward Rivers, at your eternal service.'

115

She dropped him a slow and mocking curtsey. 'You do me too much honour, Mr Rivers.'

'Stop!' He took a step towards her. 'Don't move. Stand absolutely still.'

Something in his voice drained her of challenge and she stood motionless, eyes wide and watchful, pulse beating fast, while very slowly he reached out a hand towards her, his eyes not on her face, but on her throat. 'Don't move,' he breathed and she waited obediently, quivering with the effort of keeping still. She felt the warmth of his breath on her cheek. His fine-boned face was suntanned and frowning with concentration. The dark hair at his temples glistened from the afternoon's tennis and his lashes were surprisingly thick. Like a Renaissance nobleman, she thought, or Hillyard's young courtier without the Elizabethan finery.

Then his fingers brushed her throat with a touch which set her heart racing and suddenly he smiled. 'There!' he said triumphantly, holding up a minute wriggling creature between finger and thumb. 'You had a red ant on your neck. They can give a nasty bite.'

'Is that all!' Rose was unaccountably disappointed and at the same time angry with herself for being so. 'I thought at least it was a boa constrictor!'

'I think even an unworldly artist would have noticed that for herself,' he said drily, dropping the ant into a bush.

'Thank you anyway,' she said, retrieving manners. 'But I had better go back to the house.' She picked up her hat and turned away, but he stepped in front of her to block her path.

'I will go with you,' he said calmly, 'That way.' He pointed back along the path which led from the copse to a cornfield in the distance. 'There is a path which follows the edge of the woods and comes out behind the stables. It is not far, but a pleasant walk, and I like to show new guests my small estate, such as it is.'

'Who am I to argue with my host?' she asked the trees and added, with theatrical humility, 'I shall in all my best obey you, sir.'

'I doubt it. You seem to me to be a girl who obeys only when orders coincide with inclination. Am I right, Miss Millard?'

'You were going to show me your estate,' she reminded, not wanting him to see the pulse of excitement which beat disconcertingly fast at his words. 'But if you hope to have any of those much vaunted cucumber sandwiches, we had better hurry before the vultures eat the lot.'

'True.' He added, with a look that quite disconcerted her, 'But there are other kinds of hunger less easy to assuage.'

Dumbfounded, she chose to ignore the remark, but she could not

116

ignore its implications, or her own reactions to it. When he took her hand she let him lead her through the tangled woods towards that sunlit patch ahead, while the warmth of his hand merged with hers and she felt an excitement undreamt of, even in those adolescent fantasies she had woven with Claire of romance and courtship. Pure body chemistry, she told herself firmly. Nothing to do with the heart, or the head. But chemistry was a dull subject, more fitted to the laboratory than to life. What part had it to play on a summer's afternoon? To walk hand in hand with an agreeable companion was a harmless pleasure and one which she was quite entitled to prolong. It did not occur to her that had her companion been Percival Woodstock she would have fled instantly for the safety of the tea-table.

Edward Rivers was an interesting companion. Not only did he point out the different trees, flowers, butterflies and wild life that they passed, but added anecdotes of folk lore or local history, and sometimes of his own family. 'There is where we trapped the vixen that took old Davy's hens,' 'That is the tree we used to play in as children – till Phoebe fell out and broke her collar bone,' and 'Through there, down that grassy ride, is a dell where you can pick delectable mushrooms, if you get up early enough in the morning.' They saw squirrels in the high branches, a barn owl, wings folded, asleep on a mossy stump and, once, a scuttling hedgehog. Pigeons crooned and murmured overhead and the trees were lanced with dappled sunlight. There were tiny woodland flowers, beechmast underfoot, and fairytale toadstools, scarlet and white-spotted. And not another person in sight.

A hen pheasant, startled, clattered out of the brushwood almost under their feet. Rose gasped, then laughed with relief.

'So you are human after all,' said Edward. 'When I saw you asleep on the grass, you looked like something out of a beautiful painting. I was trying to remember which, when you woke and caught me out. A Renoir, perhaps, or a Sisley.'

'Do you know Renoir? But of course! You have been to Paris *en route* for the Grand Tour. I remember you looking remarkably bored in Dieppe!'

'And you, no doubt, are never bored?'

'I do not have the leisure, Mr Rivers, to be bored. Besides, I am not in Society and am consequently free to be enthusiastic where I choose. I would dearly love to go to Paris and the galleries, to Montmartre and then south, to Arles. Afterwards, when I was sated with France, into Italy, both to study and to paint. They say it is excellent practice to copy from the masters and perhaps it is, but once the copy is done, then all one wants to do is create...'

Suddenly they were at the fringe of the woods and she stopped, enchanted. A cornfield rippled in a sea of gold, poppy-speckled, and dappled at the edges with white marguerites and dog-violets. And in the distance, on the clear horizon, a clump of trees, dark against the glare, and the stretched arms of a windmill.

'If only I had my sketchpad,' she breathed, on a sigh of longing.

'You must come again,' he said quietly. 'I would like that.'

She glanced up at him and found him looking at her with an expression that brought the colour to her cheeks. 'So would I,' she admitted and added hastily, 'To paint.'

The track which ran round the edge of the cornfield was narrow and tangled with hedgerow flowers, so that now and then they had to walk in single file, but still Edward held her hand firmly in his and, liberated woman that she aspired to be, she was glad. Once, they stopped while he picked a spray of forget-me-nots and threaded them in her hair.

'So much more appropriate than that silly hat,' he said, as if talking of the weather.

'*Let me be dressed fine as I will, Flies, worms and flowers exceed me still.* Goodbye vanity!'

'Butterflies perhaps,' he said, considering. 'But not bluebottles, or horseflies. As for worms, I have yet to come across a vermiform Adonis, or a Venus either.'

'Worms, Mr Rivers, are hermaphrodite, except of course the human variety.' She turned her back.

'Really, Miss Millard? I cannot say I have studied them closely enough to see.'

On a snort of suppressed laughter, the last of her prejudice drained away. 'Oh well. I suppose, given the choice, I should be grateful you chose flowers!'

The cornfield ended and the home meadow began – a tranquil stretch of lush grass, thick with daisies and buttercups and in the centre, a huge chestnut, its lower branches neatly clipped to cow level. Cattle grazed in its shade, tails lazily swishing against the flies, jaws grinding endlessly, with slow deliberation. One or two of them lifted their heads and watched from thick-lashed eyes as they passed.

They lingered more than necessary on the path through the meadow, till by the time they reached the gate onto the track which led to the stables and the old brewery, they were loth to move at all. They leant on the gate, side by side, studying the meadow with superficial eyes, while they talked on and on, as if they had a lifetime's communion to pack into one afternoon. Tea was forgotten, cucumber sandwiches ignored.

'I remember when I first saw you,' he said, looking at her sideways from veiled eyes. 'I had had a disagreeable morning and was anticipating an even more disagreeable afternoon.'

'And?' prompted Rose, who knew perfectly well what he was going to say. Or thought she did.

'Then I saw you and your sister, giggling and twittering like a pair of silly songbirds.'

'I was *not* giggling!'

'Then it must have been your sister. How could I tell? All I could see of you was a tilted hat and a striped dress straight out of Renoir, with a profusion of glorious, red-glinting hair.' He reached out and withdrew the single hairpin. 'Loose,' he finished, 'as it is now.' Before she could draw away he had lifted the heavy hair and let it ripple, glinting, through his fingers. The movement was as intimate as a caress. But instead of blushing, as she ought to have done, Rose felt exhilarated.

'And what of Amaryllis?' she said, with cool challange.

'Ah ... I think ... yes. You refer to Milton and the occupations of normal, unpoetical young men who *sport with Amaryllis in the shade, Or with the tangles of Neaera's hair?*'

Rose laughed. 'We called you Flannel Legs in Dieppe, but I see you are not just a pair of immaculate trousers after all. You can actually read!'

'Read, learn, and inwardly digest. Talking of which, what of the cucumber sandwiches?'

'All, all are gone,' she said, striking a dramatic pose, the back of one hand against her brow. 'Gone with the wind ...'

But he did not smile. Instead, he said quietly, 'Ernest Dowson. A sad poem. *They are not long, the weeping and the laughter, Love and desire and hate; I think they have no portion in us after We pass the gate.*'

'*They are not long, the days of wine and roses,*' she said, suddenly sober. '*Out of a misty dream Our path emerges for a while, then closes Within a dream.*'

There was a moment's silence, then he said, 'I shall be in town, after Harvest Home. May I see you?'

But Rose had recovered. 'Why not? All gentlemen are welcome at Millard and Blunt's. I work there when they need me and when they do not, I share Georgina's studio, and her pursuit of Art.'

'Yes, I heard her father had indulged her to that extent.'

'Do I assume, from that remark, that you regard Georgina's work as some kind of harmless hobby?'

119

'Work? You mean her sculpture?'

'You have answered my question, Mr Rivers. Perhaps I should warn you that I share Georgina's attitude to artistic creation. It is not merely something to be indulged and patronised by well-meaning parents.'

'No,' said Edward Rivers solemnly. 'Quite the contrary. It is something to be treated with all the pomp and reverence normally accorded to the Holy Grail.'

'Of course not, idiot!' said Rose, laughing. 'But could you not compromise and allow us a little common respect?'

'When you plead so eloquently, how could any man refuse?' Then he took her hand and said, with quiet seriousness, 'Please, Rose. May I call upon you in your studio when next I am in Town?'

'It is Georgina's studio, not mine, but I am sure she would not object, if you wish. And have nothing better to do.'

'Then, may I take you to the theatre?'

'As long as it is not to some frivolous music hall vulgarity of the kind your cousin favours, where female company would be *de trop*, yes please.'

'I promise to find the most solemn and uplifting play in Town, especially for you, Miss Millard.'

'Then I hope it will not take you out of your depth, Mr Rivers!' but her idle remark reminded her of the circumstances of their first meeting and she added quickly, 'That was a silly thing to say. I am sorry. And though the past is officially forgotten, unofficially I remember your bravery and presence of mind with humble gratitude.'

'Please don't,' he said, embarrassed. 'Look, tea will be over now, the sandwiches, as you said, all gone and we have propped up this gate long enough. Why don't you let me show you the brewery? Father had great plans for the brewery, though whether he would have carried them out is another matter. But before he died, last year, unexpectedly,' and there was something in his voice that discouraged questions, 'he had converted part of the building into an office. I have my own ideas about the upper storey, but I would be interested to hear your comments, seen with an artist's eye.'

The gate from the meadow led into a barn-yard one side of which was flanked by what Edward had called the brewery. It was an old building, in crumbling Suffolk brick, with a deep arch at one end, high enough to accommodate a hay cart or a loaded dray. Through the arch, Rose could see the stable block and the yard with the dairy on the far side and the back regions of the house. Doves purled contentedly from somewhere overhead and a handful of

120

hens scratched among the dust of the stable yard, quietly gossiping. There was a timeless quality about the scene which for a moment caught the breath in Rose's throat. In the old tiled roof were a pair of rusted skylights, and the windows in the ground floor of the brewery building were so meshed with cobwebs, bird lime and accumulated dirt that it was impossible to see inside. Under the archway, some sort of chain and tackle hung over an immobile wheel.

'This place used to produce all the harvest beer in my grandfather's day,' said Edward. 'Twice a year he would buy in malt and hops and brew enough to make the farm workers and servants forget their hard work and low wages and actually enjoy themselves. I can remember the smell of the mash tub even now, and the taste of the "small beer" my grandfather let me sample. The mash tubs are still there and the "tunnels" and dippers. Even the copper boiler, but the beer kegs have long disappeared. And, of course, their contents! But my father gave up the practice. Principally, I think, because he didn't like the product. Now, if the process could have been adapted to produce a vintage claret or a good, rich, full-bodied burgundy, it might have been different. He did try rhubarb wine once, but the result was so lethal, Grandmama forbade him to repeat the process!'

'And what about the workers' beer?'

'Bought – on account, like so much else.' He frowned at what was obviously a painful memory. 'And paid for, eventually, with yet another slice of land. Too much of the Wychwood estate has been sold over the years, as I fear those woods we have just walked through may have to be.'

Rose stopped in her tracks, appalled. 'But you *can't*! They're beautiful!'

'Beauty does not pay death duties.'

'But ...' Rose stopped. It was, after all, no business of hers. 'Tell me about the brewery,' she said, to change the subject.

'My father was going to convert it, though he never decided into what. First it was to be a workshop for craftsman-made furniture. Then a guesthouse. Swiss Alps style.'

'*Swiss Alps?*'

'You may well laugh, with Suffolk's reputation for flatlands, but my father was a genuine eccentric. I forget what ousted the Alpine idea, though I know a Parisian-style night-club featured somewhere along the line. And a museum of Suffolk antiquities. That was the year he found the fossils. But before he died, it was to be a photographic studio, with offices and a dark room and upstairs, a

121

'studio' where clients could be photographed against a choice of exotic backgrounds, from the Niagara Falls, complete with rocks and running water, to the Sahara desert. He was working on the eastern harem backdrop the day he died.'

Rose dared not laugh, until she looked up and caught Edward's eye. Then, unexpectedly, they both erupted into snorting glee.

'He sounds delightful,' she said, recovering.

'He was. Delightful and impossible – which is why my mother lives in Venice – and utterly and ruinously impractical. Do you know he actually ordered a pillar of Carrara marble for his classical background? To be sent all the way from Italy. No one knew till it arrived two months after his death, together with an exorbitant bill.'

'And where is it now?' asked Rose, remembering Georgina.

'Oh, somewhere about. In the dark room, I think. Not that it is a dark room. All my father had done on that score was to close the shutters! But I will show you.'

He opened a door to the right of the archway and held it open for Rose to enter. She found herself in a sort of barn, with sacks of animal feed along one wall, one or two cobwebbed wooden tubs, ancient straw dust underfoot, and crusted bird lime on the rafters where generations of swallows had nested, undisturbed. A collection of cobweb-festooned implements of dubious purpose hung from the beams. The air smelled musty, but warm with a scent of apples. As she stepped inside, a startled rat sat up on its haunches by a tiny pyramid of spilled grain, grey paws in front of grey chest and whiskers bristling. Then, with a glare of outrage, it dropped to all four feet and scuttled away.

'We store hen food here,' said Edward unnecessarily. 'And apples, though this year's crop has not yet been gathered.'

On the inner wall of the barn were two doors, one to the office, a small room with a desk, a chair and an empty shelf, the other to a shadowy hole of similar proportions, containing a shrouded lump – presumably the redundant marble. Edward closed the door again and turned away.

'This is what I really wanted to show you.' He pointed to a ladder which led upwards to a dim square in the roof where the heavy timbers had been floored with planks to make a loft.

'Your father did not expect clients to climb up *that*?' said Rose, astonished.

'I don't think practicalities were of much concern to him,' said Edward solemnly. 'Though I agree, a handrail might help.'

'Or a light.'

122

'I will follow you up, in case you slip.'

But Rose had always been sure-footed and the ladder was firm enough. When she emerged into the vaulted peace of the empty loft, she felt she would have climbed a rope, if necessary, to get there. She watched Edward's dark head emerge through the square, then his shoulders, and his white flannelled legs. Incongruous perhaps, but no longer ridiculous.

'Well? What do you think?' He stood beside her, almost touching, and looked over the slanting depth of the loft, which was like Georgina's studio and yet not like. Cobwebs latticed the skylights, hung in dust-laden festoons from the joists of the roof and where the sunlight filtered through, dust motes danced like a myriad tiny fairy folk, rejoicing. There were butterfly wings on the boards at her feet.

'It is beautiful,' she breathed, in awe.

'I thought you would like it.' After a moment he said quietly, 'Would you say it was haunted?'

'Oh yes, but not in any terrifying way. There is sadness,' she went on slowly, 'but no violence. Only an aura of . . .'

'Of what?' he prompted, his breath warm on her cheek.

She turned to look at him, her eyes dark with expectation, the tiny blue flowers still meshed in her hair. 'Of peace, and timelessness and wisdom,' she said slowly, her eyes meeting his, 'And fecundity and love.' Though she spoke the last word almost under her breath, he heard her.

'Yes. I felt that too.' They stood in silence while the implications of their words wove invisible threads around them, drawing them closer . . . closer . . . till Rose could hear the beat of his heart almost against her breast . . . almost . . . then the trembling moment was shattered by a cheerful shout from the yard below.

'Edward! Coo-ee! Where are you, Edward? We need you for the final game. *Edward*!' They heard a door open below and the voice came now from directly underneath.

'Edward? Are you in here?'

He put a finger on her lips and suddenly she wanted to laugh aloud. Instead, she bit his finger so that he gasped, swore under his breath, and snatched her so close her breasts were crushed against his chest. She could hear the strong thudding of his heart-beat, feel his body warmth through the cotton, sense the faint scent of perspiration which was at the same time masculine and exciting.

'Coo-ee! Edward!'

They were both laughing now, in jubilant silence. Then the door closed below them. She broke away and scrambled for the ladder.

123

'Escaped, with the skin of our teeth!'

'No. Let me.' He swung round and descended first so that when she followed, feet carefully feeling for the rungs, he was waiting to catch her round the waist and swing her from the last few rungs to the ground.

'Tell me, Rose,' he said, still holding her. 'Do you think it possible for a place to be haunted by the *future*?' Then he kissed her on the lips, so quickly and lightly that she wondered afterwards if she had imagined it, took her by the hand and led her, silent-footed, into the yard.

A moment later they were strolling, unhurried, round the corner of the brewery block and into the drive. They could hear Georgina's voice from the direction of the meadow, still calling.

'Shouldn't you answer?' said Rose, 'before poor Georgina gets a sore throat?'

'What do you think?'

'I think it is unfair to let her go on looking when . . .'

'And *I* think,' he interrupted, straight-faced, 'that we have been drinking lemonade under the copper beech and that we could not possibly hear her from there.' Then suddenly, he was gone and Rose stood alone in the shade of the big chestnut tree that bordered the drive.

She saw him later by the tennis lawn, talking easily to a trio of girls in frilled white muslins, neat little boaters tied on with ribbons, and tennis racquets in their hands. The girls were sparkling for his benefit.

'And where did you disappear to?' demanded Georgina when she reappeared, red-faced and perspiring, some ten minutes later. 'I have been looking everywhere for you.'

'I went exploring. I am sorry if I was anti-social, but you know what I'm like when I get an idea.' Rose did not know why she avoided the truth.

Georgina's criticism evaporated instantly and, true friend that she was, she asked no more questions. An idea in embryo, as they both knew, could be murdered or maimed by too early exposure to another's eye, however sympathetic.

Rose assuaged any guilt by adding, 'By the way, did you know Mr Rivers has a marble column he doesn't want?'

CHAPTER 5

It was the end of September before the theatre invitation came and when it did, it caused a major storm. This time Rebecca was on Claire's side and took Rose firmly to task.

'It is all very well for you to enjoy your artistic contacts, Rose, but you do have other responsibilities. Have you forgotten your sisters? It is months since you first met Miss Woodstock and so far you have produced *not one* introduction for Claire. It cannot go on.'

'But Georgina is my friend, Mamma. Not a marriage broker.'

'Do not be impertinent, girl! Friend she may be, but she is also well connected, with a busy social life. Is it too much to ask that you include Claire in that life?'

'But Mamma, I do not include myself in it, let alone...'

'Nonsense. You have been to a house party, haven't you? Though precious little you told us about it, I must say. Now, apparently, you intend to go to the theatre, and with *Edward Rivers!*'

'I was invited to make up the numbers, Mamma, that is all. Georgina arranged it.' And God pardon my lie, she added silently, but she could not bear to have her mother match-making on her behalf.

'Then Georgina must *arrange* for Claire to go too. And if you will not ask her, then I will!'

'Mamma, you can't!' cried Rose, horrified.

'Indeed I can. And will. Your precious Georgina will arrange for Claire to be included or I shall seriously consider, Rose, whether you have misused the freedom I have allowed you during the summer. Perhaps a studio was not a good idea after all. At least when you worked only at Millards you were not *selfish*.'

Rose understood the threat as clearly as if her mother had spoken it in as many words and so did Claire, who was smiling with satisfaction. Find Claire an invitation or go back to work full time at the shop. It was a threat she could not ignore – and equally could not comply with.

'Then as it causes you so much distress, Mamma, I will refuse the invitation.'

125

'Don't be ridiculous, girl. I *forbid* you to refuse! I merely want Claire to go too. What is the play?'

'*Hamlet.*'

'At the Lyceum? With Forbes-Robertson and Mrs Patrick Campbell? Then Claire will certainly go. Arrange it. That is an order, Rose.'

'Very well, Mamma,' she sighed. 'I will do my best.'

'Your best had better be good enough, Rose, or you will have me to answer to.'

Rose recognised defeat. There was nothing for it but to appeal to Georgina for help. 'I don't know what has got into Mamma,' she explained, 'But she suddenly insists on a chaperon, of all things. I may not go to a wicked theatre, even if it is Shakespeare, without my mother or my sister. I dare not defy her or she will forbid me to come here and I could not bear that. Besides, I do so want to see Mrs Patrick Campbell, when Mr Rivers has gone to so much trouble to procure me a ticket. What am I to do?'

'Don't worry, Rose. I will speak to Aunt Clem.'

'No! Please don't. I would hate anyone to think that . . .'

'My lips are sealed,' interrupted Georgina cheerfully. 'No one will know, I promise you. Edward will be dining with her anyway and Aunt Clem always tries to fix up at least one theatre party for Harry and me, bless her misguided old heart. It shall be *Hamlet* and Harry must endure it as best he can. You wouldn't mind,' she added with an off-hand manner which in no way deceived Rose, 'if I asked Percy too? Then Percy must bring a friend, of course, and we will need to balance numbers.'

'Bless you, Georgina. You are a dear friend.'

On an evening a week later Rose was painting in the studio when she heard the door open. Without looking up, she said, 'Georgina's gone home, I'm afraid. You must look for her there.'

'It is not Georgina I want,' said a voice which halted her brush in mid-stroke. 'I wanted to apologise, Rose. I arrange a quiet outing for myself and a friend and find I am taken over, re-organised and ordered to head a raiding party of half a score! I wanted you to know that it was you I invited. But when Aunt Clem found out, God knows how, she insisted we make a party of it – and no one thwarts Aunt Clem.'

'No matter. The play's the thing.'

'*In which to catch the conscience of the King?* But Aunt Clementina, I am afraid, has no conscience.'

'Neither had the king. But you understand me.' She turned back

126

to her painting – a scene of the mews below, with tiled roofs and stone steps in a hundred delicate gradations of colour.

'No, I do not,' said Edward. Deliberately, he drew off his gloves, folded them, placed them with his hat and cane on a side table and sat down on the ottoman. He stared at her in silence for a full two minutes, then began to whistle softly *Plaisir d'amour*. Still she seemed oblivious to his presence though had he known her better he would have noted the heightened colour of her cheeks. 'If I may interrupt your concentration for one brief moment,' he said at last, 'kindly explain to me why a girl like you spends hours alone, painting, when she could be out in the world, spreading joy and laughter.'

'Because I like to paint. Why else?'

'So do other girls. But they keep their hobby in proper perspective.'

'*Hobby?*' Rose whirled on him in fury. 'How dare you bracket me with all those silly, simpering ninnies who pose against artistic backgrounds with their little sketching pads, solely to be admired!'

Edward said, with infuriating calm, 'That riled you, Miss Millard. I knew it would.'

'How very perceptive of you! But there is one thing you had better understand, Mr Rivers, if we are to remain friends. I am a painter, not a poseuse.'

'*Methinks the lady doth protest too much.*'

'You ... you ... *viper*! I meant it! And if you will not believe me, get out!' She cast around her for a missile and Edward laughed. 'Dieppe. On the terrace. I knew you had a temper. But you are even more beautiful in anger.' He ducked to avoid the paint-jar and threw up his hands in capitulation. 'Please. Forgive me. I meant no harm.' Then, in a different voice, he added, 'Are you going to bite me again?'

'Certainly not. You do not deserve it. Now please go away and let me work in peace.' Rose was both angry and flustered and at the same time exhilarated with an excitement she dared not acknowledge. It was as if the studio was suddenly charged with magnetic energy. Assuming an expression of aloof concentration she endeavoured to work at her painting, but her hand was trembling and after a moment she said, 'Drat! I can't paint when you stare at me like that.'

'Like what? I am only watching a dedicated artist at her work. In Montmartre all the artists expect it.'

'This is not Montmartre and ...'

'And what?' He stood up, with slow, deliberate grace and came

127

towards her till he was standing as close as they had been in the loft at Wychwood. 'And what?' he repeated softly.

Whatever she had been going to say deserted her. 'I ... forget.'

'Then *since there's no help, come let us kiss...*' This time there was no question of a dream. His mouth was gentle at first, to be sure, but when his lips parted hers, when one hand twined in her hair and the other found the small of her back, then moved lower, to press her hips against his, there was no doubting his ardour, or her own melting response.

'*... and part,*' she finished weakly when at last he let her go. But her voice lacked all conviction.

'Very well – if you insist. But only till Friday. I will send the carriage.' Then he was gone, closing the studio door behind him. A moment later, she heard him whistling cheerfully in the yard below.

She stood a moment, bemused, her eyes unnaturally bright and her heart beating with a high excitement which kept the smile on her lips however she strove to compose herself. Then she turned back to the studio, took up her brush and addressed herself to her painting.

But though she persevered for another hour, she got little further with her street scene. In the end she put it aside and instead attempted a crayon sketch from memory of a male head with strong cheekbones, dark-shadowed eyes, a velvet-soft moustache and sensuous lips.

When she arrived home she found the household plunged into grim-faced silence. A small fire burnt in the front parlour where a gas lamp had been lit so that Charlotte and Maud, heads bent over school exercise books, could work under Rebecca's watchful eye. On the window seat, Claire was stitching the bodice of a cambric undergarment in equal silence. Sara was nowhere to be seen. Rose caught Claire's eye and raised an eyebrow. Imperceptibly, Claire shook her head. Later, as they filed into the dining room for cold mutton and junket, Claire managed to whisper, 'She was caught with a wicked book.'

'I hope,' said Rebecca into the silence at the end of the uncomfortable and unpalatable meal, 'that no daughter of mine will ever again sully her hands or her mind with such filth.'

'No, Mamma,' they chorused in obedience. Then Rose dared to ask, 'What was it?'

There was a delighted hiss of indrawn breath as all eyes turned to Rebecca. For a moment, Rose thought her mother would explode, then Rebecca said carefully, 'The book need not concern you. Sara is young and has been misled. She sees the error of her ways. But you, Rose, of all my daughters are perhaps the most vulnerable, the most in need of caution, and the least equipped to combat such poison. I know your propensity for the artistic life and what you call "modern" ideas, but when it comes to so-called "modern" morals, beware! Mark my words, all of you. One step along that path and you are a *fallen woman*! Spurned by society, utterly *cast out*. By the way, Rose, there is still no sign of that invitation ... I hope you have not forgotten what I said?'

'No, Mamma,' said Rose, eyes lowered in submission. 'It will arrive, I promise you.'

'Good. Now go to your rooms, all of you, and pray to God to guide and forgive poor Sara, and yourselves.'

'What on earth had Sara got hold of?' asked Rose the moment she and Claire were safely in their room and the door closed.

'A wicked novel lent to her by a precocious friend at school.'

'Not Ouida?'

'Oh no. Much worse. *The Woman Who Did!*'

'Oh, is that all?' said Rose, deliberately unconcerned.

'All?' said Claire, astonished. 'But Mamma says the heroine gives herself, without a wedding ring!'

'So?'

'Rose, you are impossible!' cried Claire, blushing. 'You only do it to annoy.'

'Do what?'

'You know perfectly well what I mean!' Later, when they were in bed and the candles snuffed, Claire said, in the concealing darkness, 'What do you suppose it is like, giving oneself, I mean?'

Rose remembered the studio and Edward Rivers and the trembling longing of his embrace, but all she said was, 'Juliet liked it. And Cleopatra. And think of all the poets.'

'But Shakespeare was a man,' said Claire. 'It is different for them.' After a moment, she said uncertainly, 'When you are married, Rose, do you suppose you have to give yourself often?'

'How would I know?' She did not want Claire discussing such things, spoiling them, making them tawdry and public. She added, brutally, 'Why not ask Mamma?'

They lay in silence for some time while Claire followed her own thoughts and Rose thought of Edward Rivers, of his hands caressing her spine, her hips, the nape of her neck, of the tingling sensations which had spread through her body till she ached to be part of him completely ...

129

Then Claire brought her firmly back to earth. 'Mamma says no man would marry a girl who gave herself before marriage. I certainly shan't do anything like that, for I intend to marry well. I'm not at all sure I will even let him kiss me.'

'Why ever not?' said Rose in astonishment. 'Kissing isn't wicked, surely?'

'No,' agreed Claire, without conviction. 'But it is unnecessary. Unless, of course, I let him kiss me once, to tantalise him, then not again until he has given me a ring.'

'Claire, you are impossible! How can you be so cold-blooded about it?'

'Not cold-blooded at all. Merely practical.'

'Then I pity the poor fellow, whoever he is, married to a cold fish like you. Don't you *want* to be kissed, caressed, to feel his hands . . .' but Claire had stopped her ears.

'I want to be *married*,' she said loudly. 'That's all. And I want to marry *well*.'

Across the room in the darkness, Rose lay marvelling at Claire's composure. How could she be so matter-of-fact whereas Rose had only to remember the pulse beat in Edward's throat and the soft gentleness of his hands to feel her whole body ache with longing?

'You did arrange that invitation, didn't you?' said Claire into the silence. 'Because if not, there'll be trouble.'

Claire was jubilant when the invitation finally came, Rebecca quietly satisfied. 'Good. I am glad you understand me, Rose. And now we must pay close attention to your dress. You are sure to be sitting in a box, in full public view, and we have a reputation to establish.'

Claire was already working on a cream silk gown of her mother's which she was remodelling into a more up-to-date style for herself. Claire had become remarkably proficient with her needle, and the eye for good style which had first emerged at the Jubilee procession had sharpened to shrewd observation. Moreover, she had learnt, by trial and error, to execute such alterations in her own limited wardrobe as to make an old dress unrecognisable and, by judicious use of lace or ribbon, to transform the drab into the, almost, *haute couture*. Rebecca, dedicated like her Queen to widow's weeds for life, had given Claire the run of her wardrobe. Now, she recommended an old blue taffeta for Rose's use.

But in spite of all Rebecca's arguments, Rose insisted on wearing peacock silk harem trousers and tunic top, a trailing silk bandana in her hair.

'You look a freak, Rose,' cried Claire in horror. 'Whatever will

130

people say? Is it any wonder you are not invited anywhere? I only hope you do not let people think that *I* dress like that.'

'I don't *let* people think anything,' retorted Rose, needled in spite of her proclaimed indifference to public opinion. 'No one is interested in you.'

'They will be, I promise you,' said Claire, with narrowed eyes. 'Your friends may think they care only for Culture and Art, but any man is interested in an attractive woman, if she wants him to be. And *I do*.'

Rose felt a momentary unease. Claire had changed over the summer. Since her failure with Harry Price-Hill and Rose's success with Georgina Woodstock, a hard edge had touched the sisters' relationship. Whether of envy, malice, or injured pride Rose did not know, but she sensed a threat that had not been there before. 'Play the coquette if you must,' she said now, 'but do not expect me to sink to your level.'

Nevertheless, though Claire had not recognised it, Rose had dressed with particular care. The peacock silk had been chosen to bring out the red lights in her hair and the trousers, though unusual, were stylish and becoming. The 'eastern' look was acceptable high fashion in artistic circles and Rose knew it suited her. Even her mother acknowledged that.

'At least, they will notice you, Rose, if nothing else.'

Edward certainly did. When they alighted at the theatre he stepped forward to meet them and after the necessary courtesy to Claire had eyes only for Rose. If she had not been so elated by the occasion and the company, Rose might have spotted the danger signals in Claire's face. As it was, she remained happily unaware as the sparkling pleasure of the evening enveloped her.

They joined the others under the chandelier in the upstairs salon and Harry Price-Hill, with great gallantry, complimented first Rose, then Claire on their respective beauty. The order was another mistake. Claire prettily inclined her head, smiling up at Harry with ingenuous eyes, but behind the feminine softness there was the glint of steel.

'We have not met, I think, Mr Price-Hill, since you so gallantly lent us your window on the occasion of the Royal Procession. Though I am not at all sure I shall speak to you after all, since you have avoided me ever since! Or were you hoping to *bump into* me, unexpectedly? Your parasol,' she added, lowering her voice in conspiratorial intimacy, 'is still so very pretty...'

'As is its owner,' he replied with practised charm. Then, to Claire's secret fury, turned to a pert-faced girl with black hair and a brazen

131

decolletage, who had apparently just joined him. 'I say, Boo-Boo, let me introduce you to Claire and Rose Millard, Georgie's friends, you know. Boo-Boo is here with the Tavistock party. What a stroke of luck, eh? But she's going to sit with us, at least for the first act.'

Boo-Boo looked them over in shameless appraisal, her knowing, boot-button eyes travelling from ribboned head to silk-shod foot, before turning her back. But she had paid Rose the compliment of a double scrutiny. Claire simmered, the light of battle dangerous in her eyes, but before she could retaliate Georgina and Percy arrived, with a young man who was introduced merely as 'Fitz' and who seemed incapable of coherent speech. Claire sparkled for the new-comers with just the right mixture of modesty and wit as they made their way to the red plush box in the dress circle. A waiter brought champagne in ice-cold glasses and the lights from the chandelier sparkled a thousand times over in the bubbling goblets.

'*A vos beaux yeux*,' said Harry, lifting his glass to the ladies and draining it in one. 'I say, old chap, you had better fill me up if you want me to behave at all decently. I'm not used to a diet of culture. Suet pudding to me I'm afraid. Left all that behind me at school, thank God. Prefer something much livelier, what?' and he smacked Boo-Boo's well-rounded rump with the proprietorial air of a race-horse owner with a prize filly. Boo-Boo whinnied and pretended to strike her thigh with a riding crop. Georgina said, too brightly, 'Suet pudding is good for you once in a while, Harry, so I do hope you are going to behave youself and eat it all up.'

'Will Nanny smack me if I don't?' he said with a wink at Boo-Boo and an expression that brought the blush to Claire's cheeks.

'Behave yourself, Harry!' said Edward, 'And remember there are *some* ladies present.' This time it was Boo-Boo who flushed, but at that moment the warning bell rang and they took their seats. Rose found herself next to Edward, with Percy on her left and beyond him, Claire. The others sat behind them, though as the play pro-gressed the gold-lacquered chairs became disarranged till Harry's and his partner's were in deep shadow at the rear of the box. Rose was increasingly aware of whispering, surreptitious scuffles and suppressed laughter.

'Cousin Harry, I fear, is incurably frivolous,' murmured Edward in Rose's ear. His arm lay idly across the back of her chair, which was close up against his. 'Ophelia cannot compete with present company for attention, not even in the person of the divine Mrs Campbell.' When she did not answer, he added softly, 'I feel some-thing of the same.'

She looked up to see him regarding her intently, though in the shadowed auditorium she could not read his eyes. His arm brushed her shoulder and she drew away under the pretence of searching for her opera glass. 'Then you are less of an aesthete than I thought. Perhaps you would find more enjoyment if you kept your eyes on the stage.' She leant forward and trained the tiny opera glass on the actors but in spite of herself her hand trembled. She was acutely aware of Edward's presence beside her, of the warmth of his arm at her back, the starched gleam of his shirt-front, the proximity of his tight-muscled thigh, correct in dark striped evening trousers.

Her concentration was disturbed not only on her own account, but also on Georgina's. It must be such mortifying pain to hear her beloved Harry philandering less than a yard behind her and with that brazen flibberty-gibbet who was obviously everything Georgina was not. And yet, perhaps it would be more painful were the girl more like Georgina? A sister, for instance? Unaccountably, Rose shivered and concentrated firmly on the stage till the words caught her up in their familiar magic and carried her away. When they reached the entry of the players she mouthed Hamlet's lines with an absorption so complete that, when the curtain closed for the interval it took her a moment to remember where she was. Edward touched her arm to attract her attention and she saw that everyone else in the party was already standing up and moving into the passage and the upstairs salon.

'I had heard you were an accomplished actress,' he said, leading her to join them and putting a glass of champagne into her hand, 'But not that you were the rival of Mrs Campbell herself.'

'A cat may look at a king,' she began, but Claire cut in sweetly at her side. 'You see, Mr Rivers, we know the words.'

'It seems to me, you Millard girls know a great deal and much of it unseemly.'

'And what is unseemly about Shakespeare, Mr Rivers?' challenged Claire, looking particularly lovely in trailing cream lace against the sparkling opulence of crystal and crimson velvet. She lifted the glass to her lips and drank with rash enjoyment.

'Any knowledge is unseemly if it makes others feel inferior,' said Rivers with grave gallantry.

'La, sir, how you do flatter me,' trilled Claire and giggled on a hiccup.

'If you mean yourself Mr Rivers, I doubt anything could make you feel inferior,' said Rose. 'You are merely patronising us. Why don't you say what you really mean – that women should not be educated at all?'

133

'Because if I did you would not speak to me for the rest of the evening.'

'I probably won't anyway,' she retorted. 'The play is far more interesting.'

'Even though you already know the words?'

'Of course. There are so many different ways of saying them and so many different interpretations. For instance, when Hamlet...'

'Rose, dear,' interrupted Claire sweetly. 'We are not in the schoolroom, now.' She held out her glass to Edward Rivers and smiled with radiant appeal. 'Besides,' she said, her eyes holding his, 'I fear we are boring the gentlemen.'

'No gentleman could ever be bored in the company of a Miss Millard,' said Rivers solemnly and bowed. Over his bent head, Claire flashed Rose a look of triumph.

'Hear, hear,' echoed Percy, refilling Rose's glass and regarding her with open adoration.

'Thank you, Percy dear,' said Rose, 'You are such a *very parfit gentle knight.*'

'And *fresh as is the month of May,*' giggled Claire, not to be outdone.

Percy looked unhappily aware that he was being teased somehow and Rose, hearing laughter from Harry's group which Georgina and Fitz had joined, suppressed the thought that he might be less out of his depth in that quarter. 'It's all right, Percy,' she said, 'We are only quoting Chaucer at each other. Take no notice.' She found his devotion both touching and irritating. But Claire saw it as an open challenge.

'Captain Woodstock,' she said, laying that slender hand on his arm, 'It is "Captain", isn't it? Or do I call you "Mr"?'

'P ... P ... Percy will do, Miss Millard, that is, if you...'

'Of course I will,' she said sweetly, leaning trustingly against him. 'And you must call me Claire and tell me all about your estate and your partridges and things. But first, fill my dear little glass, too?'

'You have had enough champagne,' warned Rose, furious.

'Nonsense. No one can ever have enough of such a lovely drink, can they, Percy?'

'I am afraid they can,' interrupted Edward, steering her back into their box, 'At least on this occasion. That was the bell for the next act.'

Rose saw with surprise that, champagne or not, Claire had managed to position herself between Percy and Edward and at the same time engage the attention of both.

'I think my dress is caught under your chair, Mr Rivers,' she

134

said, requiring a manoeuvre which occasioned close proximity of breast and cheek. Not content with that, she added, 'I am so very sorry to inconvenience you, Captain Woodstock – Percy – but I think I have dropped my fan.'

Percy bent to search under the chair just as Claire herself bent forward and their heads collided with an audible crack.

Claire squealed, giggled, said, 'Oh, Percy, I hope I have not hurt you!' While heads turned in the neighbouring box and there was a rustle of disapproval. Rose was scarlet with mortification. 'For pity's sake, Claire,' she hissed, leaning across Edward, 'Behave! Or you will have us put out of the theatre!'

'I think the management has suffered louder interruptions in its time,' said Edward and Rose realised he had seized the opportunity given him when she leant forward to slip his arm around her waist. 'And who could dream of ejecting so charming a companion,' he added soothingly, to Claire. 'As for you,' he murmured, in Rose's ear, 'it would be a brave man who tried.'

'You be quiet too,' snapped Rose. 'Or if you must whisper, do it somewhere else. I, for one, would prefer to hear the play!'

Edward Rivers removed his arm and obliged, but if ever she glanced up, she caught him looking at her with a steady contemplation which began to make her uncomfortable. At the second interval, she challenged him. 'Have I paint on my nose, or a dirty face?'

'You have a lovely face, Rose,' said Percy, overhearing, 'And he is a blackguard who says otherwise.'

'Lie down, Percy, like a good dog,' soothed Edward, summoning canapés and more champagne. 'The lady does not need defending. She is quite capable of doing that for herself.'

'Thank you Mr Rivers. That is the first sensible thing you have said this evening.' Everyone laughed, even the awful Boo-Boo.

Then Claire said sweetly, 'You must not mind Rose, Mr Rivers.' She slipped her arm through her sister's in a public demonstration of affection. 'It is only the artistic temperament that makes her so disagreeable, and she is *so* talented. We must all make allowances.'

'Georgina is artistic,' offered Percy into the sudden silence. 'Aren't you, old girl?'

'Oh Percy, don't be such as ass! I am not a patch on Rose and I know it, even if you do not.'

'Never mind, Percy,' said Claire, abandoning Rose's arm for his. 'Your loyalty does you great credit. I wish *I* had a brother to defend me as you defend your sister.'

'Oh I say...' blushed Percy and Rose turned away, disgusted.

135

The noise level rose as glasses chinked and sparkled, champagne frothed and airy pastry morsels flaked into the thick pile carpet. Everyone except Rose seemed to be laughing.

'What is it?' asked a low voice in her ear and the warmth of his hand on her arm set her blood racing. 'The weight of the world's sadness – or a headache?'

'Neither. Or perhaps both. I don't know. But it is very hot in here.'

'Shall we walk a while, in the foyer?' Before she could answer, he had steered her deftly through the doorway and out onto the sweeping cool of the stairway, then down to the foyer and out, past the braided and brass-buttoned commissionaire, onto the steps of the theatre, where the night air blessed her cheeks and the lamplight cast a benison over passing carriage and darkened street.

'Well?'

Rose did not answer. What was there to say?

'I had not planned it like this.'

'No.'

'Will you forgive me?'

'For what? For offering an evening of Shakespeare beautifully acted? What more could I ask?'

'May I visit you again at the studio?' For a moment she thought she had mis-heard, or imagined the words, but the intensity was real enough, and her own reaction to it.

'Drat chemistry!' she said, with sudden vehemence. 'All I want to do is paint.' But when he said, in that voice she thought of as dark velvet, 'Please, Rose? If I promise not to ... disturb ... you too much?' She had no choice but to say, 'Yes.'

Once spoken, the possibilities her words endorsed wove like perfumed incense around them, filling her with a new excitement and a melting longing which the warmth of his arm around her waist only increased. They stood together, in speaking silence, till the bell shrilled for the last act.

Claire fell prettily asleep, her head on Percy's shoulder, the moment the lights were dimmed and did not wake till Young Fortinbras with conquest came from Poland and Hamlet lay dead. But when she did jerk into consciousness she looked quickly from one escort to the other and murmured in self-deprecation, *Sleep that knits up the ravelled sleeve of care.*'

Edward grinned in admiration, but Rose said fiercely, 'Care? What does she know of care? Her life's a bed of roses!'

'And why not? *They are not long, the days of wine and roses...*'

'No.' Rose felt unaccountable loneliness wash over her and when Edward's hand found hers under the concealment of her trailing silks, she held it as if he alone were her lifeline to content, while the bodies were carried off with theatrical solemnity and the dead march played.

'Well,' said Claire with satisfaction when the brougham had delivered them safely home and Annie had barred and bolted the heavy front door behind them. 'That was an excellent evening's work. I think we can count on a flow of invitations from now on. That will be all, Annie,' she said as the maid hovered eagerly for titbits of gossip. 'Go to bed.' When Annie had shuffled away, grumbling, into the back regions, Claire spun round, once, under the single gas lamp before adding, with triumph, 'I accepted for the Charity Ball next month, a shooting weekend at the Woodstocks and when Fitz mentioned the Promenade concerts I said if he wanted to make up a party, we would be delighted.'

'Claire, you didn't!' Rose was appalled.

'I most certainly did.'

'Then I am even more ashamed of you than I was in the theatre when you fell asleep! And you drank too much!'

'*What?* Just because I laughed and was good company instead of glowering like you and giving boring little lectures?'

'Good company? You were outrageous. Fancy actually *asking* for an invitation!'

'And why not?' Claire executed another, gleeful pirouette, before coming to a panting stop in front of her disapproving sister. 'Don't be such a prude, Rose. It does not do to pass up a chance, and false pride got nobody anywhere. Besides,' she added, with quiet triumph, 'I think I have found the one . . . Oh Mamma!' All dignity forgotten, she looped her skirts and ran up the stairs to where Rebecca had appeared, regal in night attire, a lighted candle in her hand, 'Such an evening as you would not credit! Champagne and diamonds and everybody who is anybody was there. There were fully four eligible bachelors in our party. Mr Price-Hill is a trifle frivolous, but so debonair! And when the wild oats are sown, he will make some girl a very tolerable husband – and he has a splendid country estate! But then so has Captain Woodstock, as well as a house in Town, and as for Mr Rivers – they say his pheasants are the best this season and even the Prince of Wales shoots on his estate! And, Mamma, they are all of them *rich*.'

'Not Mr Rivers, dear,' said Rebecca who had made discreet inquiries the results of which Mr Proudfoot had conveyed to her that very day. 'Apparently Wychwood is shockingly encumbered with debt and his father . . .'

'No matter,' interrupted Claire, still borne up on the froth of champagne. 'He is a friend of Princes and handsome, as they all are. I believe Fitz might be the richest of all, but maybe not as he is only a third son and he is so very silent it is not easy to find out. But all eligible, Mamma. I can't understand Rose keeping so quiet about them – unless to keep them from me! But now I have met them, I mean to have one of them for myself. Just think, Mamma! This time next year I might be *married*! You did say I could have a dowry, didn't you?'

'Apart from all that, Mamma,' said Rose drily, 'As I am sure you are longing to know, the play was a great success.'

They did not hear her. Instead, Rebecca led Claire, still bubbling with champagne-fed exuberance, into the master bedroom where, from the squeals of excitement which greeted her entrance, it seemed the younger sisters had been allowed to wait up till their return. The door closed, only to open again on an afterthought.

'Are you coming in too, Rose, to tell us all about it?'

'No thank you, Mamma. I leave the embroidery to Claire. I think, if you will excuse me, I will go to bed.'

'As you wish, dear. But remember to turn out the light.'

She lay a long time awake, with the sounds of distant chatter drifting up from her mother's bedroom and the clearer, more intimate sound of Edward's voice, close in her ear, saying, 'May I visit you?'

She was drifting at last into sleep when the door creaked open and Sara came in. She wore a high-necked cotton nightgown with broderie anglaise at the neck and wrists and her fair hair rippled loose to her waist. Rose was struck for the first time by her sister's beauty, though Sara's eyes were anxious and her lips suspiciously trembling.

'What is it, Sara? Have you had a bad dream?'

'Oh no. I have not been to bed. But I wanted to see you, quick, before Claire comes up. They have been saying dreadful things about Mr Price-Hill.'

'Really? What sort of things?'

'That he lives only for pleasure and loose ladies and Maud's face went all red and she said he was *wicked*. Then Claire said wicked or not he was still an Honourable and that ... that ...'

Rose propped herself on one elbow. 'And what, Sara? Tell me.'

'That he is on her list! Oh Rose, she has picked one of them tonight, but she won't say which! Only that she has first choice and we must wait and see. If she chooses Harry, I will kill her!'

138

'She won't,' soothed Rose, while her mind raced with possibilities. 'I happen to know that Harry does not intend to marry for years and years and will certainly not marry Claire.'

'Are you sure?' Sara looked so pathetically anxious that Rose's heart twisted with compassion, as it used to do in those bygone nursery days when Claire's bullying got out of hand. But Sara would soon be fifteen – almost a grown woman.

'Quite sure,' she said firmly. 'Because Harry is already engaged – to Georgina.' Quietly, she explained the situation while Sara's pale face grew paler and she bit her lower lip, hard. 'There is no saying when they will marry – or even if,' finished Rose, 'But you do see how it is?'

'I see.' Sara was silent for a moment, then she said, 'But they may *never* marry. Miss Woodstock may grow tired of waiting and marry someone else, mightn't she?'

'Yes, I suppose she might,' agreed Rose, with reluctance.

It was enough for Sara. 'Thank you, Rose,' she said, smiling. Then she bent down and kissed Rose's cheek. 'I have always liked you best.'

When Sara had gone, to the attic room she shared with Maud and Charlotte, Rose found that sleep eluded her. Sara's anxieties had somehow seeped into her own mind and, absurd though it was, she found herself asking over and over who Claire had selected for her prey. When the door at last creaked open, and Claire tiptoed in, candle in hand, Rose asked her.

'I thought you were asleep,' said Claire, putting down the candle on the bedside table. She began to unhook her dress.

'I am not asleep, and kindly answer the question, if only so we all know where we are.'

'You will know when the time comes,' said Claire, loosening her hair from its pins and tossing it free. She looked jubilant, excited, and absolutely self-assured. Turning her back, she sat down at the dressing table, took up the tortoiseshell-backed brush and, in the flickering light of the single candle, addressed Rose's reflection in the glass. 'Just remember, Rose, that *I* have first choice.' She began to brush her hair, with long steady strokes.

'Do you?' For a long moment they stared at each other in the shadowed glass till Claire suddenly tossed her hair forward and, head down and reddening face concealed, embarked on the second part of the nightly ritual. 'Fifty-one, fifty-two, fifty-three . . .'

Deliberately, Rose snuffed the candle.

CHAPTER 6

'It won't do, old chap,' said Harry, sighting carefully along the billiard cue. His evening tail-coat had been tossed aside long ago in the solemn business of the billiard room and his starched white cuffs flashed emeralds set in gold. He struck the ball with practised skill and stood up, triumphant. 'Pocketed in one.'

'What do you mean, it won't do?' Edward circled the table, sighting his shot, then leant forward, hands elegantly balancing the cue. He, too, was in shirt-sleeves, a cummerbund of deep Florentine blue keeping the starched shirt front and evening trousers together.

When the theatre party had dispersed, the men had adjourned to the billiard room at Edward's club to round off the evening. But Fitz had left half an hour ago and Percy Woodstock was asleep, slumped in a carved oak chair in one corner, feet outstretched, arms dangling, mouth comically open. The rest of the building had long been sunk in somnolent silence, but Edward and Harry continued, with indolent expertise, to alternate brandy with billiards in a fog of tobacco smoke.

The green baize glowed under the shaded gas lamps, the dark red wallpaper gave the feeling of comfortable incarceration and in the grate below the heavy oak mantelpiece the remnants of a generous fire still flickered with faithful hospitality.

'I mean,' said Harry, watching Edward's hands with concentrated attention, 'that you are after the wrong quarry. Those Millard girls are bright, I grant you that, and God knows they are attractive, but take the word of an old campaigner and watch out. There may be money there, of course, if that's what you're after. But the mother's a tartar. Absolutely ruthless.'

'Don't be absurd, Harry,' said Edward, successfully completing his shot. He moved to the fireside, retrieved a brandy bowl from the mantelshelf and drank. 'Mrs Millard is a harmless widow.'

'No mother of unmarried daughters is harmless, old boy. Believe me, I know. And so should you after how many seasons running the matrimonial gauntlet. That widow has probably planned the wedding breakfast already, with you as the main dish.' He helped himself to more brandy from the decanter on the sideboard. 'I must say, cousin Edward, your club keeps a good cellar. This cognac is excellent.' He drank with relish and added, 'Don't say I didn't warn you.'

'My dear boy,' said Edward with studied nonchalance, 'I have no intention of marrying anyone for quite some time.'

'I am relieved to hear it, old chap. I noticed how those Millard girls vied for your attention this evening and you enjoyed it, you sly devil. But I am glad marriage is not what you have in mind. It couldn't be,' he went on when Edward made no answer. 'Not to a gentlemen's outfitter's daughter, even though Millard shares, rumour has it, are definitely a good bet. So if it isn't marriage?' He looked at Edward over the rim of his brandy glass. 'Don't tell me my upright model of a gentleman cousin is planning to seduce the lady?'

'Don't be an ass, Harry!'

'Because if so,' went on Harry, impervious, 'You will get nowhere with one and possibly, just possibly, everywhere with the other.'

'Really, Harry!' protested Edward, flushing. 'It is damned ungentlemanly of you to speculate about such things.'

'Not at all, old chap. Merely practical. Life is too short to waste on a fruitless chase. I'm just sorry I can't advise you more, but it's a breed new to me.'

'What is?' snapped Edward with irritation.

'The socially ambitious daughter of Trade. Ordinary Trade are simple – they don't expect you to marry them. They'll be content with jewellery and intimate dinners and when you want to move on to pastures new, all you need do is pay if they're in trouble, find them a job or a new patron and wave them goodbye. It's all they expect, old boy, and they accept it. But nowadays the better-heeled Trade think themselves good enough to marry whoever they choose, blue blood, title and all. The Millards are *that* breed and they have their collective eye on you. So remember there are five of them, and be warned.'

'Don't be such a crashing snob, Harry.'

'Why not? I merely say what everyone else thinks and is too hypocritical to put into words. I saw how they pursued you.'

'Pursue? You make it sound like a hunt.'

'That is exactly what it is old boy, with you as the prey. I know you have lectured me for years on my dissolute ways, but at least I know how to escape the matrimonial clutches. I have experience – unlike you. So take my advice. Get yourself engaged, quick, to a respectable country girl who's in no hurry to marry. Otherwise, if you are not careful, you will find yourself caught, eviscerated, and

141

your brush triumphantly wound round a Millard girl's neck – I wouldn't like to bet on which one.'

Edward could not bring himself to answer. There was too much truth for comfort in what Harry said. He had not meant to fall in love with Rose. It had happened in the flip of a heart beat, when he saw her asleep in the woods, and since that brief interlude in Georgina's studio that love had grown to an aching longing: now he wanted her as he had never wanted any woman before. But, as Harry said, marriage was out of the question.

Rose was an artist, with interests and ambitions of her own, and he had seen in his own painfully insecure childhood what that could do to a marriage. His father, amiably eccentric though he was, had expected his wife to be a proper wife and instead she had gone her own defiant and unorthodox way – 'artistic' parties, poetical and literary young men. Though Edward had been too young to understand the details, he had caught the whiff of scandal, of derision and betrayal, had seen his father's pain. And when his mother, full of vitality and rebellion, had taken herself off to Venice and left her children virtually motherless, Edward had wept, as he suspected his father had wept, in secret loneliness and longing.

In the years that followed – disorganised years with no apparent backbone or solid flesh and which her dutiful annual visits, invariably fraught with tensions and disappointments, did nothing to soothe – Edward had missed his mother with a sense of undiminished loss. Not that they had ever been close – he could not remember one single occasion when she had even kissed him – but a home needed a woman at the helm, and a child needed a mother. Edward had vowed then, and still held firm to that view, that when he married it would be to someone who would be the foundation stone of his house – a docile, loving woman with no ambitions of her own, who would be content to be his wife and the mother of his children and whose world would be bounded by the boundaries of Wychwood.

Docility, however, was not the only requirement. When Edward married, further considerations would determine his choice, the principal one, bearing in mind those crippling death duties, being money. But even if the Millards were rich, money was not enough. There were all sorts of intricate social considerations, difficult to ennumerate to an outsider, but perfectly plain to those involved – his mother was an expert – and his mother, Edward remembered with the usual apprehension, was due home for her annual visitation any day now. Lady Portia invariably arrived in a storm of complaint, disaster, bizarre misunderstandings and high drama.

142

Remembering Harry's awe of Lady Portia he said innocently, 'Harry, I almost forgot. Will you join us at Wychwood when my mother arrives? I expect her imminently.'

'Good God no! She freezes the blood in my veins. One look from her and I feel five years old and in permanent disgrace.'

'How appropriate,' said Rivers and struck the ball with malicious triumph. It ricocheted from the table edge with a series of staccato cracks like rifle fire and, with a cry of 'What? What?' Percy shot bolt upright in his chair, eyes wide with terror.

They had forgotten their sleeping companion.

'Lie down old boy,' soothed Harry, laying a restraining hand on Percy's shoulder. 'It's only Rivers here, going berserk.'

'Oh.' Percy grinned feebly with relief. 'I was having a deuced uncomfortable dream. Hordes of enemy chaps pouring over a hill-top and our bullets went right through them with no damage at all. Just came on and on, unstoppable.'

'Unlike Rivers here,' said Harry gleefully, circling the billiard table, eyes narrowed in calculation. 'Who ... I think ... is about to be ... beaten!' he finished in triumph as he cracked the ball smoothly home. 'Bad luck, old boy. That's what comes of having women on the brain.'

'It would serve you right,' said Edward viciously, 'If you fell in love yourself one day. Really fell. Not your usual light-hearted philandering, but a blind, gut-wrenching, sacrificial love that sucked the life-blood from your veins and stopped your heart in its tracks.'

'I say, that's going it a bit strong, old boy. Are you sure you're feeling all right?'

'No,' snarled Edward. 'I am not.' He slammed out of the room.

Harry was right, of course, thought Edward when, two days later, he stood at the uncurtained window of his bedroom and looked out over the silence of the Wychwood estate. Bats wove soundless patterns against a moonless sky, a barn owl called from the home woods and the black shape of a cat darted suddenly across his line of vision and disappeared. Marriage was out of the question.

To his left, out of sight, the tennis lawn stretched down to the woods and the cornfields where he had walked that first day, with Rose. And to his right, beyond the chestnut tree, was the dark block of the old brewery with its strange, love-haunted loft. Rose had felt it too, as if it were her loft, her ghost ... Impatiently he closed the curtains and lit the lamp.

But as he removed cuff links and collar stud and prepared for bed, he found he could not shut Rose Millard out of his mind with

143

the mere closing of a curtain. She was inside the room with him, hovering like an exotic bird, just beyond vision, mocking, elusive, tantalising. The same aura had clung to her in the London studio – an attraction strong as a magnetic force which drew them inexorably together, and which he could feel even now, more than eighty miles away.

He remembered the welcome of her lips, the quivering promise that he knew waited only for him to claim – and the abrasive antagonism which surfaced when he least expected it to spice the sweetness with barbed fire, like chilli peppers on the tongue. She was alluring, challenging, defiant, and, he was almost certain, his. His only rival was her art.

He stared thoughtfully into the mirror and wondered, briefly, if she would consider him worthy of a portrait. But he had not the time nor the patience to sit for hours, even in contemplation of Rose – and she would be lost in her precious painting . . . Perversely, that very self-sufficiency attracted him, challenged him as no other woman had. And she had said he might visit her.

What did it matter what Harry said? It was no business of his anyway.

CHAPTER 7

It was a week after the theatre visit that Sara read the advertisement in *The Times*. 'King's College, London, Ladies Department. 13, Kensington Square. Lectures adapted to students above the age of 16. Oct. 14 at 3 p.m. Inaugural lecture by Mr F. W. Myers, M.A. on "The Poetry of William Morris", to which all students and their friends are invited.' 'For further information apply to Vice-Principal Miss L. M. Faithfull.'

Sara read the piece over and over till she knew the words by heart, then folded the paper neatly, replaced it on her mother's work-table, and went quietly upstairs. Rose and Claire were both at Millards. Since Claire's announced intention to be married within a year, Mrs Millard had launched into a new surge of business energy. She planned to extend their stock, introduce a new line in ladies' outerwear and extend the Mourning department with a guarantee of twenty-four hours delivery. Rose was needed for the Art Work, Claire for the cash room to release her mother, suitably sombre and sympathetic in her own widow's weeds, to oversee Mourning.

Maud and Charlotte were at the Dame school, back-boards in place, deportment impeccable, reading the day's lesson from the Bible prior to writing in careful copperplate the day's lesson in the French language and embroidering the day's ration of improving sampler.

Sara was now a daughter at home. She was tall, slender, beautifully proportioned, with ethereally fair hair and dreamy hazel eyes. The bosom she had longed for in childhood had arrived almost unnoticed. One day she had been flat-chested and gawky; the next, it seemed, miraculously graceful with shapely curves at breast and hip. She was still shy, unsure and solitary, but she had the knack of noticing detail, of catching and fitting together scraps of disjointed conversation and making deductions which gave her the illusion of belonging: for though she might have few friends, at least she knew everything that was going on – and, apparently, everything that the school could teach her, for, after only a week or two of the new term, they had suggested, tactfully, to Mrs Millard that her daughter was ready, 'to move out into the world.' That, to Mrs Millard, meant only one thing – it was time for Sara to help in the shop.

Sara had refused. She needed the time for study.

'Then if you refuse to work at Millards,' said Rebecca tartly, 'you will help in the house. Claire will direct you. There will be time enough for study after the linen is mended, the silver polished and the preserves made.'

So, when her mother left the house, Sara dutifully did with all speed what had to be done – or rather, what her mother would notice were it left undone – so that she could have the day free for her real love, reading. She read voraciously any and everything, from the *Girls' Own Paper* to John Ruskin and John Stuart Mill. She devoured Dickens, Trollope, George Eliot, Scott and, secretly, struggled with a lexicon and the first principles of classical Greek. Greek was necessary for the Cambridge Tripos and if she was ever to get to Cambridge University, as she fully meant to do, she would need to be conversant with the classics. Newnham students, she knew, could by-pass the Latin and Greek papers and shorten their course, thus filling the gaping need for women teachers with the minimum of delay, but Sara meant to go to Girton College and take precisely the same course as the men students did. At not quite 15 she knew she was still too young to be considered for a place among the privileged hundred or so Girtonians, but in two years time, perhaps, she would write to Miss Welsh, the Mistress, and ask to be admitted.

Meanwhile, the lecture at King's College sounded ideal.

'I wonder . . .' said Sara thoughtfully, staring at her own reflection in the glass. Then she bundled her hair up into a Grecian knot, secured it with a handful of pins and regarded the result with frowning concentration. 'Will I pass for sixteen?' Deciding that a hat would complete the aging process, she purloined one of Claire's, added a fur tippet, and, satisfied with the result, stepped out of the house before Annie or anyone else should see her.

'You did what?' demanded Mrs Millard, laying aside her spoon. A thin vapour rose from the soup plate in front of her where a skin was already netting over the chicken consommé. All round the table, spoons were suspended, breath held, then Sara spoke.

'I enrolled for the lecture course at King's College Ladies Department, Mamma. We begin on the 14th.'

'*We?* And who gave you permission to leave the house and walk the streets of London alone, madam? Who gave you permission to *enrol* as you put it in a college?'

'Papa said . . .'

'What your father said or did not say need not concern you!' interrupted Rebecca furiously. 'It is what *I* say now!' She caught her husband's reproachful eyes watching her from the silver-framed photograph on the dresser and her anger faltered, but only for a moment. Herbert had always looked to her to keep the girls in order.

'Papa wanted me to study,' persisted Sara. 'He said I was clever. He promised . . .'

'Yes,' sighed Rebecca. 'He promised. He also promised Rose a studio and Claire a splendid dowry. But that was before, when things were different. Your father's death changed things. I would have thought you especially would have realised that, Sara.'

'What do you mean, "me especially"? Do you mean I killed Papa? Do you mean it is all my fault?' Sara was on her feet now, her voice hysterically high.

'No, dear, of course I don't,' soothed Rebecca, alarmed by Sara's vehemence, but the child took no notice.

'You think I am to blame for everything! It is no good denying it. I have heard you say "if only she hadn't swum too far" and "if only" this, "if only" that, but it is always *me* who is to blame! All of you thought so, even Annie and that horrid Mademoiselle and you still think it! I can see it in your faces – all of you – and it's not fair! I would not have harmed Papa for anything. I loved him!' Her voice broke on a sob. 'And he loved me – which is more than you do – any of you!' She turned and ran, weeping, from the room.

There was a moment's shocked silence, then Rose pushed back her chair and stood up.

'I will go to her, Mamma, and . . .'

'No, Rose. Stay where you are.' Rebecca took a deep breath and went on with almost perfect composure, 'I will not have the meal disrupted any further. Sara is hysterical, that is all. A period of quiet, in her own room, will serve better than any medicine – and she has had quite enough attention for one evening. Now finish your soup, all of you, before it is entirely spoilt.'

Obediently they ate in a silence broken only by the clink of spoon on china and the faint noise of swallowing. Then Rebecca rang the small brass hand-bell for Annie to clear away and bring in the boiled beef.

'I visited Mr Proudfoot today,' she said when the plates had been loaded and set in front of them, Sara's being left conspicuously empty. 'We discussed arrangements for a dowry should such a thing be needed in the near future and I think I can promise you, Claire,

147

that you will be sufficiently provided for.'

'Thank you, Mamma. I knew you would arrange something.' Claire beamed her satisfaction, then a small frown darkened her brow. 'The thing is, how best to let people know about it? We must spread the word, discreetly but thoroughly, so that there can be no doubt. I know! Rose must do it. Rose shall let slip to the Woodstock girl, preferably when her brother is there, that we Millard girls are worth a few thousand.'

'I will do nothing of the kind,' said Rose. 'It is vulgar to talk of money.'

'Only when you have not got it,' giggled Charlotte and was promptly squashed by the ever-vigilant Maud.

'I see no reason why you should not let it be known,' said Rebecca. 'Discreetly, of course. As for being vulgar, Rose, it is merely practical. A prospective husband needs to know the stakes before he makes a move.'

'You make it sound like a game of black-jack or whist,' said Rose in disgust. 'Why not advertise in *The Times* and let the whole world know? "The Millard daughters are now available to any man rich, healthy, and preferably titled, offering marriage with town house and country estate, in return for a dowry of ..." how much, Mamma? Five thousand? Or shall we make it ten?'

'Really, Rose, you are impossible,' snapped her mother while Charlotte and Maud tried not to laugh and Claire grew pink in the face with fury.

'If you had your way, Rose, we would none of us marry anyone,' she cried. 'I don't care what you do yourself, but I want a husband and I will not have you spoiling my chances.'

'You can spoil your own with no help from me,' retorted Rose. 'Just get tipsy on other people's champagne and make an exhibition of yourself at the theatre.'

'I did *not*,' cried Claire, aghast.

'You slept all through the last act, with your mouth open,' said Rose cruelly. 'And you snored.'

'Ooooh!' Claire would have tugged Rose's hair out by the roots if she could have reached across the table, but had to content herself with a kick at Rose's ankles.

'That is enough,' thundered Rebecca. 'I will not have my dinner table turned into a bear garden. Charlotte, stop laughing. Maud, sit up straight. Claire, you are behaving like a fishwife. As for you, Rose, I despair ... And Claire is right. Whether you choose to marry or not is immaterial, but you will not spoil your sister's chances. You will spread the word, discreetly, as she suggests – a "substantial" dowry is the expression to use – and that is an order. Do you understand?'

'Yes, Mamma.' Rose looked her mother calmly in the eyes and added, 'But if we Millard girls are worth a few thousand, why cannot Sara have a mere hundred to go to College?'

'Because ... because...' floundered Rebecca helplessly. Again she caught her husband's accusing sepia eyes. 'Because she is too young,' she finished, 'and that's an end to it. When she is eighteen, I will reconsider the matter. Now may we finish our meal in at least a semblance of civilised calm?'

The studio was pale with autumn sunlight which picked out the rich tones of Rose's paintings, gave a softer sheen to Georgina's sculptured heads and laid a veil of gold over Rose's newest work, on an easel at the far end of the room, a full-length portrait of her friend, seated at her work bench with a litter of pencil sketches before her and an uncut block of marble in the background, though the marble was imaginary, its original still shrouded under a dust-sheet in the Wychwood brewery. The shadows were soft browns and blues, the folds of Georgina's dress a vibrant gold and the whole thing illuminated by a shaft of light from the skylight overhead. Rose called it 'Inspiration' and had been working at it steadily for weeks.

But that afternoon when, released early from Millards, she arrived to resume work on the picture, she found Edward Rivers in the studio, seated on the shabby Afghan rug which draped the ottoman, one leg crossed lazily over the other and an aromatic haze of cigar smoke mingling with the late October sunlight.

'I know where Georgina keeps the key,' he said, uncrossing his legs and standing up. 'And you said I might come.' He looked at her steadily and she felt excitement surge through her till her very finger tips tingled.

'So I did.' Calmly she loosed her mantle and threw it over a chair, then reached for the long white apron she usually wore for painting. She had come straight from Millards and was still in her 'office' clothes. His hand closed over hers and held it.

'Don't put that on yet,' he said softly.

'Why not? I have come to work.'

'But I haven't. And how do you expect me to kiss you through a barricade of oil paint?'

'I don't expect anything of the kind,' she said, pulling her hand away. 'I expect to be allowed to paint in my own studio undisturbed. Was not that the bargain?'

149

'Ah ... yes ... I had forgotten.' Smiling, he resumed his seat and his cigar and as she donned the apron and set out her paints he watched her with a deliberate intensity which made her at the same time angry, excited, and self-conscious.

'There is no need to stare like that,' she snapped at last. 'Or are you hoping that I will paint your portrait free? You could do a lot worse,' she went on as he made no answer, but continued to study her, with amusement now. 'I intend to exhibit at the Academy one day.'

'Do the Academy know?' he asked, with mock solemnity.

'I can see it is pointless talking to you,' said Rose with a flash of real anger. 'Why don't you go and leave me in peace?'

'Because...' He shrugged, then said in quite a different voice, 'Unfortunately, I think I love you.'

'Unfortunately? What sort of a declaration is that? Anyone would think you had caught the plague!'

'Of all the plagues with which the world is curst, Of every ill, a woman is the worst,' he spread his hands in surrender. 'You see I can hide behind quotations too.'

'Thank you,' she said, with scathing sarcasm. 'You will be telling me next, like d'Arcy in *Pride and Prejudice*, that you know I am your inferior in wealth and breeding, but that you love me against your better judgement. That in spite of all endeavour you have been unable to conquer this inconvenient and painful emotion and must therefore swallow pride and beg for my unworthy hand in marriage.'

She saw his face flush with alarm. 'But I only meant...'

'Oh, you need not look so hunted, my fine wooer. You are quite safe. I have no intention of marrying anyone for quite some time, if at all. I have other things to do with my time.'

Other things to do with my time. That innocent phrase triggered a memory and brought back a scene he thought he had successfully forgotten. He had been small, less than banister height, and through the rungs he had seen his mother, beautiful and angry, in some outlandish costume for a fancy dress party, and his father pleading. 'Must you go? Surely your bohemian friends can wait? I had hoped we might spend the evening quietly together for once...' and his mother had laughed, a wild, scornful laugh which made his father flinch. 'A quiet evening together? I have better things to do with my time than waste it in a dreary country dining room with a dreary country squire.' She had gone then, long beads swinging and bangles jangling, and afterwards his father had stood a long time, motionless, while the grandfather clock ticked relentlessly on. Edward had not dared to look at his father's face for fear of

150

what he would see there, for his father's shame had been his, and insupportable. He had crept silently to bed and buried his face in his pillow, vowing never to marry. Never, as long as he lived.

That had been childish, of course. A man must marry one day and Edward wanted children. But he wanted stability for those children and peace and obedience and a calm country life in the house he loved. Unfortunately, he also wanted Rose, who offered none of those things. But she had said herself she did not plan to marry – and neither did he, for a long time yet.

'Of course,' said Rose, deliberately teasing, 'If you were thinking of a *long* engagement . . .'

He swallowed, flushed deeper, but at least there would be truth between them. 'No, I was not.'

'I see,' she said slowly and her eyes challenged his to look away. 'It was not marriage you had in mind. Am I right?' Before he could answer, or begin to explain, she said, 'Then *a plague on both your houses* – I assume, like the rest of your sort, you have two?'

'No,' he said and his face closed like a slammed door. 'Only Wychwood. The other was sold, for death duties.'

Rose felt suddenly ashamed of herself and petty. 'I am sorry. I was trying to be too clever.'

'No, do not apologise. I deserved it.' After a moment, he said in a low voice, 'Rose, what are we to do, you and I?'

She looked at him – a handsome man, ten years older than she, experienced, a little world-weary, and a look in his eyes which melted her very bones. Abruptly she looked away.

'You will sit there and smoke cigars until it is time for you to go to your club. I shall paint. I meant it when I spoke of the Academy.' She turned back to the portrait of Georgina and was mixing paint for the flesh tones with a hand that trembled only slightly when she realised he had left his seat and was standing behind her.

'You have made her . . . beautiful,' he said with surprise and a touch of awe. 'And yet, it is still Georgina whom most people consider plain.'

'Most people are ignorant boobies,' said Rose, without looking round. 'I agree with Constable that light, shade and perspective can make anything beautiful.'

'Perhaps. But you bring something more than that to your painting – a kind of intensity – and love. That was what first attracted me to you – the awareness of what you would give to someone you cared for. Your lover would never be cold. Do you remember the old brewery? I knew then, and you knew it too, so there is no use in denying it, or fighting to suppress it.'

151

Startled, she turned her head and his face was so close she felt his breath warm on her cheek. When she looked into his eyes she saw in their velvet depths that love-haunted loft, with eaves like these and silence, butterfly-wings in the dancing dust and slow sunlight . . . and a voice inside her heart saying, 'Is it possible for a place to be haunted by the future . . .' But her future was now, here, in a different loft.

'Put down your brush a moment,' he said softly. 'Please?' When, obediently she did so, he began to untie the bow of her painting-apron strings and at the first touch of his fingers she quivered with surging desire. Before she could remind herself of the common treachery of body chemistry it was too late. He had removed her apron, drawn her close against his chest, and kissed her with a gentleness and poignancy which stilled all protest. When at last he freed her, she said weakly, *'What of soul was left, I wonder, when the kissing had to stop?'*

'Must you always retreat into other men's words?'

'Retreat?' Rose was taken aback. 'But they say things so much better than I could . . .'

'Retreat,' repeated Edward, regarding her with passionate eyes in which she read reproach and hurt. 'Can you not honour me with your own feelings instead of always someone else's, however eminent? I would rather one loving word coined by Rose Millard than a volume of Shakespeare or Browning.'

'There speaks the Philistine,' she said, but her voice faltered and she added, humbly, 'I am sorry. It is a habit Claire and I developed years ago.'

The moment she spoke Claire's name, she wished it unsaid. It brought an alien presence into the room, with the memory of Claire's face in that shadowed mirror as she said, 'Remember, I have first choice.' To obliterate that memory, Rose reached up and kissed him and the action obliterated not only memory, but sense, resolution, everything except desire and love and longing . . . until he scooped her suddenly up in his arms and with a low cry of exultation carried her to the ottoman. Then he turned away.

'Where are you going?' She snatched at his hand.

'Only to lock the door.'

'But you can't do that! Suppose Georgina were to come?'

'But that is precisely why, my dearest,' he murmured, his fingers undoing the buttons of her high-necked blouse one by one. Then he slid a hand under the shoulder of her undergarment and pulled the material down over her arm till her breast was exposed, full and firm as Aphrodite's marble bosom, but the nipple when he knelt to kiss it was warm and brown.

'God, but you are beautiful.'

'Artists have recognised the beauty of the female form for centuries,' said Rose, but her voice trembled. She looked down at the thick silken sheen of his hair then closed her eyes as desire flowed through her with a sudden douche of fire. Her hands threaded his hair, held his head there, against her breast till her limbs ached with need. His hand found the hem of her skirts and drew them higher, stroking, caressing, with inexorable progress . . .

'No!' Rose broke away, sat up and turned her back in one fluid, startled movement. Then she sat quivering, head bowed, arms crossed protectively across her naked breast.

'Now let me lock the door?' he murmured, kissing the nape of her neck. 'Please?'

'No.' She shook herself violently, as if to shake off lingering temptation and added, with anguish, 'It would not be right.'

'Not right? What could be more right when two people find each other in such accord, such love, such need? I thought you despised conventional repression, conventional prudery and "all the coquettries of the matrimonial transaction"? I thought you believed in Free Love?'

'I do, but . . .' He pulled her roughly to her feet and kissed her, with a mixture of anger and passion which left her gasping.

'Now do you understand me? I love you, woman. I want you!'

'And I you.' Then beyond his shoulder she saw Georgina's reproachful, painted face. 'But *not here*. I promised Georgina I would use the studio only for Art.'

'For God's sake, woman, is not love a kind of art? The Karma Sutra . . .'

There was a sudden sound behind them and the door flew open on a rush of evening air. After a moment's shocked silence, a small voice said, 'I am sorry to disturb you, but I am looking for Miss Woodstock.'

'Damn, damn, damn,' breathed Edward, keeping his back to the door while he straightened clothing with exemplary speed. Then he turned, keeping himself carefully between Rose and the doorway and said, with studied nonchalance, 'Georgina? I am afraid she is not here, but we expect her at any moment. Please come in and wait.'

Demurely, eyes downcast, Sara Millard stepped over the threshold, but under those lowered lashes she saw every detail of the sacred studio – the paintings, the ottoman, the portrait of Georgina

Woodstock on the easel, and Rose, with one breast bare, her hair dishevelled and her eyes unnaturally bright. Then she looked up and Rose was Rose again, calm, sure, her garments modestly in place.

'What on earth are you doing here, Sara, and why are you looking for Georgina?' said Rose, with no attempt at explanation. Edward Rivers turned his back and lit a cigar, with the third unsteady match.

Sara watched him till the first puff of cigar smoke scented the air then said, 'I came to find Miss Woodstock, as I said. You know what Mamma said about the University and how strict she is. But there is to be an inaugural lecture on William Morris and I do so want to go and I thought if I asked Miss Woodstock to take me, then Mamma could not possibly say no. Miss Woodstock may be a Liberated Woman but she is also Society and Mamma approves of that.' When no one spoke, Sara went on, uncertainly, 'But perhaps you will take me instead, Rose? Mr Morris is a designer as well as a poet and I know you study all kinds of art.'

She spoke with apparent innocence, but something in the way she said the last four words brought a prickle to the back of Rose's neck.

'But it would be much better,' went on Sara, 'if Mr Rivers were to ask Mamma if he could take us both. She could not refuse *him*. No one could, could they, Rose?'

Sara looked from one to the other, knowing they were angry with her, knowing she was excluded, but knowing what she knew. When Rose made no answer, Sara, after a moment's awkward silence summoned the courage of desperation and looking Rose in the face, said boldly, as to an equal, 'And Mr Rivers must tell Mamma that Girton College is quite the place these days for gentlewomen's daughters – and very respectable.'

'And if he does not?' sighed Rose, waiting.

Sara cast off the last shreds of childhood. 'That would be such a pity. I would have to ask Mamma what Karma Sutra means.'

In the event, it was Georgina who chaperoned Sara to the lecture, with Rose as voluntary companion. After all, as Sara had said, William Morris was an artist. Mr Rivers, Georgina reported, would make inquiries about Sara's college. At present, he was heavily involved in estate work and could not be in town as his mother's arrival was imminent.

'And when she arrives, she will demand entertainment,' said Georgina cheerfully. 'Or heads will roll. There will be weekend parties, dinners and the like. I expect he will ask you, Rose, and Claire too, now that he knows you. But he sent you an apology.' She handed Rose a sealed note. 'Well, aren't you going to open it?'

Rose was saved by the appearance of the lecturer on the platform and in the introductory remarks and polite applause the note was forgotten, by Georgina anyway. Much later, in the privacy of her bedroom, when Claire was safely asleep, she opened it.

'Why dids't thou promise such a beauteous day
And make me travel forth without my cloak?'

I am cold without you.

It was signed simply 'E'.

CHAPTER 8

Things went wrong from the start. When the invitation arrived at the Millard house, Claire pounced on it as both her personal triumph, and her passport to matrimony. She talked incessantly of 'dear Mr Rivers' and 'dear Edward' and spent hours studying the *Illustrated London News* and *The Queen* for guidelines on behaviour and dress appropriate for a country weekend. She intended to be the epitome of elegance and, apart from a brief anxiety that Rose might disgrace her, was totally absorbed in her own appearance from the moment the invitation arrived till the moment she fastened the catch of her travelling portmanteau. She seemed impervious to the fact that there would be at least a dozen guests at Wychwood – the invitation was Edward's to herself alone.

Rose feigned indifference, but Sara's solemn gaze invariably reminded her of that afternoon in the studio, and the complicity in Sara's hazel eyes only served to discompose her further. Rose knew the invitation was to her alone, knew that Wychwood was to be their consummation, knew that Claire and her predatory vanities were irrelevant, yet she could not stifle the unease which grew as the day of their departure approached.

They were to take the train from Liverpool Street on Friday afternoon.

Wintelsham was a tiny station with a one-roomed office and a level crossing operated by the stationmaster from his rose-smothered cottage, though the flowers were long over and even the rose-hips past their best. It had been a grey day and they stepped from their 'Ladies Only' carriage into a winter deluge of unexpected rain. Claire's umbrella would not open. When it did, she kept it to herself, leaving Rose unprotected. The stationmaster appeared briefly to lift their luggage down onto the platform, then busied himself at the guard's van, unloading what looked like an entire barnyard of day-old-chicks. No one else alighted from the train and there was no-one to meet them. They stood in the small shelter of the station doorway while the stationmaster took an interminable time to close doors, blow his whistle and wave his flag, and waited again while he made his ponderous, careful way to the level crossing gates and opened them. Then at last he returned.

'You'm be the ladies for Wychwood? Master Edward say you'm to wait here till the trap return. It be taking a party to the house now, come by the down train from Norwich way. That'll be back directly.'

'Directly' turned out to be ten minutes, by which time Claire's hem, she insisted, was ruined. 'And I planned to make such an entrance!' Rose was annoyed – with Claire, with Edward, with the stationmaster and with the heavens which chose the moment of the trap's arrival to dry up and bathe them in a sparkling sunlight which revealed every muddy splotch on their travelling clothes. She was further annoyed that the driver of the belated trap was not Edward, but a servant, and her temper was not improved on arrival at Wychwood to find the house in apparent chaos and neither host nor hostess in sight. Edward's mother, it seemed, had lost one of her many travelling bags and had ordered the entire house to be searched, though her maid insisted Lady Portia had left the bag in question at home in Venice. Rose was further annoyed to find she was to share a room with Claire, though the housemaid who conducted them there very kindly promised to deal with their muddy skirts at once. 'Then you'm to go to the drawing room, Miss, for tea.'

They descended the oak staircase some half an hour later in considerable trepidation, and made their way across the panelled hall towards the drawing room door. They passed a brass gong on a stand, an oak chest and, on an oak table, a great Chinese vase of Michaelmas daisies, chrysanthemums and honesty. A wide dish of *pot pourri* scented the air with tea roses and lavender and from somewhere beyond the foot of the stairs came the reproving tock of a grandfather clock. Claire put her hand on the doorknob, took a deep breath and opened it.

'Oh, there you are at last.' A gaunt woman in trailing Venetian shawls and a great deal of jewellery lifted a lorgnette to her patrician nose and stared. 'Well, come in and sit down. You on the sofa, you on that chair beside the tea tray.' She directed them with a folded fan. 'You will be glad to hear that my flannel petticoat has been found. It is an essential part of my winter plumage, as are these shawls. I am a migratory bird – a winter visitor, you might say, come to do whatever birds do in the winter and escape from those dreary canals. In the spring I shall return to my Venetian nest.'

Claire and Rose remained admirably straight-faced and the arrival of Edward's sister Phoebe Burgess saved them the necessity of a reply. Introductions were hardly over when Fitz and his sister

157

Adelaide, a palely pretty girl, were ushered into the room by Edward himself and there was a great deal of activity as tea was poured, tiny triangular sandwiches offered, seed cake and fruit cake disposed of. The conversation relaxed into informality with one group around Lady Portia, another with Edward at its centre, and a free exchange of ideas between the two. Edward and Rose had barely spoken after the first meeting, but she felt the current as strong as ever between them. Once, inadvertently, she almost met his eye and had to look away lest they betray themselves, but the memory of their last meeting filled her with aching expectation and made her impatient with company. The longer the tea-ceremony extended, the shorter her temper became and she retreated into restless silence.

Claire, on the other hand, was patently enjoying herself. Lady Portia (a Lady in her own right who, her family claimed, had married beneath her, though the Rivers family thought otherwise), after some remark about keeping abreast of the latest intellectual folly, had introduced the daring subject of female emancipation, and had further astonished the company by mentioning *The Woman Who Did*.

Claire saw her chance. 'You may think me old-fashioned and naïve, Lady Portia, but it seems to me that this modern thinking is dangerous,' she said, with an expression which managed to combine innocence and intelligence in a particularly appealing way. 'I quite understand how any gentleman, however tolerant of progress, might shy away from such "freedom". Surely, he must ask himself, if the lady is so unfettered by convention before marriage, may she not be equally free afterwards? And there can be few husbands who would view such, shall we call it for the sake of modesty, such generosity, with equilibrium. Freedom from convention is all very well for artists and similar Bohemians, but Society requires, and deserves, more modesty from its matrons. Would you not agree, Mr Rivers?'

Before he could answer, Rose snapped, 'It is ridiculous to lump all artists together as Bohemians and therefore promiscuous libertines. Some artists actually paint.'

'Oh dear, Mr Rivers, I should not have spoken as I did. Rose is so very prickly on the subject of painting – a positive briar.' Claire gave a particularly irritating little laugh which stung Rose beyond caution.

'Don't be idiotic, Claire. And you know as well as I do that I paint because I must – not as an excuse to throw off my morals with my clothes.'

There was a hiss of indrawn breath and at least two of the

company blushed, though Lady Portia was heard to say, 'Well said.' Rose went on impervious. 'I paint because I do it well. I will go on painting because I intend to do it better. If other girls choose to spend their time simpering at themselves in the mirror, by all means let them do so – only don't sneer at those with better things to do.'

'Oh dear, I think I have upset her,' said Claire, turning away from Rose and moving closer to Edward as if for protection. 'And to tell you the truth,' she went on, lowering her voice confidingly, 'Rose is very clever. Her crayon portraits are really excellent. Everyone says so. But painting is all she thinks of. She has no time for ordinary human relationships. Except, of course, Miss Woodstock. But then she is an artist too. I sometimes think the pair of them should go off together on a pilgrimage. To Paris, for Rose's pictures, then on to Greece for Georgina's statuary, then perhaps the islands – Delphos, Poros, Lesbos.' She looked up at Edward with a mixture of innocence and complicity which left him wondering whether she knew what she was saying. If she did, she was not the innocent she pretended to be and certainly no friend to her sister; if she did not, it was a strange choice of destinations.

'You must excuse me,' he said abruptly. 'I have estate matters to attend to before dinner.' He tried to catch Rose's eye, but she was staring studiously out of the window across the sweep of pale lawn towards the winter woods. At the door he turned. 'I see you are admiring our winter landscape, Miss Millard. Do take your sketch book and explore as much as you wish.'

'Thank you, I will,' she said, turning to look at him. That, of course, was her mistake. She should have continued to avoid his eyes as she had so far admirably succeeded in doing, for the contact, brief though it was, set her pulse racing.

'... Though I fear the woods might be a little cold,' he was saying, 'without a cloak.'

She caught the reference, as he had known she would, and all irritation left her. 'Then I shall make sure I have one, Mr Rivers.'

'If you mean to walk in the woods,' said Claire brightly, 'then I shall come with you, Rose dear. The air and exercise will serve to blow away the last shreds of London's grimy cobwebs and bring us back refreshed for the evening's entertainments.'

'You know very well I prefer to be alone when I paint.'

'But surely you will not be painting, Rose dear? It will be twilight before we know it. The days are not long at this time of year.'

They are not long, the days of wine and roses . . .

Rose looked across the room to where Edward still stood in the doorway, watching her, the unspoken words throbbing between them. Then he turned on his heel and left.

'I would like to see your work, young lady,' said Lady Portia, summoning Rose to her side. 'Do you have any with you? Then fetch it. Now.'

'Yes, Lady Portia.' Rose hurried from the room in time to see Edward's back disappearing into the library which doubled as his office, a dark-panelled room off the hall, to the left of the front door. He turned at the sound of her footsteps and stood waiting in the open doorway. She hesitated, her foot on the lowest stair, then with a shrug of self-deprecation, came towards him.

'The woods?' he said, not touching her, but his voice, soft and urgent, was intimate as any caress. 'In half an hour? Alone?'

'I may not be able to get away. Your mother wants to see my work.'

'Make an excuse.'

She could not resist flippancy. 'And perhaps lose a valuable commission?' For answer he pulled her roughly inside the door and kissed her. When, breathless, she broke away, she said with quick intensity, 'I will try.' Then, jubilant, she sped upstairs on the interrupted errand.

From the darkened doorway Edward Rivers watched her move like a brilliant tropical bird against the dark oak panelling until she turned the corner of the stairway and disappeared. Then he took down from the hall stand the old overcoat he kept for estate work, added tweed cap and walking stick, whistled for his dog, and strode out of the house.

In the drawing room, Fitz and his sister excused themselves: they had promised to call on a retired family servant before dinner. When they had gone, Lady Portia rang for more tea. 'Miss Rose Millard,' she said, fixing Rose with her agate eye, 'I intend to put you through your paces. Phoebe, pour more tea and don't fidget. That Frenchwoman of yours will see to the children, and the Woodstocks and Mr Price-Hill are not expected till dinner. Miss Claire Millard,' she said, noticing Claire edging towards the door. 'Where are you going?'

'For a little exercise,' said Claire boldly.

'Nonsense. You will stay here. Edward is quite capable of inspecting his own estate without female encumbrances.'

Claire blushed scarlet and Rose smothered a smile. But Lady Portia was too shrewd for comfort. It would not be easy to elude her gimlet eye.

'In fact,' she said now, regarding Claire through narrowed eyes, 'I think Rose had best start with you. I shall enjoy my tea and watch. I give you ten minutes,' she went on, turning to Rose. 'That is what the street artists of Montmartre promise. Ten minutes to do a likeness of your sister – in charcoal, crayon or pencil, whichever you prefer.'

Rose did it in five – but then she had sketched Claire all her painting life. There was a new quality, however, which Rose had not noticed before. It was many months, she thought with shock, since she had painted Claire, and in the interval her sister had changed from a frivolously pretty girl to an elegant, self-assured young woman. But in the process the sweet, receptive innocence of her beauty had hardened to something resolute, even ruthless. Eyeing the line of Claire's profile, Rose saw her sister with new eyes and what she saw made her own confidence falter. But not her hand.

'There,' she said, handing the finished piece to Lady Portia. 'Claire Millard, a crayon sketch, November 1897.'

Lady Portia studied it in silence, lorgnette in place. Then laid it slowly aside. 'Rose Millard, you have an uncomfortable talent. I fear you see what many people would prefer to keep hidden.'

'Whatever do you mean, Mummy?' said Phoebe Burgess, taking up the picture. 'This is lovely! You have made your sister look beautiful. But then, of course, she is,' she added hastily, in case her incredulity should be taken to refer to the beauty rather than the skill. 'You must paint my children. I insist. On commission, of course. I have had their likenesses done in oils and at the photographic studio, but this is something quite different. It is as if the portrait speaks.'

'And what do you think she is saying?' said Lady Portia grimly. 'No matter,' she went on, impatient with her daughter's lack of perception. 'Rose will do a splendid job on your children, I am sure. But for the moment I intend to submit myself to her dismembering crayon. Ten minutes, young woman, and no flattery. I want *roughnesses, pimples, warts and everything as you see me.*'

'But Mummy dear, you have a lovely complexion.'

'Don't be such a fool, Phoebe!' snapped Lady Portia. 'Or if you must, at least keep it to yourself.'

'Oliver Cromwell said it to Mr Lely,' whispered Claire.

'I am thankful at least some young women are educated,' said Lady Portia, regarding Claire with faint surprise. 'Are you the young woman who wants to go to Girton?'

'Oh no. That is my sister Sara. She told me that Mr Rivers had promised to find out about it for her...'

Rose felt a stir of unease. What else had Sara told Claire?

'... I am afraid she has set her heart on going and no one can dissuade her.'

'Dissuade? I should hope not. Of course the child must go and you may tell your mother I said so. Phoebe, ring the bell. I refuse to sit any longer in a litter of tea-cups and if Rose is to see even one of my "roughnesses", let alone all, we had better have the lamps lit.'

Beyond the french windows, the pale sky was streaked with evening and the first star hung solitary above the home woods. Shadows of trees lay black and cold across the tennis lawn. Most of the branches were bare, though here and there an evergreen added a denser patch of darkness. It would be cold and damp in the woods, alone...

The maid put fresh coals on the fire, turned up the lamps and, at a nod from Lady Portia, drew the heavy velvet curtains across to close out the twilight. It was too late to go to Edward now.

'Proceed,' ordered Lady Portia.

Phoebe Burgess settled comfortably on the sofa, produced a wooden embroidery hoop and began to stitch. Claire picked up a copy of the *Illustrated London News* from a side table and joined her. The firelight flickered gently over their bent heads, edging them with gold. Rose would have liked to sketch them both together, instead of Edward's intimidating mother, ramrod-straight in the high-backed chair on the far side of the fire, near the window. But the heavy red curtains made a perfect backdrop to her white hair and the dark wood of the chair back edged her profile with patrician clarity. It was, she saw, a good composition. Rose took a clean sheet of paper and began.

There was silence in the room as Rose worked, even Edward Rivers forgotten and, after the first tentative strokes, Lady Portia too. All that concerned Rose was the relationship between artist, crayon and subject, and the need to establish an uninterrupted flow of communication so that what the artist's eye perceived, the artist's material should encapsulate on the page. When she finished, a little more than fifteen minutes later, she felt drained and, as often when she had expended all her creative energy on one object, sad with the grief the French called *tristesse*. She did not even care what Lady Portia thought of the result. It was enough for Rose herself to know that it was good.

'Humph,' frowned Lady Portia, studying the portrait. No one spoke. 'Humph,' she said again, with less outrage, and finally, 'Well, young woman, you certainly took me at my word. An imperious despot, with a certain faded beauty, and too clever for her own or other people's comfort. It serves me right.'

Rose said nothing, Claire looked anxious, and Phoebe Burgess, combining curiosity with loyal outrage, demanded to see. She took up the drawing and studied it. 'But Mummy dearest, it is you exactly! I don't see why you are complaining. It is really very good. I shall certainly commission pictures of the children.'

As if on cue, the door opened and a plain-faced woman of thirty or so, in a neat grey high-necked blouse and grey alpaca skirt, ushered a pair of fresh-scrubbed children into the room. Then the look of careful deference on the woman's face froze into shock as she saw the Millard girls.

'Ah, Mademoiselle!' cried Phoebe Burgess. 'How very fortunate. I was just talking of the children. But of course!' she went on, looking from her governess to Rose and Claire, 'You know each other. How silly of me. I was quite forgetting. You remember Mademoiselle, I am sure? Your poor Mamma must have been so sad to have to part with her, especially after her splendid bravery when she saved your sister from drowning.'

'Of course we remember her,' said Claire with splendid equanimity. *'Bonsoir, Mademoiselle. J'espère que vous vous trouvez bien?'*

'Oui, Mademoiselle Claire,' managed Mademoiselle, a hunted look behind her hard, closed features.

'Do you remember Dieppe, Mademoiselle?' went on Claire sweetly, the light of devilment in her eyes. 'It is so long ago now, but I still remember every detail of that dreadful afternoon.'

'And so does Mademoiselle, I am sure,' beamed Mrs Burgess proudly. It was not every family that could boast a proven life-saver as a governess. 'She was so devoted to your little sisters. We have heard all about it from Harry, though Mademoiselle is far too modest to confess it herself, is that not so Mademoiselle?'

'Madame is too kind,' muttered that lady, flushing under Claire's open stare. But Claire was remembering the scene in Millard's when Harry Price-Hill had come up behind a woman at the schools counter and . . . Her eyes went to Mademoiselle's well-rounded behind. There had been two children, a boy and a girl, much like this pair. And Mrs Burgess had 'heard all about it' from Harry, or rather, had heard Harry's version. She turned to Rose.

'You remember that afternoon, Rose, when Sara almost drowned and Mr Price-Hill . . .' she stopped. 'But I must not revive painful memories. We are so pleased to meet you again, Mademoiselle. Mamma will be most interested to hear that you have such an enviable position, with such precious children in your charge.'

163

'Precious or not, it is past their bedtime,' said Phoebe with motherly indulgence. 'But let Miss Millard look at you for a moment, my darlings. She is going to draw lovely pictures of you both for Mummy to hang on her wall.'

'Not again,' groaned Georgie and Marina added, whining, 'Must we?'

'You see what a delightful picture they will make,' went on Mrs Burgess, impervious. 'Perhaps together? Or separately? But we can decide that later. The dressing gong will sound at any moment. Say your good-nights now, and run along, my dears.'

When they had gone again, and Mademoiselle with them, Phoebe smiled with satisfaction. 'Such a reliable governess. I am quite delighted with her. No nonsense. No silly frivolities. And . . .' She lowered her voice. 'No gentleman followers. I shall be quite sad when she leaves us.'

'Oh?' Claire looked interested. 'Is she likely to leave?'

'Marina will not need a governess indefinitely, Claire, but I hope Mademoiselle stays with us for some time. Mr Burgess is quite impressed with her. She is saving up to start a school of her own one day, she told him, and asked his advice on investments. There now! But I suppose that is the French for you all over.'

'Investments?' said Claire, suprised. 'How extraordinary. I would not have thought . . .' She stopped, realising too late where that line of argument was leading.

'If you think we under-pay her, Miss Millard,' said Phoebe coldly, 'You may readjust your ideas. We reward excellence when we find it and Mr Burgess is happy to advise her on the merits of South African diamonds or South African gold or anything else she has in mind.'

'I wish someone would advise dear Mamma,' sighed Claire. 'It is hard for a widow to know what to do for the best and one cannot help but suspect that some men take advantage. But if Mr Burgess could tell her how to get the best return on, let us say for the sake of argument, a sum of £30,000, I am sure she would be most grateful.'

At that moment the dressing gong sounded and the ladies dispersed to their rooms to change for dinner.

'Why ever did you say £30,000?' demanded Rose the moment they were alone.

'Why not? It is as good a figure as any.'

'But we have not got anything like that amount.'

'I did not say we had,' said Claire airily. She sat down at the dressing table and began to unpin her hair. 'But if they choose to think it, who am I to contradict? Besides,' she went on dreamily, 'We might have one day – and I wanted them to sit up and take notice.'

'Them? Lady Portia and her daughter?'

'Why not? They will tell their menfolk, you can be sure of it, and it will be all over the London clubs by this time next week. "It might be worth looking over the Millard girls, what? Money there, you know." ' Claire gave a comical imitation of an upper crust accent and laughed. 'I say, Rose,' she said, in the old, familiar way, swirling round on her stool to face her sister, 'do you suppose we will have charades tonight? I do hope so.'

Rose shrugged. She found it impossible to summon up enthusiasm for the evening ahead. She was emotionally drained, despondent, hopeless, filled with an aching need. But how, in a house full of fellow guests, could she and Edward hope to have any time alone together without the whole world knowing? And if the whole world knew, half of it (Edward's half) would condemn, and the other half (her mother's) hold an emotional shotgun to Edward's head and rejoice that Rose had made such a splendid "catch". She could not bear the idea. Yet a secret meeting seemed impossible. She should have foreseen as much from the start.

There was a quick tap on their door and, without waiting for an answer, Mademoiselle slipped into the room and closed the door behind her. She leant against it with an expression of mingled defiance and entreaty.

'Please, Miss Claire. Please Miss Rose. I did not tell the lie. It was Mr Price-Hill and I did not know until it was too late. If you tell, I will be dismissed at once. It was hard enough after Dieppe. No work, no money, no references. Now, it would be disgrace. Oh *mon Dieu!*' She clutched her heart in agitation at the mere thought. 'Please, I beg of you, keep my secret? It is no harm to you, yes?'

Rose said, 'Of course we w . . .' but Claire interrupted.

'I am glad you came to us, Mademoiselle.' She spoke with the air of a lady of the manor. 'I was surprised and *shocked* to hear the lies you had countenanced, but *for the moment* we will say nothing. I do not wish to upset Mrs Burgess. Later, we will consult Mamma as to what is to be done.'

'No, please. Do not tell your mother. She is such a righteous lady.'

Claire stared for a calculating minute before saying, with a sweet smile, 'Very well. Rose and I will say nothing. Yet. Perhaps, one day, you will be able to repay us? Now please leave us. The dinner gong will ring at any moment.'

When the door closed again behind Mademoiselle's retreating back, Claire smiled with satisfaction. 'That will keep her guessing. And one never knows when such a contact might be useful.'

'You are callous, Claire. The poor woman did you no harm.'

'No. But I mean her to do me some good!'

Rose turned her back in disgust.

She dressed for dinner with mechanical detachment, putting on the dark red silk her mother had produced from the lavender-scented trunk where she kept such relics of her richer, pre-widowhood days, her only adornment a gold locket her father had given her. Her thick, red-glinting hair was piled in a heavy coil from which a froth of unruly curls escaped at the temples. Her eyes were sombre, her full lips sad.

Claire, in contrast, scintillated. Her gown was a froth of cream satin flounces and trailing lace, under which no one would have recognised the same cream dress she had worn to the theatre. At her throat, on a golden chain, she wore the pink cameo her father had given her on her fifteenth birthday, four years ago. She looked excited and radiantly lovely. When the gong sounded, they descended the stairs together, hand in hand, towards the high-pitched chatter of the drawing room.

'You did not come,' said Edward under cover of handing Rose a glass of sherry. 'I waited twenty minutes for you.' He sounded hurt and angry.

'I am sorry, but I told you I might not be able to get away. I was drawing your mother's portrait.'

'Oh yes? Could you not have left that till after dinner, with the other frivolities?' Before she could reply he had turned his back and was talking smoothly to Adelaide Fitzsimmons.

Frivolity! thought Rose with fury. How dare he denigrate her talent like that. She sought out Georgina who had just arrived, to soothe her spirits with talk of the College and the progress of her friend's latest work. It did not improve matters to see that Claire was moving serenely among the company, as if she had been born to the life, smiling, talking, collecting laughter and admiration around her.

It was no better when they went in to dinner. Normally Rose would have relished the beauty of crystal against polished wood, of delicate Sevres china and gleaming silver. There were candelabra on the long table and flowers, white chrysanthemums and lilies. She was unaware that the setting gave a perfect backdrop to her own red dress and red-glinting hair, or that in sadness her beauty was doubled. Edward saw it from the head of the table and his jealous anger increased with his frustration, especially as at the last moment his mother had altered the placings, as previously she had altered the room arrangements, and had removed Rose from Edward's end of the table to her own. Abruptly he turned to Claire who had taken her sister's place and set out to charm her instead.

Rose saw, understood, and suffered. Phoebe Burgess's husband Robert, sitting opposite, was talking knowledgeably about investments to the estate manager Guy Morton, a pleasant man of thirty or so sitting on Rose's right.

'. . . but of course there is no saying what effect this trouble in the Transvaal will have. The Boers are a contentious tribe. Look how they tried to claim Natal way back in '45 and still they will not accept that we have sovereignty over the whole of the south part of Africa. They have two states, after all – the Transvaal and the Orange river – and we built railways for them.'

'I thought the railways were in order to exploit the diamond mines,' said Rose.

Burgess ignored her. '. . . and dealt with the Zulus and the Basutos. We settled Piet Joubert's rising, though in my opinion that peace settlement was a mistake. And if Kruger is re-elected next year there will be trouble.'

'Do you mean war, Mr Burgess?' asked Percy. Since the Queen had removed to Balmoral for her annual visit his guard duties were less onerous.

'I fear so. Those damned Boers are not going to lie down without a fight and the Jameson business did not help.'

'I say,' said Harry whose glass had been emptied and refilled twice as often as anyone else's in order, he claimed, to counteract his fear of Lady Portia, 'That might be a lark, what? I see myself in scarlet uniform galloping across the veldt to rescue a gold mine.'

'They do not wear scarlet any more,' said someone. 'Besides, Harry would not know a gold mine from a coal bucket.'

There was general laughter, then Robert Burgess and Lady Portia discussed investments and the advisability or otherwise of hanging onto South African gold. Harry embarked on a particularly silly flirtation with the Fitzsimmons girl across the table while Georgina beside him talked earnestly to her opposite neighbour Guy Morton. Rose found herself left with Percy for conversation. She glanced to the far end of the table and saw Claire and Edward, heads close, murmuring together. Then they laughed, Edward signalled to the servant to refill Claire's glass and looking round the table for any similarly empty glasses, caught Rose's eye. Deliberately he turned back to Claire and Rose set her teeth in resolution. If he chose to

167

sulk, it only diminished him in her sight. She would ignore Edward Rivers and her silly, flirtatious sister. She would show him his behaviour left her undisturbed. She set out to charm poor Percy Woodstock and when her efforts left him tongue-tied with bliss, she turned to Guy Morton and asked him about the estate.

Against all expectation, she found him genuinely interesting. He had a fund of local knowledge spanning legend, folk-remedies, ancient customs and old wives's tales, ploughing, brewing and even cheese. 'Which they call "the dreaded Suffolk thump". *Those who made me were uncivil, for they made me harder than the devil. Knives won't cut me, fire won't sweat me, dogs bark at me but can't eat me.* Believe me, Miss Millard, there is truth in many an old rhyme. There was once a farmer over Tuddenham way...'

In the fascination of his stories Rose almost forgot Edward's anger and her face grew alive again with interest. Georgina joined in and the animated conversation carried them through the dessert.

Edward caught enough to realise their talk was of more interest than Phoebe's domestic prattle or Claire's tireless wit, but it was more than pride would allow to admit it. If Rose chose to enjoy herself by ignoring him, then he would do the same. And he could ask Morton for that tale about the south meadow when the women had left them to their port.

'Isn't Edward Rivers charming?' bubbled Claire the moment they were in the drawing room. She had cornered Rose by the curtained french windows where she knew her own cream dress would be shown off to advantage. 'And some of the things he says are really quite risqué.'

Rose did not answer. Claire had drunk too much again.

'I think...' began Claire, in a confiding whisper, 'I think he might just be...'

'Coffee, Miss Millard?' Mrs Burgess had appeared unnoticed at her side, a tray of delicate bone china coffee cups in her hands. 'We never entrust these to the servants,' she explained. 'Family heirlooms, you know. Your sister was telling me all about Dieppe,' she went on, addressing Rose. 'What a tragic end to your holiday. Edward is always so reticent about it though I know he was there, with Harry. Such a shock.' She moved on in a trail of taffeta flounces to the next group.

'All?' said Rose with raised eyebrows.

'Of course not. But isn't it a scream? And Edward was so solemn and straightfaced. He never once gave himself away though I thought I would burst with the effort not to laugh. Then when Phoebe was talking to someone else, he was so charming and

168

witty and entertaining. He told me so many little private, *intimate* things...' She looked Rose in the eye as she had done on that occasion after the theatre, in their bedroom, and might just as well have said aloud the words her look conveyed: *I am staking my claim – keep off!* 'But you don't want to hear all our little confidences, do you, Rose dear?' she finished sweetly. 'What were you talking about at your end of the table?'

Before Rose could frame a sufficiently scathing reply, the door opened on a wave of male laughter and cigar smoke and the gentlemen joined them.

In the ensuing pleasantries Rose lost Claire to the menfolk and there was a general shifting of seats and moving from group to group. Morton came over to speak to Rose and a moment later a familiar voice at her shoulder said, 'May I fetch you more coffee, Miss Millard?'

'Thank you.' She turned and held out her cup. As he reached to take it, his fingers brushed hers and instantly the current raced between them. She knew he felt it too, though his face was expressionless. When Morton turned away to answer someone's question, he said, in a low, urgent voice, 'I must see you, Rose. Outside, under the chestnut? When I leave, give me half an hour, then *come.*'

Before she could answer, Claire appeared at Rose's side and slipping an arm through her sister's said, 'Secrets? Do tell.'

'It would not be a secret if I did.'

'Don't be disagreeable, Rose,' pouted Claire. 'I declare you grow more cross every day. You will tell me what you were talking about, won't you, Mr Rivers?' and she gave him her most appealing smile.

'Certainly. I was asking your sister whether she preferred one lump or two in her coffee. Not perhaps of world-shattering import, but necessary all the same. I still have not had her answer.'

'What, not even a quotation? Come, Rose, you are dull this evening.'

Rose looked at him, straightfaced, and said, 'My answer is yes. Two lumps please.'

'At your service, madam.' He bowed over her hand. 'Two lumps it shall be. And you Miss Millard?' he said, turning to Claire. 'May I refill your cup, too?'

'Oh yes please, Mr Rivers, but no sugar for...' but before she could finish he had gone. 'Oh well.' She shrugged and, covering her annoyance at the snub with admirable aplomb, turned brightly to Guy Morton with some remark about tomorrow's shoot. When Edward returned with the coffee he did not stay. Instead he joined

169

his mother's group at the fireside and conversation continued in a pleasant, if desultory fashion. Phoebe Burgess played the piano. Adelaide sang. Claire was asked to sing too, but modestly declined. Then someone suggested charades and they began to choose teams. Abruptly Edward excused himself.

'I have estate work to discuss with Morton – last minute details for tomorrow.' With a nod, he summoned Morton and left.

'He has to be up at six, poor lamb,' said Mrs Burgess in apology.

'So have I,' cried Harry, 'but I'm not going to let that spoil my evening. Rose, come and join my team. We will choose the most riproaring word and baffle the lot of them, what?'

'You had far better ask Claire,' she said. 'She is much cleverer at acting than I am. She can deceive absolutely anyone, can't you Claire?' Before Claire could answer the two-edged compliment, Rose went on, 'I would prefer to watch and perhaps sketch a little. I am really rather tired.'

After that it was easy. Some twenty minutes later, when the others were still whispering and giggling over preparations for their charades, she gathered up her sketching things, made her excuses and withdrew into the quiet darkness of the hall. A single lamp burned at the foot of the stairs and cast shadows over oak panelling and dark-framed oils. The window on the stairs was uncurtained and moonlight added its pale rays to the lamp's warmer glow, illuminating the face of the grandfather clock with eerie light. Its slow tick seemed like the world's heartbeat . . .

From the direction of the old brewery she heard a barn owl call and shivered. Then she saw there was light under the door of Edward's library. She moved closer until she could hear voices within: Morton was still there. But Edward had said half an hour and she was early. She went upstairs and along the darkened landing to her room. The fire still glimmered with lingering warmth and the counterpane had been turned down on the big oak bed she was to share with Claire. A hump near the foot of the bed indicated the presence of a stone hot water jar.

Rose put away her sketches in the portfolio she used for the purpose, slipped on her dark woollen travelling cloak and opened the bedroom door. At that moment she heard a door open below and voices erupt into the hall. Morton was leaving. She heard Edward say, 'I'll walk with you a little way,' then the front door closed. Rose waited, counting how long it would take them to reach the chestnut tree and the turn into the main sweep of the drive. Then she walked, silent-footed, down the stairs, past the grandfather clock, past the oak chest and the Chinese vase of flowers, across

170

the turkey-carpeted entrance hall towards the door. The inner door into the porch was open, the hat stand a dark shape of heaped overcoats, felt hats, a bristle of walking sticks and umbrellas. She heard muted laughter from the drawing room, a girl's voice declaiming, more laughter ... Slowly she turned the great brass door knob and eased the heavy door carefully open – and as carefully closed it again behind her.

She stood alone in the darkness, letting her eyes grow accustomed to the night, feeling the air cold on her cheek, hearing the sigh of the wind in the leafless trees, the soft rustlings and patterings of night creatures in the autumn undergrowth, the distant cry of a night owl ... The old brewery was a dark block against the sky to her right, the chestnut a mesh of bones touched palely by the moon. Then on the night air came the scent of cigar smoke, warm and masculine and a soft voice saying, 'Rose?' She moved towards the voice. A shape detached itself from the darkness of the tree's shadow, crushed the remains of a cigar underfoot, drew her into the darker shadows, and kissed her with the pent-up hunger of a lifetime's longing.

'I love you, Rose,' he said softly and kissed her again. 'Love you, love you...' He parted her cloak and kissed her throat, the soft curve of her breast above the cloth, her throat again, her lips. 'I have longed for you ever since that day in the studio ... God, you were so beautiful.'

'Were?' said Rose, teasing.

'Are, damn you. *Are*. I would like to carry you to my room, tear off those fripperies, one by one and...'

'And what?'

For answer he kissed her again with a savagery that left her gasping. Then he said, 'Come to the loft, now, tonight. Oh God, Rose you know it is inevitable. You and I are *one flesh*.'

'Yes. I know it,' she said with wonder and a serene acceptance in which there was no sense of moral wrong. 'I have known it since that moment in your father's loft. But not surreptitiously, Edward. Not in the darkness, in a hurry lest people miss us. What of your mother? And Claire? Suppose she goes to bed and I am not there?'

'Damn Claire and damn my mother. I had planned to put you in a convenient little attic room on the back stairs, but she bagged it for her private entourage and I could not resist for fear of...'

'Of what? Of advertising to the world your wicked intentions?'

'Do you really think they are wicked?' he breathed, his lips against her ear.

'Oh yes ... wicked and glorious and, as you say, inevitable.'

171

'Then come with me, now.'

'No.' It was the hardest decision of her life, but she made it, for the greater glory of what was to come. 'I want you, Edward . . .' She broke off as he kissed her, hungrily, subverting all her arguments, but at last she managed to break free enough to say, 'Please . . . not now. I ache for you with every fibre of my body, but when we become one flesh, as we inevitably must, I want it to be glorious! I want us to have time and laughter, with no eye on the clock or over our shoulders for interruption. It may be immodest of me, Edward – you may put it down to the artistic temperament if you wish – but I want to see you, naked, and I want you to see me . . . all of me.'

For answer, he kissed her with a lingering, sighing gentleness that told her he accepted her terms and understood. 'Such a paradise is worth waiting for, my darling,' he murmured, closing her cloak like a door and folding it tight about her. Then he drew her under his arm, held her head against his chest, and leaning against the trunk of the chestnut, said, 'I am sorry. It was a mistake to ask you here with *them*.' The word was both scornful and dismissive. 'I have condemned you to the social whirl, vacuous, frenetic, empty, and public. I look at you across their worthy heads and ache with longing. I want only to touch you and kiss you, strip you naked and . . . and instead I must make polite conversation and refill your coffee cup!'

'You managed to entertain my sister perfectly well through dinner.' It was a stupid thing to say and she was sorry the moment she had said it, and sorry again when he said lightly, 'I enjoyed it. She was good company and the next best thing to you. You are very alike, in many ways.'

'We are not at all alike,' snapped Rose and Edward laughed.

'No. She has not your talents.' He bent to kiss her and when she turned her head away, cupped her chin in his hand and forced her lips to meet his. A long time later, he murmured, 'There is really no need to be jealous, Rose. It is you I love.'

But at last Rose broke away and said reluctantly, 'I must go in. It would not do if Claire came to bed and found it empty.'

'No. But what I would give to be in her place! Next time you come, Rose, there will be only you and I. Mother will not stay long. As soon as she has gone back to Venice, promise you will come to me?'

'I promise.' Their kiss was solemn as a marriage vow and both knew it.

'Will I see you tomorrow?' asked Rose. 'Or will you be mine host all day and public property?'

172

'It will be difficult, but do a little sketching in the woods – alone. I will try to get away. If not, we will both have to live on memories – like this one.'

It took all Rose's resolution to break away and only the thought of Claire's prying and spoiling were she to discover the bedroom empty succeeded in drawing her at last, reluctantly, inside.

The next day the men left at dawn for the shoot. The womenfolk were to meet them for lunch, at the home farm, where a picnic would be laid ready in the barn.

Rose spent the morning sketching in the grounds, alone. Edward did not come, but she had not really expected it. From beyond the woods came the intermittent crack of gunshots and from time to time the faint scent of cordite on the air. Edward was about his social business, and she must be content with memory, and with the absorbing work of her brush and palette.

Lunch was a jumbled affair with a dozen extra guests, much laughter, stamping of feet, slapping of backs and discussion of the morning's 'bag'. Edward spent much of the time in consultation with his gamekeeper and Rose hardly saw him. When the beef stew, the dumplings, the slabs of pie and the cheeses had been disposed of, with the fruit cake and bramble pie and claret, the men resumed the business of the day and the ladies returned to the house to rest, or read, or stroll in the neighbouring lanes until it was time to dress for dinner. Claire had struck up a friendship with Adelaide Fitzsimmons and they played duets together in the drawing room while Rose sketched and the long afternoon dragged tediously towards evening, until at last they were released by the dressing gong.

This time Rose was placed beside Edward, and Claire banished to Lady Portia's end of the table where the talk turned eventually to sculpture and that useless piece of marble in the barn.

'Perhaps Georgina could do something with it?' suggested Percy. 'She is frightfully clever really.'

Lady Portia sniffed. 'She couldn't turn it into a decent bird-bath! Your sister would benefit from a spell of study in a real studio instead of those ladylike afternoon classes she goes to. Six months with an expert, in Rome or Florence, could be the making of her – and if it wasn't, then she'd best take up embroidery, like Phoebe.'

'I say, did you hear that, Georgie?' called Percy across the table to where his sister was talking earnestly to the silent Fitz. 'Lady Portia thinks you should take a jaunt to Rome.'

'Rose would agree with Lady Portia,' said Claire earnestly. 'She

173

is always saying the best way to learn is to watch the experts and whereas our own Academy can boast some excellent works there is no doubt the continent has much to teach us, especially in the field of painting. Rose would give anything to go to Europe, wouldn't you Rose?'

Neither Rose nor Edward heard her. They were engrossed in each other's company, comparing notes of the day, questioning, explaining, arguing, as if the rest of the table did not exist.

It was unfortunate that Claire should look in their direction just as Edward's hand closed over Rose's, unfortunate that she should see the look they exchanged, and unfortunate that though she could not see Edward's knee against Rose's under the table, she sensed the particular intimacy of their communion. Her eyes narrowed and her chin tilted a fraction higher. Claire was not the eldest Millard for nothing.

CHAPTER 9

The next weeks were some of the happiest in Rose's life. Her work was going well. The portrait of Georgina was almost finished and her preliminary sketches for the Burgess children had met with rapturous approval. Rose had agreed to visit the Burgess house in Brompton Square for the purpose and often, surprisingly, Claire went with her, until she became as much at home there as Rose. Claire and Phoebe Burgess talked together and drank tea while Rose worked and the children fidgeted and grumbled until they were allowed to escape again upstairs. Occasionally they glimpsed Mademoiselle, but for the most part she kept discreetly out of sight.

'It is such fun,' said Claire gleefully one afternoon when they had been ushered into the drawing room of the house in Brompton Square and asked to wait while Mademoiselle fetched Master Georgie and Miss Marina. 'She does not know I gave Edward my word to keep his secret, and every time she sees me with Mrs Burgess she wonders if her end has come. It serves her right.'

'I believe you are quite heartless, Claire. Don't you feel any pity for her?'

'None. As she would have none for me, were the roles reversed.'

'I do believe you come here just to torment her, Claire,' said Rose with a flash of annoyance. She herself disliked the visits and would have preferred the children to come to the studio. Unlike Claire who revelled in it, Rose found the air of smug affluence stifling, Mrs Burgess's gentility irritating and the atmosphere of these drawing room sessions both patronising and dull.

'Not at all,' said Claire serenely. 'I come to see Phoebe.' She selected a chair and subsided elegantly into it. Then she arranged the pale blue folds of her skirt to reveal one small silk-shod foot. Mrs Millard, on Mr Burgess's advice, had made a timely investment whose swift profits had been ploughed straight into Claire's wardrobe 'as an investment of a different kind'. Rose noticed that with her new dress allowance, small though it was, her sister's clothes grew more like Mrs Burgess's every day: the cut of the skirt, the style of the bodice, small touches of lace or braid which gave an expensive elegance to an otherwise plain ensemble, but Claire had a genius for making a single shilling do the work of ten, whether in housekeeping or in the more serious matter of clothes. Claire spoke more like Phoebe, too, though Rose continued to be astonished that Claire found anything at all to say to Edward's sister.

'But Phoebe Burgess is so dull! Whatever do you talk about, Claire? All I ever hear is a catalogue of names.'

'We talk about people,' said Claire with equanimity. 'Mrs Burgess knows everyone worth knowing and though I have yet to meet them, I know as much about their lives as she does. When I move into her social circles I shall be well equipped.'

'When? It would be more appropriate to ask how?'

'You will see,' said Claire enigmatically and refused to say more. A few moments later, Mrs Burgess and the children arrived and the afternoon's session began.

Had Rose not been so absorbed in her own secret she might have suspected Claire was up to something. As it was, she was so buoyed up with private happiness that nothing touched her.

Edward did not come up to Town. His mother, he said, required his presence and besides, he could not bear to meet her in the constrictions of London: he would rather wait for the glorious fulfilment of her promise, at Wychwood. Instead, he wrote to her at the studio, dear, loving letters of poetry and passion, and she replied, drawing on Donne and Browning, Shakespeare and Rossetti, but always, remembering his Philistine preferences, using them only to illustrate her own outpourings. She told him of her paintings, of her struggle to capture Georgie Burgess's 'dear, loving nature' as his mother put it, 'but really Edward, and though he is your nephew I must say it, he is a tiresome little imp.' She told him the winter was high summer in her heart because every day brought nearer the day of his mother's departure and her own return to Wychwood, and to him.

He wrote of estate matters: wind had brought down the chestnut in the home meadow, one of his cattle had taken a prize at Smithfield, the foxes were bad again and he and Morton had spent three nights in a row, with the rest of the men from the estate, hunting the vermin down. He missed her, ached for her, dreamed of her constantly.

His mother, he wrote, planned to leave in February. Earlier if her mood changed, or the weather irritated her unduly.

Rose kept his letters locked away in the studio, where she could take them out and read them in secret, though she knew every word by heart. And while she waited, as he did, for that blessed day when his mother would go back to Venice, she worked every spare hour

176

at her painting. Her own mother was surprisingly accommodating, even suggesting that Millards could do without her for three full days a week if she needed the time 'for those beautiful pictures of the Burgess children.'

But it was Georgina's portrait that absorbed her greatest energies. She worked at it with a combination of intensity and meticulous care which resulted in what she knew to be the best thing she had done. Percy certainly thought so.

'It's beautiful, Rose,' he told her, on one of his regular visits to the studio where he would sit and talk of family matters to Georgina or, if she was not there, watch Rose at work. She no longer minded his devotion, but treated him with gentleness and understanding. She teased him a little sometimes, when he was particularly exasperating, but never cruelly – her own heart was too vulnerably happy to inflict pain on anyone who loved as she did. The fact that Percy loved her in vain only made her treat him with especial kindness. She did not notice the effect that kindness had: nor did it occur to her that he might misconstrue her meaning. She noticed only that he seemed less tongue-tied and more self-assured.

On this particular afternoon, when his sister was out at one of her innumerable classes, he stood studying the portrait of Georgina with open admiration.

'It is beautiful,' he said again. 'Quite stunning. I know little about art, but I do know no one could look at that and remain unmoved. And no one could do justice to Georgina as you have done. She's a dashed fine sister to me and a dashed fine girl. I don't know what that ass Price-Hill's about, sowing his wild oats all these years when he could have had a girl like Georgie. She'd make any man a splendid wife.'

'Yes,' agreed Rose, and added, without conviction, 'One day perhaps he will see it.'

'Not him. She'd be best to look elsewhere and forget the bounder. Trouble is, he's such a charming rogue – too much energy, that's the trouble, and not enough to do. Perhaps if this business with the Boers develops into anything...' He stopped. 'But I was talking of your painting. I wish you would let me buy it to present to the parents. They'd be delighted to have it, I know.'

'I am sorry, Percy. It is not for sale. But I promise you if I ever change my mind, you shall have first refusal.'

'Thank you, Rose.' He gulped, blushed, took hold of her hand and said, in a rush, 'I know you do not intend to marry, Rose, for years and years, and that your art comes first, but if you ... when you ... I mean, when the time comes, I wish you would promise me first refusal then, too.'

'Dear Percy,' she said, gently disengaging her hand, 'I am very fond of you, but as you rightly say, my art comes first. It would be rash to promise anything so far in the future.'

'At least tell me I may hope?' She was afraid for a moment that he would go down on one knee to her, and that she would laugh – or weep because he was not Edward. But Percy was offering her marriage. With great self-control she said, 'Who am I to forbid anyone hope?'

He took that as encouragement as she should have known he would, but it was too late and it would have been heartless to disabuse him. Afterwards she was glad, for misguided though his happiness was, it was warmer than an empty heart.

When he had left, humming happily to himself and with new pride in his step, she turned back to the portrait. When it was finished she intended, daringly, to submit 'Inspiration' to the Academy, and afterwards, successful or not, to give it to Georgina in thanks for all her encouragement and help.

Dear Georgina – her own work had sadly stagnated. The terracotta heads were no better than they had been when they first met, in spite of constant attendance at a variety of studios and classes. 'You need a change of direction,' Rose told her. 'Even a change of scene. Something to show you things from a different angle. Then you'll be fine.'

Rose remembered those words when, on a day of watery sunshine towards the end of February, Georgina returned early to the studio, a look of great excitement on her face.

'Rose dear, I have such splendid news!' She took both Rose's hands in hers. 'You will never guess what it is. I know you will not because we have been planning it for weeks and you never so much as suspected anything, did you? No, I can see you did not. But Claire assured me you would say yes, and your Mamma gave her consent, so I have made all the arrangements. Rose, I want you to come to Italy with me!'

'*Italy?*' Rose's face was a picture of shock.

'Yes, Italy. We will go to France first, of course, and you may stop wherever you like – Paris, Avignon, Arles. Then we will go on to Florence and Rome and finally to Lady Portia, in Venice. I will pay for everything – I am twenty-one this year and have plenty of money for both of us. You will be my chaperon because of course I cannot travel alone and oh, Rose, isn't it a marvellous notion?'

Rose could formulate no words. Her thoughts were in turmoil.

One part of her was jubilant, another appalled. At last she could fulfil her dream and go to Paris, Florence, wherever she wanted, something she had longed for, dreamed of, most of her life; she could soak herself in the art of the great masters, pay her homage to Michelangelo, Donatello, Canaletto and Rubens, study the great French Impressionists, visit the artists' quarter in Montmartre, copy, study, imitate, learn. She could live and breathe art with no interruption, day after blessed day, and her own painting would burgeon and flourish as it could never do in London. She would sketch any and everything that caught her artistic eye – landscapes, street scenes, people – until her portfolio was brimming. But what of her heart? What of Edward and Wychwood, where a love-haunted loft of butterfly wings and silence waited for her to fulfil its prophecy?

'Well, Rose? Aren't you going to say anything? You do want to come with me, don't you?' Georgina's pleasure faltered.

'Yes, of course I do, but ... It has been a shock, that is all.' Rose turned away lest Georgina see her confusion. But after all, as soon as his mother left, she could go to Wychwood just the same and then, when it was time to travel, she would explain to him. Edward would understand. What was absence between true lovers? The beat of a moth's wing, that was all. And she *must* go, not just for Georgina's sake, but for her own. It was a chance that would not come her way again and she knew in her bones that her artistic future depended upon it. If he truly loved her, Edward would understand. And her homecoming would be doubly sweet.

'I told Claire the moment she suggested it that we should ask you first,' said Georgina anxiously, 'but she was adamant. It was to be a surprise. I had hoped, a pleasant one.'

'Oh Georgina it is!' cried Rose, clasping her friend in a spontaneous embrace. 'And I am an old fuddy-duddy to be so slow to realise it. Since I was a little child I have dreamed of such a thing – but since Papa died I thought it was impossible. And now you come to me with your usual generosity and offer to take me and I have not even the grace to thank you! It would serve me right if you took Claire instead.'

'I don't think she would come,' smiled Georgina. 'She is far too taken up with ladies' tea parties – and anyway, it is you I want, Rose. We think the same, we share the same ideals, we confide in each other ... Oh, Rose, we will have such fun.'

Rose felt momentary guilt. Georgina was too open, too trusting, and in return Rose had given no hint of her own secret.

'When do we go?' she asked. 'Next month?'

179

'Oh no. Next week.'

This time Rose could not keep the horror from her face. 'But I *can't*. Not next week. There are the Burgess portraits to finish and my painting and . . .' She faltered into silence as Georgina broke in.

'It must be next week because we are to travel to Paris with Lady Portia. Claire said your mother would never agree otherwise and neither would mine and it seemed so convenient. I heard from Lady Portia only this afternoon and our seats are already reserved, on the Orient Express!'

'Oh God, Georgie I . . .' Rose covered her face with her hands to hide the turmoil which raged inside her. She *couldn't* go so soon. It was impossible. Her work, her plans – and Edward, waiting for her, in Wychwood. No, she could not do it. And yet . . . Paris, Florence, Venice. The tour of her dreams. How could she turn her back on that? Surely Edward would understand? Or come with her? Meet her in Paris, perhaps? Or Venice? No, his mother would be in Venice. But there must be *some* solution, somewhere.

'What is it, Rose?' Asked Georgina in a quiet voice from which all excitement had drained away. 'I can cancel everything if you would rather not go. Or go by myself.' But the bleakness in her friend's voice cleared Rose's mind as nothing else had.

'You will do no such thing,' she said, with sudden decision. 'Just give me time to see straight, that is all.' She took her hands from her face, shook herself as if to shake her ideas into place, smiled at Georgina and after a moment's silence said tentatively, 'And it must be next week?' Georgina nodded. 'Then so be it.' Suddenly she laughed and clasped Georgina's hands in hers. 'You are a dear, generous friend and I thank you with all my heart. What fun we will have, and what adventures. But I will have so many things to do before I go that you must excuse me if I start this very minute.'

'Of course,' beamed Georgina. 'Oh Rose, I am so excited you are coming with me, and so glad . . .' Then she was gone, in a whirl of happiness which confirmed Rose in her decision. And Edward, dear Edward, would understand.

She tore a page from her sketch pad and, in a state of turmoil and high excitement, wrote: *My darling Edward, I must see you. Such a thing has happened as I never dreamt of. Dear Georgina is taking me to France and on to Italy! It was all arranged in secret and I had no inkling of it until today, but we are to travel next week. Were it not for the thought of leaving you I would be quite distraught with happiness – as it is, come to me, please? I must see you before I go, hold you, kiss you, love you . . . I must have memories to warm me in the long months I am away and I cannot come to you while*

180

your mother is still with you, except by invitation. But if you cannot come to me, only ask and I will come flying to you on the instant, willingly, openly, shamelessly. Please, Edward? I love you and long for you with all my being and there is so little time. Be just one hour mine and I shall walk on air for ever after. Come, my darling, 'live with me and be my love and we will all the pleasures prove.' And if we have not time for all of them, we will save the rest for when I return, in the autumn. Dearest Edward, I hunger for you. Feed my longing.

It was shameless, even brazen, but she did not care. And when he came, she would tell Georgina everything, Georgina would leave them alone together, in the studio, and there would be no more barriers between them. She signed the letter 'R' and posted it herself. Then she ran back to the studio and painted in a frenzy of jubilant expectation until the light faded. It would be two days at the least before he came, perhaps three, but whenever it was, she would be waiting.

The following morning she arrived early at the studio, eager to put the final touches to the Burgess portraits so that the rest of her time might be free for 'Inspiration', but the door was already unlocked. Surprised, she pushed it open and stepped inside. 'Georgina?'

Then she saw him. He was standing with his back to her, apparently studying the portrait of Georgina, but she knew every line of his beloved body. '*Edward!*' she cried in joyful disbelief, then 'My darling, my dear, sweet love, how could you come so soon? I only posted...' The loving welcome froze on her lips as he turned and she saw his face.

'I hear,' he said, in a voice of steel, 'that you plan to travel abroad. Your mother wrote to mine saying "dear Rose is too excited to write herself, but she is overjoyed – *overjoyed* – at the chance to go abroad again at last and with Georgina who is such a dear, close friend. Like Georgina, Rose lives only for her art," your mother said, "and the Bohemian life of Italy has always called."'

'Edward, you must listen to me,' cried Rose, clutching at his arm, but he shook her off with the blind fury of jealousy and betrayal.

'Italy called my mother, too,' he shouted. 'And look what that did! Killed my father and ruined my estate. And now you plan to go off with *her* of all people. To Venice!'

'Edward, please. You must listen to me. I promise you I...'

'*Promise?* I hear, from my own mother, that her departure is to be the signal not for you to visit Wychwood, *as you promised,* but for you to leave the country, with her. *Is this true?*'

'Edward, I keep trying to tell you, I wrote you a letter. I posted

181

it last night. Georgina came to me yesterday and said she had arranged it all as a surprise and I swear I knew nothing till then.' She faltered to a stop as he regarded her with a cold fury in which there was no hint of love.

'Georgina. I see.' There was something in the way he said the words that triggered both her own anger and an awful, sinking fear.

'You do not see at all,' she cried. 'Georgina is generous and kind. She planned it as a surprise for me. She knew I have always longed to go abroad and when she told me I was to go as her companion, how could I refuse her?'

'Obviously, you could not. One word from your Bohemian friend and all previous commitments are of no account. The small matter of a broken promise to me is immaterial. But of course, you have better things to do with your time. Why waste it with a dreary country squire on a dreary country estate when Italy calls? You said when my mother left...' He stepped forward and gripped her shoulders so tight the fingers dug into her flesh. '*You promised you would come to me.*' His face was so close she could have kissed him, except that his mouth was twisted, his eyes blazing and his whole face contorted with fury. One hint of tenderness in that mask and she would have melted, given herself there and then, abandoned Georgina and the European tour for ever. But there was no such hint.

'I have not forgotten,' she managed, 'and I will come to you, Edward, gladly, but...'

'But you must go to Italy first, with *Georgina*!'

'No, not first, Edward! I wrote to you. I said...' but he flung her away from him and turned his back and she realised he was trembling as she was, with violent emotion. But his action had brought him face to face with the cause of his jealousy.

'Of course,' he said, with scathing sarcasm. 'I should have known your precious painting must come before everything, even love. But then you do not know the meaning of the word.'

'Edward, listen to me. I wrote to you. I asked you to come to me. I promised to...'

'Promised? I know your promises. Empty air.'

'Please, Edward, let me explain. I love you!' She tried to touch him, embrace him, show him how wrong he was, but he thrust her roughly away.

'It seems to me that Rose Millard loves only herself and her own convenience. Certainly where your *so-called* art is concerned all other considerations fly out of the window. Georgina comes to you

182

with the offer of a free holiday and you instantly forget all your promises to *me*.'

'*So-called?*' cried Rose, forgetting all attempts at propitiation.

'So-called,' he repeated with deliberate hurt. 'Look at that ridiculous table leg, and her nose is too long.' He stabbed at the canvas with a derisive finger.

'Don't touch it!' Rose struck his hand away and he grabbed her wrist so tight she gasped.

'Do not strike me, woman.'

'Then do not touch my painting! I've worked on that for weeks and the oil is still wet.' His face so close to hers was almost unrecognisable, distorted as it was with jealousy and rage, and yet the smallest shift and Rose knew beyond doubt that all that powerful emotion could still be channelled into love. If she could only tip that tiny balance . . . then he moved and it was too late.

Deliberately, with his free hand, still gripping her wrist with the other and holding her helpless, he picked up the nearest brush and drew it across Georgina's painted face, smearing the pigment into a deep, disfiguring trough. Rose gasped in agonised dismay, her face drained of all colour.

'I will never forgive you for that. Never.'

'Good. That makes us partners at least in hate.' He tossed the brush aside, loosed her wrist, dusted his hands together as after a job well done, picked up his hat and cane and strode for the door. In the doorway he turned to look back. She stood defeated, ashen-faced, achingly vulnerable, in front of that lovely canvas he had flawed, yet with a core of brave defiance that wrung his heart. He saw the red weal his fingers had made on her wrist, the tears she refused to shed blurring her accusing eyes, the lovely curve of her breasts under the dark material. He remembered their beauty, naked, remembered her welcoming lips and the melting promise of her body under his hands. His own body burned with hunger for her – yet she deliberately left him unfed, as his mother had left his father, for a painting trip abroad with the Woodstock girl. Jealousy and hurt and wounded pride crashed shut the door on his compassion. With a curt bow, he left.

When Georgina arrived at the studio later that morning she found Rose strangely quiet, but with a new air of resolution about her.

'I am glad you have come, Georgina,' she said without looking round. 'I need you.' She was working on 'Inspiration' and for a moment her aproned figure blocked Georgina's view. Then Rose moved to mix more pigment and her friend cried out in horror.

183

'Rose! What ever has happened to the portrait? I know it flattered me, but the face was lovely as it was, and now...' She faltered to a halt as she saw Rose's expression.

'I know. It was my own fault, but the canvas slipped. I cannot have wedged it properly on the easel. And I am afraid my brush slipped with it. I could have wept...' She broke off and bit her lip before going on, more firmly, 'So I am glad you have come. Would you mind awfully sitting for me again? Just till I repair the damage?'

In shocked silence, Georgina sat, while in a different silence Rose worked on through the morning, afternoon and into early evening until she had repainted every detail of that poor, scarred face, and obliterated all trace of Edward's cruelty. Then at last, wearily, she laid aside her brush.

'That will have to do for today. I will work on it again tomorrow, but at least the groundwork is done. I am sorry, Georgina, to have kept you so long. You are my dear, patient friend.' Then, to Georgina's dismay, Rose broke down and wept.

It was a subdued party that gathered at the boat train in Victoria station on that blustery March morning. When Rose and Georgina, accompanied by a porter with their luggage, arrived at the carriage that had been reserved for them, Lady Portia and her maid were already installed and Edward Rivers, to Rose's relief, nowhere to be seen.

'Said he had to buy a newspaper,' grumbled Lady Portia, 'as if *The Times* won't be waiting for him at home. He's growing dull in his old age. And it will certainly make no difference to the Transvaal whether Edward reads about it or not.'

Lady Portia was in irritable mood – Edward, she told them, had been unfit to live with for the past week, swearing, shouting at the servants, without a civil word to say to anyone. 'And to crown all he dismissed the workmen from the old brewery when the work was only half done. He's getting as bad as his father...'

Rose occupied herself with packing her painting equipment safely into the luggage rack above the seats and left it to Georgina to make suitable comment. On that awful day, Georgina had asked no questions, merely given sympathy and comfort. It would have spoiled Georgina's pleasure in the projected trip to tell her of Rose's troubles. Besides, what would be the point? It was over between her and Edward. Over for ever. She knew now what Georgina had felt when Harry Price-Hill's 'friend' had desecrated her terracotta head with a carrot – only that piece of silly vandalism had been the result of drunken high-spirits, quite without malice. Edward's had

184

been deliberate – and unforgivable. She could still hear his voice sneering 'so-called art', still feel the pain of his fingers on her wrist, and the different, searing pain as he defiled her picture. No man could do that to someone he truly loved.

After that outburst of weeping – which Georgina rightly surmised, though for the wrong reasons, was caused by 'Inspiration's' damage – Rose had not wept again. She was calm, resolute, a little pale perhaps, but unbowed. Edward had accused her of putting her painting before all other considerations. Now that she had no others, she could dedicate the rest of her life, if she chose, to art.

When Edward Rivers eventually reappeared, the indispensable newspaper, neatly folded, protruding from an overcoat pocket, Rose was able to look him in the face without expression. When he wished her a courteous '*bon voyage*' she thanked him with equal courtesy. But she made certain her hand should not touch his.

Mrs Millard and all Rose's sisters had come to see her off. Percy and Harry Price-Hill were there to send Georgina on her way, and with Edward Rivers they formed quite a little crowd. As the time for departure approached, all around them on the platform handkerchiefs waved or were held to brimming eyes, hurrying porters shepherded last-minute trolleys heaped high with cabin-trunks, hatboxes and assorted paraphernalia, groups of people collected, parted, flowed on again. Then carriage doors banged up and down the train and windows were lowered for final farewells.

'Goodbye, Rose. Write to me.' Sara hugged Rose tight and tried not to cry. Then it was Maudie's turn and little Charlotte's.

Maudie, white-faced and anxious, begged Rose to take care and not to drink the water. 'I packed a special medicine box for you, in your leather suitcase,' she said as she kissed Rose goodbye. 'With instructions.'

Charlotte had no such anxieties, but bubbled with excitement. 'Bring me back a present, Rose,' she cried. 'Something pretty.'

'You are quite pretty enough already,' said Harry, overhearing, and Charlotte blushed with delight.

'Goodbye, Rose,' said Claire. She leant forward carefully, so as not to disarrange her hat and kissed Rose on the cheek. 'How I envy you! What a glorious opportunity.' Claire looked particularly lovely in a new spring walking suit of a soft blue shade, with a cream lace jabot and a tight-waisted jacket which emphasised her curves. She had an air of suppressed excitement about her, but certainly no tinge of envy.

'Goodbye, dear,' said Mrs Millard, embracing her with unac-

185

customed affection. 'Make the most of your opportunities.' In case Rose might interpret this too freely, she added, 'And remember you are an Englishwoman and a lady.'

Under cover of the general leave-taking as Georgina and Lady Portia made their own farewells, Percy clasped her hand and murmured, with fervour, 'I'll not forget you, Rose. I will think of you every single day until you come home again.'

'Dear Percy...' Then the guard's whistle shrilled its final warning and the last door banged shut. Green flags signalled, and the boat train snorted and grunted into chugging motion in a rush of escaping steam and billowing, soot-laden smoke.

Rose's last glimpse of Edward Rivers was of a man of medium height, well-dressed, correct, his handsome face the closed mask of a stranger. He was standing a little apart from the others, as if their fluttering handkerchiefs and tearful farewells were no concern of his. He raised his cane, once, in brief farewell then, as the train gathered speed, she saw him turn and offer his arm to Claire. Claire smiled up at him, took it, and they walked away together, arm in arm, without a backward glance.

Part 3

Home and Abroad, 1898

CHAPTER 1

To: *Miss Rose Millard, Hotel des Deux Mondes, Avenue de l'Opera, Paris*

Dear Rose,

It is quiet at home since you left us, or perhaps it would be more accurate, dear sister, to say that it is dull. Mamma still desires me to work in Millards, especially since you are no longer there, but I will not. I know that if once I allow her to drag me into Papa's 'emporium' I will never escape and whatever she says, I know he would not have made me.

Claire has become insufferable since you left. She is forever altering her garments and requiring us to help her turn a hem or tuck a bodice. She annoints her face with cucumber lotion and her hands with lemon juice till she smells like a greengrocer's shop. She goes to ladies' tea parties, too, whenever she chooses and because they are in the Phoebe Burgess circle Mamma never complains. I believe Claire never works in Millards now. She goes in, perhaps, but only to 'supervise' as she calls it and once she 'modelled' one of the tea gowns from Mamma's newest department – Ladies' Half-Mourning. It is to be a natural step, Mamma says, to a fully-fledged Ladies Department which will stock exclusive gowns for the Best Circles. Claire, of course, is advising Mamma which these are.

As to my studies, Mr Rivers spoke to Mamma, as he promised he would do, and though she will not let me go to regular lectures here in London, she has consented to let me write to Miss Welsh at Girton College to inquire. Mr Rivers was very courteous and correct when he called, but it was an awkward visit. I wish you had been there, Rose dear, then perhaps Claire would not have behaved as she did. I was mortified and would not speak to her. Maudie would not speak to him. Charlotte said 'Why have you put on your Sunday dress when it is only Tuesday, Claire?' and afterwards Claire made her cry.

Mr Rivers told me I must study Latin and Greek and read as much as I can and if I still want to apply in a year's time, he will recommend me to the Mistress of Girton who is apparently a distant cousin of his mother's. He will call again, he said, when he has further information.

189

I asked if he would like me to convey any message from him in my letter to you, but he said no, though I was, of course, free to pass on to you his regards. He was very stern and correct. But April has been a disconcerting month. March truly went out like a lamb, but though April has brought sun, there is no much-needed rain and the season is distinctly behindhand. But the sticky horse-chestnut buds are opening, the plum trees are in blossom and yesterday I saw little wild hyacinths in Kensington gardens, so spring is trying its best in spite of the frosts. But many of the crops are backward and much in need of moisture and Mrs Burgess told Claire that Mr Rivers has dreadful money worries concerning the estate.

Millards continues to prosper. I cannot imagine why so many people want to buy so many clothes but they do and Claire says shares are up another 2% which apparently is very good so her precious dowry will be as lavish as she could wish. I am afraid Claire is becoming very trivial.

The war between America and Spain concerning Cuba has affected dealings on the Stock Exchange and for a while Mamma was worried. But Mr Burgess, fortunately, is advising her and she sold her American stock and bought Canadian Railway instead. They, apparently, are good, and with her Consols and her Rio Tinto she is very pleased. 'At last my goal is in sight,' she said, so perhaps when her moneybags are full enough she will let me go to College?

I wonder where you are at this moment? I saw in The Times *a report of the* vernissage *(that is what they call the opening day, is it not?) of the Salons of Painting and Sculpture in Paris. I wonder if you were there? The reporter made little comment on the art, but much on the crowds and the stifling, dust-laden atmosphere. I know your priorities would be the opposite. Dear Rose, I hope you are drinking deep in the cup of life and extending your horizons. I know that you will seize every opportunity and will look on every new sight with receptive eyes. It was always your dream. How happy you must be to have achieved it, as I shall be happy when I achieve mine.*

As to Claire's ambition, she says she would like a summer wedding, but Mamma told her, quite sharply, that there would be time to talk of that when she had secured her man. I am glad it is not to be Harry. If I thought for a moment that it was, I would urge him to go to Cuba and fight the Spaniards at once, to keep him out of harm's way. Claire is so predatory. But she is very beautiful these days. She has a new dress, just like Sarah Bernhardt's, in lovely creamy lace. Mrs Burgess lent her her very own dressmaker, though Mamma and Claire could quite easily have cut it out and stitched it themselves. But Mamma says the dividends are good and that Claire's dress is an investment.

190

Claire says that everyone admires the portraits you did of the Burgess children. They hang in the drawing room in Brompton Square and there will be many similar commissions waiting for you when you return to London. I overheard Mrs Burgess saying 'Of course when they are older, it must be Sargent, but until then the Millard girl is really very good, and so much cheaper'! Claire says visitors always comment most favourably and she is proud to acknowledge you as her sister. Is not that high praise?

Next week I am to go with Claire, in a party, to the theatre, to see The Gondoliers *preceded by* Old Sarah. *The latter title is very apt in my case. I grow more serious daily. Claire, on the other hand, grows the reverse, especially after champagne. I do hope she does not disgrace me.*

Mamma asks me to include her affectionate greetings to you and of course to Miss Woodstock. Your ever-loving sister. Sara.

To Miss Rose Millard, Poste Restante, Avignon.

Dear Rose,

By now you and Georgie will be in the south of France. I trust your journey was comfortable and that you are enjoying seeing foreign parts. I am sure you will see subjects to paint wherever you look and that the results will be as delightful as anything in the Louvre or any other gallery you may visit. But please paint and draw and study and do whatever else you must do very soon. London is dull without you and Georgina. The only excitement is the news from Cuba, but one grows tired of other people's wars. Mr Gladstone's funeral was a solemn and sombre affair – no flowers or ceremonial, by request – and the Royal Military Tournament was held in pouring rain, so you see I have little to cheer me.

Harry Price-Hill and I spent a weekend at Rivers' place recently, but the weather was very disappointing. Cold, drenching rain, and Rivers and Morton spent the whole time discussing crops and insects and such like, or the purchase of pheasants' eggs. The charades were not at all the same without you, though Phoebe Burgess brought a party of young things. You know how she always tries to pair poor Rivers off whether he likes it or not, but Rivers has been like a bear with a sore head since his mother left. I could not help wishing you had been there.

I see from your itinerary that you will soon be in Italy. I hope the statues in the Italian cities will be inspiring for Georgina. She is so clever that I am sure she could do anything she set her hand to. I hope

191

Rome gives her new ideas. I am told the Trevi fountain is splendid.

A fellow I met the other day admired your portraits of the Burgess children and said when you had enough work completed, you should give an exhibition. What do you think of that? I want you to know that I will back you, Rose, in whatever you do and all I ask in return is the right to buy any – or all – of your pictures before the public is allowed in.

Your faithful admirer and devoted servant, Percival Woodstock.

Miss Rose Millard, Hotel Alba, Florence.

Dearest sister Rose,

By now you will be strolling by the Arno admiring the antique quaintness of the Ponte Vecchio and revelling in the pictorial feast of the Uffizi. How I wish I were with you to savour the rich banquet of colour and technique, the changing styles, the throbbing lustre of the Old Masters.

Rose dear, you must be sure to see all the important paintings, frescoes, and triptychs, and Georgina all the bas reliefs, busts and statues possible before you even think of coming home. There is your own painting to consider, too, and Georgina's sculpture. There may be studios where you can apprentice yourselves and learn more in a month than in a year at home. I am sure six months will be too short a time into which to cram all the fascinating essentials. So carpe diem as Horace says. Seize your opportunity, or if you prefer, Gather ye rosebuds while ye may. I certainly intend to do so.

Mamma is well, Millards is flourishing and there is no need at all for you to worry about us poor stay-at-homes. We are only happy that you at least are fulfilling your dream. When you come home, we expect to see a full sketch book of all the places you have seen and admired.

London is dull at present. Harry Price-Hill won handsomely in the Derby, but lost most of it again on the Oaks two days later. Mr Rivers took a medal in the Shire Horse section of the Suffolk show and one of his estate workers won a prize for butter, but Phoebe said the tub he sent her was decidedly rancid. Probably the weather turned it, as it has been very thundery lately.

The Queen held a State concert at Buckingham Palace the other day and Captain Woodstock was in the Guards detachment on escort duty for the Prince of Wales. He looked very handsome in his uniform, the dear boy, and blushed with pleasure when I said as much.

192

Dear Phoebe got up a party to a matinee next week – Forbes Robertson and Mrs Patrick Campbell in The Second Mrs Tanqueray *. Do you remember that splendid performance of* Hamlet *last year? It was our introduction to Society and how excited we were! Now I can hardly remember a time when we did not know Phoebe and Percival and all our dear friends. But all the best people are out of town and there is very little going on in London now. Still, I hope to be out of town myself very soon and am busy preparing my wardrobe.*

Your affectionate sister, Claire.

To: Miss Rose Millard, Hotel Alba, Florence.

Dear Rosie-Posie,

Maudie says I must write to you to tell you we are all well and to ask how you are enjoying your tour. Here it is hot at last and everyone wishes it was not (after wishing it was for weeks!). Mamma has told Claire she may go to the country with Mrs Burgess, but it is not fair. She gets all the new clothes and we get nothing. My last year's dress is much too tight for me, but Mamma says nonsense it only needs the seams letting out. Please Rose will you bring me something really pretty from Italy or France? A hat with flowers on it or a length of lace? And I would like French bonbons, too, and Maudie says there are biscuits in Italy which are delicious, called Amaretti, I think. I would like some of those, too. And pretty little gloves? Harry Price-Hill gave me a big box of chocolates when he won at the races, but Maudie was angry with me and said I should not have accepted them even though they were for her to share. I don't see why as they were lovely chocolates even though I was sick in the night afterwards, but that was my fault for eating too many at once. He gave Mamma some too, and Claire and Sara got little phials of perfume. It was very generous of him, but Mamma said it was imprudent and that he spends money like water. I said How can you spend *water? I thought you could only* pass *it and was sent to bed in disgrace!*

One day we went on a picnic to Henley with the Burgess family and Harry was there too. He punted one of the boats and got lost and it was ages before he appeared again and Mademoiselle had lost her hat and her face was all red from the sun. Then Maudie felt sick and we had to go home.

Your affectionate and ever-loving sister, Charlotte.
Postscript: I would like a little phial of perfume, too. French *perfume, please.*

193

Post postscript: Mamma bought Claire a bathing costume as well as all her other new clothes. It is blue and white with frills on and very pretty but Claire cannot even swim! It is not fair. I wish I was the eldest.

CHAPTER 2

It had been a bad spring at Wychwood. Gales, frost, and a fluctuating temperature were not conducive to growth, and the April drought had not helped. May had brought welcome rains, the grasslands had freshened and the hay crop promised to be excellent, but other crops were still behindhand. Then rough winds stripped the plum and pear trees of blossom. Fortunately the orchard trees were slow and there should be magnificent bloom on the apple, but what was needed most of all was a spell of warm weather. The hawthorn blossom was practically stationary and though the oaks were laden with catkins, they were laden also with oak apples, an ominous sign of pests to come.

Altogether it had been a depressing time, even without the other burden which weighed heavy on Edward Rivers' mind. His bankers were pressing him again. Death duties and his father's folly had left him heavily in debt and he could see no way out of the relentless spiral of borrowing, interest repayments, more borrowing, until there was nothing left for him to mortgage or to sell. It would not have mattered if he could have sold up and left – bought a smaller place perhaps, with fewer overheads. His mother would not care and his sisters had places of their own anyway. But he wanted Wychwood for his children and their children after them. Wychwood was part of him and he loved the place with a dogged loyalty which had made him scrimp and borrow to keep his head above water and the estate intact. But now, even he acknowledged that it could not go on. Wychwood in a good year and with good management might just support him and any family he might have – but not pay off his father's debts as well.

Then to add to his depression there was Rose Millard. His brow darkened at the mere thought of her name. She had teased him, encouraged him, led him to the brink of fulfilment, and cheerfully turned her back on him the moment a better opportunity occurred. Deliberately he ignored that passionate letter she had sent him and which he had destroyed as 'lies, lies, lies'. She was faithless, worthless, she did not warrant a moment's regret, and yet every day he thought of her, with mingled anger and desire. He relived that scene in her studio over and over in his mind, but every time with an undiminished sense of betrayal and loss which was a physical pain. He knew now, as he had previously only imperfectly known, how his own father had felt when Lady Portia left him. His mother and Rose were birds of a feather. As to Rose's canvas, perhaps he should not have vented his rage that way, but had he not, it might have been her that he struck. He did not regret it. She had wounded him as deeply by her rejection.

Her cool demeanour at the railway station had only confirmed him in his resolve to cut her completely from his heart. If she had shown the slightest hint of regret, or of sorrow at parting, his resolve might have crumbled. As it was, if she chose art before him, then art she should have and be damned. He would show her she meant nothing to him.

He had offered his arm to her sister in a spirit of defiance and also, if he were honest, in order to hurt Rose. But Claire had been pleasant enough company. She had reminded him of her sister Sara's interest in Girton College and he had promised to call and discuss it with Mrs Millard on a more suitable occasion. After that, he seemed to meet her whenever he came up to town, and usually with Phoebe: in Phoebe's party at the theatre, at her At Home, even, once, at dinner. He could not avoid her and, after the first pain of reminder, found that revenge made her company welcome. She was very like Rose, after all, though without Rose's abrasiveness, and without her unfeminine ambition. Besides, should anyone suspect that Rose's absence had wounded him, they would soon see otherwise. Should anyone report to Rose herself, she would learn that she meant nothing to him, nothing at all. And Claire was invariably charming.

In spite of the drenching rain, May remained cold, the ground chilled. The unusually low temperatures retarded both growth and the progress of field work and estate matters kept him increasingly busy, with little time for regret, or for excursions to town. June was better, though sunny days still alternated with dull. The countryside looked fresh and green, the hawthorn blossom was magnificent, the broom ablaze. But the caterpillars were rampant everywhere and the aphids a plague.

Nevertheless, by mid-month hay-making was in full swing and 'Cut in wet, cart in dry' proved a good maxim. It was certainly an excellent crop and Rivers ordered up an extra keg of beer from the brewers in Ipswich and distributed it to the field workers as a token of his appreciation. He even helped with a pitchfork himself. He liked haymaking, with the sweet scent of new-mown grass in his nostrils, the sun warm in his face, the swishing rhythm of the scythe and the different rhythm of the pitchforks, spearing the bundles and tossing them onto the stack while bees murmured in the hedgerows, a dozen different field birds pecked over the stubble and his dog sniffed among the uncut grass for field mice or voles. Most farmers had reaping machines now, of course, but at Wychwood they still, of necessity, stuck to the old methods. Machinery was expensive. Besides, even with a reaping machine the outer swathes still had to be cut manually and if a sudden storm flattened the crop, then the reaper would be useless and the whole field would have to be scythed by hand.

By the end of June, the haymaking was over, though not all of it gathered in. It was a magnificent crop, and, given a spell of hot weather, the corn might equal it. There were poppies in the cornfields, dog roses scented the country lanes and cottage gardens, and the nightingale sang superbly, night and day. Perhaps it would not be such a bad summer after all.

On a day in July, Edward Rivers strode through the woods towards the home meadows, his labrador at his heels, and saw that the trees were in full summer leaf, luxurious and fecund. From beyond the woods came the lazy gossiping of hens in the stable yard and the contented crooning of doves. It had been glorious weather for a fortnight now and at last the ground was warm through and through, last year's leaves dust-dry underfoot. He reached the fringe of the woods and stopped, as always, at the sudden vista of open fields with the little windmill dark against the skyline in the far distance and that vast canopy of sky. From his feet stretched a glorious swathe of standing corn, like cloth of gold, patterned with wild poppies and marguerites and stirring softly in the gentle breeze. For a vivid moment he heard Rose sighing 'If only I had my sketch pad,' and himself saying 'You must come again.'

But that had been almost a year ago and even then she had said, 'To paint.' Abruptly he closed his mind against her. Phoebe was arriving this afternoon, with her children and governess, and he had promised Cook to have a word with Dan Bird about extra milk, and to remind the gardener to send up fresh flowers for the house. He could have sent a stable lad with a message, of course, but he preferred to go himself. That way he could walk through his woods, his meadows, his cornfields and see for himself that all was well. Or as well as it could be, with that debt, like a financial sword of Damocles, hanging over him. He had better tell the gardener to clip the lawn again, too, and mark it for tennis. Phoebe would be sure to organise a game. Idly, he wondered what else she would

197

organise during her sojourn at Wychwood. But whatever it was, it had better not interfere with the harvest.

'It is time you thought of marriage,' said Phoebe when, dinner over, they adjourned to the tranquil evening shadows of the drawing room. Before he could comment, she went on, with a swift change of subject as the maid entered with coffee, 'I am so glad you have not succumbed to pressure, Edward, and installed electric lighting. Lamplight is so flattering.' Phoebe herself had 'electrified' her entire house in London the moment it became fashionable to do so. 'But think about what I say,' she continued, pouring coffee, when the maid, with an obedient curtsey, had left. 'I have written to Diana and she entirely agrees with me.' Diana was their other sister, who lived in Berwickshire. 'It is time you considered marriage. Seriously considered it. After all, you are almost thirty and if you wait much longer you will cease to be entirely eligible.'

'Thirty is hardly decrepitude,' said Edward, only half listening. He had made his sister's arrival the occasion for opening a particularly good bottle of claret, a pre-phylloxera Château Margaux, and whereas she had hardly tasted it, hc had appreciated its delicate perfume and exquisite flavour to the full. His father, whatever his faults, had known a good wine from a bad. Now he stretched out his feet contentedly towards the fire which had been lit, in spite of summer, to add the finishing touch to hospitality. The french windows were open to the warm night air and from across the darkened lawn came the clean scent of fresh cut grass and the distant call of an owl. The room was scented with roses from a heaped Chinese bowl on the sofa table, and the gently smouldering logs gave off a faint tang of pine. Edward cupped the brandy bowl in his hands and studied its silken depths with anticipatory pleasure. A superb claret deserved a superb cognac to follow.

'Don't be evasive,' said his sister briskly. 'It is plain to see that you and Wychwood are in need of money and, to come straight if rather vulgarly to the point, a rich wife could provide it.'

'I don't know any rich wives, would-be or otherwise.' Edward held his glass up to the lamplight and studied the splendid richness of texture and tone. Then he breathed in the bouquet with a sigh of content. 'Martell '78,' he said, with reverence, 'and quite superb. At least the old man knew what he was about when he stocked his cellar.'

'A pity he did not pay his bills at the same time! Daddy, bless him, has a lot to answer for, Edward, and it is no good pretending to me that all is well, because it patently is not.' Having once started the subject, Phoebe was now in full cry, with a mixture of self-righteousness and sisterly indignation. 'The brougham needs repainting, the gate into the home meadow is a disgrace, and as for the old brewery ...'

'That is my affair,' interrupted Edward. 'You and Diana have your settlements, and Mother her annuity. How I run the estate is entirely my own concern.'

'Nonsense. It is everybody's concern. We cannot stand by and see you falling deeper and deeper into debt while the estate decays around your ears. It will be worth nothing in ten years time if you go on as you are doing. Robert says ...'

'Kindly tell Robert to mind his own business,' snapped Edward. 'I do not interefere with his bank, do I?'

'No, Edward dear,' soothed his sister. 'But there is no need to be so prickly. We are only trying to help.'

'I do not need your help. At least,' he amended, resorting to flippancy, 'not unless it is a present of thirty thousand or so.'

'But that is what I am saying, Edward dear,' Phoebe looked quickly over her shoulder as if she expected to find eavesdroppers behind the sofa and, satisfied, lowered her voice to a confidential murmur. 'You must find a wife. A rich wife.'

For a moment there was silence. The logs stirred in the hearth, from the hall came the muffled tock of the grandfather clock and inside the room the steady breathing of Edward's dog, stretched out contentedly on the hearthrug and, from the trembling twitches of his paws and the occasional whimper, dreaming of rabbits and the chase.

A wife. Edward considered the notion, as he had done, on and off, for the past five years. He was not averse to the idea, provided she was the right wife. But what constituted rightness? He thought fleetingly of Rose Millard. She had beauty, passion, talent, interest, but she was fickle. She would always put her art first, never him. She would be like his own mother, taking off to foreign parts whenever she felt like it, leaving his children and himself without a qualm to flounder on alone while she enjoyed herself in Italy with her precious painting and her 'arty' friends. Hadn't she proved as much? His wife, when he took one, must be utterly reliable, utterly devoted to Wychwood, to his children, and to himself. She must be beautiful, of course. That went without saying. Though there were many different kinds of beauty and he was not prejudiced in any way. Cultured, poised, with impeccable social manners. And in the bedroom, totally innocent, but receptive and willing. After all, there was always London if he felt the need for stronger meat, and a wife would give him a child. A son, to inherit the estate – always supposing there was still an estate to inherit.

When he had thought about marriage before, it had been in general terms. Now under Phoebe's insistence, he considered the particular. In their mother's long, unpredictable absences abroad, Phoebe, as eldest, has always taken charge, as she seemed bent on doing now. He looked up and caught her studying him. With a shrug and a half-smile, he said, 'Who have you in mind?'

'Ah!' Phoebe was suddenly all attention, the first hurdle safely past. 'There is Adelaide, of course. She is a sweet girl and impeccably bred, but there are three sons to provide for and I doubt her settlement will be much. Whatever it is, you could hope for nothing more from the estate on her father's death. Young Fitz will be lucky to get enough to scrape by on and there will certainly be nothing for the girls. Then there is Georgina – undoubtedly rich, but not to everyone's taste and there is that awkward business of her so-called engagement to Harry. Not that anything will come of it, but I believe the poor girl still hopes. I could find you several other Adelaides tomorrow, but ...' She paused, then went on firmly, 'I must say this, Edward, for everyone's good. You are not as eligible as you once were. You are still good looking of course, healthy, and of good stock. But, though it pains me to say it, and I would not do so in any company but this, we are not of the first circles. We have no title in our family tree, except I believe one of our great-great-uncles married a Lady someone, and, of course, Mummy, but everyone knows she married beneath her and they know why ...' Again she looked around her, inspecting the room for spies, before saying, with blushing directness, 'You and I both know, Edward, that Mummy was not exactly respectable in her youth. There was that shocking affair when her father had to fetch her back from Naples and that was only the first. There were others, both before and after Daddy married her, and though they tried to keep it from nursery ears, I knew long ago why Mummy lived in Italy. Her health was the official reason, but it was to keep her behaviour decently out of sight.'

'Lies. Malicious lies. I am astonished you repeat them.'

'Yes dear, you may be right,' soothed Phoebe hastily, 'and of course for years, ever since that last Italian "friend" of hers died, poor Mummy has by all accounts led a blameless life. But that sort of thing does stick and people do like to know the sort of antecedents they are marrying. Aristocratic eccentricity is one thing, a drawing master or a foreign flunkey quite another.'

'Are you suggesting ...' began Edward, with dangerous calm.

but Phoebe hastily interrupted, 'No dear, of course not. People have only to look at you to know you are Daddy's son, but it does mean Mummy's side of things is not exactly tempting and though both Diana and I were presented, we were very much the also-rans. I never said so, of course, but I *felt* it and so, I am sure, did she.'

'So?' said Edward, for whom rank did not hold the fascination it held for Phoebe.

'So you are not at the top of every mother-of-a-marriageable-daughter's list. In fact, I suspect you are very near the bottom, if included at all. Not just Mummy, of course. That would not matter a jot if you were rich enough. But news has got about, you know. Such things cannot be kept quiet and it is common knowledge that Wychwood has had to draw in the reins.'

'So?' said Edward again, an edge of irritation to his voice. Phoebe was right, of course, but it did not help to hear her state the case so baldly.

'So,' she said carefully, 'I have been thinking. Impoverished gentlewomen are no help to you, however charming they may be, and I fear it is only the impoverished who will consider such an alliance as things stand. Therefore, if you will allow me to advise you, Edward dear, I have something rather different in mind.'

'Oh?' Edward reached lazily for the brandy and poured himself another measure. It promised to be a long evening and he knew it was no good inventing excuses and fleeing to his library. Phoebe would hunt him down sooner or later, so why not now, while he was comfortable, well-fed, with his father's best brandy at his elbow? 'Go on.'

'You know Lord Delaville married that actress the other day? And the Fortesque boy married a pickle king's daughter? Well, no one has ostracised them for it. So you see, patterns are changing and it is really no disgrace to bring in new blood, as long as money comes too.'

'Did the actress have money? I thought what she had was something quite different.'

'*Edward!* You are not at your club now. Please try to listen seriously to what I am saying.'

'I am, I am. But what exactly are you leading up to, Phoebe? Have you found me a soap princess, or the widow of a boot-blacking king? A squat, square creature, with legs like a piano and moneybags enough to sink a ship?'

'Don't be ridiculous, Edward. You always were a booby where girls were concerned and this is not a matter for jest. No,' she went on firmly, 'I have something much more elegant in mind.' She

201

paused, took a deep breath, and said carefully, 'Robert tells me that Mrs Millard, under his guidance, has made excellent private investments and most satisfactory profits. Moreover, Millard and Blunt's is on a sound business footing, with dividends steadily rising, and the Millard family still own more than half the shares. You could do a great deal worse than consider one of the Millard girls. Claire, in fact.' When he made no reply, but stared, frowning, into his brandy, she went on, 'Claire is a delightful girl, intelligent, quick to learn. As you know, she has become a dear friend of mine since we met, here at Wychwood, almost a year ago. During that time I have watched her change from an attractive but rather gauche young lady to a beautiful and accomplished woman whom I would confidently introduce into any society. She comes from the wrong background, of course, but she knows that and has set out to correct it.'

'How can anyone *correct* their background, for goodness sake?' snapped Edward in the irritation born of turbulent emotion. Phoebe had actually suggested a Millard girl! A year ago he would not have credited it. He remembered Harry's suave superiority as he said, 'They are a breed new to me, the ambitious daughters of trade,' and later, 'You will get nowhere with one and possibly, just possibly, everywhere with the other.' He had certainly got nowhere with Rose.

'I meant, Edward dear, she has corrected the effects of her background. She has only to see a person eat oysters once, for instance, to know perfectly how to do it herself, and she never makes the slightest slip on introductions, always so difficult to the incomer. I have watched her progress and am really most impressed. Besides, she is an excellent manager and housewife. She runs the Millard household, you know, while her mother handles the business, and does so with admirable competence and thrift. A useful accomplishment, Edward, especially for Wychwood – and not one that every girl possesses. She is not one of us, of course, and never can be, but a sweet, affectionate girl, quite without guile. Moreover, she is healthy, presentable, and if what Robert says is only half true, rich.'

'I thought there were five daughters,' said Edward, playing for time while his mind sorted through what his sister had told him, rearranging, reassessing. 'There will need to be a tidy sum to provide five dowries.'

'I have thought of that. But from what Claire has let slip, I doubt her sister Rose will ever marry. Her art, Claire says, always comes first and no man would stand for that in marriage, would he? Then I gather the third one, Sara, has set her heart on being a blue-stocking. So unattractive to men. She will no doubt become a school-marm and perpetuate the blue-stocking breed that way. Another, Maud I believe, is not entirely well. She may die before she reaches maturity.'

'And how have you disposed of the youngest obstacle to your plan?' said Edward, with a sarcasm exaggerated for his sister's benefit. Phoebe's intelligence was not of the brightest.

'Charlotte? Oh, she is only nine. There is plenty of time for dividends to double and double again before it is her turn and the shop will provide for all of them, very lavishly, so Robert says. Millards, it seems, has quite cornered the market in black crepe and mourning attire. They made a small fortune when the Duchess of Teck died, and when our dear Queen passes on, as she inevitably must, they will make a second fortune overnight.'

'And how much of that fortune does Robert think Millards will part with to rid themselves of this paragon of a daughter?'

'Ah ... that is rather a delicate matter, but I believe the sum will be "lavish". Robert is trying to find out.'

'Then I suggest he does so, before you pursue your ideas any further. And now, if you will excuse me, I have work to do.'

He drained his brandy in one gulp, stood up, snapped a finger to summon his dog, and strode from the room. But he did not go to the library. Instead, he went out into the night, to stand under the chestnut tree and listen to the mournful cry of the barn owl from the home woods. He remembered Rose, coming to him under this very tree, remembered her kiss, the warmth of her body, his own aching desire. He had told her he loved her, and she had said immodest, glorious things. She had blatantly, joyously, promised herself to him ... and broken that promise like a twig underfoot!

Abruptly he thrust memory aside. He was done with love and treachery and the pain it brought. One girl was much like another and it would serve her right if he did marry her sister. Deliberately he studied the outline of the old brewery against the night sky. That loft was to have been their temple. But he had dismissed the workmen, filled the ground floor with sacks of chicken meal and assorted farm machinery, and sealed up the loft, for ever. That chapter of his life was closed.

Unless, he course, he pulled the building down and replaced it with a new, modern barn and stable block? That would show her exactly what he thought of her. He could get a couple more Shire horses, perhaps breed from them. Better still, he could buy one of the new reaping machines. He would need money, of course. Slowly, the seed Phoebe had planted took hold.

CHAPTER 3

This time the brougham was waiting when their train arrived at Wintelsham station that sleepy summer afternoon, and Edward himself stepped forward to welcome them when they drew up fifteen minutes later at the door of Wychwood.

Claire had spent days preparing for the visit. It was one thing to go to a weekend house party, quite another to go away for three whole weeks, and Sara was no help at all.

'I do not see why I have to come, too,' she had grumbled when the invitation arrived. 'I would far rather stay here and study.'

'You have to chaperone me, of course,' said Claire with an edge of sharpness to her voice. 'And you can study at Wychwood. There is a good library and I thought you regarded Mr Rivers as your mentor where Cambridge was concerned.'

'I do, but ...'

'Then I fail to see the difficulty. Do you, Mamma?'

Claire knew her mother would back her in this and every dispute if it helped to put Claire in a position to achieve her precious aim. Claire was twenty – very nearly on the shelf – and this summer visit might be her last chance. There was always the faithful Mr Blunt, of course, but she would rather die a spinster than descend to his level again, after achieving such social heights as Phoebe Burgess's drawing room. But Claire recognised, as her mother did, that if she could not secure an engagement ring in her three-week holiday, she might as well give up the attempt. As a result her nerves were vulnerable, her temper uncertain, and her anxiety about her wardrobe and possible social tactics gave her sleepless nights. The resulting dark circles under her eyes were an added worry so that when Charlotte told her she looked like a prize-fighter, Claire smacked her so hard Charlotte cried.

It was not that Claire lacked confidence in herself. She knew her clothes were elegant, her manner equally so, her conversation both correct and entertaining, and her social poise equal to most occasions. She did not doubt for a moment that she was beautiful – but what she did doubt was the susceptibility of her prey. In spite of their many meetings, he remained an enigma and as a result she was baffled as to what tactics to employ. But she would have to do *something*.

It was to be a small house party, with a succession of larger gatherings. Phoebe, in her mother's absence, was acting as Edward's hostess – Mr Burgess would spend what time he could at Wychwood while continuing to work in town – and had told Claire that she planned several tennis parties, a picnic or two, and possibly, weather permitting, a day at the sea. Claire must bring suitable clothing, including, if she wished, a bathing costume. Harry Price-Hill would be there, with Percy and Fitz, and, of course, Edward Rivers.

It was Claire's best chance, but also, she feared, her last. She must tread carefully till she knew her ground, but not so carefully that she got nowhere at all.

Her mother's advice was to 'Be yourself, dear. Do not be forward, but at the same time, let him know that you are, shall we say, interested?' Charlotte said, in the middle of dinner, 'Why don't you let him kiss you, then he will have to marry you, won't he? Annie says that the baker's boy will have to marry the next door kitchen-maid and she let him kiss her. I saw. They were on the area steps in the dark and he ...'

'Charlotte! Leave the table at once and go to your room!' Nevertheless, in spite of Rebecca's outrage and Claire's dutifully lowered eyes, there might be something in what Charlotte said. The difficulty was to offer enough to allure, without appearing forward, or giving the wrong impression.

In the end, Claire decided to be serenely unaware until she had a better idea of how best to achieve her end.

So when Edward handed her down from the carriage at the door of Wychwood, she gave him a gentle smile, thanked him, and taking Sara's arm, walked past him into the house in search, she said, of Phoebe. The fact that the manœuvre gave him an excellent view of her trim waist and enticingly rounded hips was apparently coincidental.

For the next week, Edward watched her, at first with amusement, then with a touch of awe, as she played the part of the perfect house guest. She played with Phoebe's children, asked after Cook's rheumatism, complimented Dan Bird's wife on her excellent butter – 'I am not in the least surprised that it won first prize at the Show. I have never tasted better.'

At dinner her conversation was impeccable: entertaining without being contentious, and he noticed that if ever a subject arose which threatened to turn into argument, she was adept at changing the subject. Last year, he remembered, she had giggled too much and on occasions been pert, but he had forgotten how engaging she could be. His initial amusement sharpened to interest.

When the tennis party ended in charades, she had the company in stitches with her impersonation of Queen Victoria and they applauded her with different though equal appreciation when she adopted a cockney accent and daringly impersonated Marie Lloyd.

'Well?' whispered Phoebe in his ear. For answer, he clapped loudly and cried 'Bravo!' But he did not seek her out. Instead he watched and waited, fascinated as to what she would do next. He knew she would do something – Phoebe would make her, if her own instinct did not, for he had no doubt that Phoebe had confided her plans for Edward to the lady concerned. Or if not confided, then dropped a delicate hint. For himself, he was detached, amused, even a little curious, but emotionally untouched. Besides, it was harvest time and he had more important matters to attend to.

Towards the end of the second week of Claire's visit, he and Morton agreed that the time was right to begin harvesting the corn. The fine weather might break at any minute and heavy rain would devastate the standing corn. At least if the corn were cut it would come to less harm. Again, Claire behaved as if born to the life. When she and Phoebe, in elegant straw hats and pale muslin skirts, strolled down to the corn field with baskets of bread and cheese for the workers, he saw her moving among the womenfolk, asking after their ailments and their families, addressing the labourers and even some of the children by name.

It was the mid-day break and many of the women had infants to feed or babies to put to the breast. Small girls scarcely out of nappies themselves staggered across the stubble from the village under the weight of infant siblings until relieved of their burden by one of the red-faced, perspiring women who sprawled under the hedgerow in what little shade the tangled briar and hawthorn afforded. Then the woman would unbutton her bodice and suckle the child while the older sister stood patiently waiting, until someone gave her bread or a mug of milk, or ale. Then, the break over, each returned to his task so that the field could be finished before sundown.

It was a busy, happy scene and one which never failed to stir Edward Rivers' heart: the rippling corn, liquid gold under the sun, the village workers, whole families of them, hired willingly for the harvest, the larksong and the chatter, the inquisitive, foraging dogs, the children, and the men with their firm, weather-tanned arms and gaiters of leather or bound sacking, their blades honed sharp on the whetstone. First the clean cut of the scythe, rows of them in rhythm as the men moved forward, then the dip and bend of the women following, binding the sheaves for others to stack in rows of golden stooks above the naked stubble. The field would be shaved, from the outside inwards, till the last standing square of corn remained, and all the neighbourhood boys gathered, stick in hand, waiting. Then as the blades sliced into their last refuge, the rabbits would break cover and race in a wild dash for freedom with the whooping, yelling boys at their terrified heels. The village pots would be full that evening, the village air aromatic with rabbit stew.

Then, at the end of the day, the last corn cut, the gleaners would move in – women of all ages, collecting what was by ancient custom rightfully theirs.

Edward was standing under an oak tree, in the last of the pink evening light, watching them when he heard a footfall and turned to find Claire at his side.

'Have you seen Sara?' she asked innocently. 'I had thought to find her here, but perhaps she went back to the house a different way.'

'Did you try the library?' His eyes were on the cornfield, bare now of workers, except for the handful of gleaners that remained, their shadows long across the stubble. A rabbit, a solitary survivor of the afternoon's onslaught, lolloped cautiously across the space between one stook and the next, birds foraged in the newly-bared ground and the rows of fresh stooks cast dark shadows over the shorn field. To the west, behind the woods, the sky was afire with gold and streaked with trailing shreds of turquoise and vermilion. Overhead the oak leaves stirred in a soft evening breeze and the air was suddenly cool on his cheek.

'No,' said Claire. She stood beside him, following his eyes across the harvested field before saying quietly. '*It is a beauteous evening, calm and free. The holy time is quiet as a nun, breathless with adoration ...*'

For a moment he thought it was Rose beside him – the same voice, the same perfume – and the surge of joy and desire almost took his breath away. Then he remembered. But when he turned his head, he saw the same full breasts, the same neat waist and in the evening shadows he could almost imagine the same dark eyes and full, welcoming lips. Claire was, after all, very like her sister, and the desire which that artless quotation had aroused still lingered. What was the point of resisting further? And Claire, unlike Rose, was utterly reliable. After a long moment he said, with a sort of tired resignation, 'Yes.' Then he turned and offered her his arm. 'Shall we walk home through the woods? It is the shortest route.'

'Thank you.' Gravely, Claire took his arm.

In the clearing, where he had first seen Rose asleep in a tumble of immodest skirts and flowing hair, he stopped. Rose's presence was all around him, her voice, her laugh, her sweet, welcoming lips which set his blood racing with desire. In the magic of the woodland shadows past and present merged. He turned, lifted her chin with his forefinger and kissed her on the lips.

With a startled gasp, she jerked away and the spell was broken. It was not Rose after all, but a stranger. 'I am sorry,' he said wearily. 'I forgot myself. Please forgive me.'

'No, please, I mean . . .' Claire's agitation seemed entirely genuine. 'It is the first time I have been kissed by a man.' She spoke, not looking at him, but at her own twisting hands, but after a moment she looked up, blushing, and said, 'I was startled, that is all – and unschooled.' She put out a hand and touched his arm. 'Please . . . teach me?'

He smelt the perfume of her hair, the warmth of her breasts, with the faintest undertone of perspiration. She was undoubtedly beautiful and when she murmured 'Please?' with those deliciously full lips, he drew her close, removed her hat, and kissed her again. This time she did not resist. Her lips were cool and soft, her face shadowed by the twilight so he could not read her eyes. He closed his own and imagined she was Rose, soft, welcoming, burgeoning under his hands with a desire equal to his own. But when his hand found her breast, she struggled, broke free and cried, 'Mr Rivers! How dare you?' Trembling with shock, she found her hat and tied it firmly back in place, not meeting his eyes.

Was her outrage tactical or real? He did not know and did not care. 'Forgive me. I had thought . . .' He turned abruptly away as despair engulfed him. What a fool he was, what a fool he had been. Of course this was not Rose. This was the other one, like Rose but not Rose. This one would not offer herself to him on a plate, even if her breasts were as deliciously round and full, her lips as soft, her thighs. . . But of course this one did not have thighs. No lady had until she was married. But, a wedding ring on her finger, this one surely would be as gloriously welcoming as the other? And, unlike the other, be utterly faithful? That other had offered herself, teased him till he was mad with desire, and left him. This one had refused him with all proper decorum, but would give him everything once she was his wife. Everything – *and*, he heard Phoebe's prompting voice, a dowry. Phoebe was right. He needed a wife; a useful, reliable wife. He had even found himself eyeing some of those harvest women with lust, and just now, if he had lost control . . . 'That was most ungentlemanly of me,' he said quietly, his back to her. 'I forgot myself. But you really should not be so ... beautiful.'

For a long moment there was silence. Through the massed leaves overhead the sky was now a deep red trail of setting glory, but here, under the trees, it was already twilight. An evening dampness rose from underfoot where years of layered leafmould sheltered little woodland creatures, speckled mosses, toadstools, and star-bright wood anemones. The dark shape of a hedgehog blundered across their path and disappeared in a whispering of stirred leaf.

From the direction of the village came the tang of woodsmoke with the first of the evening cooking smells and, from closer at hand, the voices of the gleaners in the field, but in the clearing itself there was only the sound of her breathing, slower now as she regained composure. Then she spoke.

'I am sorry,' she said, looking down at her hands. 'But I did not expect ... I mean ...' She faltered to a stop.

With an effort, he said, 'Will you forgive me?'

'There is nothing to forgive, Mr Rivers. Nothing at all. But you took me by surprise, and ... I did not know your intentions.'

'I hardly know them myself,' he said, his back still towards her. Then he turned, coming to a decision, and said quietly, 'But I rather think they are honourable.' He offered her his arm and they walked, in silence, to the house.

That night Claire lay a long time awake, her mind a turmoil of triumph, apprehension, and excitement. He had said his intentions were honourable. Surely that could only mean marriage? Or did it mean simply that he did *not* intend to seduce her, whatever that involved? Then when his lips had pressed hard against hers, why had he tried to part them with his tongue? She had not let him, of course, but why had he tried to in the first place? Was that what people did? Was that 'giving oneself'? If so, she did not care for it much. As for touching her breast ... she shuddered with abhorrence. That must have been a mistake. Though perhaps things like that came into the 'giving'? She hoped not. It was so immodest, so embarrassing. For once, Claire wished Rose had been there so that she could have asked her, after dark of course so that no one could see her face. But then Rose would only have mocked, or pretended she knew all about it anyway.

She could not possibly ask Sara. Sara was clever and spent every day studying, but she was only fifteen and could not be expected to know about such things. Even if she did know, Claire could not stoop to ask her. Resolutely Claire pushed the question of fondled breasts aside. The important thing was that he had kissed her, though there had been a point when she thought she had bungled things, jerking away like that. But she couldn't help it, and she had managed to retrieve the situation. Now all she need concern herself with was a proposal, then quickly, to clinch matters, an announcement in *The Times*. Intentions were one thing, an actual engagement quite another. And there was only one more week to go.

'Well?' said Phoebe, cornering Edward in the library after dinner.

'Well what?' snapped Edward crossly. He had successfully avoided Claire's company all evening.

'You know perfectly well what I mean. And in case you are still doubtful, Robert assures me she will have at least £15,000 and probably double that. I had a letter this morning.'

'And how does Robert know?'

'He asked Mrs Millard outright. Apparently she came to him at the bank to inquire about some investment of hers – diamond mines, I think – and he asked her. "What provision are you hoping to make for your daughter," he said and she said, "Oh . . . well into five figures".'

'Hoping? That is not the same thing as doing.'

'No dear, but you must admit it sounds very promising. And remember Claire mentioned £30,000 that time she stayed here last year? Properly invested – and with Robert's help it has been – think what that figure must be now. And you do like her, don't you? You remember she is going home in a week's time?' She paused for him to draw his own conclusions, then went on carefully, 'I thought we might all go on a picnic tomorrow, if the weather holds, to Felixstowe. The bathing there is excellent and with Mademoiselle such an expert at life-preserving, we need have no fears on that score.'

'No,' said Edward solemnly. 'None at all.'

The little ones did not swim, of course, but splashed noisily in the shallows and Mademoiselle was most solicitous that they stay well within their depth.

'Such a reliable young woman,' said Phoebe as she and the Millard girls changed into their swimming costumes in the bathing hut. Claire gave Sara a warning glance and made no comment. It was the first time that Sara had swum since that dreadful day at Dieppe four years ago, but on Claire's insistence – and her mother's advice – she had brought a bathing costume with her. So had Claire, though she had no intention of going in above her knees; But she had chosen her costume with great care – a flattering garment in blue and white striped cambric with broderie anglaise frills at the knees and a dear little cap to match. Tight waisted and cut daringly low at the front she knew it suited her. Sara's was more utilitarian, being black and plain, with a white bandanna to tie up her hair.

Harry was of the party, of course, and Edward, and when Sara stood hesitantly at the fringe of the water, watching the foam curl over the shingle and retreat, Harry came to stand beside her and took her hand.

'There is no need to be frightened, old girl,' he said kindly. He was nicer to her every time they met, but it was enough for Sara that he even spoke to her. 'I know what happened, Sara,' he went on. 'So do we all. But Edward and I are both here. Don't be afraid. Look, I will hold your hand and we will walk in together.'

It was the most intimate thing Harry had ever said to her and when he held her hand and pulled her gently into the water, she followed, at first with reluctance, then with joyful faith. When the water reached her waist, he said, 'Now, lift your feet off the bottom and swim. I will stay close beside you, I promise.'

So she lifted her feet and swam and the old pleasure flowed back into her limbs as her arms followed the remembered strokes and her legs kicked, frog-like, behind her. With her head held carefully out of the water she could see Harry swimming beside her, as he had promised. He grinned, said 'Well done, Sara. That's the ticket,' and the last shred of fear left her. It was bliss to swim again, bliss to have Harry beside her, bliss to know that he and she for that brief time were alone together in a private world where no one else could follow.

'Oh dear,' said Phoebe anxiously. 'I had quite forgotten about poor Sara's unfortunate experience.'

Phoebe and Claire were standing in the shallows, splashing themselves now and then with scooped sea-water and watching the others. It was a day of scorching sun, the hottest yet, but with a welcome breeze coming in from the sea. The hotels on the cliffs behind them had all put out awnings and tables with striped umbrellas and the beach was crowded with bathers. All the bathing huts were taken and the fringe of the sea was dotted with children splashing and squealing while further out, their older brothers and sisters tossed rubber beach balls to each other or swam. Edward was nowhere in sight, but Sara's white-bound head and Harry's blond one were clearly visible. 'It was so thoughtless of me,' worried Phoebe, watching them. 'I do hope she will be all right.'

'Of course she will, Phoebe dear.' To be honest, Claire had forgotten it herself, being far too taken up with her own affairs, and at that moment the subject of her thoughts emerged, dripping,

211

from the sea only yards away and stood, knee deep, shaking the sea-water from his hair. His sleeved black bathing suit reached to his knees and was decorous enough, except that, soaked, it clung to every muscle and fold of his body. He was a well-built man and his outdoor life kept him so. His biceps were firm, his shoulders strong and muscular, and the hairs on his chest where the top button had come undone glistened with sea-drops. But when her eyes inadvertently followed the line of his body downwards, Claire felt herself blush and looked hastily away. It was only recently that mixed bathing had been allowed on English beaches and Claire was not at all sure it was a good idea. Mr Rivers might as well have been *nude*.

'We were just saying how worried we were about Sara,' said Phoebe. 'You will keep an eye on her, won't you Edward dear?'

'Don't fuss, Phoebe,' said Edward, studying Claire with obvious approval. She had a superb figure, voluptuous and trim in all the right places, and what breasts! 'Besides, Harry is with her.'

'And of course,' said Claire with composure, 'there is always Mademoiselle,' She looked solemnly at Edward and he returned her look with grave complicity. Then, suddenly cheerful, he reached forward and caught Claire's hand.

'Come on in, reluctant Nereid. The sea is big enough for everyone.'

'But I can't swim!' she cried, all sophistication forgotten in the terror of the moment.

'Then I will teach you.'

'Really, Edward, are you sure it is quite proper?' protested Phoebe.

'Mixed bathing? Of course it is proper – and in this case eminently sensible. Unless you would prefer Claire to drown?'

'No,' protested Claire in genuine fear, as he pulled her deeper into the sea. 'I can't ... I ... oh!' She slipped, fell, floundered in terror as the water closed over her head in a string of bubbles, then felt herself pulled to her feet again in the waist-high water, coughing and choking, her hair plastered flat round her head and her pretty hat gone.

'Oh ... you beast!' she spluttered in fury, for a moment forgetting her role as the perfect gentlewoman. 'You did that on purpose, you vile, disagreeable ...' Then she saw him regarding her with surprise and what looked very like amusement. Hastily she turned her back and mumbled something about looking for her cap.

'Leave it,' he said, grinning. 'I will buy you another. Besides, I like your hair like that. You look like Venus emerging from the waves.' It was true. She looked remarkably desirable, with her costume clinging to her every curve and her hair in disarray. Her nipples were like little covered buttons on her breasts and the curve of her stomach indicated softer curves below the water line. Besides, that flash of temper had excited him as her weeks of demure correctness had failed to do. He did not acknowledge, even in his most private thoughts, that it might be because it reminded him of Rose.

'But I am sorry,' he said gravely. 'I did not mean to go too fast.'

'No, it was my fault,' she managed. 'I lost my footing, that was all.'

'And your temper?'

'All right, that too,' she admitted, with scant grace, and added with an effort, 'I apologise. But now that I am thoroughly wet, perhaps you would teach me what to do next, Mr Rivers?'

'Another lesson?' he said, deliberately reminding her of the woods, then briskly, 'Certainly, Miss Millard. First, watch how I move my arms, hands together, push forward, slowly, like this ... Now you try. Yes, that's the way. Next, watch how I move my legs ... Now lift your feet off the bottom and try for yourself. I will hold you.' He laid a hand under her stomach to support her, another on the small of her back. He felt the warmth of her flesh even through the cold, sodden cotton and when she kicked out, her bare leg touched his. She floundered, he caught her, lifted her half out of the water by her waist, and as she slipped down again, half struggling, half laughing, he kissed her, in full view of Phoebe and the entire bathing populace of Felixstowe.

After that, of course, there was no going back.

CHAPTER 4

Miss Rose Millard, Hotel Alba, Florence. (Please forward if required.)

My dearest Rose,

The past week has flown by in such a whirlwind of joyful preparation that I have only now been able to snatch a moment of precious time to write to you, my dear, loving sister. But I know you will be so happy for me. And by now, Rose, surely you have guessed? Yes, I am to be married!

Last weekend, at Wychwood, my dear sweet Edward asked me to be his wife. I can still hardly believe it and, as you can imagine, I am walking on air. Oh Rose, he is so handsome, so distinguished, so mature and kind, so . . . dare I say it? . . . so passionate. I would blush to speak of such things to any other, but you, Rose dearest, have always been my confidante. When I remember his kisses, his caresses, his sweet, importunate ardour I still cannot quite believe my good fortune, and only the ring (a splendid sapphire set with diamonds in white gold) which he placed on my finger with such tenderness reminds me that it is not a teasing dream. Do you remember in Dieppe how we joked and laughed about such a possibility? How we squabbled over which of them should be mine? Though even I never really dreamt that such a thing could happen. And now I am to be Mrs Edward Rivers, and mistress of Wychwood! My arm is quite black and blue with pinching myself to make sure that it is really true.

We have decided against a long engagement, as there is no reason for delay and Time trots hard with a young maid between the contract of her marriage and the day it is solemnized. *Besides, my dear Edward is so impatient and so passionate that I had no choice but to succumb and agree to be married as soon as the banns have been called.*

Phoebe has offered her house in Brompton Square for the wedding breakfast (so much more spacious and convenient than our own) and she and I agree that a small, select gathering is so much more chic than a large, ostentatious affair. I would love you to be my bridesmaid, dear Rose, if you can hurry home in time, and of course Georgina is invited too, but I fear that by the time you receive this letter it will already be too late. I have quite lost track of where you plan to be and the postal service is so uncertain abroad. How I wish you were here to share my happiness, dear sister, but what cannot be, cannot be. Sadly, dear Edward's mother cannot come at such short notice, either. She is old and set in her ways and never comes home, Edward says, before October.

I will miss you, Rose, but Sara, Maud and Charlotte will attend me and Phoebe's dear Marina will be a flower girl and dear little Georgie a page. As Papa is dead and we have no brothers or uncles, Mr Burgess has kindly consented to give me away. Robert and Phoebe have been so kind, so affectionate and with my own darling Edward's love ... Oh Rose, words elude me.

I am to wear ivory satin for my wedding gown, with a bouquet of lilies and a travelling outfit of cornflower blue because Edward says it reminds him of the first time he saw me, in Dieppe. He is so romantic. He will not tell me where we are to spend our honeymoon but afterwards, when we are married and installed in Wychwood, you must come and stay and I will invite dozens of eligible young men for you to choose from, just as we agreed years ago. Oh, Rose, be happy for me. You have your precious painting, I my precious Edward. I do believe at last our dreams are coming true! We are to be married in the Church of St Martin-in-the-Fields, three weeks from today!

Your ever-loving sister, Claire Millard.

There was a post-script from her mother, urging Rose to come home by the first available train, 'so that we can all be together for this joyful event.'

Rose read the letter once, twice, a third time while the blood drained from her face and her limbs trembled with such a turbulence of emotion that she could not speak.

'What is it, Rose?' cried Georgina, alarmed. 'Has someone died?'

Silently, Rose thrust the letter into Georgina's hands, while her mind churned with horror, anguish and a dreadful realisation that she had been duped. She stared unseeing across the Piazza del Campo and the splendid vista of marble and red-brick paving, empty now of people in the sleeping afternoon, and saw instead Claire's face at the dinner table at Wychwood when Rose and Edward had been together, Claire's smile when she took his arm on the railway station and walked away.

From the umbrella-shaded comfort of a pavement cafe across the square, she had been sketching the Mangia tower and the lovely facade of the palace, its glorious colours pure 'burnt sienna' in the sunlight of late afternoon, when Georgina had found her out, with the packet newly claimed from the hotel desk. Georgina had roused the dozing waiter and ordered iced coffee for them while, in all

215

innocence, Rose opened the packet, expecting the usual harmless chatter from home. Instead she had loosed a Pandora's box of treachery and betrayal.

'She knew we were in Siena,' cried Rose as the waiter set two frosted glasses on the table in front of them, amid the litter of Rose's crayons, sketch-book and paints. The viper! The scheming, cold-blooded viper. But that was only Claire after all. The law of primogeniture operating at its worst. Rose should have known it, seen it, and been on guard.

With a cool, detached part of her mind she noticed that the corners of the uppermost page of her sketchpad were already curling in the sun's heat. She would have to press them carefully flat again when she got back to the hotel. Somewhere a baby cried and was quietened. An old man in black trousers and waistcoat emerged, scratching and yawning, from the next door *trattoria* and began to take down the shutters from his windows. Pasta, tomato paste, olives and salamis, ham smoked almost black on the bone, green-gleaming olive oil. A cat crept surreptitiously from a nearby alley, positioned itself in the mellowing sunlight and began to groom its fur, as, with a grumbled *'Ecco, Signorina,'* the waiter returned to the somnolent depths of his cafe.

'She sent it to Florence on purpose,' resumed Rose. 'Deliberately! So that by the time it caught up with us it would be too late for me to ... to ...' Her voice broke on the edge of a sob which turned unexpectedly to rage as the memories crowded in to illuminate her innocent naïvete.

She remembered Georgina saying 'Claire said ...' 'Claire suggested ...' 'Claire thought ...' Remembered Claire flirting with Edward at the theatre and again at Wychwood, and burnt indelibly on her memory was that picture of Claire in her newest finery, smiling up at Edward on the railway station while the train Claire had engineered to remove her rival, duly removed her across the Channel and out of reach. God! I've been blind! she thought with horror. Blind and gullible and stupid. And I walked straight into her trap. Oh God! Rose buried her head in her hands and rocked with silent agony as jealousy tore her heart apart, with rage and hurt and seering, impotent despair. How *could* Claire do it? And how could *he*? After all he had said, all he had done. *You and I are flesh of one flesh ... I am cold without you* ... and now....

'I am sorry, Rose,' Georgina was saying hesitantly. 'Perhaps if we caught the very next train, tonight, we could get home in time for the ceremony?'

Rose stared at her, uncomprehending, then laughed, an empty, despairing laugh too close to tears. Georgina actually thought she was upset because she could not get home in time to attend the wedding!

'Oh, Georgina, you are so kind, so ...' Rose caught herself up on the teetering edge of breakdown. She must not tell Georgina. Georgina would feel responsible, would believe she had contributed to Rose's anguish, and her generous, joyous European tour would be tarnished for ever. With a long, shuddering sigh, Rose said only, 'Thank you. But I am better now. It is just that when I saw where she had addressed the letter, when she had a day by day itinerary of where we would be and knew we were here, in Siena, I was so angry and hurt. Claire is sometimes very selfish.'

Rose drank slowly from the ice-cold glass while she collected her turbulent thoughts, then went on, after a moment, 'She was always jealous of her position as eldest. She used to make us swear the silliest vows when we were children and she never could brook competition. I expect she thought I might take some of her precious limelight.' Or her husband, she added with bleak certainty.

That was her only comfort, bitter though it was. Had Claire been absolutely certain of her man, she would have gone for a six-month engagement, Westminster Abbey, the Archbishop of Canterbury, the lot. She might not have got them, but she would have moved heaven and earth in the attempt. More *chic* indeed. Rose had seen through that one instantly. All Claire meant was more certain.

'Oh dear,' said Georgina anxiously. Georgina was of that rare breed who never feel envy. But unhappiness she could understand. Remembering, Rose added enough of the truth to explain her emotion, without blighting their tour.

'To tell you the truth, Georgina, I suppose I am a little jealous. Edward Rivers can be very charming and I believe I might have said as much to Claire. I certainly said I would love to live at Wychwood.'

'I remember,' said Georgina with a beam of new understanding. 'And you got on so well with him that last weekend we spent there. Poor Percy was quite jealous. I know a lot of girls do rather sigh for Edward. He is really quite handsome and charming too, when he puts his mind to it. But you will soon get over your disappointment, Rose dear, and I know you will find it in your loving heart to be happy for your sister. It is fruitless to yearn for the unattainable and after all, it is not as if you had nothing else to occupy your thoughts. Besides, you said yourself that you do not intend to marry for years and there is no need to look so puzzled, Rose. Percy told me. He is very faithful ...' she finished, unwittingly reminding Rose that Edward Rivers was not.

'Like his sister,' said Rose, wearily. 'It seems to be a family failing. Anyone else would have crossed Harry Price-Hill off her list years ago.'

When Georgina did not answer, Rose went on with brutal directness, 'Everyone, even Guy Morton, has written to you, but has Harry? No. Does he miss you? No. Does your presence or absence make the slightest difference to him? No. Have you even the smallest expectation of his ever "coming to heel"? No, no and no. So why, Georgina dear, is it fruitless for me to yearn for the unattainable, as you so poetically put it, but not for you to do so?'

'Because ...' floundered Georgina, blushing, then she suddenly laughed with disarming frankness. 'To tell you the truth, Rose, it has become a habit with me, that is all. And you are quite right. I cannot urge you to forget unless I follow my own advice and do the same. So, if you will, I will. From this day forward you and I are heart-free. A pact?'

'A pact,' agreed Rose, outwardly composed. But the composure was for Georgina's sake. For Georgina's sake she sat at the cafe table, sipped her iced coffee and talked much as usual of the day's doings, of the news from home, both domestic and political, and of their own plans for tomorrow. She even managed to speculate with apparent calmness about arrangements for Claire's wedding. But when Georgina eventually left her, to return to the hotel, only the fading sun and the need to paint until the last light fled from the darkening square kept her sane.

That night Georgina peacefully slept, untroubled by dreams of her renounced fiancé Harry, but across the room Rose lay a long time awake, as the jagged knife of jealousy twisted deeper and deeper into her heart. In vain she reminded herself that it had been over between herself and Edward before she had left London. In vain she conjured up that scene in the studio when he had deliberately mutilated her painting. In vain she remembered her own words, 'I will never forgive you,' and his reply, 'Good. That makes us partners at least in hate.' Neither remembered injury nor remembered hatred could blot out the sweeter memory of his gentle, passionate kisses, his caresses, his ... she buried her face in her pillow to stifle the cry of anguish which threatened to tear her apart.

And within a week, a mere five days away, he and Claire would be man and wife. Somewhere in the town a bell chimed midnight and she whispered, 'No, four days ... four nights ... from now.' But that particular path was too agonising to embark upon. Desperately she searched her rag-bag memory for comfort and when she found it, murmured over and over, in silent prayer, as if by force of repetition the aim could be achieved. *We that did nothing study but the way to love each other ... must learn the hateful art, how to forget.'*

Four days. Three days. Two days. The waiting became unbearable.

They had planned to visit Gubbio and Perugia before travelling south to Rome, but suddenly Rose found the peaceful silences of the ancient Umbrian cities too achingly moving to contemplate: she wanted noise, crowds, busy activity, anything to blot out the desolation of her thoughts.

'Georgina, let's go straight to Rome? Please?' If Georgina read the agitation behind Rose's question, she made no comment.

'Of course. We can always visit the hill cities later, if we feel like it. Besides, I have wasted far too much time already idling and enjoying the countryside.'

Rose was overcome with remorse. 'I am so sorry, Georgina. I have been thoughtless and selfish, as usual. I should have realised that for your sculpture you need more than sunlight and shadow in Tuscany, or the cobbles of an ancient Umbrian street. You should have said.'

'Why, when I was enjoying myself so much? Besides, it would have made no difference. Remember Florence and the little work I did there? I had for my examples Cellini, Verrocchio, Donatello, the splendid bas reliefs of Andrea Pisano, even Ghiberti's glorious Gate of Paradise. But instead of spurring me to attempt work of my own, they merely emphasised my small talent and showed me my limitations. It is different for you, Rose. You seem to find subjects to draw and paint wherever you go. But I, who aspire to the lofty heights of sculpture, persuade myself that no time or place is quite right for me to try my hand, except what is round the next corner! But I will have no further excuse in Rome and I hereby solemnly declare that I will find out the first studio that will have me, and enrol myself for a spell of serious study. You must hold me to that, Rose.'

'I will.'

'Good. Then I will tell the maid to pack at once.'

While the bells of St Martin-in-the-Fields rang out for Claire Millard's wedding, the bells of St Peter's added their sonorous clamour to the street sounds of Rome as Rose led Georgina on a day-long, foot-sore, exhausting tour of the Eternal City, through the maze of twisting alleys and narrow streets, the small squares and ancient palaces of the old town, in and out of churches, museums,

219

galleries, up steps and down, past fountains, statues, monuments, and finally to the silent classical splendour of the ruined Forum. Only when the sun finally set and the last light left the sky did Rose consent to take a *carrozza* back to their hotel. Whatever the time of the ceremony, for Claire had not specified, it was over now, the deed irreparably done.

Georgina, thoughtful friend that she was, ordered dinner in their room, and champagne, 'To toast the happy couple – and to drown our sorrows.'

It was a large room with gilded cornices, faded fringes everywhere and equally faded pink brocade. Heavy tasselled cords looped back heavy old-rose curtains at the two tall windows and a similar weight of old-rose weighed down the two ornately carved beds, high as thrones above the polished tiles of the floor. There were faded Venetian rugs and, in the window, a table which the waiter draped in floor-length damask before setting out a suitable weight of silver cutlery, crystal glasses and a pair of dark red roses in a silver vase. The curtains, on Georgina's orders, were left open so that they could look out over the sparkling, lamp-lit darkness of Rome, with the great dome of St Peter's gleaming with unearthly splendour under the moon.

When the waiter had gone, leaving the newly-opened champagne bottle smoking in its ice-bucket, they dutifully raised their glasses to 'Mr and Mrs Edward Rivers', then to 'absent friends', to each other, and to a succession of increasingly frivolous objects, from Georgina's bicycle to Rose's sister Sara's battered china doll.

'Claire called her Rat-face,' remembered Rose, and added 'Rat-face herself.'

'To Rat-face,' echoed Georgina solemnly and shared out the last of the champagne.

After that, it seemed only sensible to send for a bottle of the *vino locale* to accompany the silver-covered dishes of *fettucini*, and *Saltimbocca alla romana*, a deliciously rich and aromatic preparation of veal, *prosciutto* and herbs, and the array of fruits and local cheeses.

As the evening progressed they became in turn lachrymose, giggling, scintillatingly trivial and solemnly profound until their troubles had receded to some separate plain, still visible, but unconnected to their own confused, though euphoric island the surface of which had a disturbing tendency to shift and settle when one least expected it.

'I like our little restaurant,' announced Georgina, mopping up the last of the *Saltimbocca* juices with a hunk of bread. 'It may be small, but the food is superb.'

'Not small,' corrected Rose carefully. 'Select. And so much more *chic* than all those large, ostentatious affairs out there,' and she waved an expansive hand towards the window to encompass the whole of night-time Rome. Georgina choked on her bread and had to be walloped several times, hard, between the shoulder blades while her eyes streamed with laughter. When at last she could draw sufficient breath she said, gurgling, 'What did you say in your telegram?'

'Oh, the usual,' said Rose evasively. 'Congratulations and so on. In Italian, of course.' She giggled. 'Claire does not speak Italian.' There had also been a post-script, but that was something between Edward and herself alone. 'What about you?'

'I didn't think of Italian,' said Georgina, crestfallen. 'I just put best wishes for your future happiness together.' They looked at each other for a precarious moment, remembering, then Rose raised her glass and said, deliberately, 'The happy couple – into hell with them!'

Georgina almost choked a second time, before countering with 'Here's hell to Harry, too!'

To help down the chilled *zabaglione*, they sent for a bottle of dessert wine in which they drank to Art, to Friendship, and to Italy.

'Let's stay here as long as we like,' said Georgina, much later. 'I have money enough and they do not need us at home. Nobody needs us. We are free ...'

'Free,' echoed Rose. They chinked glasses, looked at each other – and disconcertingly wept, each for her lost dream. When they had embraced, recovered, dried their eyes, laughed again with determined valour, Georgina raised an unsteady glass to 'The Future' and Rose answered with 'Success'. They talked of Florence which they had visited, of Venice which they had not, and of Rome, still barely touched upon.

'We will draw the Trevi fountain tomorrow,' said Rose.

'And the figures in the Piazza Nerona.' Georgina stood up, made her unsteady way across the room and collapsed triumphantly onto her bed.

'Navona,' corrected Rose and added, after a thoughtful pause, 'I think.' But Georgina was asleep.

With slow and careful concentration, Rose pushed back her chair, stood up, and made her way to Georgina's bedside. With equally careful concentration she pulled off Georgina's shoes, arranged her limbs more tidily on the bed, and covered her with a blanket. Then

221

she went back to the table, poured the last of the wine, and stood at the uncurtained window till the first pale light of dawn edged the rooftops with gold. It would be over now.

'*The day breaks not,* she said, with bleak finality, '*It is my heart.*' Then, at last, she went to bed.

CHAPTER 5

It was a most satisfactory wedding. The sun shone, the bells rang, the small, select gathering was as *chic* as anyone could wish. The wedding breakfast sparkled with champagne and laughter, crystal, diamonds, and exotic silks. Claire's beauty was much commented upon, her gown both envied and admired, and her family did not disgrace her. Mrs Millard was magnificent in black silk with velvet ribbons and, in deference to the occasion, pearls. Sara, Maud and Charlotte looked most satisfyingly pretty, without detracting from Claire's beauty or threatening her limelight and as for Edward, no bride could have asked for a more handsome or attentive husband. To be sure the 'surprise' honeymoon had proved a disappointment – nothing more exciting than a week at Wychwood, where Edward had arranged a shoot which could not be postponed, followed by a visit to Edward's other sister, Diana, in the Borders.

'It is such lovely countryside,' Phoebe assured her as she helped Claire change out of her wedding dress and into her new travelling outfit of pale blue cashmere trimmed with velvet. 'And the heather will be fully out.'

Neither piece of information removed Claire's annoyance. She had expected a sojourn in Bournemouth or Bath, even possibly across the Channel in Boulogne. Her wardrobe had been planned accordingly and did not include anything suitable for walking in the Borders, whether or not the heather was fully out.

Perhaps it was lingering annoyance which made her recoil from Edward's embrace in the railway carriage and remind him, rather sharply, not to disarrange her hat. She tried to mend matters, of course, and said, with a sweet, pleading smile, 'Wait till we are at home, Edward dear, in privacy.'

As Edward had reserved a compartment, with curtains discreetly drawn and a bottle of chilled champagne to greet them, he could have been excused for ignoring her protests. As it was, he shrugged, drew the cork, and said curtly, 'Very well.'

Claire knew she had annoyed him and set out to charm him accordingly, with talk of the wedding, of Wychwood, of the season's shooting and with questions about his sister's house in Berwick.

She is nervous, poor girl, he thought in excuse, and refilled her glass. Nervous and excited and painfully innocent. But so voluptuously beautiful . . . his eyes ran over the full curves of her breasts and hips, the tiny, hand-span waist, and those pouting lips, so generously soft and full. It would be a delight to explore that virgin territory, to teach her dalliance and laughing love. . . . With the third glass of champagne his irritation had dissolved in tender expectation.

The pony and trap awaited them at Wintelsham station, with a new knee rug for Madam and the harness bright with polish. At Wychwood there was a fire in the dining room and a cold supper, with claret for the Master and for Madam, should she prefer it, a chilled hock. There was a fire in the drawing room, too, and banks of fresh flowers – gladioli, dahlias and lovely, scented lilies, so that there was every excuse for lingering in such fire-lit, perfumed comfort. Edward drank his brandy, Claire her coffee. Edward smoked a cigar and watched her, in silence, as she sat, self-conscious and increasingly embarrassed, bereft of both conversation and excuse. The grandfather clock in the hall struck eleven, then the quarter hour, and still she sat, pretending unconcern.

Edward stood up, tossed his cigar end into the dying embers and doused the lamps. 'Time to go to bed, Mrs Rivers.' He took her unwilling hand and led her solemnly upstairs. At the door of the master bedroom he stopped, opened it, and stood aside for her to enter.

The counterpane on the high double bed had been turned back, her new silk nightgown laid ready on one side. A wood fire simmered in a glow of crumbling ash and the warm air was scented with pine and lavender. Behind a screen in one corner she glimpsed a wash stand and ewer and what she presumed to be a night-commode.

'The maid will bring hot water,' said Edward, tugging the bell pull. 'And help you undress. You know where the bathroom is, of course, but on some occasions it is better not to have to trail along a draughty corridor.'

She swallowed and mumbled something about being very tired.

'There is no need to look so nervous, darling,' he said softly, tilting her chin and kissing her lightly on the lips. 'My dressing room is through that connecting door. I will give you fifteen minutes to compose yourself, but I warn you, sixteen minutes will be too long.' Then he went into his dressing room and closed the door behind him.

For one panic-stricken moment Claire was tempted to turn the key, then reminded herself that after all he was her husband and he had his rights. Besides, hadn't Mrs Ruskin been able to divorce her husband because he had *not* exercised those rights in their marriage? Apparently a church ceremony was not enough and a marriage must be consummated to be truly binding. Claire was not at all clear what that consummation involved, but she was determined that her own marriage should be binding 'unto death'.

She remembered her mother's vague and lofty instructions to, 'Be guided by your husband, Claire, in all things. You are expected to be ignorant, he is not. Just remember you are his wife. You owe him obedience, and also a little pleasure. There is really nothing to worry about, as long as you remember that.' With those enigmatic instructions, Rebecca had changed the subject, to their mutual relief. Now Edward had told her to prepare for bed and she must obey.

The maid brought hot water, helped her out of her dress and stays, unpinned and brushed her waist-length hair, while all the time Claire kept a nervous eye over her shoulder in case he should come back unexpectedly and catch her in deshabille. But surely he would not come in as long as her maid was here? She took as long as possible to wash, then, in her nightgown, to cream her hands, buff her nails, and touch eau-de-Cologne to temple and throat. But at last she could find no further excuse. Besides, if she were too long, he would be angry. Reluctantly, she dismissed her maid and slipped into bed, pulling the sheets high under her chin. As an afterthought, she turned down the lamp. Then she lay feigning sleep, every sense alert, till she heard the door of the dressing room open and a soft voice say, 'Open your eyes.'

Obediently, she opened them – and quickly snapped them shut with a shudder of dismay. Edward Rivers was standing in the doorway of the dressing room *naked*.

'I said open them, wife. Remember you promised to obey me?' He was closer now, his voice teasing, and when she obediently opened her eyes a nervous crack she saw that he was standing beside her, barely a foot away. Her eyes slid hastily away from his nakedness and she blushed, while her mouth went dry with distaste. Then, before she could stop him, he had peeled back the sheets. He looked at her for what she could only think of as a gloating moment, then said, 'Take that garment off.'

She folded her arms tight across her chest and said, 'But Edward dearest, I embroidered it specially. Threading the ribbon alone took me a whole morning and . . .'

'And taking it off will take no time at all.' He undid the little pearl buttons one by one, then slid his hand inside her bodice and cupped her breast. She flinched involuntarily, but he kept it there,

225

murmuring 'You are my wife now, remember. Modesty is inappropriate.'

'Then at least,' she managed, fighting back her outrage, 'at least turn out the light.'

'And miss the sight of such beauty when it is a feast my eyes have longed for?' To her horror he turned the light up, till the bedroom leapt with shadows, then he peeled off her nightgown and left her with no retreat and no defence except to close her eyes, tight. He kissed her eyelids, then her lips, then the curve of her throat, saying softly, 'I can see that I must teach you everything, right from the beginning.' When he slid into bed beside her and began the lesson, she reminded herself firmly that it was her duty to 'give herself'. She only hoped it would not take long.

Afterwards she understood exactly why her mother had not explained. No woman could speak of such an embarrassing, uncomfortable and downright unseemly process, even to her daughter. Especially to her daughter. Claire shuddered with remembered affront. But at least the marriage was consummated now and she could sleep in peace. Putting everything else from her mind, she began to plan the dinner parties she would give now that she was mistress of Wychwood.

Later, when she slept, Edward stood at the unshuttered window, looking out into the darkness of woods and stars as he had done on that evening a year ago, and told himself that his wife was innocent, ignorant, modest, untaught. It would be better next time. She would relax and learn. She would welcome him, her love answering his, and give him rest. To his right, beyond the chestnut tree, was the dark block of the old brewery, with that love-haunted loft where he and Rose had hidden, locked in laughing silence, while Georgina coo-eed underneath. For a vivid moment he remembered Rose's lips, her warmth, her voluptuous, melting sensuality, her laughter, then he slammed the door hard, on memory. Rose had rejected him. For all her pretended love and desire, she had given him nothing, whereas Claire was his wife.

He turned to look at her asleep in the moonlit silence of that shadowed bridal bed. The fire had died long ago in colourless ashes and the night air was chill. The tumbled bed was a monochrome of sadness and loss; even the flowers on the little writing desk were reduced to different shades of grey. From the depths of the sleeping house came the slow, muffled chime of the grandfather clock ... one ... two. Was it only two o'clock? He had thought an age had passed since he opened the dressing room door and saw her feigning sleep. Suddenly he felt overwhelming loneliness.

226

Claire stirred, murmured something incoherent and settled again, but the movement had dislodged the sheets and bared one of her breasts. Her hair was a dishevelled cloud about her head, one arm carelessly outflung and that glorious dome of a breast rose, nipple-crowned and quivering with each sleeping breath. She looked young and vulnerable and achingly beautiful, like a sleeping goddess, her skin pale and smooth as marble in the eerie light. But a sleeper could be awakened. He crossed the room on soundless feet, slipped in beside her and kissed the soft skin of her throat. 'Claire?' This time, surely, love would answer love?

A hopeless, lonely, spent time later he lay drained and sleepless, staring unseeing at the ceiling, knowing with blinding certainty that no amount of teaching could turn marble into melting flesh, no amount of loving find answering love in an empty well.

He remembered his mother's letter in reply to his own: *Fool*, she had written, *If you had to marry one of the Millard girls you might at least have had the sense to choose the right one. No, I shall certainly not come home to your wedding. I shall not come home at all this winter. Or if I do, I shall stay in London with Phoebe. I only hope the money your wife brought you makes it worth it.'*

The wind sighed in the chestnut tree and somewhere a fox barked at the waning moon. At last, when the first birds signalled approaching day, he slipped wearily out of bed and moved, silent-footed, to his dressing-room, closing the door behind him. Ten minutes later he was in the darkened hall, drawing back the heavy bolt of the front door. He snapped his fingers, once, and his dog appeared, yawning and stretching, from the back regions. Carefully he opened the door, stepped outside, and closed it soundlessly behind him.

The morning was grey and sombre, the drab air mournful under the autumn mist which trailed sad fingers through the chestnut tree and beaded the tennis lawn with tears. The old brewery crouched like a neglected animal in the half-light and even the doves were silent. Then a cock crew indignantly in the kitchen yard and from somewhere across the meadow a cow answered, long and slow. Already the mist was lifting. Beyond the woods the stubble fields were pale gold ridged with red in the strengthening light, the brambles in the hedgerow purple-gleaming. And even as he watched, the dull, uniform brown of rosehip and elderberry brightened to scarlet. Thistledown quivered in the ditches and the bracken curled brown at the edges. They would be milking the cows already at Bird's farm, then the brimming churns would be loaded up onto the cart for the morning's delivery. All over the village and the neighbouring estate assorted jugs and churns stood empty on doorsteps or beside gateposts waiting to be filled, housemaids or housewives tended morning fires and kettles, babies cried, children gathered eggs or mushrooms, men took up axe or spade or harnessed horses, and the countryside yawned and stretched into another day. As always the beauty of Wychwood spread like balm over his wounded spirit until he felt almost whole again.

At least his beloved woods were safe now from debt.

Five minutes later he was striding through the familiar trees, his dog at his heels, seeking he knew not what, knowing only that he must walk, alone, till the clean wind blew the last shred of despair and yearning from his soul.

And in Italy Rose had the consolation of her Art.

Part 4

Wychwood, 1899

CHAPTER 1

Autumn in Venice was glorious. Lady Portia had welcomed them with abrasive impatience, handed over the keys with a generosity which gave them free run of the palazzo from balcony to wine-cellar until her return, and promptly left for England 'Where I suppose I must visit that idiot son of mine and inspect his wife.'

In fact, she stayed in Suffolk only long enough to greet Edward and Claire on their return from the Borders, to announce to the new Mrs Rivers, in public, 'Welcome to Wychwood, but of course, as you are well aware, it is your house now, not mine,' and to Edward, in private, in a voice sufficiently penetrating for the whole household to hear, 'How much did they pay you to take her, you great booby? Because if it wasn't a fortune, there is no excuse!' Then she ordered her bags to be packed and left again for the more familiar irritations of her daughter Phoebe's house and a winter season in London.

In Venice, mist hung low over the Grand Canal, twined wraith-like through the loggias of the Doge's palace and shrouded the island of San Giorgio Maggiore in mystery. 'We will go there,' said Rose one crisp December morning when, breakfast over, they dared the balcony of the palazzo and watched the water traffic weaving beneath them. 'I want to paint the palace from across the water – at twilight. Or perhaps with the winter sun reflecting every golden inch of its facade in the water of the canal. I want to catch and hold every tint of gold and blue and violet and ... oh, Georgina, isn't the light extraordinary? It is like nothing I have seen before. I see now why Whistler came so often, and why Turner saw everything here in a series of infinitely varied nuances of light and colour. I want to attempt what they did, to catch for ever on my canvas the very soul of the city.'

Georgina was silent, apparently studying the black wooden gondola, shaped like some ancient pointed shoe, which was creaking its way beneath their window, a heap of brilliant oranges in its maw. The gondolier shouted *'Buon giorno, signorina,'* and grinned. He deftly held his oar steady with one hand and with the other

231

snatched up a choice orange and offered it. '*Arancia! Belissima come la signorina!* You want?'

He seemed in no way offended when Georgina shook her head, but tossed the fruit back onto the pile and continued his creaking way in a ripple of slapping water, shouting his wares with musical resonance as he went.

'Isn't it glorious?' breathed Rose. 'Ruskin was surely thinking of Venetian architecture when he said *when we build, let us think that we build for ever.* There is a timeless beauty everywhere I look.'

'He was wrong about Whistler, though, wasn't he?' teased Georgina, throwing off whatever had oppressed her. 'Coxcomb, was it?'

'For *flinging a pot of paint in the public's face* – but how exquisitely he flung it and, as he said himself, with the knowledge of a lifetime behind his hand!'

'Knowledge is not always enough,' said Georgina quietly, but Rose was too absorbed in the winter beauties of the Grand Canal to notice. She saw a composition of gondola and mooring poles against the marbled facade of the buildings opposite, gilded by centuries of sun and reflected in lapping golden discs in the wintry water. Then a racing storm cloud swept away the sun and suddenly the Grand Canal was a turbulence of tossing wavelets, small boats dipping and dancing in a confused palette of rainbow colours. Rose turned to her companion with a face of awe and wonder. 'If I stayed here a lifetime,' she said, 'I could find something fresh to paint ten times a day.'

'Then we had better start at once,' said Georgina. 'I will order the gondola. You to your seascape, I to my clay.' Georgina, true to her promise, had found herself a tutor, in a studio behind the vegetable market. Sometimes Rose went with her, sometimes she stayed in the palazzo painting the view from the balcony, sometimes she went alone into the canal-threaded city, exploring churches, hidden squares and bridges, the Rialto, the Bridge of Sighs, San Moise, Santa Maria della Salute, the Fenice and Dogana and Accademia, but always she returned to the heart of the city, to the Doge's palace and the great Piazza San Marco.

It was here on a chill morning in late February that Georgina found her, at their usual table in the only pavement cafe still prepared to submit its furniture to the vagaries of winter weather. There were not many people abroad, but Georgina and Rose had been up since first light. Rose, well-wrapped against the cold in woollen shawl, thick woollen skirts and knitted mittens, was sketching San Marco with a clutch of resting gondolas at the waterfront and a brooding stretch of lagoon. It was the morning light she wanted particularly to capture. In the afternoon she was working on a different view, from the balcony of the palazzo d'Estarte – a gift for Lady Portia whose arrival was imminent. At the thought of that lady's return, Rose grew feverishly impatient with the short winter days. 'How shall I ever paint all I want to before she arrives?' she wailed, and crammed every waking moment with her work against the day when she must leave.

It had been a convenient arrangement. Rose and Georgina had kept the palazzo well warmed and aired, had made sure the servants did what they were paid to do and that Lady Portia's dog was fed, and in return had had a perfect base from which to pursue their artistic endeavours. The palazzo itself was spartan enough, even decrepit in parts, but with a gondola stage at the door and a vista of the Grand Canal, who could ask for more? Certainly not Rose, who had embarked on a series of canal scenes at different times of day and in all kinds of weather. Meanwhile Georgina had attended her classes with admirable perseverance, though when Rose asked to see the result of her endeavours as like as not Georgina would confess she had destroyed it, or decided to start again.

Now, however, Georgina had forgotten artistic frustrations in the pleasure of a packet of letters from home. 'Three for you, Rose, and three for me.' She tossed them onto the table, then disappeared into the cafe behind them to order *cappuccino* and fresh bread. Rose, making a space amidst her painting paraphernalia, opened the first letter.

Rose's mother wrote of Millards – profits still excellent, though there had been a hiccup in the market in January; of Sara's unhelpfulness – her nose always in a book, often not altogether suitable; of Maudie's chest – worse with the winter fogs; and of Charlotte's fondness for sweets *which Mr Blunt will indulge though I tell him not to, but then he is always so generous to the girls.* Then the usual plea to Rose to come home. *You are needed in Millards – the art work has sadly deteriorated since you left and we cannot use your old designs indefinitely. After all, you have been away almost a year. Besides, you could be such a help to Claire. The baby is due in June.*

Rose stopped abruptly, the letter trembling in her hand. A baby . . . but of course, it was inevitable when two people . . . She slammed the door quickly on that train of thought. Had she entertained any silly delusion that their union might have been platonic, the baby confirmed for all the world to see the idiocy of such an idea. Resolutely, she read on. *It would be nice if you were here to help Claire through her last tedious months. I am sure she would welcome your companionship. You always got on so well when you were children and now you could be such a comfort to her. She knows so few people at Wychwood, and Edward is often called to Town on business. It is not good for her to be alone at such a time, so I shall expect you home as soon as Lady Portia returns to Venice.* The phrase triggered a memory she thought she had successfully subdued: herself and Edward, vowing their love, and making that tryst which was never kept.

'What is it?' said Georgina, returning to the table. 'Bad news?'

'Oh no. At least ... I am to be an aunt in June.' Determinedly she smiled. 'But Mamma wants me to go home – and I am enjoying myself too much here.'

'Then we will not go,' said Georgina cheerfully. 'We will stay as long as we like. If only for this gorgeous coffee.'

The waiter had arrived with two cream-frothed and chocolate-dusted bowls of *cappuccino* which he placed carefully before them. With a sigh of pure content, Georgina closed her eyes and drank.

'Agreed,' said Rose, and followed suit. Then they returned to their letters.

'Rose!' Georgina looked up, white-faced and anxious, from the letter in her hand. 'Daddy is not very well.'

'Oh dear,' said Rose in quick sympathy. For all Georgina's pretended irritation, she knew her friend was fond of her father. 'What is it? His heart?'

'Mummy doesn't say. Just that ... that the doctor calls regularly and Daddy is making progress. I am not to worry, but, oh Rose, she asks when I am planning to go home. Do you think she means ...?'

'I don't know what she means,' said Rose calmly, reaching across the table to where Georgina had laid down her post. 'But I think you should read what Percy has to say before you decide anything at all. That is his writing, is it not?'

Rose had good reason to recognise it, for Percy the faithful had written regularly to her throughout her time abroad, in spite of her own regrettable lack of response, though she had answered on occasions, with brief, impersonal notes about the places they had seen, or her paintings. Now she saw, without surprise, that she too had a letter from Georgina's brother.

Dearest Rose, he began. *Forgive me for addressing you in such familiar terms, but you have long known how I feel about you and at times such as these I need your understanding and your sympathy more than ever. My father took a toss from that car of his and hurt his spine, as well as cracking a couple of ribs. Now he has an infection on the chest and I very much fear he may not recover. Though the doctor did not tell my mother so, he told me and I think Georgie ought to come home without delay. I have told her so myself and, dearest Rose, I beg you to come with her. I confess I have a selfish motive for asking you, as well as genuine anxiety for my father. You may have heard that affairs in South Africa are not going well and it seems likely that something not altogether pleasant might develop. As it is, I fear I may be drafted into the contingent due to go out there for consultation and once there, there is no saying when I may return. It is so long since I saw you, Rose, but my feelings for you are unchanged. If anything, they are stronger than ever. No distance, however great, can change my love for you, Rose dearest.*

There, I have said it and I am not ashamed. I love you. I will love you always. You told me once that I might hope, and I do, every moment of the day and night. But on the eve of what may be a departure into who knows what conflict, it would strengthen and sustain me so very much to see you again before I go. I will demand no promises and I will not stand in the way of your painting. On the contrary, for I love all your paintings, good and bad, (though there are few of those) because your hand painted them, your eyes studied them, your heart conceived them. Rose, I would not dare to write to you so freely in any other circumstances, but my heart is in turmoil. I only hope I am not required to leave for South Africa before (here he had written Father and crossed it out) *Georgina arrives home to be with Father. Come with her. Please? Besides, I think I may have a surprise for you. In any case, please see she comes home* quickly. *Your ever-faithful and devoted Percival Woodstock.*

Rose's eyes were grave when she had finished reading. She was sitting motionless, eyes downcast, considering the implications of Percy's letter, when Georgina cried out, 'Rose, I must go home at once!'

'Your father . . .?'

'Yes. Poor Daddy. Percy says he is so very ill. But not only that. After writing at great length about Daddy and Mummy and almost everything else under the sun, the dear boy tells me at the very end, where I might almost have missed it, that he might be sent abroad at any moment – to South Africa. Rose, I haven't seen my brother for almost a whole year. I could not bear it if I arrived home too late and found him gone.'

'No,' agreed Rose, 'that would be dreadful for you.'

'There is no need for you to come with me, Rose dear,' said Georgina awkwardly, 'though Percy will, of course, be disap-

235

pointed. But you know how he admires your painting and would never stand in your way and you said yourself you have so much left to do here. I am sure Lady Portia would be happy for you to stay on with her in the palazzo. She likes you, you know, but if you did not want to commit yourself to her company, I would be happy to rent rooms for you in Venice, anywhere you choose.'

It was a temptation. Rose knew Georgina was right and that Lady Portia would not turn her out. To stay on in Venice, with the sunlight glinting on the waters of canal and lagoon, the serenity of Venetian palaces and churches, the gondolas and busy water life, the tryptychs and murals, the richness of Venetian painting and always that matchless interaction of water and sky ... But she had learnt more than enough for the moment. It was time to consolidate and build. If she were to stay it must be for the rest of her painting life. Otherwise, it was merely postponing the inevitable. Yet when she thought of what awaited her at home, in England, it was a beguiling temptation, offering instead a life of wine and roses.

They are not long, the days of wine and roses. Memory pierced her with physical pain – and made up her mind for her.

'Thank you, Georgina, but I will come home with you. I have been away long enough. I cannot put off my return for ever.'

Nor her meeting with Edward Rivers. Percy Woodstock she could deal with, she hoped, without too much hurt, but Edward was a different matter. Claire, in every effusively domestic letter, asked when 'dearest Rose' was going to visit her and 'my darling Edward' at Wychwood. The visit could be avoided, but with Phoebe Burgess in London, a meeting one day was inevitable. It might as well be sooner as later. Besides, they had parted long ago and would meet as strangers, uninvolved. His marriage to Claire had cancelled all their vows. She had told him as much in her telegram, if he had the wit to see it. *And when we meet at any time again. Be it not seen in either of our brows. That we one jot of former love retain.* And of course she didn't – not one jot or proverbial tittle. So there was really nothing at all to worry about.

As for Claire, she was beneath contempt.

They called for the reckoning and while Rose put the final touches to her piazza scene, Georgina made the necessary travel arrangements, informed the servants, left suitably effusive explanations and apologies to greet Lady Portia on her arrival, and sent telegrams home.

'I do hope we reach home in time,' said Georgina anxiously as they boarded the train for London the following morning. 'I could not bear it if darling Percy sailed before I could say goodbye.'

'No,' agreed Rose. But it will be far easier for me, she thought, if he does.

Neither of them voiced that other fear, concerning Mr Woodstock, but at least they were speeding home without delay.

CHAPTER 2

Wychwood was prospering. With his wife's money and his wife's shrewd housekeeping, Edward had to admit that the change was remarkable. In their six months of marriage Claire had proved to be a determined woman and a born manager. She revelled in her new position as Edward's wife, and intended him to move from the wings of county society into the forefront, with all decorous speed. Edward should become a J.P. and possibly even an M.P. (though that might take him too often up to Town, she said sweetly, unless of course they bought a town house). But certainly she intended that he, and she, should achieve prominence. Claire was adept at getting other people to do what she called 'little favours' for her and several of her dinner parties (most correct and elegant occasions) had resulted in benefits of one kind or another to Edward's estate. Yet as the fences were repaired, the broken gates replaced, the peeling paint renewed and even the woods trimmed and tidied, he felt, illogically, that something of the old charm had been destroyed. His estate was spruce, clean, prosperous-looking, even elegant, but it felt strangely empty, as if it were no longer his. He almost missed the worries of those tangled, debt-ridden times when Wychwood was a beloved ache, deep in his heart, and when he had no wish nor means to go up to Town. Now, increasingly, on one pretext or another, he spent days at a time at his Club.

In public, Claire was a model wife, elegant, efficient, well-informed, even witty on occasions, while at the same time deferring to Edward's superior knowledge and experience. In private she could be petulant and irritable, especially if things had not gone her way, and he had long since ceased to look for any answering response to his love-making. Yet if she was not enthusiastic, she was compliant. However, since the confirmation of her pregnancy Claire had been increasingly prone to plead fatigue or a female malaise when bedtime approached. Then, when they had been married a mere four months, she actually said, in response to his tender approaches, 'Will it take long, dear? I am really very tired.' After that, he had renewed acquaintance with the discreet establishment he had patronised in his bachelor days. But though his physical needs were adequately catered for, the emptiness remained.

It was as he came out of this same establishment, in a street behind Leicester Square, on a bleak evening at the end of February that he bumped, literally, into Harry Price-Hill.

It was a moonless night of thick cloud and insidious fog. The gas lamps strung at intervals along the street were merely smudges of pale light in a greater gloom in which passers-by were no more than black shapes, moving hurriedly for home. Harry himself looked incongruously festive in evening dress, complete with flamboyant evening cloak and opera hat. His starched white shirt front gleamed in the lamplight, as did his teeth as he grinned at Edward's shock.

'You sly devil!' he cried, with a delighted slap on the back. 'So used to your home comforts now that you can't do without it for even a night, eh? You are a dark horse – or should I say stallion? But who would have thought to see my virtuous cousin emerging from a house of ill repute? Unless, of course, you were reading the inmates a sermon? I well remember that time in Venice when ...'

'Shut up, blast you!' interrupted Edward, 'And mind your own business.'

'Sorry, old chap. No offence. Glad to see you're human like the rest of us.' But he looked at Edward with surprise and a hint of puzzlement. Edward had not been married six months and no one could say his wife was plain. 'What about a drink to show there's no hard feeling? I would advise you to take me up on the offer. You might not get another chance.'

'What do you mean by that?' growled Edward morosely. He already regretted his outburst. Harry, after all, was sufficiently urbane not to have thought twice about the incident if Edward had not drawn attention to it by losing his temper. He should have smiled, made some light-hearted quip, slapped Harry on the back and been the one to offer the drink. Then Harry would have forgotten the whole thing. Now he would probably come out with the story at some drunken party and in no time it would be all over Town.

'I mean,' said Harry, with a comically martyred look, 'that the Sword of Damocles dangles. Georgina is on her way home and you know what that means. Mother will arrange all sorts of painfully worthy get-togethers, Georgina will look embarrassed, I will feel guilty, and end up behaving worse than before. My only hope of reprieve is her old man's illness. No ill-will to the old buffer you understand, but it might keep her safely in the country. If not, it will be the West Indies for me this time if I don't do the decent thing. Or Tasmania.'

239

'Then why don't you do the decent thing?' said Edward irritably while his mind turned over the implications of Harry's news. Claire had made no mention of her sister's return. But then Claire was surprisingly reticent on the subject of Rose.

'Me?' Harry roared with laughter. 'Can you see me married? Let alone to dear old Georgie. It would be like marrying the family nanny. Bordering on incest, old man. All right for poets and all that, but not for yours truly. So,' he glanced from side to side in a comical parody of a conspirator on the run and said, 'I may have to flee the country if things get too hot. I could always enlist, of course. Trot off to South Africa to defend the flag and all that. Might even be quite a lark. But tonight, a certain little party is waiting for me backstage at a certain theatre, not a hundred yards from here. Then I am going to find the crowd and make a night of it while I still have the chance. Want to come along? No? Oh well, I suppose you married men haven't the stamina.' With that parting shot Harry strolled off, whistling cheerfully, into the night.

Belatedly Edward hailed a hansom and repaired to his club where he ordered brandy and subsided morosely into the dark leather silence of the lounge. One or two other members sat similarly sombre over brandy or port or lingering cigars, each lost in his private thoughts. If Georgina was coming home, he thought, staring into the molten depths of the glass, then Rose Millard would come with her and there would be no way out of it for either of them. She would come to Wychwood. He would have to greet her as a sister-in-law, kiss her affectionately on the cheek, sit down to meals with her, walk with her, talk with her.... But he was letting his imagination run too freely. She had been cool enough on Victoria station a year ago and so had he. When they met this time, it would be as cold strangers. He had absolutely nothing to worry about.

CHAPTER 3

Rose refused to go to Wychwood. 'Percy Woodstock has found a gallery for me,' she explained to her mother. 'And if I am to have the smallest chance of assembling enough paintings before May, then I must work in the studio at every spare moment.'

'Really Rose, you are extraordinary!' declared Mrs Millard. 'A whole year away and you cannot even spare the time to visit your favourite sister, and in her condition, too. You know very well she cannot visit you. Travelling would be most unwise. I would have thought the very least you could do would be to pay her an extended visit and divert her with tales of your travels.'

'She has quite enough diversion as it is,' said Rose, 'with a husband and home of her own. She has managed perfectly well without me for a year. A few more weeks will not break her heart. Claire has got what she wanted. She has no need of me.'

'Don't be so unfeeling, Rose. Every woman in her condition needs a sister.'

'Then she can have Sara,' retorted Rose and refused to be moved. 'I will go nowhere till my exhibition is over.'

That had been Percy's surprise. He had been at Victoria station to meet them off the boat train and when he had swept Georgina off her feet in a bear hug of welcome, taken Rose's hands, adoringly, in his and kissed her on the cheek, he linked an arm with each of them and led them to the waiting carriage, insisting that he must take Rose home before conveying Georgina to her father's house.

'I told your mother I would meet you,' he explained, blushing. 'The truth is, I wanted to see you alone before Georgie and I go home. No, Georgie, there is no need for you to leave us,' he cried, catching his sister by the waist and holding her tight. 'It is not a secret from you – but I thought Rose would prefer to hear what I have to say in private.'

Oh dear, thought Rose with apprehension. Surely he cannot be going to propose to me in front of Georgina, on Victoria station? 'And what is that, Percy?' she said in as matter-of-fact a voice as she could manage. She must have overdone it, for the joy left his face and he looked suddenly unsure.

241

'Just that ... it is not definite yet and you need not feel obliged in any way at all, but ... well, I came across a fellow – old school friend of mine, came into a bit of money, decided to start up his own gallery – and, well, I said I knew just the thing for his opening exhibition.' He paused, and this time he could not keep the excitement from his voice. 'A talented young artist, just back from Venice, with a superb collection of paintings. Rose, I have reserved the gallery for *you*.'

She stared at him in open-mouthed, speechless astonishment, and after a moment, when she still made no comment, he said uncertainly, 'I thought it was what you wanted. It is, isn't it?'

'Of course it is, you great booby!' She kissed him with spontaneous gratitude. 'I could not believe my ears, that is all. It is a dream come true.'

Percy blushed crimson, stuttered, 'Oh I say,' and retreated into euphoric silence while Georgina leant her head against his shoulder saying, 'You are a dear, generous brother, the best in the world.'

But Georgina's words shook Rose out of her dream world into cold reality. 'But, Percy, what about the gallery fee? Surely they will not lend me their walls for nothing?'

'Call it my investment in your talent.'

But Rose was beholden enough to him already. 'No, Percy. I will not do it if I cannot pay my way.'

'But you will, Rose, when you sell your pictures.'

'And suppose no one buys any, then what?'

'But they *will*,' cried Percy and Georgina together and Rose allowed herself to be persuaded.

Since then Rose's happy excitement had changed to apprehension and a gathering conviction that none of her paintings was worthy of showing to anyone, let alone the critical London public. 'Not one, Georgina,' she wailed a week later when her friend had taken a day's respite from her father's sickbed to come up to Town. 'Look at them! All pitiful, amateur daubs unworthy of the pavement, let alone a public gallery. What am I to do? I cannot possibly exhibit these!'

'Yes you can,' said Georgina calmly, running her critical eye over the assorted canvases and watercolour sketches that Rose had propped against the studio wall. 'You must group the Venetian ones together at one end, the London ones at the other, the French in the middle. It will be like a rainbow, from muted grey at one end to glorious blazing gold at the other with a score of brilliant butterfly shades between. You have a clear six weeks and eight till opening day – time to put the finishing touches to all of them. You will need

242

to have them properly framed of course. I will take care of that. There is a man I know at the Slade who is excellent. Just tell me which are ready to go and I will take them round to him at once. There will be the catalogue to do, but I will help with that too and in any way I can, if only to take my mind off poor Daddy.'

'How is he?' asked Rose with contrition. She had almost forgotten old Mr Woodstock's illness.

'Cantankerous as ever, the poor pet, and no better. Mummy has a dreadful time with him, but I do what I can. His lung is punctured, apparently. Dr Allen says there is nothing to do but wait now, and pray ...'

When Georgina had gone, taking three of Rose's canvases with her, Rose stared thoughtfully at what remained – all landscapes of one kind or another – before moving resolutely to the far corner of the studio where a large canvas stood, face to the wall and shrouded in a piece of tattered bedspread. Rose had not looked at 'Inspiration' since her return, knowing what memories it would revive, but now, remembering all Georgina's kindness and loving friendship, she determined to do as she had always intended and, if it was worthy, exhibit 'Inspiration' too.

It was better than she remembered, the damage invisible to anyone who did not know, and, she thought critically, seeing it with new eyes after a year's absense, not at all bad. Bits of the background could be bettered: the marble column for instance, looked more like painted wood, and that table leg was not quite right.

Clearly from the past came that derisive voice saying 'So-called art! Look at that ridiculous table-leg!' With a long, shuddering breath Rose made her decision. She would work on 'Inspiration' till every detail was perfect – and make it the centre-piece of her exhibition. That, in some obscure way, would settle the account. He might have been right about the table-leg, but she would show him and all the world that he was wrong about the 'so-called'. And she would not go to Wychwood, or anywhere else, till every picture was perfected, framed, labelled and hung in place.

'No, Mamma,' she said when Mrs Millard raised the subject yet again. 'How many times must I tell you? My art comes first.'

'Even before your sister and her unborn child?'

'First,' repeated Rose, unmoved.

'I never thought a daughter of mine could be so heartless!' Mrs Millard glared at Rose with open dislike. 'I don't know what your Papa would have said.'

'I do!' cried Sara. 'He would say Rose is quite right. And it is Claire who is heartless. She sent Rose away on purpose so that she could steal Edward for herself and ...'

'Sara! How dare you say such wicked things! Go to your room at once and stay there. As for you, Rose, I despair. Have you no family feeling? Whatever will people think when they learn you have been *weeks* in London and have not been near your sister since her wedding? They will call you a heartless, selfish Bohemian – or worse! I *require* you to visit Claire, do you hear me?'

Rose, however, remained obdurate and it was Sara who nobly went with Mrs Millard to Wychwood when Claire's letter arrived, requesting company.

I am so dull here, Mamma, she wrote, and the weather is so dreary. All the crops are late and the trees scarcely in bud, let alone in blossom. I declare I think spring will never come and Edward is forever discussing ploughing and winter barley and such like with Guy Morton so that I hardly see him. Even dear Phoebe has deserted me. That sly Mademoiselle suddenly gave a week's notice and left. A week's notice after how many years in the family? And then under false pretences. But she made a profit, apparently, on the stock exchange – with Robert's help of course – selling out of South African gold and into something else before everyone else did. I do hope Robert advised you to do the same, Mamma. Anyway, the odious Mademoiselle has bought her precious school in France. She offered Phoebe's Marina free schooling there, apparently! The cheek of the woman – though Phoebe says she may well accept the offer when the time comes. I might even consider sending a daughter of mine there myself one day. After all, Mademoiselle owes me a favour and a good French accent is so important, don't you agree? But of course Phoebe cannot leave London till she has found a suitable replacement.

Percy Woodstock's father is no better. Opinion has it that he will not last out the spring, and then young Percy will be quite a catch. If he has not been transported to South Africa by then. They say there will be trouble there and that extra soldiers may be sent. Guy Morton is in the Reserves, apparently, and if things get really bad he may be called upon to go too. That would be a blow to dear Edward. But enough of that. Percy Woodstock is still with us and I wonder whether it would be bad form, in view of his father's illness, to ask him and Georgina over to dinner one day? Perhaps when Sara is staying here? Or Rose, of course, if she ever deigns to come. Dear Mamma, I really do not mind who comes as long as someone does. There is no society to speak of hereabouts at this time of year and I am reduced to taking tea with the vicar's wife for diversion. Of course, everything will be different when my child is born and I am free to travel about once more. Meanwhile, I beg you, Mamma, to spare a few days to visit me

244

or I declare I shall go mad with boredom. Your affectionate daughter, Claire Rivers.

Sara raised no objection when it was decided she should visit Wychwood, with her mother. She prepared for the visit with a good grace and made no mention of classes missed (she had a Greek tutor now) or studying still to be done. 'I am doing this for you, Rose,' she confided, as she kissed her sister goodbye. 'You can rely on me. And I promise I will be back in time for your exhibition. I know it will be the best in London.'

'I doubt it,' said Rose honestly, 'but I hope it will not disgrace me. Or the gallery.'

'Mind you keep the young ones in good order,' warned Mrs Millard. 'Maudie is to be sure to take her tonic and Charlotte must practise at the pianoforte every day. Do not let Annie be wasteful with the housekeeping and remember you are to run your eye once more over the new catalogue. I am still not happy about the Ladies Section. Some of the drawings are rather daring. Finally, if you are worried about anything at all, consult Mr Blunt and he will deal with it. He is such a help.'

'It is all right, Mamma,' soothed Rose, with an edge of irritation to her voice. 'After all, you are only going away for a week.'

At Wychwood the week began badly. On Monday it rained steadily till well after mid-day. Ditches at the roadside filled and spilled over onto the rutted surfaces so that the highways swam with rivulets and brimming potholes. The wheels of the brougham which met them at the station showered mud in great arcs behind them and the rain blew in under the roof so that both Mrs Millard and Sara were mud-spattered and dishevelled by the time they arrived at Wychwood. The fire had been smoking all day and the latest kitchenmaid had been caught stealing raisins. Claire had dismissed her on the spot, but as a result had a nervous headache and was decidedly irritable. It was the third maid she had dismissed in as many weeks and she knew Edward would disapprove. Edward himself had been called out to inspect one of the cottages at Wychwood Bottom where the thatch was leaking so badly, they said, that a child had almost drowned in its cradle.

'Rubbish, of course,' said Claire as she poured tea. 'They only complain in order to get their rents reduced. But Edward is so patient with them, I tell him it is no wonder the estate is out of pocket when he is forever paying for repairs other landlords would make them do for themselves. But that is dear Edward all over. Such a philanthropist.'

245

At that moment dear Edward joined them and the talk turned to plans for the week. 'If ever this dashed rain stops,' he said, glowering through the streaming window at the waterlogged lawn, 'we might take a spin over to Cambridge and show Sara the colleges.'

'Oh, I would love that,' cried Sara, her eyes suddenly sparkling so that the introverted look quite vanished.

'Out of the question, Edward dear,' said Claire, handing her mother the plate of scones. 'You know I cannot travel.'

'I was not suggesting that you did,' said her husband. 'Presumably you could manage to survive one day here alone? If this business in the Transvaal develops much further, the Government will have to send more troops and that is sure to mean a run on good horses. It would be wise to buy in a few while we can and there is a fellow in Maddingley with a fine pair of greys for sale. I thought I could drop Sara off at Girton, which is practically next door, and collect her when my business is done.'

'Yes please, Edward,' said Sara eagerly. 'I have written to Miss Welsh and she says I am welcome to talk to her at any time.'

'Then there is really no hurry is there,' said Claire sweetly. 'We can arrange your trip on some other occasion.' But Sara had recognised the old light in her sister's eyes and the old, remembered hatred flooded back.

'Of course, Claire dear,' she said, with deceptive meekness. 'I was forgetting how clever you are at arranging such things for other people. Look how carefully you arranged everything for Rose to go abroad and she knew nothing about it till the very last minute. I wonder even now if she realises it was all your doing and not really Georgina's at all.'

'Is this true, Claire?' Edward's face was taut with shock, his whole body rigid with the need to conceal the turbulence of emotion Sara's words had unleashed.

'I declare I don't know what Sara means,' said Claire, but her cheeks were flushed and her disarming laugh was decidedly brittle. 'It was nothing to do with me at all.'

'Then I am glad to hear it,' said Edward gravely and turned away, but with a feeling of growing dread he wondered if Sara had indeed spoken the truth. If so, it would explain so much.

'Perhaps I was mistaken, Claire dear,' said Sara meekly. 'Perhaps merely *thy wish was father to that thought.*'

'Sara!' reproved her mother sharply. 'You are being precocious.'

'Then I am sorry, Mamma.' Sara smiled in sweet apology and a hunted look came into Claire's eyes. She glanced quickly at Edward, but he was standing at the closed french windows, his back to the room, apparently studying the waterways of the lawn. She knew beyond doubt that Sara was up to something. The child had never looked more innocently lovely. She was wondering whether to feel suddenly faint, or to have an attack of diplomatic heartburn, when Sara spoke again and it was already too late.

'Not an altogether apt quotation, I admit,' she said humbly. 'You could do much better, Claire, and always could. I remember how you and Rose used to quote endlessly from more poets and drama- tists than I even knew existed. You were both so clever, and under- stood each other so well.'

Claire began to relax, her supremacy restored. She reached out for the silver cake knife and the caraway sponge – and was arrested in mid slice by Sara's next words.

'Even that telegram she sent you for the wedding was perfectly chosen. How did it go? *Tanti felicitaziones* of course and then *I am glad yea glad with all my heart.* Such a beautiful sonnet. I have been studying Drayton and ...'

'I thought you had to concentrate on your Greek,' interrupted Claire, spearing Sara with a look of venom. But for the first time in their lives together Sara noted an edge of uncertainty to what the sisters called Claire's primo-stare.

Satisfied, Sara said meekly, 'Yes, I do. Thank you so much for reminding me.' She stood up, excused herself politely and declared she would go to her room, 'to study a little before dinner'. In the doorway she paused, turned, and said, 'When the rain stops, Edward, please will you take me to Cambridge?'

Without turning his head, he said, 'Yes.'

Edward Rivers' thoughts were in turmoil. Sara's apparently inno- cent words had stirred a hornet's nest of memories, in the foremost of which was Rose, in that Kensington studio, protesting her ignor- ance of the planned trip, declaring that Georgina had planned it as a surprise. He remembered Rose's passionate, shameless letter which he had torn into a thousand shreds – and her anguish and defiance when he had desecrated her painting. He remembered that other time in her studio when he had said, *Since there's no help, come let us kiss* ... and afterwards she had capped the quotation with the next line. But didn't the sonnet continue *And I am glad, yea glad ...?*

'Excuse me,' he said to Mrs Millard. 'Like Sara, I have work to do before dinner.'

'But Edward dear, you have not finished your ...'.

He shut the door on Claire's sentence and walked unseeing past

247

the massed white hyacinths in the Chinese bowl, the gleaming dinner gong, the polished Jacobean chest, and on to his library. There he went straight to one of the bookshelves which completely covered the four walls from floor to ceiling and took out a volume of Elizabethan sonnets.

> *... yea glad with all my heart*
> *That thus so cleanly I myself can free.*
> *Shake hands for ever, cancel all our vows,*
> *And when we meet at any time again,*
> *Be it not seen in either of our brows,*
> *That we one jot of former love retain....*

When he had read to the end, Edward remained a long time in silence. Then he snapped the book shut, threw open the door, shouted for his dog and strode, hatless, into the drenching rain.

It was two days before the rain stopped and Edward took Sara to Cambridge. They spoke little. Edward's business went well. Sara's likewise. Her name was now on the waiting list for Girton College. The return journey passed in silence. Then, as the carriage turned into the gateway of Wychwood, Sara said, 'Did you know Rose is to have an Exhibition, in a Bond Street gallery? It opens in May and will be very good.'

CHAPTER 4

Affairs in the Transvaal, as Edward Rivers divined, were not going well. The long history of discontent between the English-speaking colonists and the Dutch-speaking colonists, who had been 'sold' by Holland into British rule, with the territory, after the Napoleonic wars, was coming to a head.

The main bone of contention was that of rights for the Uitlanders, or foreigners, who had flooded into the Transvaal with the gold rush, and the period of residence required before they could claim equal voting rights in the Transvaal election. Correspondence was exchanged, the stately dance of diplomacy played out to the last manoeuvre, until finally it was agreed that President Kruger and Sir Alred Milner, High Commissioner for the Cape, should meet in conference in Bloemfontein, in May.

Meanwhile, South African shares were depressed, British subjects in Johannesburg petitioned the Queen to urge their interests and questions were asked in the House about increasing the military forces in South Africa. More had not yet been asked for, was the reply, but more were being sent.

Captain Percy Woodstock was not, after all, posted to the Cape. Harry Price-Hill's mother, it was said, knew someone who knew someone on the relevant Board and in view of Mr Woodstock's decline, did not want poor Georgina to be left unsupported when the sad time came. Harry himself, it was left unsaid, could not be relied upon to step in and offer a 'fiancé's' support to the bereaved and rather than let the family down by such open dereliction on Harry's part, steps should be taken to ensure Percy's presence. So whether by coincidence, or by discreet string-pulling in the necessary quarters, Percy was sent to Aldershot instead, where a rigorous programme of training, for infantry and cavalry alike, was already in progress. No one, it appeared, was optimistic about the outcome of the talks and it behoved Her Majesty's army to be ready for whatever might ensue.

'Percy says there is sure to be war before the year is out,' said Georgina worriedly, 'and if there is, then whether Daddy is ill or not, Percy will have to go.'

Meanwhile, Rose was glad Percy's duties kept him occupied in Aldershot. She had quite enough to do completing her paintings in time for the opening without his declarations of love to contend with. He had been good about it, recognised her priorities, assured her he understood, but his silent devotion unnerved her almost as much as his words would have done till she dreaded his visits, rare though they became. She spent every waking hour in Georgina's studio now. Georgina herself travelled to and fro between studio, gallery and her father's bedside, with little time for her own pursuits.

'I do not mind in the least,' she told Rose. 'Mummy needs me to take turns nursing Daddy, so that she can rest. He can be very trying, poor dear. He does so hate to be helpless, but he treats the nurses so badly that none of them will stay. Except Nanny, of course. She is a real brick and she is why I can still come up to Town and make sure everything is ready for your Opening.'

Rose did not answer. As the day approached when her paintings would be exposed to the coldly critical eye of the world she felt her confidence dwindle and die. Percy planned a champagne opening, with smoked salmon and caviar. He had not only invited all the art critics in London, but also all his relatives and friends, as well as all hers, including Edward Rivers and Claire. They would not come of course, she told herself over and over, not with Claire so near her time. But the possibility, remote though it was, lingered at the back of her mind and would not be squashed.

Then, a week before the day of the Opening, Mr Woodstock died.

'You will cancel the Opening, of course,' said Mrs Millard, as if it were a foregone conclusion. 'And when you speak to Miss Woodstock, do remind her, discreetly of course, that Millards can supply all her mourning needs "With the maximum sympathy and the minimum delay". Such a clever tag. We have Mr Blunt to thank for that one, the dear man.'

'I will do nothing of the kind,' snapped Rose, appalled by her own reactions. She was genuinely sorry for old Mr Woodstock, though as Georgina had said several times in the last fortnight, at least death would put an end to his pain. And, remembering her sadness when her own father died, she genuinely grieved with her friends. But at the same time a selfish voice inside her cried over and over, why now? Why not next week, when my Opening would have been safely over? Because of course, as her mother said, the Opening would have to be cancelled. And without an Opening, who would bother to come?

She had reckoned without Percy's devotion and Georgina's loyal support.

'Of course we will not cancel it,' declared Percy, when he called at the studio the following day. He was white-faced and sombre and already in deep mourning. 'Georgina cannot leave her mother or she too would be here with me to assure you that everything must go ahead as planned. It is Freeman's gallery after all, not mine, and there will be no disrespect. Though you will excuse us, I know, if Georgina and I stay away. The funeral is to be the day before and there will be family matters to attend to.'

'Of course, Percy dear.' She had already expressed her sympathy, in words and letters, but his dignified sorrow moved her afresh and she realised, for the first time, that he was now head of his family, and carrying the responsibility well. The thought awed her a little and she looked at him with new respect. 'But are you sure you would not rather cancel everything? It seems so unfair to celebrate when you and Georgina are ...'

'Certainly not,' he interrupted. 'After all, it is entirely thanks to the dear old man that I am here at all and not in South Africa. His suffering would have been in vain if we cancelled everything now.'

Before his devious logic, Rose was silent, and Percy went on, with solemn emphasis, 'I always intended to launch you with style, Rose, and it will still be done. Everyone will come, I promise you.'

'If they can spare time from the Guildhall Gallery where they can see real pictures,' she said. 'Turner and his contemporaries attract 4,000 visitors a day.'

'There you are then,' said Percy, undaunted. 'They will come and see your pictures, too. Especially on the opening day. It is going to be the party of the year, even without Georgie and me, and I count on you to dispel the gloom and make it so. For my sake and Georgina's, if not for your own.'

But old Mr Woodstock's death had cast a shadow over everything and Rose could not even summon up the smallest smile. 'At least the champagne will be good,' she said, looking bleakly round the studio where the last half dozen of her paintings stood framed and ready to be transported to New Bond Street, 'And the frames. The public, if they come at all, will have *something* good to look at.'

'Nonsense. It is the pictures inside that count. Don't look so dejected, Rose. We have all of us invested too much in the venture for you to back down now, so cheer up and make the best of it. Parcel up those last canvases while I fetch a cab. I will take you to the gallery myself, though I am afraid I cannot stay as I have an appointment with the family solicitor. But Freeman will be there, and all you have to do is decide the final hanging order.'

Hanging order is right, thought Rose with dread. And it is my neck in the noose. But at least the Woodstock funeral would ensure that no one came from Wychwood.

It was the season for openings. The usual Vernissage in Paris, the Royal Academy at Burlington House, a host of smaller exhibitions, and even a motor car show at the Crystal Palace. At the Royal Academy, the sculpture was pronounced 'good', the portraits and landscapes 'average' and the figure subjects 'somewhere below it'. The exhibition of Turner and his Contemporaries attracted, as well as the 4,000 daily visitors, the carping criticism that the adjective 'contemporary' had been misused. At the Paris Vernissage the atmosphere was 'painful in the extreme' owing to the crowds and the dust, the paintings unmentioned.

In New Bond Street, the exhibition of works by R. A. Millard attracted a large and noisy crowd on the opening day, due in large part to the offer of free champagne, a brief paragraph in *The Times* on a 'promising debut by this talented young artist', no doubt as a result of the same free offer, and a steady trickle of passers-by thereafter, tempted first by the portrait in the window and then by the smell of free coffee from inside.

That had been another of Percy's ideas. His anxiety that Rose's exhibition should be a success had tapped a surprising vein he did not know he possessed and already several of her smaller sketches had been sold. Others, by his orders, were not for sale, including the oil painting in the window. In a heavy gilded frame, on a small easel, alone against a background of draped velvet, was the portrait of a girl at a littered table, with sunlight slanting in on her bent head, a marble column behind her. It was a picture of arresting beauty, tranquillity and resolution and no one walked past the window without hesitating, if only momentarily, in order to look at it again.

On an evening in early June, when the exhibition was drawing to the end of its fourth week, a handsome man of medium height, well-dressed, with the look of a country gentleman about him, passed the window, hesitated, turned back, and stood a long time studying the portrait. Finally, as if coming to an unwilling decision, he opened the door and stepped inside.

May had been a dreary month. Even when the sun shone and blossom-laden breezes carried the promise of summer to come, Edward Rivers seemed restless and dissatisfied. Claire put his restlessness down to her approaching lying-in and was by turns irritated and smugly complacent. It was only proper that he should be anxious on her behalf, but at the same time he ought to think of her own anxieties and sufferings and do his best to divert her.

This he increasingly failed to do. He attended the Woodstock funeral, quite properly, without her but when, the following day, she wanted a detailed description of the event and the people there, he dismissed her with a curt, 'It was a family funeral, dignified and sad. That is all.' When she persisted, demanding a description of Mrs Woodstock's and Georgina's gowns, he slammed out of the room without a word.

He had been unpredictable, she realised with sudden apprehension, ever since that unfortunate occasion when Sara had accused Claire of 'arranging' Rose's absence. Sara had not repeated the accusation and had gone back to London with her mother soon after, but she had left uneasiness behind her. Claire had protested her innocence, of course, at the time, but now, remembering his tempers, she was no longer sure that Edward had believed her.

So when her husband eventually reappeared after a day spent on estate business, she tried to make it up to him by being particularly charming and solicitous, ordering his favourite dishes for dinner, asking after the estate. She even read out interesting snippets from *The Times*.

'Listen to this, Edward dear. The Marquis of Salisbury, speaking at the Royal Academy banquet, made fun of lady bicyclists! *My belief is that if there was a Dante to write an artistic* Inferno *its lowest circles would be assigned to the ladies who dress themselves in the divided skirt or knickerbockers (laughter)* and though it was, as usual, an entirely male audience from whom laughter could be expected, I am not at all surprised. I have always thought trousers look ridiculous on the female sex. Don't you agree, dear?'

'They would certainly look ridiculous on you,' he grunted, which was not at all what Claire wanted to hear. Her girth was enough of an anxiety to her as it was without such unfeeling comments. How she would ever fit her corset again she did not know. But Edward had had a long and no doubt arduous day. She allowed herself the luxury of sulking for a scant five minutes, before offering, in propitiation, 'What are you reading, Edward?'

'The Journal of the Royal Agricultural Society. An article on "The mare and the foal" of particular interest to breeders.'

That was no better, and Claire lapsed again into silence. Until, casting her eye over the newspaper, she saw a small paragraph entitled 'Freeman Gallery'. 'Well, well,' she said brightly. 'There is a paragraph about Rose's exhibition. Such a pity we could not go, though as Mamma said it would have been so much more seemly to cancel it, under the circumstances.' When Edward made no comment, she went on, 'The writer calls her "promising".'

'Yes. I read it.'

'You did not say,' she said, aggrieved, and after a moment, 'Is "promising" encouraging, do you think, or merely damning with faint praise? I hope it is encouraging. Poor Rose lives only for her painting these days. Mamma says she is becoming a positive recluse and has no time for normal life at all. She certainly has no time to visit *me* . . .'

Edward closed the journal and stood up. 'I have work to do. I will be in the library if anyone needs me.'

But the report, small though it was, of Rose's exhibition had unsettled him, as Sara's visit had unsettled him, and he found he could not get it out of his mind. The weather did not help, promising sun one minute and showers the next and whereas normally this would have made no difference to his interest in the running of the estate – on the contrary, would have sharpened it – the uncertain season seemed to reflect his own restlessness and increase it. He saw a similar unrest in the news from abroad: bubonic plague in Hong Kong, South African shares depressed, the interminable Dreyfus trial and the developing dispute over the Franchise question in Bloemfontein. Nothing seemed stable any more. Even the Queen's eightieth birthday seemed to him an occasion not of rejoicing, but of foreboding, and when at last he smelt summer on the wind he felt no joy.

He had not meant to attend this year, with Claire's lying-in so close, but before May was out he had changed his mind: the Royal Counties Agricultural Show at Windsor would be his excuse for a trip up to Town. Claire, of course, could not accompany him, but that did not prevent his planning to spend the whole four days of the show away from home.

'Edward! How can you leave me at such a time!' cried Claire, aghast. She clasped her hands over her swollen stomach in a gesture of unconscious protection and he saw that, behind the affront, her fear was real enough.

'You will be quite safe,' he said, unmoved. 'The staff will care for you and I understand you have another month to go before the child is due. The Agricultural Show is of particular interest to me this year. The Shire horse section promises to be outstanding.' He

254

stilled further protest by saying firmly, 'I shall be away four or five days. If it will make you happier, invite your mother to keep you company.'

Suddenly, it was magnificent weather. After the miseries of May, June ushered in a summer of welcome heat, serene, untroubled skies and perfect hay-making weather. The hedgerows were heavy with dog-roses and everywhere the cuckoo sang. Nevertheless, Edward Rivers found the attractions of a sun-bathed Wychwood insufficient to keep him at home and made his way to the Royal Agricultural Show as arranged.

Sun blessed the opening day with splendour. The Show attracted more people than ever and with the State apartments open longer than usual, the Band of the Royal Marines in the showyard, the horse-shoeing competition, the butter-making competition in the working dairy, the poultry plucking and cheese stalls and gleaming new machinery, there was an air of holiday everywhere. The Shire horse judging was of particular interest, and the cattle, especially the Channel Island breeds. Edward also inspected the sheep and pigs, and took a second look at the agricultural machinery, in particular the reaping machines. Then, abruptly, after a mere two days, he left his lodgings in Windsor and returned to Town. He told himself he needed time in London, time to assess the situation regarding the Transvaal quarrel, to tap informed opinion about investments, to test the financial waters. If he was to go ahead with certain improvements at Wychwood, he needed reassurance that war, if it came, would not interfere with his plans. These were his official reasons. His real reason was something different.

It was this other reason that led him to Mayfair on a gentle summer evening and, eventually, after much procrastination and unnecessary wandering through side streets, into Berkeley Square and thence, via Bruton Street, into New Bond Street. Here, he made his way northwards until he was almost at his destination. Even then he lost his nerve at the last minute and walked on. But a meeting was inevitable. It might as well be sooner as later. Besides, she might not even be there and it was her pictures he was interested to see. He turned back – and saw the portrait. As he looked at the seated figure, golden against a background of soft browns and blues, with that shaft of illuminating light and the marble column in the background, memory thrust through the gates he had closed upon it and filled his brain, his eyes, his heart.

'I will never forgive you,' she had said, and he had answered, 'Good. That makes us partners in hate.' But the face in the picture was serene and beautiful, with no trace of his cruel desecration.

He stood a long time remembering, then resolutely moved to the door.

Rose did not usually come to the gallery. After the first few days of activity when visitors came in and out with satisfying, if not lucrative, frequency, numbers had dwindled to a manageable trickle. The gallery was no more than one room, with a rear office where Freeman, an earnest and cultured young man of genuinely artistic leanings, worked at the book he was preparing on cloisonné enamels and from which he could oversee his gallery unaided. But on this particular evening she had felt the need to reassure herself that her art was worth continuing. She had had a bad morning at Millards – in her mother's absence at Wychwood, Rose was required to work there in the manager's office every day till noon – and a worse afternoon at the studio where nothing seemed to go right.

The weather was oppressively hot and in spite of changing into the cooler garments she kept there for the purpose and opening every skylight, the studio was stifling. Georgina had not been in all week which could only mean her mother needed her, and looking at Georgina's neglected clay and modelling stands Rose felt guilty, and guilty again that she herself had produced so little in her afternoon's endeavours. Phoebe Burgess had already approached her with the names of several valuable clients whose children, she said, would make adorable little portraits, and who would pay well. But Rose had spent the last year painting landscapes and inanimate objects and had lost her nerve for portraiture. 'Later,' she told Phoebe, 'When I am back in the way of things.' But this afternoon the self-portrait she had attempted in front of a mirror bought for the purpose had refused to coalesce.

'It is no good,' she said aloud. 'I shall have to resort to Charlotte or Maud.' She prepared to go home, but, because a welcome breeze had blown in from nowhere to freshen her spirits, because it was a summer evening of birdsong and trailing gossamer clouds in a pink and turquoise sky, she pedalled her bicycle into Berkeley Square and thence to the gallery where she left her machine in a side alley and went inside. She would ask if anyone had bought anything, check that her pictures still hung straight on the walls, and then go home. But Mr Freeman had asked her to 'hold the fort' while he had a quick word with a friend of his at Sotheby's so that when the door opened and a man stepped inside, she assumed it was him coming back. Until Edward spoke, and stopped the breath in her throat.

'Good evening, Rose.'

He was as she remembered him, the same fine-boned features, the same dark hair and brooding, deep-set eyes. But his voice, like his expression, was coldly polite. She stood up, came round from behind the desk, held out her hand. She would not have done so had she known the effect even such brief contact would have, but it was too late.

'Good evening, Edward.' Her voice was as cool as his, but her heart was suddenly beating uncomfortably fast.

He looked at her in silence, seeing a young woman of arresting beauty, clear-eyed, resolute, her red-glinting hair escaping in dishevelled coils from its binding ribbon. She wore a Moorish tunic top over silken trousers of the kind Lord Salisbury and Claire had mocked, a silk sash bound at her waist. She looked alluringly feminine, with a quality of individuality and warmth he had forgotten. How ever could he have thought that she and Claire were alike?

But his silence and his unwavering eyes unnerved her. 'I have yet to congratulate you on your marriage,' she said politely, turning away and busying herself with papers on the desk. 'How is Claire?'

'She is well.' After a desolate moment, he added, 'Did you enjoy your sojourn abroad?'

'Very much.' A pause. Outside in the street a carriage clattered past in a cheerful jingling of harness, two people strolled, arm in arm, past the window and stopped to admire 'Inspiration'. Please come inside, *please*, she begged inside her head, but they moved on again, talking together. The lady laughed. 'I hope all is well at Wychwood?' she managed, with outward composure.

'It is. Thank you.'

Another pause, worse than before. Even the street was empty while inside the little gallery the tension of his presence grew intolerable. 'The gallery will be closing as soon as Mr Freeman returns,' she said, brightly, as to a stranger, 'but do look round if you wish.'

'Thank you.' He turned away to study the nearest painting, a view of the Grand Canal from his mother's palazzo.

There was silence as he moved, without comment, from one painting to the next. But it was a silence charged with awareness of each other's slightest move. Rose resumed her seat at the desk, her back a little too straight, her cheeks a little too pink, and began to turn the pages of a catalogue for the exhibition which would follow hers, though her eyes saw nothing and her ears heard only the creak of polished floorboards and the faint sound of his breathing. The silence stretched to unbearable tension. Then, with his back to her, he spoke.

'My informant was right.'

257

'About my so-called painting? And what did your informant say?' Rose spoke calmly, but her heart was thudding painfully fast. If he caught the reference, he ignored it.

'That your work was not only promising, but good. I agree.'

Rose could not resist the chance to wound, as he had done. 'Really? I am surprised. Or is the Vandal school of criticism out-moded now?'

There was a different silence while Edward Rivers apparently studied a watercolour of a back street in Florence and Rose continued to study her catalogue, with empty triumph. When he next spoke it was so quietly she thought at first she had mis-heard. 'I am sorry.'

The words hung trembling in the silence between them. Then he turned and looked at her. She should not have met his eyes, should not have listened as he said, with low intensity, 'I was sorry even then. I could not help myself. Forgive me, Rose? I know now it was not your fault, not as I thought, but I was blinded by jealousy, frustration and ...' he stopped.

'Love?' supplied Rose with unexpected bitterness. 'It is a strange love that destroys.'

'*Destroys*?' His eyes looked deep into hers and she was powerless to look away. 'Your painting has improved beyond all expectation, and as for you, sorrow has made you lovelier than ever.'

'Who spoke of sorrow?' But it was empty vaunting, and when he continued to look at her with the old, remembered eyes, she cried angrily, 'You should not have come! It is *too late*!'

He took a step towards her and she pushed back the chair and stood up, keeping the desk safely between them. She was white-faced and trembling now. 'Please go.'

He took another step, held out his hand, palm upwards, for hers and said, 'Not until you have said you forgive me.'

'For what? For defiling my painting, or for marrying my sister?'

He dropped his hand and turned away, an expression of such despair in his eyes that she almost relented. 'Have you had so little joy?' He sounded suddenly old and tired.

'No,' she said, truthfully. 'I have lived for my painting and found fulfilment. I have known friendship and laughter and I have seen beauty in so many places – as you must have done, at Wychwood. I have found joy enough.'

'Enough?' he repeated sadly and again her heart lurched with the old ache.

'Enough,' she lied. 'Did you not glean my message?'

'*Shake hands for ever, cancel all our vows?*'

'Yes, and I meant it.'

'Have you forgotten how the sonnet ends, Rose? *Now, if thou wouldst ...*'

But the door opened suddenly behind them and Mr Freeman came in.

'My brother-in-law Edward Rivers,' Rose said with hardly a falter, and even managed a smile. 'He was waiting especially to meet you. He is a friend of Percy's, from Wintelsham.' She made the necessary introductions, spoke a meaningless social sentence or two, then made her excuses to leave.

'Let me call a cab and see you home,' said Edward, with practised courtesy. His eyes willed her not to leave with so much still unsaid. She refused the entreaty. 'Thank you. I have my own transport. Perhaps I could offer *you* a lift, dear brother? On my bicycle?' With that flippant retort she whisked out of the door and round the corner, before he could follow and break the brittle shell of her composure.

CHAPTER 5

Three weeks later, at the end of June, Claire's daughter was born and named Rebecca Fay. She was a lusty child with strong lungs, a profusion of dark hair, and an apparently equable disposition, being content to eat and sleep and be cooed over, unprotesting, by a succession of dewy-eyed female relations. Though less than dewy-eyed, Rose, inevitably, was of that number.

Her exhibition had closed two days before the news came and with her pictures removed from the gallery, either by their purchasers or by Rose herself, there was no further excuse on that score. Her studio was back to normal and she had no urgent work in hand. The only 'urgent' work was at Millards in preparation for the annual July sale.

'I realise you cannot – must not – be away from home for long, Rose dear,' wrote Mrs Millard from Wychwood where she had hurried on hearing of the baby's imminent arrival and where she was now installed as the indispensable grandmother of the new-born wonder, *'but I know you will be overjoyed at the safe arrival of dear little Fay and every bit as impatient to see her as everyone else is. So I have written to Mr Blunt and you are to leave everything to him and take two days off from Millards to come to Wychwood, and bring Sara with you. The others must wait until dear Claire is stronger, but I shall expect you and Sara on Friday, by the usual train ...'*

What was the use of resisting? thought Rose, with a mixture of dread and excitement. *What will be, will be ...*

'Don't you mind?' asked Sara, as the train gathered speed through the summer countryside. They had their 'Ladies Only' carriage to themselves, their small portmanteaux hung in spacious comfort in the netted luggage rack, and the antimacassars on the plush seat backs were sparkling clean. Rose had let down the window a little so that the swaying summer air streamed in, with smuts and dust and the clatter of wheels, and the scent of new-mown hay. June had ended in rainstorms, with even hail in places, but the sun which followed had dried out the land and left it greener, lusher, and more bright with flowers. Thatched cottages and roses, hay ricks, apple orchards, flower-filled country gardens, rivers, country lanes, and field after field of glorious ripening corn peeled away in tranquil sunshine on either side as the train carried them inexorably forward, to Wintelsham and Wychwood.

Rose knew exactly what her sister meant.

'What is the use of minding what cannot be helped?' she said with apparent cheerfulness.

'If it was me,' said Sara, 'I would want to kill Claire.'

Sara spoke with chilling composure, as if commenting on the weather, and Rose, in spite of her sister's fair-haired, ethereal beauty and innocent face, knew that she meant every word in literal truth.

'Nonsense,' said Rose. 'What good would that do? Besides, she was only being Claire.'

'The rights of primogeniture, you mean? But no one ever took that seriously except her. You told me so yourself, years ago.'

'Yes.' After a pause, she added, flippantly, 'I hope she does not instil the same principle into the hapless Fay.'

'But it would not matter for *her*,' said Sara, with vehemence. 'It would be the others who would suffer.'

'If there are any others. You know how worried Claire is already about her precious waistline!'

'More like a bumblebee than a wasp!' giggled Sara and the moment passed.

But the reminder had unsettled Rose. *Now if thou would'st ...* Then, in time to the wheels of the train, a different scrap of literary history chanted over and over in her mind: *If it be now, tis not to come. If it be not to come, it will be now. If it be not now, yet it will come. The readiness is all ...* And she was ready, with all her defences...

Besides, there would be people enough everywhere for there to be no danger of finding herself alone with Edward. But Claire was a different matter. Her last view of Claire had been on Victoria station almost eighteen months ago, when Claire had hidden her duplicity behind a display of sisterly affection. But that crocodile-teared leavetaking had been followed on the instant by a display of a different kind as Claire smiled up at Edward Rivers and took his arm. Would Claire feel any guilt? If so, would it make her placatory or belligerent? Or would she merely feel the triumph of a plot well laid and be correspondingly smug? Did she know Rose knew? If so, would she give a little laugh of pretended apology, kiss Rose with extravagant affection and say *All's fair in love and war.* Or....
But speculation was useless. The train was approaching Wintelsham and Rose would know soon enough.

The train slowed, squeaking and clanking, drew into the tiny

261

station, and sighed to a stop. Doors banged, whistles blew, flags waved, and then, too soon, it was labouring out again in a cloud of chugging, coal-flecked smoke, leaving Rose and Sara alone on the deserted platform.

Dephiniums and hollyhocks crammed the flower beds by the stationmaster's office, the railway fence was a mass of scented roses and where the platform ended, the burnt grass under the hedge was brilliant with buttercups in the afternoon sunlight. It was oppressively hot. The stationmaster was busy with the gates of the level crossing, and as they swung open to unlock the road again, she saw Edward walking towards them from beyond the hollyhocks.

'Hello, Sara,' he said, kissing her on the cheek and taking her small portmanteau from her. 'You look lovely as ever. And so do you, Rose.' He offered his gloved hand and she touched it politely with hers. He did not kiss her cheek and she was glad. 'I trust you had a comfortable journey?'

'Very, thank you.' 'Thank you' seems to make up our conversation these days, she thought wryly, but it is a safe and useful phrase. 'How is Claire?' she asked as he handed Sara into the trap. He did not offer her, nor did she desire, a similar courtesy.

'She is well.'

'And the baby?'

'Doing all the things a baby is supposed to do, I understand, but if your mother is to be only half believed, doing them exceptionally well.'

'Naturally. Surely you know that every firstborn is a wonder child?'

'With very special rights,' put in Sara, with solemn eyes.

'Ah, that explains it. And no doubt those rights devolve upon the grandparent too? I know that I, as a mere father, am not allowed to participate in the sacred mysteries of the nursery.'

'Then you must assert yourself,' said Rose, looking straight ahead at the gently curving road and shadowed hedgerows on either side, and trying not to see the firm set of his shoulders as he held the reins, the ripple of thigh muscles under the taut cloth as he braced his feet against the foot board, the grace of his gloved hands, the wind lifting his hair at the forehead when he turned his head. 'That is, if you ever hope to be allowed to play with the clockwork train and the building blocks. But of course, Fay will have a doll's house, though I think I shall give her a box of coloured crayons as soon as she can hold them, so that she may scribble all over her nursery wall.'

262

'Her nanny will not thank you for that,' said Edward, turning towards her with a half-smile.

'But posterity might.' Inside her head she moaned, Oh God why did I come? 'She may grow up to be a famous artist then you will be able to sell the nursery walls to the nation.'

'And you could convert that lovely old brewery into a studio for her,' said Sara artlessly. No one answered. Rose stared brightly ahead, as if she had not heard. Edward touched the horse's flank with a none too gentle whip, and they trotted faster, in a rising cloud of dust from the sun-parched lane. The hedgerows on either side were dust-grimed, the dog-roses powdered white, the foliage grey, but overhead, above the range of carriage wheels, the leaves were still green and cool. With vivid clarity Rose remembered her first visit to Wychwood, two years ago, when she had lain in that woodland glade and studied the sky, until Edward had found her, sleeping ...

They travelled on in extended silence until, to everyone's relief, the chestnut trees of Wychwood swung round the approaching corner towards them and five minutes later they were alighting at the door.

Rebecca Millard met them in the hall, where the welcome cool was redolent of roses and lavender, the oak wood gleaming, the grandfather clock still measuring its timeless time with slow authority.

'Ah, there you are,' said Mrs Millard with a mixture of relief and irritation. 'I was afraid the train might be late.' She looked tired and a little drawn behind the satisfaction which the absence of Edward's mother had given her. Claire was not the easiest of invalids to please, and though the baby was undoubtedly perfect, Claire herself could have behaved with more dignified acceptance of the process necessary to bring the little thing into the world. Some of the remarks she had let slip had been positively disturbing. Since the child's birth, Claire had recovered much of her usual composure, though still restless and fretful on occasions, but Rebecca herself felt decidedly drained. Now she gave her daughters each an automatic kiss before studying them through narrowed eyes. 'Hmm. You had best wash and tidy yourselves before you see the baby. You don't want to irritate Claire. The dust everywhere annoys her enough as it is. Was everything well at Millards when you left, Rose?'

'Yes, Mamma. The summer sale is well under way and promises to be exceptionally profitable this year.' She spoke as by rote. 'Mr Blunt said I was to be sure to tell you that the new line in cricketing blazers is completely sold already. And to say that he has managed to obtain tickets for *Lucia di Lammermoor* for when you return.'

'How very kind of him.' Unexpectedly, Rebecca blushed, and hurried on, 'I have always wanted to hear Melba sing. But we can decide who is to go later, when we are at home. I told Claire we would all join her for tea.'

Claire, of course, was still in bed and expected to stay there for at least a month.

She looked languid and lovely, lying back against a mound of pillows, her chestnut hair in one long heavy plait, its curling ends dark against the ivory satin of her high-necked, pleated and embroidered nightgown. Her hands, Rose noticed, were white and soft, the nails buffed pearly pink and filed to perfect ovals. A huge bowl of sweet peas stood on the writing table in the window, there were more beside her bed, and in the fireplace, masking the empty grate, a deep brass jug of roses. The wide oak floorboards were polished mirror-black where the soft pink Chinese carpet did not cover them, and pink chintz curtains hung motionless at the open window. The sound of pigeons crooning in the home woods drifted in with the sunlight, and the distant sound of hens from someone's yard. The heat of high summer had permeated the very floorboards of the room and the air was warm to the cheek and flower-scented. Rose wondered, briefly, if Claire had staged the picture especially for her. It was a perfect composition. Then the subject of that composition spoke.

'Rose darling! At last!' She lifted her white, lady's hands and held them out in welcome. 'Come and kiss me after all this time!'

So, thought Rose, it is to be unsullied sisterly affection. So be it. And when they had kissed and laughed and asked each other questions, when little Fay had been carried in, admired, and carried out again, when tea had been poured and drunk, it was almost as it had been between them, long ago, before Wychwood. Except that both were acting a part. Mrs Millard and Sara joined in this game of happy families, and they talked of London and Millards, of Wychwood, and of little Fay, and even, briefly, of Rose's sojourn abroad while the lovely summer evening languished into shadow and one by one the birds fell silent.

Later, Edward Rivers came to his wife's bedroom to join them. Claire held out her hand to him, Rose noticed, with exactly the same gesture she had used for Rose, and drew him to her bedside. 'Edward is so good to me,' she said, looking up at him with a gentle smile. 'I feel quite pampered.'

Rose averted her eyes. She had no wish to see any intimate

exchanges between them. But when she looked back, a reluctant moment later, Edward was seated in a chair beside the bed and had taken up a newspaper, apparently at random, and Claire had resumed her elegant position against the pillows. For the first time Rose noticed the small line of discontent on her sister's brow, and an emptiness behind her smile.

'It was such a shame, Rose dear, that we could not attend your exhibition,' said Claire, after a moment. 'Edward and I were so sorry to miss it. But you do see how impossible it was for us to come?'

'Of course.' Rose kept her face, and voice, expressionless, but she need not have worried. Edward remained, apparently, engrossed in his newspaper.

'And then with the Woodstock funeral,' went on Claire, 'poor Georgina could not come either, nor her brother. Such a pity ... When the mourning period is over,' she went on speculatively, 'I wonder whether Harry Price-Hill will marry her at last? They say both she and her brother are very rich. What do you think, Edward dear?'

'Yes, I expect they are,' he said, and turned the page.

'Really, Edward, you are so literal! I mean, do you think Harry will marry her?'

'I shouldn't think so.' Rose heard Sara's breath released in a long sigh of relief. 'I doubt if he will ever marry, and certainly not Georgina.'

'Edward! How can you say such a thing when everyone knows they are engaged.'

'Everyone may know, as you put it, but not everyone recognises it, least of all Harry.' He shrugged, said 'These things happen,' and returned to his paper.

A few minutes later he stood up, folded the newspaper, and left, pleading estate work which needed his attention before dinner. He had not once looked at Rose.

'You will take your dinner here with me, Rose dear, won't you?' said Claire when he had gone.

'Of course.' It would be a blessed relief from the tension of his company. But Mrs Millard would hear none of it.

'Nonsense, Claire. We will all dine together downstairs and leave you in peace. You have had quite enough excitement for one day.' And though Claire pouted and protested, her mother remained adamant.

So it was that when the gong rang for dinner, Rose descended the polished oak stairway into the remembered hall and took her place, on Edward's right, at the remembered dinner table. Her mother wore her usual black, Sara virginal white muslin, with ribbons, and Edward echoed them both in the black and white correctness of his dress. Had Rose wished to create the perfect setting for her own appearance, she could not have chosen better. But for once she was too preoccupied to be aware that her dark red dress and thick, red-glinting hair, bound with a red silk band, stood out in arresting contrast from the monotones around her, and thrust her into lovely, if unwelcome prominence.

There were candelabra as there had been on that last occasion, and carnations, crystal and heavy silver, and the extra leaf had been taken out of the table so that there was not too large an expanse of polished wood between the mere four diners. But what there was, Rose welcomed. At least it set a distance between her and her neighbour.

The curtains, and the windows, were open to the evening, and light spilled from the room onto the darkened lawn beyond. Somewhere beyond the light the first bats wove and dipped in the summer darkness and suddenly across the woods came the mournful cry of an owl. She was reminded of that other evening, before Claire, and snapped shut her memory, hard.

'What is the news of the negotiations in the Transvaal?' asked Rose when the iced consommé had been served and what desultory conversation there had been had lapsed. Mrs Millard was tired, Sara withdrawn, Edward apparently preoccupied and Rose driven to desperation both by his proximity and by the words that hung unspoken between them.

He seemed grateful for her question and launched into an explanation of what had happened so far between the two sides and of the difficulty of finding a compromise acceptable to both. 'Nothing can be done until the *Volksraad* resumes next week,' he explained, 'but when it does, there is no saying there will be agreement. The retrospective clause concerning residents of five years and more will be the crux. But a meeting of ex-Volunteers in Johannesburg has already offered military support to the British Government in the event of war.'

'And will there be war? I understood there to be a considerable body of opinion in this country against such a course.'

'And the usual pleas to the 'uninformed' to keep quiet, in the national interest! There was a letter in *The Times* only the other day along such lines. "The average Transvaal Boer" the writer stated, as if he were the world's authority on the matter, "seems prepared to enter upon a conflict with this Empire with the lightest of hearts." Apparently, this Average Boer, as if there could possibly be such a thing, believes us to be cowardly beyond contempt and any honest expression of an opinion other than the official one is merely evidence for their case.'

'And is official opinion in favour of war?'

'Official opinion, as I understand it, is that nobody wants war, but that nobody will acquiesce in the permanent subjection of Englishmen in a land where England is the paramount power. If moral persuasion fails, they will reluctantly sanction "other methods". Make of that what you will.'

'All this talk of war is very unsettling,' said Mrs Millard. 'Look how that American squabble with Spain last year affected investments, though it was nothing to do with us. Mr Burgess says South African stock will undoubtedly suffer. It is most worrying.'

'Percy Woodstock may have to go and fight,' put in Sara, 'and that is much more worrying, certainly for Percy and Georgina.'

'And if the Volunteers are called upon, then so, I am afraid, may Guy Morton,' said Edward with a frown. 'And he can ill be spared. Reinforcements have already been sent out to the Cape, "to secure our frontiers", with a clutch of special service officers to organise local forces on the spot, and Woodstock says plans are well in hand for an expeditionary force on a much larger scale.'

'Then let us hope the Average Boer will see sense and make peace before it is too late,' said Rose. 'We cannot have all our friends disappearing across the seas.'

'And certainly not before the corn harvest,' said Edward. 'I need Morton here.'

Talk turned to the backward state of crops since the dry weather set in, to the new Shop Assistants bill due for its second reading in the Lords – 'We are expected to provide *chairs* for our female assistants to sit upon,' said Mrs Millard indignantly. 'Think what an impression that will give to the customer!' – to the current season at Covent Garden where Melba was singing, and the different attractions of the 'Savage South Africa Greater Britain Exhibition,' where one could see a real stage coach attacked by Matabele tribesmen, horses plunging over precipitous cliffs, zebras, wildebeasts, baboons and even a herd of elephants and a Kaffir Kraal.

So the meal ran its impersonal course until it was time to adjourn to the drawing room for coffee. Edward came with them, was solicitous with coffee pot and cream jug, then settled into a chair with a copy of the *Agricultural Review* and began to read.

Mrs Millard and Sara sat on the sofa together and soon the former had launched into a day by day account of the baby's

267

development, interspersed with references to and comparisons with her own children's infancy. After the first few minutes, neither Rose nor Sara listened. Rose took out her inevitable sketch pad and began to draw while Sara appeared lost in her own thoughts. But eventually, Mrs Millard announced that she was going upstairs, 'To say goodnight to dear Claire and to retire for the night.'

'I will come with you,' said Rose quickly, closing her sketch book and standing up. 'It has been a long day and I am rather tired.' She dropped a pencil in her haste and it rolled under Edward's chair. 'It does not matter,' she said, moving for the door. 'I will find it in the morning.' But he stood up, tipped back the chair and retrieved it. He held it out to her in the palm of his hand and she had no choice but to take it, though the contact, brief as it was, quite shattered her composure. 'Thank you,' she said, avoiding his eye, and fled.

'You too, Sara,' ordered her mother. 'It is quite late enough.'

'I will be up directly, Mamma. I left a book in Edward's library which I must retrieve, then I will catch you up.'

'Very well, but do not loiter. Edward has work to do.'

When they were gone, Edward resumed his seat, his brandy glass and the *Agricultural Review*. But after five minutes of reading the same article over and over without registering a word of it, he laid it aside, took up his glass and stared into its mesmerising depths, seeing scenes from the past which came to him unbidden and which he knew he must forget.

'So be it,' he said wearily, drained his glass and stood up. 'So it *must* be.' He turned down the lights and went out of the room. He had time for an hour's work before bed.

When Sara opened the door of the bedroom she was to share with Rose, she found her sister at the open window, leaning on the sill.

'What are you doing, Rose?'

'Nothing, just watching the night. It is so beautiful. *In such a night as this, When the sweet wind did gently kiss the trees And they did make no noise, in such a night* . . .' She stopped, but Sara supplied the words she had not wanted to hear.

'*Troilus methinks mounted the Trojan walls And sigh'd his soul toward the Grecian tents, Where Cressid lay* . . . I have been studying *The Merchant of Venice*,' she offered, in excuse.

Rose did not answer, but continued to lean on the sill breathing the soft night air, listening to the faint stirring of the leaves on the chestnut tree, the scuttling of little night creatures under the stars, the sudden snorting breath and stamp of hooves from the stable block. Over the dark bulk of the old brewery bats wove soundless patterns against the velvet sky and she could almost hear the earth breathe.

'Aren't you afraid a bat will get tangled in your hair?' asked Sara, shivering.

'No. And if it did, I think the little creature would be far more terrified than I.' *In such a night* . . . she lingered, dreaming.

Suddenly her nose caught the scent of cigar smoke on the air. Under the chestnut tree a shadow moved. 'Perhaps you are right.' Quickly she closed the curtains and shut out the night.

The following morning, when they came downstairs, Edward had already left for the hay field and was out about estate business all day. Rose took turns to sit with Claire, and when she was not in Claire's room, she took her sketch pad into the garden, but she made sure she did not stray beyond the tennis lawn and always stayed within full sight of the house.

The evening was a repetition of the previous one, though this time the conversation covered such topics as the recent thunderstorms, the excessive heat and drought, and whether or not the summer would prove, as someone had suggested, to be unparalleled for thirty years.

'It would be lovely to go swimming,' sighed Sara. 'I wish we could stay longer.'

'You may, of course, stay as long as you wish,' said Edward with automatic courtesy. He looked tired and drawn, his face pale under the flush of the day's unrelenting sun.

'Thank you,' said Rose, yet again. 'But we must return to London tomorrow, by the earliest available train. At least,' she amended, 'I cannot speak for Sara, but I have work to do.'

'But you could paint here, Rose,' said Sara earnestly. 'You could do a portrait of Claire, or of baby Fay.'

'Don't be ridiculous, Sara,' reproved Mrs Millard. 'Rose meant she had work to do for Millards. Mr Blunt cannot manage everything, you know, and the sale does not finish for another week.'

For once Rose did not contradict her and Sara did not urge the point.

Edward excused himself the moment the meal was over. He had an appointment, he said, with Morton and would not be back till late. He avoided her eyes as he had done all evening. Rose took her coffee upstairs, to drink with Claire, and went early to bed.

'Come again, Rose, soon,' said Claire when Rose went to say goodbye the following morning. She had her baby in her arms,

269

posing for the Madonna and child, thought Rose sourly. 'Please, Rose dear? I want you to do a portrait of Fay for me.'

'Then you must wait,' said Rose. 'At her age, one baby is much like another.'

'Don't listen to your cruel Aunty,' crooned Claire, nuzzling her child who was swathed in layers of frilled white garments, her tiny face half hidden by a bonnet. 'You're the most beautiful little baby in the world.'

'Perhaps,' snapped Rose, 'But no one can see enough of her to tell. I could do you a portrait of her bonnet, if you like, but I certainly can't hope to paint her picture for at least six months. I would prefer a year, or even two. By then she might be an individual.'

'I think you are very hard,' pouted Claire. 'Since you had your precious exhibition and your private commissions, your own family, I suppose, is not good enough for you to paint.'

'Don't be absurd, Claire. You know perfectly well that I am right.'

At that moment Edward came to say the trap was waiting and time was running short if they were to catch the morning train.

'Tell her, Edward,' said Claire, catching hold of his hand. 'Tell Rose she must come again very soon, and paint a picture of Fay for us.' Standing by the bedside and looking over his wife's head, Edward said quietly, 'You heard what Claire said. You must come again, very soon.' For the first time he looked her deliberately in the eyes.

'You could find a room for her somewhere in the stables, couldn't you, Edward?' continued Claire. 'A room she could use as a studio.'

'I could find room,' he said, still holding Rose's eyes with his. Then he dropped Claire's hands and broke the spell. 'But at the moment I am more concerned that Rose should catch her train.'

'At least you will come to the christening, won't you, Rose, and you can draw Fay then.'

'Goodbye,' said Rose firmly and left.

He drove them to the station himself. He lifted their bags into the train for them, kissed Sara on the cheek and proferred Rose his hand. *Now if thou would'st* ... The words hung unspoken between them. Then with a curt, 'Goodbye,' he turned and strode away.

'Claire does not love him,' said Sara when they had travelled in silence for some half an hour. 'Only his position and his home. And he does not love her.'

270

'What Claire and Edward feel or do not feel for each other is no business of ours. They are *married!* Now for pity's sake, leave me in peace,' Rose snapped.

CHAPTER 6

The summer heat grew excessive, and so intense in parts that even
the hardened labourers were driven from the fields. The grass on
the tennis lawn at Wychwood was scorched an unlovely brown, the
country lanes rutted and pitted with dangerous potholes, dust rose
in choking clouds under carriage wheels and usually agile horses
lost their footing on the treacherous surface. Even the birds in the
woods were mute in the unaccustomed drought and the glow-
wormed evenings brought no respite. Inside and out the air was
heavy and oppressive and harvest work was seriously hindered.

At Wychwood Claire was listless and fretful, in spite of the status
her new motherhood had given her and the admiration her infant
daughter received, particularly, surprisingly, from Edward who
seemed positively to dote on the child. This, instead of pleasing
Claire, merely irritated her and she kept to her bed or, if she left it,
lay inert, white hand trailing, on the drawing room sofa. Phoebe
Burgess had taken her family to Bournemouth for a month, the
Fitzsimmons were in the south of France and even the vicar's wife
had gone away to visit a sister. Claire forgot to be the perfect wife
and instead complained of being neglected and deprived. Edward
was at first patient, understanding and considerate, then increasingly short-tempered in the oppressive heat.

They argued over the godparents. Edward suggested Percy
Woodstock, 'a good, reliable fellow,' while Claire wanted Harry
Price-Hill. 'After all, he is your cousin,' and, though she did not
say so, an Honourable. As for the godmothers, Edward suggested
Georgina, Claire refused outright and wanted the Fitzsimmons girl.
Neither of them mentioned Rose, Edward because he assumed it
to be a foregone conclusion, Claire because she had other plans in
mind.

They argued over the infant's christening. Claire had wanted
strawberries and champagne on the lawn and a summer ceremony.
'But what would be the use with no lawn to speak of and the cream
curdled before it leaves the dairy? We had better settle for early
September instead.' But Edward wanted to wait till October, when
his mother arrived from Venice. 'She missed our wedding. The least

272

we can do is to include her in her grand-daughter's christening. We will arrange the ceremony to coincide with the shooting season – if there are any birds left to shoot.' The drought was so bad that water had to be carted from dawn to dusk for the stock, at a time when all hands were needed for the harvest, and the milk supply had dwindled till there was scarcely enough for butter or cheese.

Even the placid Fay became fretful under her swaddling clothes and her little body erupted into an unsightly heat rash which quite spoiled her looks.

'There!' cried Claire at this final insult. 'What did I tell you? This summer is impossible. I refuse to make any arrangements at all until she is presentable again.' She scolded the nurse, who scolded the nursery maid and the general disaffection spread.

There was disaffection in the Millard household, too. Mrs Millard spent much of her time at Wychwood, summoned peremptorily by Claire. She was sometimes accompanied by Sara, sometimes by Charlotte or Maud, but Rose steadfastly refused to go again. Only her continuing work at Millard's, in her mother's absence, redeemed what Rebecca saw as Rose's 'callous disregard for your poor sister's feelings.' Claire, she implied, was languishing solely for want of Rose's company and was mortified in the eyes of the neighbours by her sister's neglect. The latter, reflected Rose, was certainly possible: the former unlikely. If Claire missed Rose's company it could only be because it deprived her of the opportunity to crow. As for Rose herself; it would be time enough to face Edward at the christening, when she had no choice. Until then, the plain truth was she dare not go. *Now if thou would'st* echoed in her head with relentless enticement, breaking down resentment, virtue, loyalty, pride, till her sole defence was solitude, which, whenever Millards allowed, she sought, and found, in her studio.

Since Georgina's removal to the country, to keep her widowed mother company, Rose saw nobody but family for days on end, and when she was immersed in her painting, scarcely noticed even them. She had returned from Wychwood with a need to lose herself completely in her work and as her exhibition had closed with a reassuring seven pictures and three small sketches sold, she had accepted one of Phoebe's commissions and agreed to draw the eight-year-old daughter of someone in Robert Burgess's bank. This involved sketching the child in her home in Grosvenor Square, but Rose did much of the finishing work in the studio, especially when the child was removed with her family for a spell in the country, and, as the summer lengthened, the studio grew more and more her own. Georgina's modelling stands still stood in their accustomed place, and Rose religiously made sure the covering cloth on her half-filled bin of clay was kept well-damped. But Georgina herself seldom visited and Percy even less.

Captain Woodstock's new duties at Aldershot were onerous, and grew more so as the summer progressed, with army training programmes in full swing. The news from the Transvaal became increasingly grave as the two sides negotiated the extension of the franchise against a background of heated argument, accusation, inflammatory speeches and questions in the House. Telegrams were exchanged, delaying tactics employed, with diplomatic feints and threats. Both sides moved troops into more strategic positions, counted their forces, assessed possible support. Two companies of Royal Engineers were despatched to Natal and reserves of supplies and ammunition sent out. The Commander-in-Chief put the final touches to the plan for the composition of the larger force which would be necessary if negotiations failed. This seemed daily more likely, as, while England slowly parched in the heat of the hottest, driest summer for 35 years, events in the Transvaal moved inevitably towards war.

At the beginning of September the Queen left London for Balmoral. A week later, a special Cabinet meeting was called. There was great activity at the Colonial Office and the War Office . Despatches were sent to Pretoria. It was said that the increase in British troops was merely a precaution. Calm was recommended, peace prayed and hoped for, compromise urged, while preparations continued against the alternative.

At Woolwich Arsenal and dockyard 50 tons of engine appliances and field telephone equipment were requisitioned, with the equipment for 20 field hospitals, packed into cases suitable for transport by ox-wagon and mule-pannier. Compressed forage, oxen-harness, and field kitchen appliances were assembled ready for shipping, with a team of extra veterinary officers to examine the mules and oxen that would be bought in South Africa.

Up and down the country, voices still spoke out against armed intervention in the Transvaal, but they were isolated peacemakers in a sea of patriotic fervour. Every thinking man must deprecate war, naturally, and especially war between two white races, but if war was forced upon the country by the obstinacy of the Boers, then there could be no question. It would not be easy, not a summer day's amusement, but a tough fight and a determined one. The Red Cross and the Order of St John of Jerusalem declared themselves ready for duty whenever required.

Details were published in the press of the Home forces to be sent

274

to the Transvaal if war was declared, with a list of those Brigades likely to be placed under orders at any moment. Captain Percival Woodstock's cavalry brigade was at the head of the list.

'That settles it,' declared Claire, when they heard the news. 'We must have the christening at once, before Percy and everyone else disappear.' Edward agreed. If his mother arrived in time, all well and good. If not, her absence would make little difference to the efficacy of the infant's baptism. Besides, as Claire was quick to point out, with war fever spreading daily and more and more people being caught up in its waves, there was no saying who would be where from one day to the next once war was officially declared.

Captain Woodstock was at present engaged in last minute manoeuvres with his unit on Salisbury Plain, prior to sailing for South Africa on the 23rd, with the contingent of Major General French, Commander the Cavalry Brigade. But he would have leave to come home before embarkation.

'We will combine Fay's christening with a splendidly patriotic farewell party for our departing troops,' cried Claire and looked more animated than she had done for weeks. 'It will be the talk of the neighbourhood for years to come and everybody will attend.'

Everybody, thought Edward with a sense of inevitability which left him strangely free, including Rose. . . .

Rose was absorbed in her portrait of the banker's daughter when she heard the door of the studio open and looked up to see Georgina, sombre in mourning black, her face both sad, apprehensive, and at the same time lit in a strange way by an inner light of resolution. Rose was reminded of her own portrait of Georgina, which hung now in the Woodstocks' country home, and felt an answering wave of apprehension.

'What is it, Georgina?' she asked, putting aside her paint brush and untying the strings of her apron. 'Has something happened?'

'Yes. A great deal.' Georgina drew Rose to sit beside her on the ottoman, and, keeping her hand in hers, said, 'You are to listen very carefully, Rose, and not to interrupt me. Percy is under orders to embark for South Africa and will leave in two weeks' time. No, do not speak! I want to explain things in my own way. We have known for some time, he and I, that it was inevitable, but since Daddy's death I have realised a number of things. Not least that I want to do all I can to help, so that Percy may come home safe and well when this Transvaal business is over. I cannot join the army and fight with him, nor would I wish to if I could, but there are other, more useful things that I can do and that I know I can do well.' She paused, studying Rose's face for signs of dissent or impatience, but Rose was honouring her with close attention, her eyes fixed on her friend's solemn face, for she realised Georgina had changed since her father's death, had grown stronger, more thoughtful, more mature.

'I have learnt to accept many things,' Georgina continued slowly. 'First of all, Daddy's death. I have learnt to be grateful for that, not just because it freed him from his pain, poor darling, but because in some strange way it freed me from my illusions. Not just about Harry – I had known he was unreliable for years, but would not acknowledge it. When I promised to stop yearning for the unattainable that day in Siena – do you remember, Rose, how shamelessly drunk we were later, in Rome? – it was not Harry I should have been renouncing. Though I think I suspected, even then.'

Here Rose opened her mouth to protest as she realised where Georgina's words were leading her, but her friend waved her unspoken thoughts aside.

'No, Rose. Nothing you say will change my mind, so please don't contradict me or try to jolly me out of my decision. It is too late. I enrolled at St Thomas's this morning. I am going to train as a nurse so that I can go out on the first hospital ship that needs me and nurse the wounded and the sick. I found that I was good at nursing, when I looked after Daddy.'

'But what of your mother … your career …' floundered Rose, aghast. She had thought to hear some change of direction in Georgina's work, to pottery perhaps, or even wood-carving, but nothing as drastic as this.

'Mummy will approve, I have no doubt of it, and she has Nanny to keep her company and the estate to run. As to my career, that is non-existent. Before you say anything at all, Rose, let me finish.' She paused, gathering her thoughts, and Rose waited, hearing the rattle of carriage wheels from a distant street, a costermonger's cry, children's voices. The skylights were open to the calm September evening, and Rose noticed, with surprise, a butterfly playing in a shaft of sunlight, dipping and weaving in a silent dance of crimson and royal gold. In the studio it was very quiet, the familiar smell of linseed oil and damp clay mingling with the smell of sun-warmed wooden floorboards and the lingering scent of straw from the abandoned stable underneath. She watched her friend's dear, frowning face, half expecting what she would hear, but even so Georgina's honesty took her by surprise.

'My career was always wishful thinking,' Georgina said at last and though there was sadness in her voice, there was also calm and a new resolve. 'That European trip was a revelation to me, Rose. We saw such beauty, such exquisite perfection of art in all its guises and whereas such examples were to you a spur and an inspiration, to me they merely pointed out my own woeful inadequacies. By the time we reached Venice, I knew. Oh, I could buy myself teachers who would encourage me with faint praise, but I know I can never be any good. And do not try to tell me otherwise,' she said fiercely, as Rose attempted to speak. 'I have a small talent with clay, enough to throw a reasonable pot, perhaps, or glaze a tolerable plate. But as to sculpture, I could not fashion an acceptable garden fountain! Lady Portia once said that if six months abroad was not the making of me, I had better take up embroidery. Instead, I shall be a nurse. Aunt Clementina has been splendid. She has arranged everything for me and I begin next week. At least now I will be doing something useful.'

Rose felt strangely humbled. She knew what store Georgina had set by her sculpture, what heartbreak it must have cost her to speak as she had done, but at Georgina's next words the tears stood in her eyes.

'I shall not use my studio again, Rose, but I do not intend to sell it. You shall have it to live in, paint in, and use as if it were your own. I will hear no argument, and before you protest, I have already seen my solicitor and arranged that should I by chance not return from South Africa, it will be legally yours, for ever.'

Rose could only stare at Georgina with brimming eyes, before hugging her in spontaneous gratitude. 'Dear Georgina, thank you. But I do not deserve it.'

'Nonsense.' Georgina stood up and straightened her dress. 'I wear this dreadful garment solely for Mummy's sake,' she explained apologetically. 'Daddy never cared a hoot what I wore – if he even noticed. And now, can you find a use for all this modelling equipment, because if not I shall give it to my old tutor at the College, as a small recompense for all his patient suffering!'

'Please leave the modelled heads,' said Rose, 'Unless you have other plans for them. They are so much a part of the place – and they will remind me of you.'

'Don't think you will get rid of me so easily,' said Georgina, more cheerful now that the worst was over. 'I shall be in and out of here to see you all the time – at least, whenever Matron allows. And now, I must go and arrange about my uniform so that everything will be ready to begin my new career on Monday. Dear Rose,

I shall miss our happy times together, working side by side, in companionship and understanding. You have been a good friend.'

'And you.' It was the end of a chapter, Rose realised, for both of them. Georgina was embarking on a new career. As for Rose, she was beginning to earn money and a name for herself, and her needs were small. From now on she could live in the studio if she chose, break away completely from home and Millards, and devote her life to painting.

'Please don't look so solemn, Rose, or I shall lose my courage and I know I am right. Percy thinks so too, the dear boy.' She stopped, hesitated, and said quietly, 'I know it is none of my business, Rose, but Percy is devoted to you. It would make him happy if, before he sailed for South Africa, you would ...' She stopped, grinned, and said, with something of the old Georgina, 'I sound like some dreadful marriage broker, but you know what I am trying to say.'

'I know,' sighed Rose and managed a smile. 'But your brother is a big boy now. He can speak for himself.' And will, she thought with dread.

But Georgina was leaving. In the doorway, she turned, looked for a long moment at the studio which for years had held her girlhood dreams, then shrugged. 'Goodbye, studio. It is yours now, Rose. And if I can't see you before, we will meet at Wychwood, for the christening.'

CHAPTER 7

It promised to be perfect weather for the christening. There had been rain earlier in the week – the first for many weeks and blessedly welcome. Gutters, ditches, potholes had run sweet with water till the rain-butts overflowed, the ponds filled, the worst of the dust settled and even the poor, parched grass revived. Tiny, valiant threads of green appeared in the desert of the lawn till it was no longer a bleached brown wasteland, but took on a verdant sheen against which the woods glowed bright with colour. For the leaves were turning and the changing hues of gold and brown and umber throbbed in the sunlight against a clear sky, and were echoed in the hedgerows where scarlet rose hips vied with crimson haws; On the weaving tendrils of the bramble, berries slowly changed from red to purple and the apple orchard was ripe with fruit.

In the home woods, squirrels cheerfully squabbled over the business of nut-gathering, and a pair of jays flashed arrogantly low across the tennis lawn between forays into the trees in search of acorns.

Claire sent armfuls of autumn flowers down to the village church to deck the tiny nave for the baptism, and ordered as many more to adorn the house. Lilies, michaelmas daisies, dahlias and carnations perfumed every corner, as did open dishes of lavender and fresh pot-pourri. Crisp linen sparkled on newly made-up beds, fresh curtains stirred at freshly opened windows, and the sweet scent of beeswax hovered in the air as teams of aproned house-maids scrubbed and swept and polished till every detail from tiny muslin lavender bag in freshly-lined drawer to pleated paper fan in black-leaded grate was perfect. Warming pans were polished and stone water jars set ready to air the beds, with water carafes, biscuit barrels, hot water jugs, fresh soap and towels for washstands, and in the kitchen everything scourable was scoured, everything polishable polished.

Even the piano keys in the drawing room were ministered to with an alcohol-moistened cloth.

Edward watched Claire with amusement and a touch of awe, as he had watched her that summer when she had displayed her new-

279

learnt social skills for his appraisal. And as then, he admired and approved. But it was with the admiration he accorded a ploughman for a perfect furrow, a thatcher for a perfect gable-end, or a stable boy for the perfect grooming and presentation of a horse. Had she been his farm manager or his housekeeper, he reflected, he would have given her a bonus, as token of his appreciation. As it was, when they were at dinner on the eve of their house guests' arrival, he thanked her, commended her forethought, and asked out of goodwill rather than curiosity how she planned to distribute their various house guests.

'Phoebe and her family, of course, will have their usual rooms, and I have put Mummy in the blue room, with Sara, and Charlotte and Maud next door.' Claire had taken to referring to her mother as Mummy, in imitation of Phoebe's social circle, though she had yet to test it out upon Mamma herself. 'Your mother's room, of course, must be kept ready for her, should she arrive in time.' Lady Portia had not thought fit to let Claire know one way or the other but, thought Claire grimly, that was only typical. 'I had thought of asking the Woodstocks to have Rose to stay with them, but then perhaps it would not be quite proper, under the circumstances, so I have put her in the little attic room, in the housemaid's corridor. Such a pretty little room, simple of course, but with a certain rustic charm. I am sure Rose will feel at home there, with her affinity to rafters.' Claire gave the gentle, deprecating laugh with which she usually accompanied any reference to Rose, rare though these were. 'And she can splash her paints about to her heart's content with no fear of spoiling the carpets.'

'Are you sure that is quite proper?' said Edward. 'It seems a little degrading for our daughter's godmother to be banished to the servants' quarters.'

'Godmother? Why Edward dear, whatever gave you that idea? Phoebe and Adelaide Fitzsimmons are to be godmothers, did I not tell you?'

'No, you did not.' As you well know, he could have added, but chose to refrain. He was puzzled by Claire's attitude to Rose, which seemed to him unnatural – effusively affectionate to her face, and behind her back uneasily defensive. But that would not explain Claire's deliberate passing over of her sister, when such a gesture could have been a natural olive branch. It was almost as if Claire was jealous, or deliberately excluding her sister from the family stockade.

'Then I am sorry, Edward dear,' Claire said. 'I was sure I had mentioned it, but then you are always so taken up with the estate affairs and I expect I wanted to spare you unnecessary interruption. But no matter. Everything is arranged now and, I am sure, for the best.'

That was untrue. The arrangements were a compromise and a vexing one at that. Claire had set her heart on a distinguished name for the newspaper announcement and with that in mind had approached the Honourable Harry Price-Hill.

'Me? *Godfather*?' He had looked at her in astonishment, then disconcertingly laughed, 'Oh no, Claire dear. You will not have the satisfaction of my name on your baptismal line-up, even for cousin Edward's sake. I made it a rule years ago never to stand godfather to any infant. It can lead to such unfortunate gossip and I have enough trouble avoiding paternity suits as it is. I am sorry, Claire dear, but you will have to hunt your glittering scalp elsewhere.'

Snubbed, affronted and decidedly annoyed, she had approached Edward's choice of Percy Woodstock. To her astonishment, he too declined.

'I am sorry, Claire, but I feel it would not be appropriate. As a soldier I have no control over my whereabouts and could spend years at a time overseas. I would not be able to give the child the attention she deserves.'

Attention indeed! thought Claire, fuming. It was the Woodstock money she had in mind. She asked Georgina to stand godmother and realised, too late, why Percy had refused.

'No thank you, Claire. I would not wish to take a position that is rightfully Rose's, whatever your reasons for not asking her. Though Percy and I will be delighted to come to the christening, of course.'

'Of course,' echoed Claire, 'and we will be delighted to see you.' But Georgina's outspokenness had made her uneasy. Her conscience was not entirely clear where Rose was concerned, though she told herself she had not only the right, but the positive duty to marry first. Rose knew and accepted that, and everyone knew Rose preferred painting to marriage. Nevertheless Claire was uneasily aware that others might not entirely share her point of view.

Looking at her husband's glowering face across the dinner table, Claire said, with an edge of defiance, 'Adelaide Fitzsimmons is such a kind, gentle girl, a dear friend of mine, and so fond of Fay. She will be ideal. And Robert and Phoebe are so reliable and conscientious. Whereas Rose, as you know, tolerates nothing that interferes with her painting. Why, she has only seen the child once since she was born and then was positively rude about her. Refusing to paint her dear little portrait, making fun of her bonnet. Besides, Rose may be going abroad again at any time.'

'Oh?' Edward kept his voice carefully non-committal, while he struggled to control the sudden surge of emotion her words had loosed inside him – fear, apprehension, a sense of urgency and, stronger than all of them, a deep, consuming need which he had thought dead or at least under tight control and which he realised now was neither ... He reached for the decanter and refilled his glass, not looking at Claire but waiting with every sense alert for her to continue.

'Phoebe says your mother has offered Rose the palazzo in Venice whenever she chooses, for as long as she cares to stay. Phoebe was quite hurt about it. Your mother has never invited her.' When Edward made no comment, she went on, 'Apparently Rose painted a picture of the palazzo and left it for your mother as a gift. And all Lady Portia's dowager cronies admired it so much they want similar sketches of their own decrepit ancestral homes before they sink without trace into the canals of Venice. So you see, Rose may not even be here.'

When Edward still made no comment, she continued, in growing uneasiness, 'Besides, if we are to take baptism at all seriously, it is really not appropriate to entrust our daughter's spiritual guidance to a Bohemian.'

Into Edward's mind came the memory of Rose and Claire, arguing, and Rose declaring, 'It is ridiculous to lump all artists together as Bohemian and therefore promiscuous libertines. I paint because I must, not as an excuse to throw off my morals with my clothes.'

'What exactly do you mean by that remark?' he said, with an expression she could not read.

Claire looked flustered. 'You know what I mean, Edward dear. We do not want Fay to be exposed to any unsuitably outlandish ideas.'

'And is it so outlandish to paint good pictures and to wish to continue to do so?'

'Not at all. Of course not. But we do not want our daughter to be enticed into the world of free-thinking, free-living libertines, do we?'

'And is that the world your sister inhabits? Really Claire, you surprise me. I thought she spent her mornings working for your mother in the family business, and her afternoons, alone, painting respectable portraits of respectable children, when she is not paint- ing respectable views of respectable palaces. But if that is not the

282

case, then I suggest you alert Phoebe at once, and, of course, my mother, both of whom have recommended Rose unreservedly to their friends.'

'Yes, but . . .' Claire blushed under his sarcasm, knowing she had got herself into an indefensible position, but determined to justify herself. 'Don't tease, Edward! You know perfectly well what I mean. Besides, at its most practical,' she went on rashly, goaded beyond caution, 'Rose has no money and can do little for Fay beyond what an aunt would do anyway.'

'No money? Will she not have a settlement, as you had?'

'Why should Rose need a settlement?' blustered Claire. 'She said years ago that she did not intend to marry.' Something in Claire's manner alerted Edward to new awareness. He looked at her shrewdly for a long moment before saying, 'So . . . it is to be Phoebe, Adelaide and Robert?'

'Yes, dear,' she said with relief, the matter safely closed, and rang the bell for the maid and the iced soufflé.

But in Edward's mind the matter was not closed. That the god-parents were chosen behind his back and without consultation was annoying, but not earth-shatteringly so. Such arrangements were best left to the women anyway and it was his own fault for not inquiring sooner. Had Fay been a son, he would have taken a firmer hand in the business, of course, but Claire's arrangements would no doubt serve well enough, and would not affect his daughter's wellbeing in any way. What was more disturbing was the idea of Rose that Claire's words had conjured up. Rose being passed over by her sister as not respectable enough, Rose having no money, Rose somehow pushed beyond the pale as a penniless Bohemian by her own reactionary fault.

Everything Claire said served to increase his interest in Rose, and his suspicion that she had been ill-served somehow, not least perhaps by him, or because of him. As a result, not only was the fascination she held for him redoubled, with the desire which pride and necessity had made him suppress, but his chivalry was stirred on her behalf. He resolved to tackle Mrs Millard on the subject at the first opportunity.

The meal was completed in silence.

'Shall I ring for coffee in the drawing room?' asked Claire, with wifely solicitude. She knew she had offended Edward by arranging things without consulting him, but she also knew her arrangements were faultless, as the dinner just over had been faultless, and wanted to show him that it was his wishes and his welfare she had at heart. 'Or will you take your brandy here at the table? Or perhaps you

283

would prefer port this evening? We have some excellent raisins, and the walnuts this year are . . .'

'Thank you,' interrupted Edward. 'I will take coffee in the library.' He pushed back his chair and held open the door for his wife to pass through.

'In that case, I will say goodnight, Edward dear.' She inclined her cheek for him to kiss and made her way to the drawing room to enjoy her own coffee in solitude, with the latest copy of the *Illustrated London News*. Afterwards she would play a little on the pianoforte, perhaps do a little embroidery, then retire to bed.

She did not miss his company. In fact, she felt more at ease when Edward had retired to his own pursuits. She could relax her vigilance a little, think frivolous thoughts, and be as openly calculating about the people and places she saw in the journals as she wished without fear of arousing Edward's displeasure or scorn. And without fear of arousing different, more tiresome emotions.

For Claire enjoyed the luxury of her solitary bedroom, with the ministrations of her maid to pamper her and her mirror to confirm that she was still beautiful. Her waist was growing smaller, too, and Minnie had managed to lace her a half inch tighter that very morning. Another month and she might be back to what she had been before the baby. But other aspects of her life before the baby she was less anxious to renew.

Claire studied an illustration for a floor-length dinner dress in oyster-coloured silk, tight over the hips and to below the knees, then flared out in a mermaid's tail of tiny pleats. The waistline sloped low in front, but was beautifully nipped in at the sides, with a flattering decolletage. Trains, she noted, were definitely 'out', but waists were still very much 'in' and she meant to keep hers so.

A small frown line appeared on her forehead as she remembered her daughter and her daughter's conception. Claire had been convalescent for almost three months now and though Edward had been most gratifyingly considerate, she was not at all sure how long he would remain so.

'I sleep so much better these days, Edward dear,' she had told him, her hand cool on his arm. 'In my convalescent's bed, alone. But it is so comforting to know that you are only a door's thickness away, should I need you.'

But lately Claire had grown uneasily aware that three months might be considered sufficient time for convalescence and that any husband after that time might feel justified in claiming his rights. Edward certainly might, and the prospect was not an attractive one. Recently, in the evenings, when they sat together in the drawing room after dinner, she had caught him looking at her in a quite disconcerting way. 'Speculatively' was the word that came to mind, but she dare not challenge him to reveal his thoughts lest they turn out to be what she least wanted to hear. Instead, she pretended he had already considered, respected, and understood her wishes in the matter.

'You are so understanding, Edward dear,' she said, looking up at him with soulful eyes. 'You know I could not bear to go through that again so soon ...' And she continued, prudently, to lock her door.

Alone in his library, with a glass of his father's best cognac for company, and the faint tones of the pianoforte drifting across the hall from the drawing room, Edward remembered those words. He had assumed that by 'that' Claire meant the process of childbirth, but now the idea came to him, unbidden, that perhaps her statement had been deliberately ambiguous and that by 'that' she meant not only childbirth, but what caused it. He found even the possibility daunting, but the more he remembered, the stronger became his conviction that he was right. Her flinching from him in the woods should have warned him, though she had protested ignorance as the cause; then her modesty which now seemed more like prudery, her asking 'Will it take long, dear?' and her convenient fatigues. It must be six months since he had shared her bed and, in that time, memory had blurred dissatisfactions. Every day he saw her beauty, her voluptuous curves and flawless skin, her thick, shining hair and limpid eyes, and thought that marriage and motherhood had improved her. Every day he admired her domestic efficiency, her growing confidence, her developing style. He loved his little daughter with an intensity that surprised him and yearned already for another child, and then another. Claire would soon be strong again and every day he wondered when he could legitimately reclaim her as his wife, watched her face for signs of encouragement, or even of passive acceptance. Instead, he saw an evasive withdrawal which brought back with uncomfortable clarity the memory of that sleeping marble statue.

She told him she slept so well alone, but that she was comforted by his presence 'only a door's thickness away, should I need you.' Edward had taken that as a hopeful sign, even a tentative invitation, yet as he had discovered, it was the opposite.

'Oh dear, was it locked?' she had said innocently when he rattled the handle late one night. 'It must have been Minnie. Did you want something?' But Edward knew it was not Minnie and suddenly any want he might have felt left him.

285

'It does not matter.' He went out again, closing the connecting door. He did not test his theory, but he was almost certain she crept out of bed and locked it again behind him. Besides, she let him know by a dozen tiny subterfuges and innuendoes that they were to remain husband and wife in name only until ... But the 'until' had not been indicated and Fay was almost three months old. He began to wonder if 'until' would stretch indefinitely. But that was nonsense. She was his wife. He must give her time, that was all. ...

He scarcely gave Mrs Millard time to take off her travelling clothes the following afternoon before tackling her on the subject of Rose, who was to travel down alone on the morning of the christening.

He found he could not get the idea out of his mind that Mrs Millard and Claire between them had somehow used Rose – and himself – for their own ends and until he found out one way or the other he could not settle. Since her return from Italy his feelings towards Rose had been turbulent enough and their brief meetings, first in the gallery and then at Wychwood, had done nothing to unravel them or to give him peace. He had asked her to forgive him, not an easy thing to do for a man of his pride, and so far had had no answer. Whether because they had not been alone together since, or because she bore him unflagging antagonism he did not know – all he knew was that there was unfinished business between them and that until it was resolved he would find no peace. Moreover, he was almost certain she avoided all contact with him for the same reason that he avoided contact with her – even the touch of their gloved hands was dangerous – and that should circumstances ever conspire to throw them alone together ... But that way was barred, even to imagination. He was married to her sister. And because she had no father or brother and he, as brother-in-law, was the nearest responsible male relative she had, the least he could do, he told himself firmly, was to show proper concern for her welfare.

'Mrs Millard,' he began carefully, when he had despatched Claire with her younger sisters to the drawing room and ordered tea for himself and his mother-in-law in private, in the library. 'You know that Captain Woodstock is under orders to sail next week for South Africa?'

'Yes, indeed,' said Mrs Millard. 'More and more of our brave soldiers are going every week. Why only on Saturday ...'

'I have reason to believe,' interrupted Edward firmly, suspecting smoke-screen tactics on Mrs Millard's part, 'that Captain Woodstock will approach me on the subject of your daughter Rose, and

286

I would like to be in a position to answer his questions as freely as a father might. How much can he expect Rose to bring with her, should he take her as his wife?' The idea of Rose as anyone's wife filled him with white-hot jealousy and a disturbing ache in the loins, but he knew, or thought he knew, that the question was an academic one. Mrs Millard, however, did not.

She flushed, looked flustered, made great play with the milk jug and sugar tongs, before saying evasively, 'That depends, Edward, on when the wedding might be.'

'How "depends"?' He intended to allow no evasions.

'Why, I am not quite sure. Mr Proudfoot ... Mr Burgess ... In short, there are various long-term investments which, my advisers assure me, will provide sufficient return in, say, ten years' time.'

'*Ten years?*' Am I to understand that Rose must wait ten years for a dowry?'

'But Rose does not wish to marry, Edward. She has her painting and her ...'

'Did she decide this for herself?' interrupted Edward with icy politeness, 'Or did you decide it for her, out of economic necessity?'

'I declare I don't know what you can mean,' stammered Rebecca, thrown unexpectedly into disarray by Edward's obvious anger.

'I mean,' he said slowly, each cold word an accusation, 'that one daughter with a large dowry has much more chance of a good marriage than two daughters with a small.'

'But Rose has every chance,' chattered Rebecca, avoiding the question and struggling to retrieve composure as she changed tack. 'Everyone knows how devoted to her Percy Woodstock is.'

'One large, or two small?' repeated Edward implacably. 'Was that the choice?'

'But I keep telling you, Edward dear,' said Rebecca, still floundering, but spotting one small rock she might cling to. 'Dear Percival ...'

'Will not require a dowry. Unlike me. Was that it?'

'Such a charming young man, and so devoted. And such a support to her in her artistic endeavours,' continued Mrs Millard bravely, for after all, to brazen it out was the only course open to her. 'Why he even arranged an exhibition for her and looked for no return except the pleasure of furthering her painting career. Not many men would be so understanding, so selflessly supportive, and so undemanding, but then he is an exceptional young man. Quite exceptional ...'

After the first sentence Edward hardly listened. He saw what had happened as clearly as if Mrs Millard had taken him with her to Mr Proudfoot's office. Rose's portion had been added to Claire's in order to secure Wychwood – and himself. Rose, he was certain, had not been consulted, though had she been, he doubted she would have been mercenary enough to object. Her objections would have been on quite a different score. 'Forgive you for what?' she had asked. 'For defiling my painting, or for marrying my sister?' One act was reversible, the other not, and both, perhaps, were equally unforgivable? But the fact remained that he had received two dowries.

'Rose is so unworldly,' Rebecca was saying, and then, as if that might be misconstrued to Claire's detriment, 'And Wychwood was so very much in need of maintenance. Claire was quite worried about it. So tragic if those lovely woods had had to be sold. You said so yourself.'

'I see.' He pushed back his chair and stood up. With a cold 'Excuse me,' he left Mrs Millard to her own uneasy thoughts, whistled for his dog and made for those same woods, where he strode restlessly to and fro before finding out the glade where he had first come upon Rose sleeping and where he had first kissed Claire. Rose who had been robbed of her rightful settlement and Claire who had taken it and given it to Edward, together with herself and eventually their child. At the thought of Fay his eyes softened with momentary tenderness before hardening again as he realised how he had been duped, and remembered the injustice that had been done to Rose. By Claire, by her mother, and most of all by Edward himself.

His back against a beech tree, new-fallen beech mast crunching underfoot, he lit a cigar, and stood a long time deep in tormented thought, while his dog nosed and pottered quietly in the autumn undergrowth. In the distance, doves purled contentedly above the stable block and somewhere overhead a blackbird sang full-throated into the fading light. Once, he heard the sound of a carriage in the drive, and voices. That would be Phoebe and her family arriving. Once, a hedgehog trundled, rustling, across the glade, but both dog and master ignored it. The air under the trees grew chill as the evening gathered. Then, as the first star appeared in a velvet sky, the faint sound of the dressing gong drifted across the tennis lawn from the lamplit house. Slowly he stubbed out his cigar, grinding it to cold ash under his heel.

Tomorrow would bring his daughter's christening – and Rose.

Rose arrived alone by the morning train and found the Wychwood brougham awaiting her. She was met at the door by Claire, in full glory of cream coloured silk and lace.

288

'Darling Rose,' she cried, touching her lips to Rose's cheek. 'How lovely to see you. And looking so artistic.' She studied Rose, her head on one side, for a smiling moment, before adding, 'Is that the Eastern look they talk about? Or something all your own?'

'It is the travelling-from-London-in-comfort look,' said Rose. 'Or, if you prefer, the country-weekend-for-the-unconventional look. I brought my bloomer suit for the christening.'

'You *didn't!*' Then, realising, she said, 'Really, Rose, it is hardly a matter for jest. Now, the arrangements. The men have gone over to the Woodstock place, and we ladies are to have a cold collation for luncheon. Then the ceremony is at three. Let me show you to your room so that the maid can unpack for you and press anything you need pressing.' She could not help adding, 'If you have nothing suitable I could lend you something just for the afternoon.'

'Thank you, Claire dear, but no. Besides, you know I could never fit into anything of yours.'

'Perhaps not.' Claire smiled with satisfaction and turned for the stairs. 'This way, Rose dear.' Rose refrained from pointing out that she had stayed in the house several times before and meekly followed her sister up the dark oak stairs to the first floor corridor with its polished wooden floorboards, its turkey carpets, its flower vases in leaded casements, its air of quiet comfort, reinforced by the distant ticking of the grandfather clock in the hall below.

Claire led Rose along the corridor to the right-angled bend by the housemaid's cupboard, and on past the nursery wing to the back stairs.

'Up there, dear,' said Claire. 'The last door on the left. Forgive me if I don't come with you, but I must have a word with Cook.' She turned back the way she had come and Rose, watching her, thought *How sweetly flows the liquefaction of her clothes.* But there was nothing else sweet about her sister. Claire had dug her heels in behind her hard-won position, all gentleness and courtesy outside, all calculating determination inside, and she would, as always, be ruthless in achieving her aim.

Oh well, shrugged Rose, what did it matter where she slept? And the housemaid's attic might be rather fun. She mounted the bare wooden stairs to the upper landing, coconut-matted, with white-washed walls, and was reminded of that time more than two years ago when Claire had taken them to Harry Price-Hill's house in expectation of the drawing room and they had been shown to the upstairs schoolroom instead.

But, as then, Rose found the result pleasant enough – a small, whitewashed room with a rag rug, one small skylight in the sloping

289

ceiling and a view, when she opened it and leant out, of the stable block and the old brewery. But it was airless, even with the window open, and far too small for her to paint or draw in it with any ease. She would unpack, then take her sketch pad outside.

In deference to the occasion and her mother's wishes, Rose had brought a simple blue and white striped dress, reminiscent of the one she had worn in Dieppe years ago, but more up to date, and a plain straw hat with a blue ribbon. She was spreading this dress out on the bed when she heard hurrying footsteps and Sara burst into the room.

'Hello Rose. What a lovely little room! You are lucky being alone up here, away from everyone else, while I am stuck with Mamma and the others. Maudie is being a bore, as usual. She keeps pestering Nanny to let her hold Fay or push her perambulator round the garden, when she is not lecturing Charlotte on correct behaviour, as if Maudie knew the first thing about it anyway. Charlotte is being very silly and exhibitionist and Claire, of course, is insufferable, playing Lady of the Manor and condescending to anyone within reach. I wonder Phoebe Burgess did not see through her years ago. The Burgess children, by the way, are stealing apples in the orchard and no one has noticed yet. I hope they are sick in the middle of the ceremony!' Sara giggled in anticipation. 'It is no wonder the men have all gone out! Harry looked very handsome on horseback,' she said, suddenly wistful. 'I overheard Percy Woodstock say he would make a fine cavalry officer. You don't think ...' She stopped, bit her lip, and looked down at her hands before saying, 'Last night at dinner, Mr Burgess said that Chamberlain's latest despatch to the Transvaal Government is a virtual ultimatum and that it is only a matter of days now before war will be officially declared. A hundred horse of the Royal Field Artillery are to go out next week, as well as twenty companies of the Army Service Corps.'

'But those are regular soldiers, Sara, whose job it is to fight. After that come the Reserves, then the Volunteer regiments, and only then, if they still need men, will they call on the public for volunteers. I expect the war will be over long before that stage is reached.'

'Do you really think so?' Sara looked at Rose with disconcertingly clear hazel eyes.

'I am not an expert, Sara, but so everyone says. Even Percy says so, and he ought to know.'

'Will you marry Percy?'

The question hung like a dancing dust mote in the sunlit attic room, which smelt of lavender, beeswax and clean linen – a smell that was to remind her for years after of Wychwood – while from the yard below came the sounds of distant kitchen voices, the clattering of pans and pails, the gossiping of barnyard hens and somewhere a stable lad's whistle, tuneless and cheerful in the clear September air.

'He is going to South Africa,' said Rose, avoiding the question. 'Besides, he has not asked me.' That was not entirely true, for hadn't he asked to have first refusal and mistaken her answer for yes? When Sara opened her mouth to persist, Rose said, 'It is really no business of yours – so kindly keep out of it!'

'Yes, Rose,' said Sara meekly and added, as if to make polite conversation, 'Did you know that Claire keeps the door between her room and Edward's locked? Minnie told me.'

'And who is Minnie?' said Rose, while her heart surged with unwelcome excitement and a new, incredible idea.

'Claire's maid, of course. She told me that ...'

'How often has Mamma told you not to gossip with the servants?' Rose looked, and sounded, very stern, but Sara had planted her disruptive seed and did not care.

'She is not "Mamma" any more, has not Claire told you?' she said, with a swift change of subject. 'We are all to call her "Mummy". Poor Mamma has no say in the matter. She is only on the receiving end and sister Claire is not to be gainsaid, even by the master in the matter of her bedroom door. Minnie says that when Edward ...'

'I think you are in danger of becoming a mischief-maker,' interrupted Rose, picking up her sketch pad and making for the door. 'I am going downstairs.'

'The men went by the bridle path,' said Sara with apparent innocence. 'And may return the same way. If you plan to sketch in the woods, take care not to be trampled.'

'I will,' said Rose grimly, and fled. Sara knew too much for comfort and Rose could not decide whether it was worse to be favoured by the child as Rose apparently was, or to be hated like poor Claire. Either way, one's life was not one's own. She abandoned all idea of sketching and joined the rest of the womenfolk in the safety of the drawing-room.

Lunch was a ladylike affair of chicken galantine, decorative little morsels in aspic, and similar scraps of unsatisfying conversation. Afterwards the ladies retired *en masse* to rest, refresh themselves, and dress, while the servants endeavoured to make the children equally presentable.

Rose's toilet was soon completed. She was sitting on her bed, in her freshly-pressed dress, neat shoes, and plain straw hat, its ribbons flowing loose at the back and very blue against the gleaming red of her hair, wondering whether to go downstairs to the drawing room or to stop where she was when through the open skylight came a sudden clatter of hooves from the yard below, the stamping and snorting of horses, the rattle of harness and the ring of shod boot on cobblestone. The clear September air was suddenly laced with the smells of warm leather and steaming horses, with an underlying tang of straw and fresh manure. Rose found it strangely exciting. She heard cheerful male voices and laughter. So the menfolk were back. They would come inside, talk for a few minutes perhaps, before going to their rooms to wash and change. She heard a door slam deep in the house below, distant voices, silence. If she waited another five minutes surely it would be safe to go down? She would find a spot on the edge of the woods from which to sketch the house and from where she could see the others gathering in the drawing room. She took her sketch pad and pencils, opened her door, listened, then made her way quickly down the back stairs, through the kitchen regions and into the hall – just as he came out of the library door and closed it behind him.

She saw him clearly against the polished oak of the door, like a figure in a painting: dark-haired, handsome in pale, whip-cord breeches, dark leather riding boots, tweed jacket with velvet collar and high white stock. He stood, motionless, like a dummy in Millard's window, she thought irreverently, for the space of seconds, before stepping forward to block her path.

'So you came,' he said quietly, his eyes grave and intense.

'Of course. It is my niece's christening, after all.' She made to pass him, but he side-stepped and put out a hand. Involuntarily, she flinched, but he took her arm just the same, looked swiftly to right and left, then above to the landing, and drew her into the shadow of the stairs.

'I must see you, Rose,' he said urgently. 'Alone.' When she made no answer, but tried ineffectually to break away, he said, 'We cannot spend the rest of our lives avoiding each other. It is, at the least, ridiculous. We have unfinished business, you and I. I cannot rest till it is settled, and nor, I think, can you.'

'No.' She sighed with the acceptance of the inevitable.

A door opened on the landing above. 'I must go,' he said swiftly. 'I will find a way. I am not sure where or when, but somehow. Will you be ready?'

'Oh yes ... *the readiness is all.*' Then he was gone, spirited soundlessly away into the back regions of the house, and she was left alone, in the slow-ticking quiet of the hall. It was done. She had licensed the inevitable, and behind the pain and the pride she felt jubilation. She would tell him what she thought of his behaviour, how he had misjudged and maligned her, she would rid herself of all pent-up resentments and misunderstandings till the air was pure and fresh again between them. She would tell him she was a painter now in her own right, whatever he said about 'so-called art', and that she meant to be a better. That he must accept that if they were to be friends. Accept it without condescension or patronage. Accept *her*, as she was.... Then it would be as it had been that autumn, two years ago, before she went abroad, before Claire.

At the thought of Claire, her elation flickered and dimmed, but only momentarily, before blazing high again with expectation. Claire was irrelevant. She remembered that scene in their bedroom in Kensington, when Claire had declared into the dressing-room mirror, 'Just remember, Rose that I have first choice,' and she had challenged, 'Do you?' It had been Claire who had lowered her eyes, though she pretended it was in order to brush her hair. Rose had defied Claire then and would do so again, in spite of all obstacles.

Her sketching for the moment forgotten, she made her way to the drawing room to wait for the party to assemble – and for whatever message Edward might contrive to send.

CHAPTER 8

The christening was an unqualified success. The little church looked lovely, Claire's flowers both cheerful and elegant against the quaint stone walls. The sun slanted through the stained glass window at just the right angle, and a gratifying number of tenants and villagers had gathered to catch a glimpse of the party from Wychwood and Mr Rivers' little daughter.

Fay behaved herself perfectly, giving a tiny cry of protest at the first touch of water – 'That's the devil safely out of her,' whispered the superstitious – and afterwards smiling beatifically on everyone within range.

Nanny was discreetly at hand to reclaim her charge before Madam's arm should tire or Miss Fitzsimmons' garments be crumpled, and the group at the font looked altogether charming. The Burgess children were not sick after all, or not until much later, which was more likely the result of too much chocolate cake and cream than of the stolen apples.

After the ceremony people made their way back to Wychwood variously on horseback, in carriages, or on foot. Rose half-thought Edward would contrive a meeting then, but no. He drove his wife and daughter home at the head of the procession, so that he and Claire, the perfect parents, were in position on the steps to welcome their guests to Wychwood. There, a splendid tea had been set out under a striped awning on the terrace. Cucumber sandwiches, minced chicken sandwiches, slivers of bread with caviar or smoked salmon, tiny choux buns filled with flavoured creams of this and that, meringues and petticoat tails, several different sponge cakes, and, of course, the christening cake in central splendour. There was champagne in which to drink the infant's future, and unlimited tea. Later that evening the staff and estate workers were to have their own celebration on a similar trestle table in the stable yard, but for the moment their ministrations were devoted entirely to the welfare of Wychwood's guests.

After tea, ladies and some of the gentlemen strolled the paths of the flower gardens, gossiping, children ran about squealing and for once unchecked. Maudie took charge of Fay's beribboned and lace-

294

decked perambulator and reverently wheeled it to and fro in the shade of the copper beech till Claire told her for goodness sake to keep still before she made the child sick. Maudie's face crumpled into unsightly blotches and her eyes filled, but as soon as she stopped pushing, Fay cried and Claire hastily said, 'Oh all right then, if you must,' and turned her back.

The lawn had been made ready not for tennis but for croquet, the gardener having set out the hoops while they were all at church. Rose and Percy played together against Sara and Fitz. Charlotte pestered Harry Price-Hill unmercifully until he consented to be her partner, then he promptly lost every hoop. Ten-year-old Charlotte alternately squealed with delighted laughter, or accused him of doing it on purpose and belaboured him with her fists till he threw up his hands in surrender and begged her mercy. Georgina and Guy Morton won. Then Rose took up her sketch pad again and made thumbnail sketches of most of the guests when they were not looking, and of some of them when they were.

'Rose dear, you must do a little portrait of me with Fay,' cried Claire when she saw the sketch pad. 'Maudie, wheel my little darling over here, then run and see if you can find Edward for me. Tell him to come at once, for a portrait.' She arranged herself and her infant in a basket chair under the awning and commanded Rose to begin drawing. 'But leave space to put in Edward, standing beside me.'

Edward, however, did not come. Maudie returned, breathless and red-faced, ten minutes later to say he was showing Robert Burgess the new pair of greys he had bought in Maddingley and to manage without him. 'Tell them I cannot come for the moment,' she repeated, 'but will sit for my portrait later, at a more suitable time.'

Rose carefully included Claire's frown of displeasure in her portrait with the result that Claire thought it 'Not up to your usual standard, Rose dear. I hope you are not losing your touch.'

Mrs Millard found a confidante in the vicar's wife and unburdened all the trials of widowhood and her worries about her daughters' futures into that lady's sympathetic ear. Lady Price-Hill and Mrs Woodstock retired to the drawing room 'where it is so much cooler,' with a bottle of champagne and two glasses, and settled down happily to renew acquaintance and, no doubt, discuss what was to be done about their respective offspring. Certainly Harry, seeing them together through the open french windows, decided to keep well away and suggested hide and seek to the younger ones, in the woods. Sara joined in and when Harry found her behind an oak tree and demanded a forfeit, she kissed him. Charlotte saw and wanted to kiss Harry too and he smacked her bottom and told her to run away and play and come back in ten years' time.

The woods and policies of Wychwood rang with laughter and children's voices, and the house itself purred with contented chatter till the sun sank low behind the trees and the air grew suddenly chill. Nannies collected children and shepherded them unwillingly indoors. Women sent for wraps, or followed. And at last Percy sought out Rose where she lingered at the edge of the wood, beyond the tennis lawn, sketching the view of the house which she had planned that morning and waiting, without impatience, for Edward. She knew he would come and the mere expectation was an inner strength. But it was Percy who came to stand beside her and said tentatively, 'Rose? May I talk to you?'

He looked older and less flamboyant than he did in his Guards uniform, more sober and responsible, but his fair colouring showed to advantage against the dark correctness of his dress. He was a handsome man, she realised, with Georgina's looks: the kind that grew with acquaintance and could never be called plain. She had thought him ineffectual once, but now she saw strength in his jawline, and his eyes when he looked at her were resolute, though a little afraid.

'Of course, Percy.' She continued to draw in apparent composure, though she knew what was coming and dreaded it. 'You don't mind if I finish sketching while you talk, do you? I do so want to finish this before the light goes.'

'No. Of course not.' He subsided into silence, watching her pencil dart smoothly over the page, and after a few minutes, her conscience troubling her, she looked up and said, 'What was it you wanted to say, Percy?'

'I will wait till you are finished. Then perhaps we could walk a little in the woods, before dinner?'

'What a lovely idea! I would enjoy that.' She hoped her voice did not sound as emptily jolly to him as it did to her. She spent as long as she could on her drawing while the sky changed from turquoise to glowing red and trails of autumn mist hung over the home meadow. In the stubble fields, poppies glowed scarlet in the slanting light and the first rabbits emerged, lolloping cautiously through the shadows. Still he stood patiently waiting beside her and in the end she had to close up the book.

'There!' she said brightly. 'That will do for today. What a lovely day it has been.' She slipped her hand into the crook of his arm and said, '*Where'er we walk, cool winds shall fan the glade ...*'

'Don't, Rose.'

She was taken aback. 'Don't what, Percy?'

'Don't playact. Don't pretend you don't know what I want to say to you.'

Rose was surprised and ashamed. She had regarded Percy for so long with a mixture of tolerance and kindly scorn that she had not considered he might have feelings as deep and perceptions as sharp as anyone else's.

'You are quite right. I was being frivolous and brittle. Please forgive me.'

'Rose, you know I could forgive you *anything*,' he said with an intensity she had not heard in his voice before. She looked back at the house with some vague idea of running, or of seeking some fortuitous rescue, but everyone had apparently gone inside. The lamps had been lit in the drawing room and she could see figures moving – Claire, her mother, another woman in widow's black. Upstairs, there were lights in the bedrooms and faint on the air came the smell of cooking – chicken, she thought, or possibly partridge – and the sound of a piano, playing Chopin. Then a baby's cry. Poor little Fay. She had been remarkably good. But where was Edward? She had not seen him once since tea.

Percy took her by the hand and drew her into the concealing shadows of the woods. The bridle path was well trodden, the turf almost soundless underfoot. From across the woods, towards Wychwood Bottom, came the sudden bark of a fox and Rose realised that it was later than she had thought. She remembered with relief that the dressing gong would ring before long.

It was dark under the trees, after the open vista of the lawn. Behind them, the lamps of the house shone like fallen stars between the tree trunks and ahead of them, the gold and russet shades of autumn blended into a twilight monotint of shadows. On either side of the path, bracken curled and wove in brittle autumn splendour and suddenly, from overhead, came the pure, indignant cry of a blackbird.

'I feel we are intruders,' said Rose. 'Perhaps we should retreat and leave the wood to its rightful inhabitants?'

'Not yet. There is a glade I want to show you, where toadstools grow and tiny wood anemones.'

'Oh Percy,' said Rose, suddenly desolate. Why was he here with the wrong woman, and she with the wrong man? He offered her tenderness, romantic chivalry and faithful love, when all she wanted was ... She stopped on the edge of admitting the inadmissible.

'Do not look so sad,' he said. 'I know beauty moves artists to sadness and even tears, but I will care for you. Always.' He turned

297

towards her and she said quickly, 'Show me the toadstools, before the light goes completely.'

They walked on through the gathering darkness, until the path widened into a little clearing with a patch of sky overhead and a single star.

'There,' he said, pointing. The toadstools were almost colourless in the twilight, their scarlet muted to brown. Then he took both her hands in his and said, 'Rose, I sail for South Africa on Saturday. I may never come back. No, don't protest the contrary. Every soldier recognises the possibility of death. Do you remember I wrote you a letter, in Siena?'

'Of course. It was a beautiful letter, though I did not deserve it.'

'I meant every word, and I mean it still. Rose, I love you. Please, before I sail, say that you accept my love?'

Rose was silent, searching for words which would neither wound nor encourage false hope. She was fond of Percy, loath to hurt him, humbled by his generosity and ardour, and absolutely untouched. She felt nothing in his company beyond the affection she might accord a favourite brother and, perversely, because of that was powerless to deal with the situation. It would have been simpler had she hated him, or felt positive revulsion. Besides, he was sailing for what might be a bloody and destructive war. He might even die ... for the first time, the possibility seemed horribly real. How could she kill his heart before he left?

'I know your painting comes first,' he said, misconstruing her silence. 'I understand that and am proud for your sake. I said I would demand no promises and I meant it. Instead, I ask you, Rose dearest, merely to renew that hope you gave me once? May I still hope that one day you will be my wife?'

Oh God, she thought, who am I to take that hope away? She reached up and kissed him gently on the lips. 'Make of that what you will. And ask me again when you come home.'

As before, he took prevarication for consent. 'I will,' he cried, with jubilation. 'Dearest Rose, I will write to you every day, think of you every waking moment, until I come home again, to claim my reward.' He bent his head to kiss her, but she twisted away.

'Don't be premature. You have not even sailed yet!'

At that moment, the dressing gong sounded in the distance and Rose laughed with relief. 'Saved by the gong! Now take me back to the house, quickly, or we will never be ready in time for dinner.'

She let him kiss her, once, at the edge of the trees, then broke away and ran for the safety of the house.

Alone in her attic room, she felt ashamed. She should have told him she felt nothing for him and never could. Should have told him she would never marry him. Should have told him ... what? That the only man she wanted was married already, and to her own sister?

No. She had done absolutely right. At least she had made Percy happy and, after all he had done for her, she owed him that. He would sail for South Africa, happy in the belief that she would marry him on his return. She might even do it. He would be away for at least a year, probably two, and who knew what might happen in that time? It might, after all be the best solution.

Dinner was a lively affair. They were seventeen at table and would have been twenty had Edward's mother arrived in time and had not Claire decided at the last moment that Charlotte and Maud should not eat with them after all. Charlotte had behaved in a precocious and boisterous manner all evening, especially where Harry Price-Hill was concerned, and she could not risk any disruption to her dinner. As for Maud, she had had quite enough excitement for one day anyway and would be far happier in the upstairs nursery with the rest of the children.

Edward had Mrs Woodstock and his Aunt Clementina on either side, Claire had Robert and Percy, so chosen because he was a soldier on the eve of battle. She had placed Rose beside Percy for reasons everybody knew. Hadn't she promised years ago that once married she would give house parties and invite suitable suitors for her sisters? Guy Morton, as a member of the Suffolk Volunteers, was also expecting to be summoned to the flag at any moment, but Claire conveniently ignored that particular fact. Morton was only a farm manager and would do for Georgina whom Claire disliked. So Rose found herself between Percy and Fitz, with Georgina and Guy Morton opposite.

Rose could not have spoken to Edward had she wished to, with such an expanse of laden table between them, though the conversation became so animated that he could have signalled to her unnoticed a dozen times. As it was, he had not spoken to her since that snatched moment in the hall that afternoon and had made no sign. Yet she felt the current strong between them. Words were unnecessary and Rose was content to let fate take its course. There was surprising comfort in accepting the inevitable. She grew increasingly light-headed and, as the wine flowed, the good will begun by the afternoon's champagne blossomed into full-blown enjoyment. When Percy tried to hold her hand under the table she let him for a full five seconds before drawing it away in mock reproof.

299

'Don't tell me that was one of the manoeuvres you practised on Salisbury Plain, Captain Woodstock! I thought it was drill of a far more warlike kind.'

'Is that the reconnaissance you were telling us about, old boy?' called Harry from further down the table. 'If so I think I might join the cavalry myself.' Percy blushed, and Claire, the perfect hostess, said smoothly, 'I hear that cavalry training is no longer merely an amusement for spectators, but something far more rigorous. Is that so, Percy?'

'Nonsense,' cried Harry. 'When they are not galloping all over Salisbury Plain, terrifying the natives, they spend their time playing polo, gorging themselves silly in the mess tent or indulging in a bit of *dismounted action*, eh, Percy?' Greatly amused by his own joke, Harry repeated and embellished it at his own end of the table till his mother commanded him to, 'Be quiet, Harry, or leave the table!'

'Don't take any notice of Harry,' said Rose. 'He is merely being frivolous. But please tell us what really happens, Percy? That is, if it is not a deadly secret?'

'Not at all. In fact, the more widely known the approach, the better. We have had many years of peace, with no need to train cavalry in battle tactics, and even the movements in the Cavalry Drill book have been allowed to lapse. Besides, except at places like Aldershot, many regiments have no elbow room to practise manoeuvres and the Plain is ideal. First we teach the fundamental principles of pace and direction, then we practise the long advance, followed by the "charge", "break-up" and "rally".' He went on to explain the simplification of orders to ensure efficiency, the benefits of training at regimental before brigade level, the efficacy of training cavalry for shock action.

After his first embarrassment, Percy spoke with confidence and authority and Rose realised that he was not the ineffectual gentleman-soldier she had always taken him to be, but as much an expert in his field as she hoped to be in hers. The whole of his end of the table was listening intently: from Claire with her air of courteous attention, to Guy Morton, lower down on the opposite side, with his very personal interest in things military.

'If we are to be an efficient arm in modern warfare,' Percy finished earnestly, 'then our cavalry must be trained in all aspects of warfare. For instance, the speed of dismounting and taking up firing positions is far too slow, and not enough attention is paid to the business of handling Reserves. Everyone knows Cromwell was one of the greatest cavalry leaders in history and we could learn much from him.'

'Except that he's dead, old boy,' called Harry the irrepressible, but he found himself ignored.

Percy's confident, informed description of the training he and his brigade had undergone had reminded the company of the secondary reason for their gathering – a farewell to those of the Queen's soldiers who were embarking for Natal to secure a threatened outpost of her Empire.

'Then reconnaissance is undervalued,' continued Percy, 'and must be taught and learnt. Not only that, but officers all down the line must be taught to report concisely and accurately what they have seen. And to read a message correctly.'

Here, something made Rose turn her head and she saw Edward looking at her. Had she missed his message? Or was he indicating that its delivery was imminent?

'My father,' said Edward deliberately, 'was once interested in the transmission of messages – before the photography, I think, and after the fossils.' There was indulgent laughter – old Mr Rivers' eccentricities were obviously well known. 'He even set up a heliograph in the old brewery and signalled to my mother – who very properly ignored him. After all, the messages were in a private code and he had not given her the key!'

Again there was laughter, while realisation flared in Rose's mind. It was to be the old brewery – of course. Remembering that other, haunted time she shivered suddenly with dread and resolution, with a sense of the inexorable, and something else she refused to acknowledge.

'The ordinary morse code is enough for our chaps,' said Percy beside her, 'though a second might be useful with a heliograph, if the enemy can see it too. We tried a couple of exercises against a "flagged" enemy on the Plain, but unfortunately our assembly points were so close to each other that reconnaissance was hardly necessary!'

The discussion reverted to Percy's cavalry exercises, the best method of training for reconnaissance and the advantage of foot patrols. Guy Morton raised the question of how to transport horses on a sea voyage of at least two weeks and nearer three, and he and Percy and even Edward from the far end of the table discussed the relative merits of the old, short stalls where the horse was braced, and the new long stalls where the animal was left free, and because it was Percy's embarkation dinner, Claire allowed the subject to continue long after she would normally have introduced an alternative such as the latest London concert or the ever-useful weather.

Rose sat silent, apparently following the discussion with absorbed

301

attention while inside her head the arguments pursued each other in a whirling maelstrom of discord. She ought not to go. He ought not to ask it. He was married, irrevocably married. Besides, he had rejected her long ago. He had scorned her as a second-rate amateur, and laid a vandal's hand on her painting. She could forgive him some things, but never that. Never ... hadn't they agreed to be partners in hate? Yet when she looked up and caught his eyes on hers a line of Blake's came unbidden to her mind. *Mutual forgiveness of each Vice, Such are the Gates of Paradise*, and were it not impossible, she could have sworn he heard it too. Damn, damn, damn, she thought with increasing desperation. A thousand times damn.

The men sat longer than usual over the port and when they eventually joined the ladies, they were decidedly mellow in their individual ways. The vicar found out a secluded chair and promptly fell asleep. Robert Burgess waxed garrulous and increasingly pompous, to anyone who would listen, Edward sank into brooding silence, while the younger men were boisterously merry, demanding singing and dancing, hide and seek and charades.

Claire played demurely on the piano, the vicar's wife surprisingly less so. Adelaide sang. Claire sang. Georgina and Rose sang a duet. Harry recited *The Wreck of the Hesperus* and got most of it wrong. Sara recited *Lycidas* and got all of it right. Claire sent for tea and the card tables. Percy cornered Rose behind the piano and suggested a stroll in the moonlight, which she refused. Lady Price-Hill fell asleep over her hand of cards and dropped them. Then Harry demanded dancing. He cajoled the vicar's wife into playing a waltz and threw open the french windows onto the terrace. There he danced first with Sara, then with Adelaide, then, requiring two extra pages in her diary, with Sara again. Guy Morton partnered Georgina, Fitz whoever would have him, and Percy danced with Rose. Edward excused himself and went out 'To check the servants have all they need for their party.' He was gone half an hour. When he came back, Claire summoned him to her side and whispered in his ear. They joined the dancers on the terrace and took a sedate turn before Claire suggested to the vicar's wife that her poor fingers must be aching and they could not possibly impose on her any longer. She closed the piano. Adelaide offered to take over, but Claire said the windows had been open long enough and it was growing late.

Georgina roused her mother who roused Lady Price-Hill. Someone was sent to rouse the coachman and they prepared to leave.

'Thank you for a splendid evening,' said Percy when the ladies had assembled their belongings and each other and left in the Woodstock carriage, Harry and Fitz riding escort beside them, the vicar's dog cart behind. Phoebe Burgess had already said their goodnights and goodbyes and propelled her husband upstairs to bed. Only Guy Morton lingered, exchanging last-minute cavalry talk with Percy in the hall while Edward and Claire stood politely waiting, with Mrs Millard, Sara and Rose. But farewells were finally said, good luck wished and wished again, thanks bestowed, and Guy Morton left, to walk the mile or so to his house at Wychwood End.

Yet still Percy lingered, while his horse waited patiently in the darkness outside, occasionally lifting and stamping a foot, or flicking lazily with its beautiful tail. The stable boy, tired of waiting, had hitched the bridle over a fence post and returned to the festivities in the yard.

'Good luck, old chap,' said Edward, shaking Percy's hand. 'And a safe voyage.'

The womenfolk echoed his wishes, and Claire kissed his cheek. Mrs Millard did the same, then, blushing, Sara followed. Finally it was Rose's turn.

'Walk with me to the gate?' He pleaded. Now that the parting moment had come, he was careless who should hear him.

She hesitated, dreading the darkness alone with Percy, then reproached herself for her heartlessness. He was a soldier riding into battle and if not certain, then certainly possible death.

'Go with him, dear,' said Mrs Millard, with approval. If Rose was sensible for once she could be engaged by morning. 'But you had better take a wrap. The night air is chill.'

'All right. Wait for me, Percy? I'll only be a minute.' She ran lightly for the stairs and up into the lamplit shadows of the first landing. She heard voices from the direction of the Burgess room, and from somewhere at the back of the house, a murmur of muted merriment where the servants were sitting up late.

On the second floor landing it was quiet and empty of all light but the faint light of the moon which glimmered through the landing skylight. She had forgotten to bring a candle, but the moonlight led her safely to her room. She opened the door, groped for matches and a candle, struck a light – and saw, dark against the white of the pillow, a shining metal key. She thought at first it must be the key to her travelling case, then saw that it was too big – more like the key to a door. With a thud of the heart she remembered that dinner conversation. She opened the skylight window and peered out: to her right, the lamplit shadows of the stable block where figures still moved about, clearing tables, laughing, and closer, beside it, the dark block of the old brewery. Thoughtfully, her eyes strangely bright, she lowered the window again. Then she slipped the key into the placket of her dress, took up her woollen wrap and went back downstairs.

'We will say goodnight now, Rose dear,' said Mrs Millard, shooing Sara towards the stairs, 'and will see you in the morning. There is no need to hurry. Just see you do not keep her out too long, Percy,' she added, with an indulgent smile.

Claire and Edward said their final goodbyes to Percy, then Claire kissed Rose and said, 'I will say goodnight too, Rose. Then you need not feel you have to hurry back.'

'If I leave the door on the latch,' said Edward, 'will you lock it after you when you come in?'

'Of course,' she said, and added solemnly, 'Your key is safe with me.'

'Then we will say goodnight.'

Edward took Claire's arm and steered her towards the stairs.

'Goodnight,' said Percy and Rose together. He held open the door for her, stepped out into the waiting night, and closed it firmly behind them.

Edward heard the heavy door close and felt a sudden surge of jealousy so violent it almost made him stumble. 'Your key is safe with me,' she had said. She knew, understood – but would she come? He had left the arrangement deliberately vague, deliberately tangled and obscure so that still there were loopholes through which either of them could retreat with honour and dignity intact. It was safer that way. Besides, he had a conscience.

And now she was out in the darkness, with his connivance, with that moon-struck, doting Woodstock who would no doubt try to kiss her and . . . God! If he attempted anything more Edward would kill the bounder!

But of course he had no right to do anything of the kind. Rose could bed whomever she chose. Oh God. He almost groaned aloud at the thought.

'I hope you did not drink *too* much this evening,' said Claire. 'You know it is not good for you.'

'Too much for what?' he asked, directing his frustration at the nearest object. Then, deliberately, he held her by the shoulders and kissed her. She neither responded nor withdrew, but when his hands slipped from her shoulders to her waist, she moved on up the stairs saying, 'It is so late, Edward. I had not realised. Long after midnight already. I do hope the servants will be sensible and remember that I expect them to be up in the morning exactly as usual.' She had reached her bedroom door and turned, her hand on the knob. 'Perhaps you had better just run down and remind them, Edward? Please?' She smiled with what he thought of as her 'sweet entreaty' look, though there was little 'sweet' about it.

'All right,' he sighed, 'If you insist. But I won't be long. It will give you time to undress before I return, and I will say goodnight then.'

'Of course. But just in case I am asleep.' She reached up and kissed his cheek. 'Goodnight, Edward dear. It was a most successful day.' Then she opened her bedroom door and slipped quickly inside.

Edward stood a moment on the landing, brooding. The sober, responsible part of him knew he should follow his wife into that room and into her bed and forget all other possibilities. The other, romantic side of him ached for a different, forbidden consummation which he knew was almost within his grasp. Yet even now it was not too late. He could renounce temptation, set his eyes firmly on the road of virtue, honour his wife with faithfulness and rectitude. She was an excellent wife in many respects, a first-class manager, a competent, even talented hostess, virtuous and comely to look on. If he could be content with looking he would have few complaints – and, he thought bitterly, she would have none. But he was not content. A wife owed more than mere token obedience to her husband's wishes. If she chose not to honour that obligation, then she forfeited the right to his exclusive loyalty. Suddenly he saw his way clear. He would leave the final choice to his wife. He made for the backstairs and the kitchen to fulfil her needless errand with all speed. His fate lay in Claire's hands now. If when he returned to his dressing room he found the door to her bedroom unlocked, then he would go in. He would forget temptation and spend the rest of the night in virtuous union with his wife.

And if the door was locked . . . Excitement raced at the possibility. He knew which road he longed for, which direction his body ached to take, but if fate decreed the path of virtue, then that should be his path.

It was quiet when he returned. The coverlet on the narrow bed in his dressing room was turned back, his night shirt laid ready and the lamp beside the bed turned low. There was no sound from Claire's room, no light showing under the connecting door. She must be in bed, waiting. He stood a long moment, summoning the courage to test fate's answer, then slowly turned the handle of the door.

305

Afterwards, Rose could not remember what she and Percy talked about in that last half hour together. She only knew that there was gentle moonlight and sadness, that she disappointed him by withholding her acceptance of his love and yet at the same time strengthened him, with hope and resolution. He was tender, thoughtful and grave. She promised to go with Georgina to Southampton to see him embark and, finally, she kissed him. Then she stood on the doorstep of Wychwood and watched him ride away into the night, an upright, military figure, handsome in the moonlight. He turned at the curve in the drive and raised his hand. She waved in return, though perhaps he did not see. She listened as the hoofbeats drummed further and further into the distance till they merged, throbbing, into the moonlit silence, in time with the louder throbbing of her heart.

When the night was still again, except for the busy rustling of night creatures in the undergrowth and the ceaseless weaving of bats, she stood a moment gathering her bearings. There was a lamp still burning in the stables and another by the scullery door, but the old brewery block was in darkness. She had half expected a lamp in the skylight, in imitation of his father's heliograph, but that would have been flagrantly indiscreet. Nevertheless, she had expected something. . . .

Doubt halted her step. Suppose she was mistaken? Suppose she had imagined everything and the key was nothing – something the housemaid had found and mistakenly thought was hers? After all, he had made no sign, and she could remember no door in the old brewery that needed a key. She remembered her last sight of him with his hand on Claire's arm, leading her upstairs to bed. Tonight would Claire's bedroom door be locked?

The moon came out from behind a cloud and flooded the old brewery with sudden light. It was a huge, full moon, serene and stately. She made up her mind. Moving on silent feet and keeping to the shadows, she sped along the path from the house to the old brewery block, then under the carriage arch and through the entrance into the black maw of the building itself.

There had been corn sacks, she remembered, and old farm machinery. A rat had sat up on its haunches, whiskers twitching in indignation. She hoped the rat was elsewhere, though she was strangely unafraid.

Moonlight filtered through the cobwebbed windows and made the empty brewery building seem like some ancient cathedral, victim of a forgotten Reformation and long abandoned. She stepped further inside and looked around her – two doors where she remembered them, both open, and, in place of that rickety ladder, a new flight of wooden steps with a handrail, pale in the moonlight, and at the top a door, with a lock.

From the past came Lady Portia's voice, indignant on the railway station, 'And to crown all he dismissed the workmen from the old brewery when the work was only half done ...' Other memories crowded in, of the last time she had stood at the foot of what had been a ladder then and was now a stairway and he had asked 'Do you think it possible for a place to be haunted by the future?' She stood listening, straining her ears into the silence. Nothing. Only the sound of a door closing far away in the kitchen block, a voice calling goodnight. There was a soft rustling noise in the corner of the barn and her scalp prickled for a moment before she made out the shape of a tiny four-legged creature – a field mouse, perhaps, or a vole. A bat swooped silently across the barn and out into the night. She moved resolutely for the stairs and climbed them, her hand tight on the rail. The wood was new, the steps in places hardly finished. She reached the door at the top and tried the handle. Locked. She took the key from her pocket, placed it in the lock and turned.

Inside, it was as she remembered except that where there had been bare floor boards and dust there was now a patterned carpet and a pile of cushions which gleamed silken pale and welcoming in the moonlight. Were they left over from the old time, before ... or were they newly strewn, in preparation?

The moon was high in the sky now and its light streamed steadily in through the pair of skylights making it almost light enough to read. Certainly to see. She felt in the pocket of her cloak for the little sketchpad which travelled everywhere with her and settled down on the cushions to wait. She would sketch the loft with its sloping ceiling and secret, new-made door, its patterned carpet and heaped cushions, and the moonlight throwing everything into eery relief. Then, when the moon faded, she would go back to the house, to bed.

All around her was silence, only moonlight on rafters, and the mournful cry of a barn owl from the copse beyond the Great Meadow, and still Rose worked on, while a kind of acceptance flowed into her very bones, filling her with contentment and a strange peace. *If it be not now, yet it will come....*

Then, soft through the silence, came the sound of a footfall in the depth of the barn, the creak of new wood, a step on the stair. The door slowly opened and after a long, breath-held moment, a shadow fell across her page.

'Rose,' he said softly, 'May I come in?'

CHAPTER 9

She rose, slowly, from the cushions and stood waiting, watching him across the moonlit, empty room with sombre eyes. He had changed out of his evening finery into the riding breeches and tweeds he had worn that afternoon when she came upon him in the hall. And, as then, he remained motionless, his hand on the doorknob. 'I await your answer.'

'It is your barn. Who am I to bar you entry?'

'I gave you the key,' he said, still not moving, 'so that you too could lock me out, if you chose.'

You too ... So Sara had been right! The last shred of guilt fell away in joy as Rose remembered that day in Dieppe five years ago when Claire had made her promise never to take Claire's man and Rose had added in defiance, 'Until you have finished with him.' Now Claire had removed herself from the contest and it was a contest no more. Rose was free. Then she forgot even that as she realised his pride would let him wait no longer. He was turning away.

'But I did not choose, Edward,' she said quickly, and added, taking the step beyond retreat, 'And never will.'

He came in then, moving the key from the outside of the lock to the inside. He closed the door, and slowly turned the key with a sound that echoed over and over in her head, with the throbbing of her blood.

He moved towards her through the moonlight till he stood so close she could feel his breath on her cheek. The harvest moon, she thought irrelevantly, or was it the hunter's? Either seemed appropriate.

'I asked you to forgive me,' he said, looking into her eyes. 'You gave me no answer.'

'If you cannot read the answer for yourself, you must ask again.' But her voice trembled and she could not look away.

'Then I do ask ... again.' His forefinger traced the line of her brow and cheek with a touch that set her blood racing. 'Miss Rose Millard, will you forgive me?'

'Guess.' When his finger moved over her lips she caught it between her teeth as she had done that time, long ago. After that, of course, there was no going back.

A glorious, hungry, passionate time later, as they lay naked and at peace on the moonlit silken cushions, he said quietly, 'You have forgiven me ten times over, and ten times more than I deserve. Though you did not say as much, I heard it in your singing.'

'There are times, Mr Rivers,' she said, teasing, 'when it is one's duty to forgive. And I was not singing.'

'Oh yes you were, woman. Duty indeed! Every beloved inch of you was singing, gloriously and exultantly, as I entered your gates of Paradise.'

'How very immodest of me.'

'Not at all. You have a lovely singing voice.' With a low laugh he sprang suddenly to his feet and stood, naked in the streaming moonlight, towering above her. 'Will you sing to me again?'

She looked up at him through narrowed eyes, stirred, stretched, folded her hands behind her head and said languorously, 'That depends.'

'On what, Jezebel?'

'On what song you expect me to sing.'

'The same song, over and over, to the end of time.' He held out a hand and reaching up, she ran a forefinger lightly over his palm, saying, 'You make it sound like some interminable encore,' but her eyes were laughing.

'My apologies, Madam. I should have said the same song, with variations.' He gripped her hand, drew her slowly to her feet and as slowly kissed her, then held her away from him, studying her marble whiteness in the moonlight. 'Like Venus rising from the waves, with glorious, uncovered breasts.' He bent his head to kiss them.

'I have longed for you to do that ever since that time in the studio.'

'And I ... God, Rose, but you are beautiful ...'

'Is that in our song?' she managed, gasping aloud as pleasure sent darts of fire through her blood.

'Oh yes, I think so. And so is this ... and this ...'

'I don't suppose this was quite what your father had in mind,' she said dreamily, a long time later, her hand languidly tracing the line of his chest, his hip, his thigh. 'But the harem theme is not entirely inappropriate.'

'No.'

She lay on the tumbled cushions in the shadowed, cobwebbed

loft and knew she would not have changed one dust mote, one crumbled butterfly wing, one grain of sawdust for all the luxuries of man's imaginings. Nor had any other light but the moon. She looked up at the skylight and the clear night sky beyond with its scattering of stars and murmured, '*And behold the wandering moon, riding at her highest noon* – I wonder if it is her highest?' Edward did not answer and she saw that his eyes were closed, his face relaxed in sleep. She studied him in the moonlight, naked and beautiful, memorising every curve and inch of him, to store against a barren future.

'Sweet love,' she whispered, her eyes on his sleeping face. 'What are we to do, you and I? If only we could turn back time, undo our mistakes, remodel life to fit our hearts' desire ...'

But what did her heart desire? In the languid pleasure of their cushioned bed Rose knew that Edward beside her was part of it – as an arm or leg was part of her – but not all. She needed her art, too – and that dedication had lost her Edward once. Would it lose him again? She lay, propped on one elbow, studying him, her naked breast warm against his chest, her thigh touching his. The loft held all the stored warmth of that miraculous summer, but the night air was chill now as the moon began to wane. It would be morning soon.

She watched the rise and fall of his chest, the pulse beat in his throat, the dark shadow of eyelash on cheek and wondered when they would be so at peace together again. Tomorrow – or was it today? – she would go home. She had half promised to stay longer, but that was out of the question now. She knew it was impossible for her to be in Edward's house and not in Edward's bed. A phrase from a letter of Claire's long ago flitted through her mind. *My heart is like a singing bird because my love is come to me.* Poetic lies on Claire's part. They must have been, for had her heart ever sung as Rose's heart sang now, she could never have locked her door against him.

The sky was paling fast. Soon the first bird would sing, the first cock crow, the first cow low in the meadow, the first kitchen maid rise ... She must go. She moved away from him to sit up, but he caught hold of her and clasped her tight, his eyes still closed in lingering sleep. 'Not yet.'

'*Night's candles are burnt out and jocund day stands tiptoe on the misty mountain tops* ...'

'There isn't a mountain top for a hundred miles.'

'No, but it is appropriate nonetheless.'

'Juliet to Romeo? Or the approach of day?'

310

'Both, of course. Or do you want the world to find us naked together when they collect the morning milk?'

'Ah ... the cruel practicalities of life.' But he did not stop her when she sat up and began to dress. He watched her pull her petticoat over her head and straighten it, then said quietly,

'Do you truly love me, Rose?'

She stopped, frozen in the act of buttoning her bodice, her back towards him. Then she said, 'I am not sure I know what to love "truly" means. I know I love you, Edward. I set no measure to that love. I make no promises and I ask none of you. If that is "truly", then so be it.'

He snatched her to him and kissed her with a force and passion which left her gasping. Then a bird sang suddenly sweet from the chestnut tree and was answered by another and another. 'We must go.' They dressed quickly and in silence, Rose in her last night's dinner dress, Edward in his working clothes of riding breeches and tweeds.

'I will wait till you have left, then go to the stables,' he said, 'and saddle my horse. You go in by the front door and the front stair. No one will see you at this hour.' He kissed her, lingeringly, on the lips. 'Till next time, my darling. I am hungry for you already.'

'Settle for breakfast,' she retorted, not trusting herself to more. Then she moved, silent-footed, down the wooden stairway, across the shadowed darkness of the barn, and out into the half-light of a misted September morning. She would have liked to run, singing, through the woods, to dance with the poppies in the stubble fields, to race with the rabbits in the Great Meadow, to shout her love defiantly to the whole sleeping world that they might wake and rejoice with her.

Instead, she slipped through the shadows under the chestnut tree, waited a moment, listening, at the great front door, then tiptoed inside. She crept cautiously through the sleeping household to her empty garret room where she undressed again, slipped into bed and lay sleepless, dreaming. They had said no goodbyes, made no promises, but she knew, as he must know, that they were one flesh now, unto eternity.

She was drifting into contentment when she heard hooves on cobbles in the stable yard. She saw as vividly as if she had risen from bed and looked out of the window, the horse being led out from its stall, the stable lad, still bleary-eyed with sleep, holding the bridle. Saw Edward, lithe and strong in riding breeches and leather boots, a white stock at his throat, his eyes dark with memory ... Saw him put his foot in the stirrup and swing into the saddle, touch whip to warm flank, and move out of the yard into the drive. She heard the hooves muffled on the fallen leaves under the chestnut, then louder on hard-baked earth. The steps changed from a careful, measured walk to a steady trot, and she saw him rise and fall in the saddle, rise and fall ... then in the far distance the pace quickened to a canter and she saw him crouch forward, his thighs gripping the animal's flanks, and knew he was galloping hard into the morning freedom, his heart singing as hers was.... When her washing water came she would dress and pack, then catch the morning train back to Town.

Ten minutes later she heard the first housemaid stir, then another, and the day began.

'You are looking particularly cheerful this morning,' said Mrs Millard shrewdly when they met at breakfast some three hours later. Rose had washed all over in icy water, brushed her tangled hair till it shone, and dressed demurely in the blue and white striped cotton, but nothing could douse the glow of fulfilment which lit her face with beauty and touched every line of her body with alluring grace.

Had not Mrs Millard known him better, she would have suspected Captain Woodstock of taking liberties. As it was, she said, 'Did Percy keep you outside long?'

'I didn't notice, Mamma,' said Rose, truthfully enough. 'It was such a lovely night and we had so much to talk about.'

'Did you decide anything?'

'Yes. I am going to Southampton to see him off,' said Rose, turning away to help herself to scrambled eggs from the sideboard. She had an extraordinary appetite this morning.

'Must you be so exasperating!' cried Rebecca who had had a difficult enough morning already, what with Sara mooning over that wretched diary of hers when she should have been dressing, and locking it away when she saw her mother coming, as if it contained precious secrets and her mother was an enemy spy. Then Charlotte had snapped at Maud to stop pestering her and to let her do her own hair for once and Maudie in consequence had had one of her attacks. They had all three been forbidden to speak again until they were spoken to and sat glowering but obedient over their breakfast plates. And now, it seemed, Rose was going to be equally annoying.

'You know very well what I mean, Rose. Did he *speak*?'

'Of course, Mamma. I told you we talked for hours ...' Then relenting, for after all life was too gloriously happy to spend it

312

teasing her mother, she added, 'He asked me to marry him.'

'Thank God for that,' said Mrs Millard with considerable relief. For Edward Rivers' question had unsettled her. Her conscience was not entirely clear where Rose was concerned, her financial juggling decidedly suspect. But Percy Woodstock had changed all that. Two down, three to go, she thought with satisfaction and in spite of her moods Sara was attractive enough. The Fitzsimmons boy, she was sure, was interested. 'I am very pleased, Rose dear,' she said, and kissed her. 'When is the wedding to be?'

'You are jumping to conclusions as usual, Mamma. I merely said he asked me to marry him. I did not say that I accepted.'

'But . . .' She stared at Rose aghast. 'But you must!'

'What must Rose do?' said Claire, coming into the room in a rustle of perfumed lavender silk and spotless lace. She took her place at the foot of the table and reached out a slender white hand for the silver coffee pot. 'Edward sends his apologies, but it was such a lovely morning that he went out for an early morning ride, to look over the estate. He is so conscientious, the dear boy. No, just a little toast for me, Mummy,' she said, waving aside the boiled eggs, 'and perhaps a touch of marmalade.'

'These scrambled eggs are delicious,' said Rose, 'I think I will take bacon as well. All the excitements of yesterday have given me an appetite.'

'You really should be careful, Rose,' said Claire sweetly. 'You do not want to grow fat and I have noticed that your waist is not as slender as it might be. All those loose garments you favour are not good for the figure. They provide no restraint.'

'I sometimes think those garments of yours, Claire, provide too much.' She looked solemnly at her sister and added, 'You do not want to get rigid.'

'Or break in half in the middle,' giggled Charlotte and was promptly smacked by an irate Mrs Millard.

'I told you not to speak till I gave you permission!' But of course it was Rose's fault. 'Claire! Tell your sister she must marry Percy Woodstock!'

Claire regarded Rose with faint surprise and said, 'Of course you must marry him, Rose dear.' She looked round the table and added, 'Phoebe is late today. But then perhaps she and Robert have decided to breakfast in their room, *à deux*. It is so agreeable for a husband and wife to have a little precious time alone together . . .' She gazed dreamily into space for a moment as if recalling precious times of her own, then, with a little smile, said, 'Didn't I say I would find husbands for you all, dear sisters? I want you all to enjoy the

313

happiness we married women enjoy.' Then, in a different voice, 'I knew Percy would propose last night. There was something in the air.'

'But she refused him,' cried Rebecca, furious. She turned on Rose with venom. 'I order you to marry him! Do you hear me?'

Rose laughed. 'Poor Percy. Married by order. I am much too fond of him for that, Mamma dear, and I beg of you not to interfere. What Percy and I decide together is our business and no one else's. Besides,' she added, in the interests of family harmony, 'we have agreed to decide nothing till he comes back from Natal. I wonder, Claire dear,' she continued smoothly, 'whether you would order the pony and trap to take me to the station? I find I must return to Town.'

'So soon? Certainly not!' cried Mrs Millard. 'What will people think?'

'They will think how devoted I am to our brave soldiers,' said Rose calmly. 'I have promised to be at Waterloo when the train leaves for Southampton on Saturday.'

'Of course she must go, Mummy,' said Claire, her hand already at the bell. 'But I hope you will come back very soon to do a proper portrait of Fay with her Mummy and Daddy. When you have brushed up your technique a little, of course.'

'Of course.' She looked at Claire with unwavering eyes and Claire looked steadily back, but as on that occasion after the theatre visit, it was Claire who looked away. Rose wondered if Claire remembered that other occasion. If so, did she suspect? But if she did she gave no sign, except by the alacrity with which she put the pony and trap at her sister's disposal.

Sara wanted to accompany Rose and was not allowed. 'Have you forgotten we are invited to tea with the Fitzsimmons? Adelaide is such a sweet girl and I think Fitz is quite attracted to you, Sara. I saw him looking at you last night in a most encouraging way.'

'Mamma!' cried Sara, blushing. 'I will not be paraded like a cow at an auction. I would rather go back with Rose.'

'You will do nothing of the kind, Sara. You will do as I say, or *no Cambridge!*'

For once Rose did not intercede on Sara's behalf. She wanted to be alone, to take out her memories one by one and treasure them, in solitude. She wanted to paint before that moonlit picture etched into her memory faded and blurred. And she wanted to leave Wychwood before Edward returned.

The pony and trap had almost reached the station when Rose became aware of a horseman overtaking them. As they drew into

314

the little station yard, a rider appeared at her side and dismounted to hand her down from the trap.

'So, you are fleeing the field?' His eyes caressed her.

'A diplomatic retreat.'

'Very wise. My mother has telegraphed to say she will arrive this morning.'

'Then I am wiser than I realised. My studio in Kensington is a far safer place.' She looked at him with steady meaning and his eyes became hooded with a look so charged with memory that she had to turn away lest she betray herself to all the watching world. He moved away to give the Wychwood stable lad fresh orders then took her bag and led her onto the platform.

'Forgive me if I leave you to the ministrations of young Davy Bird,' he said. 'I do not trust myself to stand beside you for another moment without outraging your modesty.'

'Surely, Mr Rivers, you know by now that I have none?'

'Oh God,' he groaned, turned on his heel and strode away. But Rose was smiling.

CHAPTER 10

Waterloo station was a scene of turbulent confusion. Everywhere was bustle and excitement, military uniforms mingling with civilian in the endless shifting crowds which thronged the platform. The special boat train, which was to take the soldiers and those of their families who could not bear to part at Waterloo to the dock at Southampton, was packed to overflowing. Georgina and Rose found themselves squashed with eight other people into a carriage that normally held six. There was an air of tension everywhere, frenetic chattering here, despairing silence there, bravado and laughter, even singing, side by side with gravity, the whispered confidences of parting, the dry-eyed misery of loss. In their carriage, a young soldier and his sweetheart sat, fingers entwined, in silence. An older man and woman talked in low, earnest voices, discussing last minute instructions concerning the trivia of housekeeping. Two lads, fresh-faced and spruce in proud new uniforms, joked and laughed.

The corridor was crammed with soldiers, with here and there a handful of wives or well-wishers and, in a special carriage, officials of the Union Line, with senior officers and the colonel of the regiment.

Then there was a shrill cacophony of whistles from the platform, green flags waved above the cheering crowds, and the engine ground into motion, its great pistons driving at first with leaden purpose, then inexorably faster. The crowds on the platform cheered, hands waved from train windows, voices shouted last minute messages and goodbyes. On the platform a woman held up a little child to its father at the moving window of the train, her face streaming tears, till the train outstripped her and she stood desolate and weeping, a small, indeterminate scrap in the debris of the station.

'Percy's train from Aldershot will be ahead of us,' said Georgina. Rose agreed. After that they hardly spoke. Rose busied herself with her sketch book, Georgina with her thoughts. Once Georgina gripped Rose's hand and squeezed it, whether to comfort herself or Rose the latter did not know.

Then, under an overcast and lowering sky, they drew into the station at Southampton docks where there was as much bustle and excitement as at Waterloo, but more colour and less confusion.

The Northumberlands, who were to travel in a newly-converted troop-ship, *The Gaul*, had arrived from Aldershot in special trains and were already embarking in ordered rows of scarlet serge, each man with pack and equipment and rifle with sheathed bayonet fixed.

'The Fighting Fifths,' said someone, in admiration, 'Straight from Omdurman and Crete.' They were certainly impressive, deep-chested, upright, resolute, filing up the gangplank and onto the troop ship with a precision of movement which had its own beauty.

'I thought they were to wear khaki,' said Georgina.

'Not issued yet,' their informant told them and Rose was glad. The river of red serge uniforms was splendid and one needed splendour as an antidote to sorrow – the more so when the over-shadowed sky burst its seams in a crack of thunder and loosed torrential rain.

However, their business was not with the Fighting Fifths, but with a mere captain of cavalry, in a party of assorted officers travelling out on a different ship of the Union Line. *The Gaul* had been requisitioned by the War Office on Monday and completely equipped as a troop ship by Friday afternoon, with rows of hooks for hammocks in great traverse beams, long deal tables, numbered and stacked athwart the ship, and countless tons of meat, flour, potatoes, fresh vegetables, in order to feed the thousand or more fighting men like fighting cocks and deliver them in peak condition.

Percy's ship had undergone no such wholesale transformation and as the officers were for the most part in mufti and barely distinguishable from the ordinary passengers on board, an unin-formed observer could have been forgiven for thinking it an ordi-nary ship on a routine voyage to the Cape. Except that the horses being led on board had a military look about them and arrange-ments for their transport were ordered and undertaken with military precision.

'There is Titan!' cried Georgina, indicating a splendid chestnut mount, with aristocratic bearing and a magnificent mane. 'Percy will not be far away.'

At that moment he came pushing through the throng towards them, calling their names. After their first greeting, he hurried them aboard, delivered them to the saloon and, with apologies, disappeared again to oversee the safe stowing of his precious mount.

The atmosphere in the saloon was not one of happy excitement at the prospect of a sea voyage to foreign lands, as might have been expected in a normal sea-going liner, but of quiet gravity. This was reflected in the faces of the officers who, many with their wives and sisters, had gathered in the saloon to spend the last short time together before the ship sailed.

There Percy joined them some twenty minutes later, and there they lingered, making determined conversation, repeating promises to write, while the rain drummed on the deck awnings and spurted up in tiny fountains all over the harbour. Rose drifted out onto the deck to leave Georgina and Percy together. Georgina fetched her back and took Rose's place. Mrs Woodstock had sensibly said her farewells in Suffolk and declared she could not stand the emotional strain of a shipboard farewell. 'All that water and creaking wood-work makes me quite ill.' Rose began to wish she had followed Mrs Woodstock's example.

Then a small party of nurses came aboard and Georgina pounced on them for information of where they were going, what hospital they trained at, how long ago they had volunteered. When she returned she was bright-eyed and excited.

'One of them has little more than a month's training,' she announced, 'and she says they are desperate for any nurses they can get. I shall speak to Aunt Clementina the moment she returns to London and ask her to pull strings. I intend to follow you, Percy, my boy, so you need not think you can escape me so easily.'

He grinned and ruffled her hair with touching affection. Rose, watching them, wished with sudden intensity that she could join that simple circle of undemanding love, forget that other torment and be happy with Percy, who loved her.

The time came for all visitors to say their final goodbyes and leave the ship. There was no hysteria, no weeping: the great British stiff upper lip prevailed, at least in public, and while most of the women and several of the men were moist-eyed, no one broke down. Across the water came a great burst of cheering from the troopship and the shore, as *The Gaul* cast loose and the tugs began to draw her out into the channel. A band on the promenade deck struck up *The British Grenadiers*.

Percy and Georgina hugged each other in farewell.

'Time to say goodbye,' said Percy, taking Rose's hands in his. 'Wait for me, till I return. And if, by some mischance, I do not, remember I love you.' Then he kissed her.

'Goodbye, and God go with you.' She wished she could have added, 'I love you too.' Instead, she said, 'Dear Percy, please take care ...'

'You are to paint, remember,' he told her, smiling, still holding

318

her hand in his. 'So that when I return we will give another Millard exhibition together, you and I. Promise?'

'I promise.'

The last warning whistle blew.

'Goodbye, my darling.' He kissed her again, then, one arm round her waist, he clasped Georgina with the other and kissed her, too. Across the water, the troopship had moved out into the channel and the band on its promenade deck changed rhythm to the slow lilt of *Auld Lang Syne*. It was the saddest thing Rose had ever heard.

Her eyes were wet as she stumbled down the gangplank to the shore, Georgina at her side. They stood with the other women, a small, forlorn group, and waited as the gangplank was raised, the signal given, ropes loosed, and engines swung into motion, until, in a churning wake of foam, the ship edged away from the quay while the distant strains of *Auld Lang Syne* trailed back to them across the harbour.

They spoke little on the return journey. The train was half empty, peopled for the most part by sad-faced women, a few whimpering children, and one or two younger boys, impatient to follow their fathers or brothers overseas, to defend Victoria's Empire.

Rose had expected Georgina to be sad. Instead she was buoyed up by a restless impatience and an eagerness to set to work at once.

'I mean to follow Percy before the year is out,' she told Rose as they neared Waterloo station. 'By fair means or foul. Aunt Clementina will help me, I know, and I will work at the hospital seven days a week, and seven nights too, if I must, just so long as I can sail out with the next batch of nurses to the Cape. The studio is empty now, Rose. Did I tell you? Empty, that is, of my possessions. All that remains is yours, including those poor old terracotta heads! I left the key on the lintel, in the usual place, but everything is yours now, to use exactly as you please.'

'Thank you, Georgina. You are a true friend.'

They parted at the station, Georgina to her hospital, Rose to her studio.

It was as she remembered it, though bare of modelling stands and clay. But the space was the same and the light, the sense of freedom and the peace. It is mine now, she thought with awe, to use as I please. I can live here, if I choose, welcome visitors and friends when I choose, love and paint as I choose, in privacy and without guilt....

She thought of the house in Kensington, empty now of everyone but Annie and the kitchenmaid until the family returned from Wychwood. Annie had welcomed her, fed her, fussed over her –

and pestered her for every detail she could squeeze out of her concerning Miss Claire's dear little baby's christening, but when she had started on Miss Rose's gentleman friend and Miss Rose's marriage prospects, Rose had sent her back to her kitchen with what Annie herself called 'a flea in her ear'. Rose knew that on her return she would have to undergo the same interrogation about her gentleman friend's embarkation, but until then she was free. And at least Annie knew nothing of that other.

No one did. And must not. She had a moment's apprehension when she remembered Sara, but the moment passed. Her family was irrelevant now. She remembered her mother's marriage plans for them all, her probing and questioning, her domineering authority, and knew that, whatever road her own life might take, she had grown beyond the house in Kensington. Besides, were her mother ever to suspect, she would class Rose with *The Woman Who Did*, brand her a fallen woman, 'spurned by Society and utterly cast out', and no doubt show her the door. Rose could at least save her mother the trouble.

Tomorrow she would bring what few things she needed here, to the studio. She would make her home here, where she belonged, and paint. . . .

She took off her hat and travelling cloak, tossed them onto the ottoman and tied the strings of her painting apron. Then she set up her easel, put her paints and pencils ready and stood, considering. There were the Wychwood notebooks to work on and today's sketches of the station and the troop ship at the quay – all fresh in her mind. She could finish the sketch of Percy she had begun this afternoon. Georgina would like that and she owed Georgina so much. Percy would like it too, as a sign that she thought of him, and she owed him even more. . . .

He would be somewhere in the Channel now, unsuspecting, on his way southwards to what they said was certain war. And when he came back . . . But she refused to think of the future with its complications and inevitable sorrows.

At Wychwood they would be lighting the lamps in the drawing room. The barn owl would call as it always did, from the woods by Wychwood Bottom, and in the old brewery, moonlight would creep in through the cobwebbed skylight and flood the secret loft with memory.

Rose took a clean sheet of paper, clipped it to her drawing board and stood a long time remembering till every line of his body was vivid in her memory. Then, smiling, she took up her pencil and began to draw.

Part 5

London and Wychwood, 1900

CHAPTER 1

By the beginning of October there was no doubt in anyone's mind that war would come. Reports had reached London of large-scale mobilisation in South Africa with troops massing on the Natal borders and more at Mafeking. A week after Percy sailed, a further 1,500 of the Queen's troops followed him for South Africa and throughout Britain preparations were vigorously under way. Army and Navy lists were published, officers appointed to new commands, troops equipped and trained, horses requisitioned, hospital ships prepared, reservists mustered, all manner of stores collected and despatched, even a consignment of fifty vats of gas for captive reconnaissance balloons. Every day the newspapers printed informative maps of the country whose leaders' intransigence had led to this justifiable dispute and when, before Percy Woodstock's ship had reached its shores, the Transvaal sent its ultimatum, there could be only one answer: Britain and the Transvaal were at war. Parliament was recalled, the reservists officially called out and mobilisation in full flow.

Shiploads of troops embarked, at intervals as regular as the necessity of supplying them with horses and equipment allowed, amid fervent, patriotic cheers and much banner waving, to secure Victoria's glorious empire for her loyal people.

But the first weeks of the South African War were an unpleasant shock to complacency. The initial invasion of British territory had been at four points (all with the useful benefit of railway lines, which could be cut), but the main thrust was into Natal, towards Ladysmith. There, after a disastrous battle at Lombard's Kop, the main British force was completely surrounded and trapped.

Casualties were high, especially among the officers, for the Boers proved to be exceptional marksmen. Even when officers were ordered to get rid of all distinguishing insignia and dress as common soldiers, the toll continued and on top of that, hundreds of troops were captured. It was plain that reinforcements were needed: and a relief force of willing reservists and volunteers was already on its way.

But patriotic fervour was not confined to the men. As the first casualty lists arrived from the front, the ladies, too, swung into action. The Dowager Countess of Lichfield organised the collection of comforts such as socks, vests, flannel shirts, caps, tobacco, pipes and cigarettes, for the men of the 1st Battalion, the Highland Light Infantry. All over the country similarly patriotic ladies followed suit. Phoebe's house in Brompton Square, to Lady Portia's annoyance, became a clearing house for such 'comforts' and, as that lady tartly put it, a mustering point for all the silliest women in Town. But Wychwood was no better, and had the prospect of a mist-laden miasma of malodorous canals not been equally distasteful to her, she would have returned hotfoot to Venice. As it was, she grumbled and endured in Brompton Square: at least Phoebe's talent for irritating was ingrown and natural: not like that infuriating wife of Edward's, always posturing and posing and aping her betters, as if such antics could ever make her a true-blue lady of the manor.

Lady Portia's antagonism towards her daughter-in-law was more than reciprocated, though Claire had the shrewd good sense not to indicate as much, even to her own mother. To that lady's exasperated cry of 'Really! I swear I shall throw something at the tiresome old battleaxe if she raises her patronising lorgnette in my direction just once more!' Claire replied soothingly, 'I know, Mummy dear, but you must remember she is eccentric and cannot help it. She was not brought up to be well mannered, as we were. We must all make allowances. Besides,' she added artlessly, 'I expect she is a teeny bit jealous of you, Mummy, especially when she sees how well you and little Fay get on together.' On the sole occasion when Lady Portia had been persuaded to hold her newest grandchild, the infant had expressed her alarm in an unfortunately dampening manner. '*Christopher Columbus!*' Lady Portia had said with, under the circumstances, remarkable restraint. Then, with withering sarcasm, 'Kindly remove this leaking creature until she had learnt at least a semblance of self control. I left Venice because of the damp.' With a glare at Claire, she finished, with patrician scorn, 'Of course, I should have *known* ...'

'I am so sorry,' said Claire sweetly. Unhurried, and with infuriating serenity, she rang the bell for Nanny then, wrapping the offending infant in an extra layer of carefully protective shawl, crooned, as she waited, 'Poor little Fay. There, there. Who is Mummy's *clever* little girl?' Lady Portia, to Claire's secret delight, had humph'ed her indignant way upstairs, to order a change of gown and an immediate removal to Town. Thus had battle been joined and, on this occasion, won: though his mother's swift retreat to London might incur Edward's displeasure, it was a risk Claire

324

was prepared to take, especially as she had ensured that in neither word nor deed could she herself be criticised.

Surprisingly, Edward neither upbraided her nor expressed displeasure. In fact, if anything, he seemed positively cheerful about it. 'Poor Mother. She grows more cantankerous every year. I expect she misses her Venetian cronies and her pesky little lap dog. Never mind. Phoebe will look after her, and, of course, I can always take a trip up to Town to visit her.'

That he had proceeded to do, somewhat to Claire's surprise, after barely two days. Though the developments in the War Office might have had something to do with that. For once the war became official, Edward seemed to be called to London with increasing frequency.

'The War Office,' he said and offered no more information than that he was required 'for consultation' – something to do with horses, he implied. He also implied that it was no business of Claire's and when, one morning in early November, after the nonchalant announcement at breakfast that he must 'take a run up to Town' yet again, she followed him into the library and dared to ask outright, said only that his business at the War Office was 'confidential'.

Claire was both baffled and annoyed: he had no business to have secrets from her, especially such important and interesting ones, in London, when she was stuck in the middle of a grey winter countryside with only a baby and the vicar's wife for company. (The rest of the local social scene she dismissed as of no account, the Woodstocks having returned to London.) She glared at Edward, wondering whether the time had come to make a firm protest, whatever the personal nocturnal consequences might be, when an idea occurred to her.

'Confidential?' she repeated, but with speculation rather than outright curiosity.

When he did not answer, but began to open and close the drawers of his desk, as if looking for something, she knew, with sudden revelation, that she was right. Of course! 'Confidential' meant secret, important, and therefore a guarantee, if not immediately, then surely before very long, of inclusion in the honours list. The thought banished all dissatisfaction and instead filled her with excitement and anticipatory pleasure. *Lady Rivers.* She would need to have new At Home cards printed, of course, and an entire new wardrobe. That went without saying. Then the dinners they would give – and attend – at which she would have precedence. *Sir Edward and Lady Rivers.* She could hear the splendid words in her ears even now, feel the pride and happiness which would swell her jewelled bosom and add that extra something to the set of her tiara-ed head. She could barely contain her excitement. And all this time she had been worrying quite unnecessarily. Nothing was wrong after all.

For Edward had been different since their daughter's christening. She could not quite put her finger on it, but it was as if he had removed himself in some subtle way. Not just from her bedroom: perhaps, upon reflection, she should not have locked him out quite so swiftly on the night of their child's christening, though he had very properly exercised his energies on horseback instead. However, when she had inadvertently forgotten to turn the key in their connecting door a few days later he had not made use of the advantage offered. She had told herself that he was respecting her wishes, but, perversely she had been displeased. It was not that she desired his attentions – quite the contrary: she merely wished him to continue to desire hers. Moreover, he had appeared healthily cheerful at breakfast the next morning whereas she had hardly slept at all. She had left the door unlocked the following night too, and the same thing happened. It was most disconcerting. He ought to be languishing for her, not finding something – or, prompted a subversive voice quickly squashed, someone? – to interest him elsewhere. For surely it could not be his mother's company that sent him home from London with that particular spring in his step? Could it?

It was no business of hers, of course, to inquire. Wives did not pry into their husbands' private affairs and she should be grateful for the respite it gave her. Nevertheless, she could not quite strangle that niggling whisper of disquiet. But War Office work, especially of a 'confidential' kind, was something different. People were knighted for services to their Queen and country, weren't they, especially in times of war? Sir Edward and Lady Rivers. The names sounded no more than natural to her already. Natural and right.

'Then of course you must go, dear.' She laid a gentle hand on his arm and looked up at him with large, submissive eyes. 'You must do whatever your country requires of you.' But she could not resist adding, 'I hope they *recognise* your services, Edward. After all, you have plenty of work of your own to do here on the estate, especially since Morton left.' When he made no answer, but busied himself with various papers on his desk, she said outright, 'I trust you will be rewarded for your devotion?'

'I am rewarded,' he said quietly, almost as if talking to himself. She could have sworn he was smiling, though she could not see his face. He took up a sheaf of papers and began leafing through them.

When she did not take the hint and go, he said after a moment, 'Did you want something, Claire?'

'Only your attention,' she snapped, for an unguarded moment. '*If* you can spare it ...' Then, taking a slow breath, she went on more calmly, 'If my husband is to spend as much time in London as at home, the least Her Majesty can do is reward him – and me – for it. You must let it be known, Edward, in the right places, that you require recognition. Public recognition – with a knighthood.'

Disconcertingly, Edward gave a shout of laughter and when she frowned and glared and finally stamped her foot in rage, he laughed even more. 'You talk as if knighthoods were sacks of apples or sides of beef! You really are a scheming little madam, Claire,' he managed at last. 'I always knew it, of course, but I was beginning to wonder if motherhood had satisfied your ambitions – or merely drained your spirits.'

'Really, Edward, what a thing to say!' But when he continued to regard her with one eyebrow raised and an expression of amusement mingled with a strangely impersonal curiosity, she felt an unwelcome prickle of that unease which, she suddenly realised, dated from the arrival at Wychwood of her sister Rose. Though she had to admit that Rose had behaved well enough, under the circumstances – for here Claire's conscience, such as it was, was not entirely clear – and had left again, with admirable promptitude, as soon as the christening party was over. But the visit had been somehow unsatisfactory. Rose had not admired as she should have, had not been submissive as befitted a younger sister to an elder. She had not accorded Claire the deference her age and married state entitled her to, had not cooed sufficiently loudly and often over the infant. In fact, Rose, as always, had been quite annoyingly self-sufficient.

At least Claire had done her duty and Rose ought to thank her for that. For it was generally understood, by Claire and Mrs Millard anyway, that Rose and Percy were now engaged, and to her mother's satisfaction Rose had, quite properly under the circumstances, followed Percy Woodstock to Southampton. Nevertheless, Claire would have liked Rose to stay. She would have enjoyed advising her on the mysteries of marriage – 'Remember how we used to speculate, all those years ago?' she would have said, with an indulgent little laugh. 'How timid and apprehensive we were, in our virginal little bedroom, sharing our hopes and secrets in the darkness? But there is really nothing at all to worry about, Rose dear.' Here, she would give a reflective smile, compounded of tolerance and affection. 'Men will be men, after all, and who are we to complain?' Something along those lines, anyway. But Rose had not looked in need of advice. In fact, she had seemed objectionably confident, even triumphant, as if reminding Claire that she too could get a man when she put her mind to it, and a rich one at that.

The fact that Percy Woodstock could buy out dear Edward twice over and still have money to burn was a sore point with Claire. She did not relish the idea of Rose being richer than herself. She knew Rose of old, knew her capacity for subversion and quiet disobedience, suspected that, in spite of a lifetime's drilling reinforced by Bible-sanctioned vows, she did not accord her elder sister the unquestioning obedience and deference Claire required. And when Rose was established as the mistress of Woodstock Hall she would be insufferable. But Percy Woodstock was in South Africa, fighting for his country, and for the moment Rose still lived in London, where, apparently, she spent days at a time in her studio, alone, in spite of Rebecca's outraged protests about propriety. But then Percy Woodstock positively doted on her, though Claire could not for the life of her see why. He would not mind what conventions Rose flouted. Edward had not seemed particularly concerned either, on the occasion Claire had mentioned it to him. 'She is an artist, after all,' he had said, and changed the subject.

Nevertheless Edward would complain soon enough if Claire behaved as Rose did, especially now ... Reassured by her recollection, Claire straightened her back and looked at her husband with new composure. The possibility of a knighthood for Edward put a different perspective on things and corrected any possible imbalance of riches. Were Rose Woodstock as rich as Croesus, Lady Rivers would still take precedence. Claire determined there and then to do all in her power to further that end.

'You can laugh as much as you like,' she said now, with the imperiousness of anticipated rank. 'But if the Queen expects you to spend more time in London than at home, she must expect to give you something in return. A knighthood would be entirely appropriate.'

'I will tell her,' he said solemnly. 'If I see her.' Perhaps it was the thought of the Queen's inevitable bounty which brought a whistle to his lips as he left for the station half an hour later, and which kept him in Town even longer than usual. Claire had no time to speculate, because by the time he returned she was involved in important war work of her own.

Claire would have liked to be in London at the heart of things in these stirring times, but as a new young mother she could hardly desert her nursery so eagerly early. Besides, her health was still not

328

entirely all it should be, or so she chose to think, and her lingeringly delicate condition made travelling unwise. So, when she read in the paper of yet another Lady Bountiful devoting her life to war work, Claire decided it was time to take patriotic action on her own account. There would be no harm in showing the world that she, Claire Rivers, was more than capable of scaling whatever lofty heights were destined for her husband, and, while so doing, of being an adornment and a helpmeet, a loyal and accomplished wife.

Accordingly, she announced her intention to use the drawing room at Wychwood as a collection point for the generous offerings of the county and invited ladies from the surrounding area to join her in assembling suitable parcels to send to 'our brave men at the Front.' Ladies who had refused her invitation in normal times and bridled at even leaving a card, accepted in the interests of patriotism and Claire blossomed with success until she was almost her old, imperious self again. She inserted an advertisement in *The Times* newspaper, and daringly gave two addresses to which donations might be sent. 'I knew you would not mind, Phoebe dearest,' she wrote, 'and there was no time to consult you first, but dear Edward will explain.'

Dear Edward was required to convey the assembled 'comforts' periodically up to Town which gave him one more reason for his visits.

'Will you be staying with Phoebe or at your club?' Claire asked, innocently enough, on one such occasion.

'Probably the club. Why?'

'No reason, dear,' said Claire hastily, noting his frown of annoyance. 'I just thought that if ever I needed to contact you, on charity business perhaps . . .'

Edward made no answer, and she did not pursue the subject. But a careful probing of Phoebe Burgess elicited the information that Edward certainly did not stay in Brompton Square. In fact, they rarely saw him. So much for visiting his mother, thought Claire, with asperity, though also with a certain satisfaction: War Office work was obviously of prior importance. 'All this war work,' wrote Phoebe, 'is so time-consuming, but really rather exciting too, don't you think?' Thinking of that nebulous knighthood, Claire had to agree.

'Exciting' was not the word that sprang to the minds of the bereaved mothers, widows and orphans of that bleak winter of '99. For in December came news of fresh setbacks, starting with the appalling slaughter at Madder river. Then, in 'Black Week' came Magersfontein, where for the first time in history a Scottish regiment actually turned and fled, then the disaster of Stormberg Junction and the retreat from Colenso. Nearly 3,000 men killed or wounded and a whole battery of field-guns lost. It was appalling and, of course, could not be tolerated.

A new commander-in-chief was appointed, the last of the reservists called up, and orders issued to set up new regiments. Volunteers flocked from every corner of the country – for it was inconceivable that Victoria's proud Empire should lose – and the New Year saw general embarkations from Liverpool, Southampton, Woolwich. Orders went out to the 7th Dragoon Guards and the 17th Lancers to be in readiness and a shipload of 530 remounts left the Albert docks. In the other direction came the wounded and the sick, while the daily casualty lists made sombre reading. In that sweltering foreign land, enteric fever was as deadly an enemy as the Boer.

'I do hope Percy remembers to boil the drinking water,' said Georgina, with determined cheerfulness. 'I have told him over and over, and very soon I hope to be able to tell him in person,' she finished, in a rush.

She had snatched an hour's precious leave from the hospital to visit Rose whom she found hard at work and pre-occupied. However, on Georgina's arrival Rose had abandoned the portrait she was painting – one of Phoebe Burgess's commissions – and brewed up coffee for them both on the paraffin stove which served as fire, kitchen range, and heater of water for Rose's simple needs. Now they relaxed, curled up on the ottoman, each with a steaming coffee cup in her hands, but Georgina's words startled Rose into close attention.

'Do you mean . . .?'

'Yes!' interrupted Georgina, her eyes bright with excitement. 'I am to go with the very next group of nurses. Probably before the month is out.'

Rose felt suddenly desolate and cold. It was January 1900: a new century, a new order. Soon, inevitably, a new monarch. Men would fight and die. Women would nurse them. Some would marry and bear children in spite of war. Others would mourn and weep. But what could the future hold for her? And now her dear friend Georgina was leaving too, to join the rest of the war-hungry in the Cape.

'I shall see Percy,' Georgina was saying, 'Or at least hear word of him. Then perhaps we will really know what has been going on. The dear boy is so evasive in his letters, though I expect that is only natural. I expect he wants to spare us anxiety.'

Rose did not answer. Percy's letters to her were a source of embarrassment and secret guilt. As Georgina said, Percy told them little of the war – merely that he was involved somehow with a local force of mounted Volunteers and was under general Buller's command. His letters to Georgina referred sometimes to the nursing: *The Boers have ambulances and women nurses, just as we do, and of course they have the added advantage of fighting in their own country so that houses can be requisitioned if necessary . . . Their care of wounded is reputed to be very good . . . Or . . . My sergeant was shot in the foot, poor fellow, and suffered as much from the sun as the pain until the stretcher-bearers arrived to remove the wounded to hospital . . .* He talked of the heat – intense; of the country – vast; of the flies – infuriating; but most of all of home.

To Rose he wrote generous-hearted, loving words which left her humble and ashamed. Georgina shared her letters with Rose, and Rose would have done the same, but Georgina refused.

'No, Rose dear. Percy's letters to you are private,' she said, curling Rose's fingers over the close-written pages. 'I would not dream of intruding.'

But the worst of it was that Rose found it impossible to reply to those letters – or rather to frame anything like the loving reassurance she knew he must look for. Instead, in desperation, she took to sending him pictures – tiny, thumbnail sketches of anything she could think of to divert and amuse him. *You must forgive me, Percy dear, if I do not write you volumes* she wrote, with shame. *But my pictures must speak for me. I know you like them and after all you yourself told me to sketch as much and as often as I could.* She sent him sketches of Georgina, in the studio, of the newspaper seller on the corner, of children and dogs in the street, a cat on a city roof, a hansom cab, a gaggle of perambulating nannies in Kensington gardens, a pair of Covent Garden porters, heads heaped high with baskets of assorted vegetables and fruit, a horse and carriage side by side with a Lanchester motor car, in fact anything to fill the page and the emptiness that should have held words of love. And when his letters arrived, brimming over with tenderness and longing, she was ashamed. But, the letter read, she forgot shame with a celerity that would have shamed her afresh had she thought of it. As it was, she plunged back, unthinking, into her euphoric, passionate and dream-like existence where nothing could touch her. Not conscience, loyalty, prudence, shame. Not even fear. But she would miss Georgina. . . .

'We will probably sail with the City Volunteers,' her friend was saying. 'Oh, Rose, I cannot wait to be out there, helping. I know

331

the sick here in London need nursing too, but there are others to do that. I want to be there, at the Front, with the wounded.' She stopped, and said in a different voice in which Rose noticed an edge of new anxiety. 'Have you heard from Percy lately?'

'No ... at least ... the last was, let me see, ten days ago now. From Colenso.'

'Mine too.' After a pause, Georgina said, 'There is a girl on my ward whose brother was killed at Colenso. She only heard yesterday. The telegram said he was wounded in the thigh and died in hospital, of gangrene. And the battle of Colenso was more than a month ago.' Rose knew what Georgina was thinking, but before she could frame a suitably reassuring reply, Georgina went on with a mixture of horror and helplessness, 'Oh, Rose, it is all so very dreadful. She told me her brother wrote in the last letter she had that the heat is appalling, the flies worse, and when the stretcher-bearers try to carry the wounded off the battle-field, the Boers just keep on firing.'

'What do you expect? It is not an exercise on Salisbury Plain,' snapped Rose. 'It is their country, after all.'

'*Theirs?*' Georgina was shocked out of her anxiety, as Rose had meant her to be. 'How can you say "theirs" when ... Oh.' She managed a smile. 'You are teasing.'

'Yes, though perhaps not entirely. It is, after all, what many people say. Mr Lloyd George among others, though no one thanks him for it. Remember the Boers were settlers in South Africa long before these gold-diggers and diamond-miners invaded the country.'

'Perhaps,' said Georgina, 'But the country is still ours. Why else is our army fighting, except to make safe the land for Britain's Empire?'

'Why else?' sighed Rose, but knew better than to continue that line of argument, though it was one of increasing concern as the casualty lists lengthened and the cash registers at Millards rang with sale after sale of mourning crepe. Too many men were dying, needlessly, when they could be alive and loving. . . .

'I am worried, Rose,' said Georgina in a quiet voice unlike her usual cheerful self. 'I shall not be happy now until I reach South Africa. At least then I shall be at hand if ...' She had no need to finish her sentence. Rose squeezed her hand in understanding. 'Percy will be all right, do not worry. And I will give you presents to take out with you. Books and photographs and cigars. Maudie always says cigar smoke keeps away flies. And a bottle of Percy's favourite brandy.'

'He would rather have you,' she said, managing a smile.

'Then he must wait.' But behind the flippancy Rose felt a twinge of customary guilt. She did not want to see Percy. Not yet. Perhaps not ever. She was immediately ashamed of the thought and was particularly affectionate when Georgina took her leave.

'Let me know as soon as you hear what ship you are sailing in and I promise to come and cheer you on your way.'

Then she closed the studio door, hitched back the curtain from the little skylight to indicate that her guest had gone, and resumed her painting. Five minutes after her friend's departure Rose had forgotten Georgina, Percy, the war in South Africa, everything – except the paintbrush in her hand and the expectation in her heart.

For in the weeks following Fay's christening her life had been a charmed and blessed paradise, secret and intense. As golden autumn merged into the greyness of winter she hardly noticed. Mists, rain, even the chilly blanket of a London fog meant nothing to her except perhaps a different palette for her paints. Snow was a brief benison, transforming as it did the familiar into the new and lovely. But when it melted into unlovely slush, she reverted to an indoor scene or a portrait without even momentary regret. What was the point of regret when she had so much to be gloriously grateful for? For in those blessed weeks Rose refused to look beyond the walls of her studio, refused to contemplate any future further than an hour away, lived only for the moment and its exquisite, forbidden bliss.

And it was bliss, a poignant, draining, utterly fulfilling pleasure which filled every inch of her till she felt gloriously replete. It only surprised her that no one noticed. Her mother, with faint surprise, said only, 'You look well, dear. Engagement obviously suits you.' Georgina said, 'You look happy, Rose. I knew the studio was a good idea.' As for the others, she hardly saw them. She did not return to Wychwood, naturally, and Claire did not come up to Town. Occasionally Rose helped out at Millard's, though since Fay's christening her mother had been surprisingly accommodating where Rose's art was concerned. Occasionally she went home, with washing perhaps, or to see Sara. Sara had applied, officially, to Miss Welsh for admission to Girton College after the summer vacation and was awaiting the reply. Occasionally Rose visited exhibitions or galleries. But for the most part she worked in her studio, totally absorbed, knowing with a serenity devoid of all impatience that he would come to her. It was a precious, charmed existence, a time, she realised afterwards, too self-absorbed, too unworldly to be allowed to last. Halcyon days, precious and fleeting – a blatant and open temptation to the gods.

For no one in Victoria's virtuous Empire could flout the conventions and go unpunished. In such flagrant individuality lay the seeds of discord – and there was discord enough as it was, across the seas. Standards of morality and rectitude must be maintained, backsliding punished, the righteous rewarded and re-established in command.

Retribution was inevitable. The little halcyon was allowed a mere fourteen days of blessed calm in which to build her nest. What had Rose ever done to deserve weeks where the kingfisher for all its darting glory had merely days? If she had spared even a moment for sober thought, Rose would have realised it. But she did not. Instead, she went hurtling, blissfully and blindly, to her own destruction.

CHAPTER 2

At the foot of the War Office steps Edward Rivers stopped to fasten his overcoat against the biting January wind before striding purposefully towards Piccadilly. He had told Claire the truth when he said he was needed on War Office business, but it was only a small part of the truth. He had become involved in the logistics of transporting cavalry horses: a job that warranted nothing higher than an OBE, he thought wrily, if that, and then only if they had one spare at the end of the list. It certainly would not bring him the knighthood which Claire dreamed of, though of course he had not told her that. He had not told her a number of things. For instance that Harry Price-Hill could have done the War Office job just as easily and probably better. Edward would cheerfully have unloaded the whole business onto his cousin, had it not provided him with the perfect excuse for spending time in Town. Also, although he felt a certain loyalty to Queen and country, his private sympathies lay with Lloyd George and the anti-war lobby, and any guilt which this entailed was salved by this contribution, small though it was, to the war effort.

But since the new year began, things had been looking pretty black. This war with the Boers was turning out to be no picnic. More a blood-bath and a dashed unpleasant one at that. Guy Morton had been sent there in October with the Suffolk Volunteers, soon after Percy Woodstock, as well as several of his farming acquaintances and friends. Every day now there was a name someone recognised in the casualty lists, if only that of a friend of a friend. If things went on as they had been, it could be only a matter of time before Morton's or young Woodstock's name appeared too. It was an unwelcome thought. Edward adjusted his silk scarf and turned up his overcoat collar as he made his way across Trafalgar Square. The wind was decidedly cold.

He had promised to join his mother for tea with Aunt Clementina. Lady Portia would grumble as usual about the war – 'But then men have been knocking each other about one way or another since the world began. Cudgels, lumps of rock, bows and arrows, Mausers – what difference does it make? They are hardly likely to listen to reason so late in the day. At least this time they have had the decency to do it somewhere out of sight.' Aunt Clementina would protest, also as usual, and talk shop about the Admiralty where her husband had some sinecure or other, or the Red Cross which, to hear her talk, you would think she had not only personally invented, but ran single-handed – with the other tied behind her back! Harry would come in for the usual roasting from both of them probably, though for different reasons. The occasion would be tedious enough, but Aunt Clementina's cakes were always excellent and afterwards when Claire asked him, as she was sure to do, he could reply with absolute truth that he had taken tea with his mother. He must remember to note what she was wearing, particularly her jewellery which seemed to hold for Claire a morbid fascination. Later, as soon as he decently could, he would make his escape to an appointment of a less licit but far more pleasurable kind.

It was very late when Edward returned to his club. He would not have returned at all except that token respectability must be maintained and should Claire have taken it into her head to ring with some trivial message, as she had done on occasions, he ought at least to be there to receive it, if only hours later, via a note in his pigeon-hole. But his pigeon-hole behind the porter's desk was reassuringly empty. He was moving towards the stairs and bed when the porter's deferential voice halted his step.

'There is a gentleman waiting to see you, Mr Rivers. In the billiard room.'

'Oh? Did he give his name?'

'No. But I believe the gentleman might be your cousin, sir.' The man managed to combine sympathy, deference and complicity in such a way as to warn Edward, before he opened the door, what he would find. Harry, resplendent in dress shirt and scarlet cummerbund, diamonds flashing from cuffs and starched shirt front, was slumped in a corner chair, bare feet outstretched on the carpet, dress trousers rolled up to the knees, dress coat in a crumpled heap on the floor, an open bottle of the club's best brandy in one hand and a billiard cue in the other – on the end of which spun his own black opera hat.

''Lo, cousin mine,' he said, grinning. 'You've been a dashed long time coming home. Ought to smack you.' He hicupped happily, spun his hat once too often and when it fell off, sent the billiard cue clattering after it. 'Where've you been anyway?'

Edward ignored the question. He retrieved the hat, dusted it off and placed it on the side-board. 'Where have *you* been seems more to the point.' He picked up the billiard cue, inspected it for damage and returned it to its fellows. 'Well?'

Harry grinned, put the bottle to his lips, drank noisily, and said, 'Here and there. Have a drink, dear cousin.' He thrust the bottle at Edward who took it, wiped the rim fastidiously with his handkerchief, found a glass in the side-board and poured himself a measure. Then he corked the bottle and placed it on the mantelshelf, out of Harry's reach.

'Well?' repeated Edward. 'To what do I owe the pleasure of this nocturnal visitation?'

'Don't be so damned po-faced, you old reprobate.' Harry wagged an unsteady finger in Edward's direction. 'I know where *you've* been, old man.' He laid a conspiratorial finger against the side of his nose and winked. Edward flushed with shock and alarm.

'Can't get enough of it these days, can you, you old stallion. I know that well-served look. Recognise it anywhere.' He collected enough coordination from somewhere to stand up and make his unsteady way to the hearth where the last of the day's fire lay dying into colourless ashes. He reached for the brandy bottle and fumbled with the cork while Edward watched, immobilised by an awful dread, unable to move or think, until he realised what his cousin was saying.

'Saw you last time. Didn't tell. Won't tell this time. All men together, what?' With a sigh of satisfaction he released the cork and put the bottle to his lips. 'Visited little place off Leicester Square myself tonight. Didn't see you though. Too busy.' He giggled, hicupped and, negotiating the carpet with comical care, slumped back into his seat, the bottle firmly held in one hand. 'Prefer Salome myself. Chicita not bad though. Or Maisie-Bell. Who d'you favour?'

Relief flooded through Edward Rivers with the benison of water to a desert. 'That would be telling,' he managed, with creditable suavity. 'Which I prefer not to do.'

'Quite right. Mum's the word. Good girls, all of 'em, bless their little dimples. And dashed good fun, what?'

Edward took a slow, measured breath, drank, and when he felt once more in control, said, 'And what has prompted this excess of, shall we say, celebration on your part? Is it someone's birthday? Or have you won at the races?'

'Neither.' Harry lay back in the chair, bare feet spread wide, shirt front escaping from silken waistband, hands, with brandy bottle, dangling to brush the floor, and drawled, eyes closed, 'I have enlisted, old boy.'

'You have *what*?' His own embarrassment was forgotten in the

337

shock of Harry's revelation. The war in the Transvaal was a soldiers' war, fought by professionals whose job it was to fight, though so far they seemed to be doing so with little success. But if they needed reinforcements there were still plenty of regular soldiers to be deployed, surely, without calling on irresponsible idiots like Harry. 'Sit up and pull yourself together.' He removed the bottle from Harry's hand, pulled his cousin upright, straightened his shirt front, retrieved his bow tie from under one ear and tugged it back into place. He picked up Harry's tail-coat, shook it straight and steered his cousin's arms into the sleeves. Then he rolled down those ridiculous trouser legs and attempted to brush them flat. 'They're wet! And where are your stockings and shoes?'

'Not an earthly, old boy,' said Harry happily. 'In the pond I expect. We went paddling.'

'We? What pond? Oh, never mind.' Edward rang the bell and when the porter appeared, ordered black coffee and sandwiches. 'And perhaps you could obtain a pair of shoes for Mr Price-Hill? Size eleven?'

Half an hour later, esconced in the leather-upholstered respectability of the club smoking room and, with the resilience of good health, comparatively sober, in a pair of highly polished leather brogues and speckled socks which stuck out incongruously from beneath his rumpled dress trousers, Harry explained, between mouthfuls of thick roast beef sandwiches and very black coffee.

'We sign on for a year. Less, if the war is over before the year is up. The Prince of Wales is overseeing the business himself and the new Imperial Yeomanry is looking for men just like me – hardy, athletic, fresh from a country life . . .'

'Fresh from a country race-course would be more to the point,' interrupted Edward. 'Or fresh from a city pond.'

Harry ignored him. 'I will have you know, cousin mine, that I am the answer to their prayers. Young, fit, unmarried, and of good character. I have witnesses to prove it! A good rider, a good marksman, and – this is the clincher, old boy – my own horse.' He bit happily into yet another sandwich. 'When I offered to supply a couple more, as remounts, they made me a lieutenant on the spot.'

'I don't believe you,' said Edward calmly, pouring more coffee from the gleaming silver pot. He had known Harry all his life.

'Don't you, by God?' Harry reached inside his jacket and withdrew a stiff, folded sheet of parchment which he tossed onto the table in front of Edward. 'Then read that.'

The document was inscribed on the outside, 'Henry Price-Hill, Gent.' – someone, whether Harry or the scribe, had forgotten to include the 'Hon.' – with, underneath, 'Lieutenant (temporary rank) Land Forces. The City of London Imperial Volunteers.' Carefully, Edward opened it to see the Queen's signature and seal on the top left-hand corner.

'Well?' challenged Harry. 'Temporary rank, admittedly, but look at this bit.' He jabbed the document with a well-manicured finger. '... *carefully and diligently to discharge your Duty in the Rank of Lieutenant or in such higher Rank as We may from time to time hereafter be pleased to promote or appoint you to.* There. I'll be promoted in no time. Just keep your eyes on the *London Gazette* and you'll soon see. And listen to this. *You are at all times to exercise and well discipline in Arms both the inferior Officers and Men serving under you and use your best endeavours to keep them in good Order and Discipline. And We do hereby Command them to Obey you as their superior Officer.* What a lark, eh? They've got to do as I tell them, or else. I reckon I'll be a colonel before you know it. Besides,' and he gave Edward a knowing wink, 'a friend of a friend of the Mater's is on the Selection Board.'

'That might not be an advantage,' said Edward drily, remembering Aunt Clementina's way of steam-rollering over anything in her path. 'Unless she actually wants you to go.'

'Oh the old girl's sure to be in favour,' said Harry disrespectfully. 'Honour of My Country. Fight for the Flag. Leadership. Responsibility. God Save the Queen. Whereas I just think it will be a splendid lark. Galloping across the veldt, playing polo, doing a bit of pig-sticking perhaps.'

'Or a bit of Boer-sticking?' said Edward sourly. He was both envious and apprehensive. He was fond of his cousin. Harry was tall, head and shoulders above the Imperial Yeomanry's required minimum of 5ft 3ins., with a firm, muscular body and the supple movements of the physically fit. He was a handsome man, even now, in the dishevelled and unflattering small hours of what had been a punishing night. On horseback, in uniform, he would look superb. He was an excellent horseman and an outstanding shot. But he was also reckless, carefree and incurably frivolous, and the daily casualty list was no respecter of persons.

'You're jealous,' accused Harry. 'But it's no good, old chap. They don't want married men.' For some reason this struck Harry as a great joke, but Edward could not even raise a smile. 'Besides, with Morton gone, who would look after Wychwood? Unless you expect your paragon of a wife to do it? Mind you, she's formidably competent by all accounts and might well do the job better than Morton. Good chap, Morton,' he went on after a moment's silence

339

in which Edward frowned at the document, as if at a bad hand at cards, 'for a farmer. Tell you what, Edward. Find me half a dozen extra mounts and I'll give you more than a fair price for them. That should get me my promotion overnight, with or without Mother's old buffer on the Board.'

Harry retrieved the precious parchment, refolded it carefully and tucked it away in an inside pocket. 'Fitz and the others will be green with envy, though I tell them they'll get drafted soon enough, especially if the Boer continues to put up any sort of a fight. When dear old Queenie sees her precious Empire crumbling she'll kick all the young hopefuls overseas to defend it for her. I can't tell you how much I'm looking forward to it, old boy. They say the social life in Cape Town is not to be missed. The girls are volunteering in droves, bless them, scrambling and scratching each other's eyes out for the privilege of shipping to South Africa to nurse the sick and mop the fevered brow. Even Boo-Boo's put her name down, though I doubt they will take her. Too disruptive an influence, what?' He winked with man-to-man complicity and unexpectedly Edward blushed. 'Not like Georgie, bless her. She's a natural. They'll make her matron in no time and there's even talk of her being included in the nursing contingent that's sailing out with the Volunteers.'

'Good for Georgina.' Edward added, straightfaced, 'And how lucky you are. You will be able to spend so much precious time together on the voyage.'

'There is safety in numbers, thank goodness. Which reminds me.' He pushed the last sandwich, whole, into his mouth, stood up and dusted the crumbs from his front, then said, through the beef, 'Too late to go to bed now, old boy. I feel a second wind blowing strong. Fancy joining me on the embankment for a dawn stroll? We'll drink the worker's tea out of tin mugs and throw crusts at the pigeons. Or we could go to Covent Garden and see how many vegetable baskets we can carry on our heads. There's a porter there who . . .'

'No thank you,' interrupted Edward. 'I have to catch the early train to Wintelsham.'

'Home with the milk, eh?' Harry winked. 'Don't worry, old chap. Man to man and all that. I won't breathe a word.'

Edward ignored the remark. 'I think you would be well advised to forget any further frivolity and go straight home to bed.'

Disconcertingly, Harry gave a shout of laughter. 'You pompous old hypocrite!' But he let Edward steer him to the door and out onto the club steps. When a solitary hansom turned a distant corner and came towards them, lamps a pair of swaying yellow pools in the darkness, wheels clattering and hooves echoing with eerie clarity in the empty night, Edward hailed it and saw Harry safely inside its leather-upholstered interior. He gave the driver Aunt Clementina's address in Stratton Street, but he suspected Harry would redirect the fellow the moment they turned the corner. Harry was as exasperating and irresponsible and incorrigible as ever. But, remembering that crackling parchment stamped with Victoria's official seal, Edward felt a new sadness as he watched the cab merge into the drab city night and disappear. He was fond of his cousin. He would not want him to come to harm. He might even go to Southampton to see him embark, when the time came.

CHAPTER 3

Rose did not go to Southampton to see Georgina sail after all. Instead, they said their farewells in private, over supper in a busy cafe near the hospital. It was a simple meal – steak and kidney pudding and tea. The decor was functional and moderately clean, the clientele cheerful, the service adequate but impersonal which suited them, making as it did no demands. They were left to themselves, in their cocoon of friendship, and once their plates had been set before them, ignored. It was what they both wanted. They had been friends for a mere two and a half years, but into that time they had packed a lifetime of companionship.

'I will miss you,' said Rose, inadequately.

'You know as well as I do, Rose, that I have to go. And it will make no difference to our friendship. I know that we will always be friends, you and I.' When Rose made no answer, but continued to stir the thick, unpalatable tea round and round as if mesmerised, Georgina reached across the table and gripped Rose's hand. 'Promise?'

Rose looked up into her friend's anxious eyes and saw integrity, concern, affection, but behind everything else the steady light of excited resolution. With an effort, Rose smiled. 'Of course, Georgina.'

'Is anything the matter, Rose? Something you have not told me?'

The words were a double reproach, especially now, but Rose said only, 'What a question, when my friend is going to war on the other side of the world.'

'Hardly! Even I know where South Africa is and it is less than three weeks away by sea. As to the war ...' But there was no reassurance to be given on that account and they both knew it. 'I will give your love to Percy,' she said instead.

'And your own to Harry?' teased Rose, pushing aside the trouble which had weighted her heart increasingly in the last days of preparation before the City Imperial Volunteers sailed.

'Certainly not. I have not forgotten that pact we made in Italy and a very sensible one it was too.'

342

'Yes,' sighed Rose, though the regret in her voice was not what Georgina thought.

'Cheer up, Rose. Very soon we will all be home again, for a splendid reunion. You have your painting, after all, and remember Percy loves you.'

Had Georgina wished to stab Rose with remorse and shame she could not have chosen better words with which to do it, though, being Georgina, she intended only comfort. 'Will you watch the Volunteers leave tomorrow?'

'I have little choice,' managed Rose, with a half-smile of self-mockery. 'The whole city has gone mad with patriotic fervour and even Mamma has ordered the shop to close till the valiant Volunteers have passed in order that the shop girls can squeal and cheer with everybody else. I expect I shall join them. Besides, I might make a sketch or two.'

'Do you remember when we first met, on the occasion of the Jubilee procession?'

'Of course. And I drew that inexpert picture of Percy on horse-back.'

'Not inexpert at all. It was very good. Your portraits now are much better, of course, but I still treasure that one of Percy. Who would have thought then that you and he ...'

Rose closed her ears. Percy was reproach enough as it was without Georgina's innocent reminder with every word she spoke. When at last Georgina stopped, Rose pushed back her chair and stood up.

'I am sorry, Georgina, but I am very tired and perhaps a little over-emotional. Let us say goodbye now, quickly, before I disgrace myself.'

'Of course.' Georgina was instantly solicitous, but Rose found even her friend's affection too much to take. She had held her emotions on a knife edge of composure for too long and knew that the smallest, most unexpected thing might tip her into the abyss. It was something she dare not risk. 'Goodbye then.' She pushed past Georgina and almost ran outside into the cold night street. There she stood a moment, trembling, breathing deep. The air was chill, laced with incipient fog and the grime of winter chimneys. But it was anonymous and undemanding and Rose craved such solitude. She could not hold out much longer. A week perhaps? In a week's time Georgina would be well on her way to South Africa. Then a week it must be. ...

The City of London Imperial Volunteers in whose newly mustered ranks the Honourable Harry Price-Hill was now a Lieutenant (temporary) left London on a wave of patriotic fervour which rivalled the Queen's own Jubilee celebrations for numbers, noise and volume. By most of the Volunteers the previous evening had been spent in various forms of carousal and enjoyment, and what remained of the night in blankets on the drill-room floor until reveille at five a.m. Then breakfast, in overcoats and wideawake hats at long tables in the same drill-room, their kitbags, rifles and other equipment heaped against one wall and overlooked by a gallery of select well-wishers, male and female, who had arrived by cab for the purpose. Last minute letters were distributed by the officers during the meal. The meal over, the men were mustered, roll-call taken, and at 'stand easy' the well-wishers streamed in to take a last farewell. Then at seven a.m. the drill-hall doors were flung open, the band of the London Rifle Brigade struck up and Colonel Cholmondeley led the Volunteers out into the cheering melée of Chiswell Street.

It was a crisp winter morning, star-bright and clear. Dawn had not yet broken, but the street-lamps were still burning and the warehouse lights flared bright along Finsbury Pavement and Moorgate Street. Mounted police headed the procession now, backing and prancing, as they struggled to clear passage for the Volunteers. Trumpets blared, drums thumped, 'Oh, listen to the band' thundered out unheeded into the roaring masses who had their own songs to sing, their own admonitions to shriek into the general hubbub. By the time they reached Mansion House the City's Imperial Volunteers were already way behind schedule – they should have been at Westminster Bridge, two miles away, by now. But the Lord Mayor and Lady Mayoress, with various Aldermen and other dignatories, all in ceremonial splendour, were cheering from the balcony of the Mansion House, beneath which balcony hung the troop's new banner – white, with a red cross, a crown and sword in one corner and the letters 'C. I. V.' – and the column had no desire to hurry. The men were enjoying their transitory fame far too much to resist their boisterous admirers' attentions. Messages were sent ahead along the route, and, as the dawn light strengthened and the street lights faded, the triumphal march continued its cacophonous way towards Westminster Bridge and the Albert Embankment.

There, as the band of the Queen's Westminster Volunteers took over and in the brief melee as one band replaced another, Sara Millard at last saw Harry. The Millards, in company with the rest of those who had thought Westminster bridge a good vantage point, had waited impatiently long after the Volunteers' expected arrival time, but to any suggestion that they might give up and go home,

344

Sara had made vehement protests. Now all discomfort and tiredness were forgotten at the sight of the approaching troop.

Harry-Price Hill was in a contingent of mounted Volunteers, erect, uniformed, wideawake hat at a jaunty angle, and every bit as handsome as his cousin Edward had predicted. Sara waved and cried out with what her mother described later as 'most unseemly forwardness' though at the time Sara's voice was lost in the general cheering and the thunderous drum-roll of the band. Charlotte squealed and bobbed on tiptoe, shrieking 'Harry! Harry!' in the intervals of wailing piteously 'I can't *see*!' Even Maudie waved her handkerchief with prim fervour, while Rebecca raised one decorous gloved hand and with the other touched the corner of her eye with a scrap of lace-edged cambric. She had a soft spot for Harry. Only Claire, thought Rose, was missing from the family group – and Edward. But they were separate now, of course, living their own lives. The thought shot her through with a pain so fierce she caught her breath on an audible gasp. Whatever had passed, whatever was to come, *he was still Claire's*. Rose might lead her rebel band against the high priestess, and had done repeatedly since childhood, but whatever her victories, nothing could topple Claire from her eminence or cancel the rights of the first-born ... She remembered, with a sudden shaft of buried memory, her father all those years ago at Dieppe, offering free tailoring to Edward and his cousin, and Claire's blushing shame. She had known what she wanted even then and never questioned her right to have it. Now Claire was Edward's wife, and Harry....

At that moment in her thoughts Lieutenant Harry Price-Hill turned his handsome head in their direction and raised a gloved hand in acknowledgement, whether of the general adulation or of the particular was not clear. Sara, however, chose to take it as the latter.

'He waved to me, Rose. He actually waved,' and the tears which neither dread nor pain at parting had allowed her to shed, stood bright in her adoring eyes.

Rose beside her had not the heart to suggest otherwise. Instead she prayed with sudden fervour, 'Please God, don't let Harry be killed.' She had only come this morning because Mamma had expected it and Sara had begged her. Rose was reminded of that time long ago in Dieppe, when Claire had similarly entreated her company, to walk the *Plage* and watch the young men from under demurely lowered eyelashes. But those young men had been on holiday, pleasure-bent, whereas these were destined for quite a different entertainment. 'Please, Rose,' Sara begged. 'We must all be there to see him go. The others will squeal and cheer as they would do for anyone in soldier's uniform, but you know what love is, Rose. *You* understand.' She had finished, with sudden intensity, 'Suppose Harry were to die and you had not even waved him goodbye?'

'Nonsense, Sara.' Rose had been relieved to be able to pass over the subtler implications of Sara's words. 'Of course he is not going to die.' But there was no real 'of course' about it. Men were dying every day, if not of Boer-inflicted wounds, then of enteric fever. For whatever Harry and his set might say of the night-life in Cape Town, Rose had little doubt that such a life would be only briefly available, and only to the few. It was proving a hard war to win – or why else were Volunteers needed?

Oh God, she thought with despair, why is everything so complicated? Then, as the column shook itself into some sort of order and began to move, in broken step, over the bridge to the cheerful blare of the band, she heard Sara's voice at her side, cheering over and over again with all the vulgar abandonment her mother had feared and deplored. When the last of the Volunteers had been sucked into the vortex and carried over the river to the far Embankment, the sisters stood in silence, watching the seething eddies of the attendant crowd divide and settle into a dozen different streams, some following the Volunteers, some finding their own short cuts across the river to meet up with the column again on the other side, some making their deflated way back to work or home.

It was then, in the sudden lull that she felt it – a sensation unknown to her, a swaying, earth-rocking sensation at the same time cosmic and intimate, piercing and sweet ... a visitation. She felt suddenly dizzy and a little faint. She stood, clutching the parapet edge, waiting for it to pass – then in that cocoon of silence which enwrapped her she heard a man's voice, cracked with age and misuse, crying in penetrating newsvendor's cadence, 'Latest casualties, General Buller's Advance! All the Spring Handicaps! Newmarket, Lincoln and Kempton Park. Read all about it!' From over the water came the thud of the receding band, from the river a ship's horn sounding in salute, from nearer at hand the groundswell of dispersing voices, carriage wheels, a motor horn, the steady clop of horses' hooves, even a baby crying in a distant street. All the usual London sounds, and, in her own cocoon of stillness, the newspaper vendor's voice, like a message piercing her heart.

'Is anything the matter, Rose?' asked Rebecca sharply.

Rose was tempted to say 'Everything,' but instead, with a huge effort of will, managed, 'That man's voice. I have not seen a newspaper today and I suddenly feared ...'

'Ah, of course. Dear Percy.' Rebecca, touched by Rose's unexpected and obvious anxiety, fumbled in her pocket for small change. 'Buy a newspaper, Sara. We will wait for you here.' Rose leant against the parapet and obediently waited, while the crowds milled and moved and went about their business and the thumping of her heart steadied to a more measured beat. From far above her head Rose heard Big Ben chime and could not even count the strokes. She knew now, beyond doubt. She only hoped Sara, with her knack of divining secrets, had not guessed the nature of that knowledge. Sara was uncomfortably good at guessing....

'Are you all right, Rose?' asked Sara anxiously when she returned.

'Yes. It was just the crowds and the pushing and then that man's voice, shouting death and racing tips with equal gusto! I can't help worrying, Sara,' she added, with truth.

'Of course you can't, Rose dear.' Her mother took the paper, ran a brisk finger down the casualty lists, and said with satisfaction, 'All's well.'

'How can you say that, Mamma, with so many men wounded and killed?' cried Sara, her face as pale as Rose's now. 'It is heartless and cruel.'

'Don't be hysterical, child! I meant, all is well *with Percy*.' She frowned her displeasure before saying, 'And now that the crowds have thinned at last, we will all go our proper business.'

Sara said, with sudden vehemence, 'Let us catch the train to Southampton! There is still time.'

'Certainly not! You are behaving like a camp follower,' and Rebecca herded her daughters sternly homewards, the day's frivolities over. Rose, after agreeing to help with Millards' new display cards later in the week, left the others for the refuge of her studio, pleading the need to complete a commissioned portrait which, she said, was already behind schedule. Edward, she knew, had gone to Southampton with the Price-Hills and a group of friends to assist at Harry's final embarkation. She did not expect to see him today. But before long he would come, and when he did, there could be no more prevarication. She must tell him the truth.

Rose arrived early in the upstairs office of Millards, four days later, to work as promised on a layout for the new advertisement her mother planned. She had come straight from her studio to find her mother had not yet arrived: surprising, but not unusual. Some domestic misdemeanour had no doubt claimed her attention, if not Annie's wasting sugar, then Charlotte's being pert or silly, or Sara's

347

sullenness. Rose laid out her drawing materials, clipped a fresh sheet of paper to the drawing board and stood in contemplative thought. How could one expect to make a work of art out of something so banal as 'Millards Outfitters – the best in Town'? But of course her mother did not want a work of art. She wanted something eye-catching but tasteful, something, as she humourlessly explained, to bring in a good class of customer with the right kind of money. 'Is your money a burden?' thought Rose mischievously. 'Millards will relieve you of it.' Or 'Too much money and not enough style? Come to Millards to redress the balance.' She was smiling at her own subversive thoughts when there was a nervous knock on the door and the assistant from 'Schools' stepped hesitantly inside, a folded newspaper clutched in one hand.

'Oh,' she said, taken aback to see Rose. 'I thought Mrs Millard was ... we just wanted to ... to say how sorry we are, Miss Rose,' she went on, gathering courage. Then, seeing Rose's cheerful face, said uncertainly, 'I am sorry if I've spoken out of turn, but I thought ... we thought ...'

Studying the woman's nervous, pitying face, Rose said quietly, 'What has happened?' When the room began to sway gently from side to side, she clutched the table edge as if to hold it in place and said again, 'What?'

The woman laid the newspaper on the table in front of Rose. It had been folded back to show the latest list of Dead and Wounded. 'I wouldn't have spoken, Miss Rose,' she said nervously, 'Only with Mrs Millard not here and then ... well, we thought you knew ...'.

Rose's finger moved slowly down the list in a suspension of sound and all other movement, till it stopped at '... Officers killed and wounded at Ladysmith ... the name which was at first indecipherable is now reported as killed, Captain Pervical Henry Arbuthnot Woodstock ...'

With a small moan, Rose slipped senseless to the ground.

Rose woke to a blurred confusion of faces and anxious voices, the spiritous bite of sal volatile in her nostrils.

'The poor thing ... it's the shock ... her fiancé and not engaged six months ...' Then she was in a cab, the lady from 'Schools' white-faced beside her, on her way home to the ministrations of her mother and the faithful Annie who, alerted by a telegram from Wychwood, already knew the dreadful news....

It was only later, when 'Schools' had been thanked, fortified with a cup of tea she was barely given time to drink, and ordered back to Millards with a message for Mr Blunt that Mrs Millard would

348

not be in today after all (and a private message she thought prudent to keep from Rose, concerning black crepe), when Sara had been despatched to the post office with a hastily written note of 'deepest sympathy' to Mrs Woodstock, and instructions to collect Maud and Charlotte early from school, and Annie was out of the room, preparing a fortifying broth for them all, that Rose, lying back on the lace-edged pillows of her mother's bed, the scent of lavender warm in the chill air, for the fire which Annie had hastily lit in the bedroom grate had not yet taken proper hold, said, with a mixture of defiance and deliberate self-torture, 'I am pregnant, Mamma.'

'You are *what*?' Had she wished to shatter her mother's composure to the four winds she had more than succeeded. Rebecca staggered, clutched a chair back and feeling her way round its outspread arms, sank into it with all the histrionic éclat of a tragedienne, though in her case shock was all too genuine.

Rose watched her for a moment, with fleeting pity. Noted the sudden ageing of her mother's face, the grey tint to the skin, the hunted look in her eyes. Rebecca Millard was forty-five, middle-aged, but still striking, with the forceful vigour of good health and the determination to get her own way. She had grown selfish, perhaps, since her husband's death, some said even mean, though that was understandable when the cares of five daughters lay on her shoulders alone. But on the whole, she had born the burden well. She had rescued her husband's business from debt and brought it through prosperity to riches. She had seen one daughter successfully married, another, as she thought, engaged, and a third on the hopeful brink – and now all her careful edifice of respectability had toppled about her ears. In that moment, Rebecca looked broken and dismayed.

'That is why I fainted, Mamma,' said Rose bitterly. 'I could not give Percy my unqualified attention even in death.'

But her mother had recovered. With a visible summoning of strength, she gripped the arms of the chair, pushed herself to her feet and stood a moment, breathing slow and deep as if to summon help from the ozone of the air. Then she crossed the room, opened the door, stepped out onto the landing and called over the bannisters with almost her old authority, 'When Sara and the others return, keep them downstairs, Annie, till I call. Miss Rose needs *absolute* rest.' Then she came back inside, closed the door, and turned the key.

'Now, Rose,' she said ominously, '*what* did you say?'

Rose closed her eyes and repeated softly, 'I am pregnant.'

There was a silence in which Rose could hear her mother's

thoughts as loudly as if she had spoken aloud. She believed it to be Percy's child, of course and was working out when they had last been together, how many weeks had already passed, when the child was due. But when she spoke, Rose was taken by surprise.

'Why didn't you tell him?' Rebecca said fiercely. 'You must have known weeks ago.'

How could she explain to her mother that she had not known, or rather that she had refused to know? In those halcyon weeks she had noticed neither date nor time. If the monthly cycle of the stars and moon left her unaware, why should she notice the mundane business of her body's functions? She had chosen to notice nothing but the glorious presence of her lover. She had closed her mind and whenever suspicion knocked had merely turned another key to keep even the smallest doubt at bay.

'Or did you tell him?' Rebecca stopped, suddenly hopeful. Then, when Rose made no answer, went off on a new tack. 'Mrs Woodstock will have to be told, of course. She must take responsibility for her son's child, whatever people say. It is only right. And now with her son dead she ...'

'No,' interrupted Rose. Her mother ignored her.

'Of course you could have been married,' she said, veering off in a fresh direction. 'That's it, of course! You *were* married. I knew there must be an explanation. You left Wychwood so hurriedly that day after the christening in order to be married by special licence before the poor boy sailed.'

'No,' said Rose again. It was a word she was to use with relentless monotony in the days to follow, but Rebecca was not to know that yet.

'You are a widow. A poor, unhappy war-widow, expecting your dead husband's child.'

'No, Mamma.'

'Yes, Rose. *You must be.* It is the only way.'

'Don't be so ridiculous, Mamma. You know very well it is not true. I refuse to go through any such charade merely you save your face.'

'*My* face?' cried her mother in fury. 'And what about Claire's face? What about her husband's knighthood and our family name? What about Sara's hopes of the Fitzsimmon's boy and your little sisters' prospects? But then you would not think of them, would you? Oh no. Only of yourself and your own pleasures. How *could* you, Rose. How could you be so wicked, so thoughtless, so ...'

Rose ceased to listen. Poor Edward, she thought bleakly. She had not planned it this way. If she had planned at all in that deliberately irresponsible time, it had been to tell him in the loving privacy of her studio. And now Edward would hear via her mother's hysterical accusations and Claire's echoing outrage. Poor Claire. Rose felt fleeting sympathy for her ambitious sister. What a blow it would be to her pride and her visiting list, though not nearly such a violent one as the whole truth would be! As for Edward....

As her mother flowed on, heaping reproach on accusation, with a heavy sprinkling of venom, she imagined how loving, how reassuring, Edward's reaction would have been in contrast if she had done as she had planned and told him herself, when they were alone together. Now of course it would be public and different, but Edward was an honourable man and he loved her. Divorced, he would be ostracised of course, black-balled at his club, and respectable folk would cross the street to avoid contamination with the mere hem of Rose's skirts, but eventually some newer scandal would catch their attention and they would forget. And Claire? Claire would be astonished, humiliated, furious, but she would turn it all to her advantage. Claire would suffer nobly as the virtuous, much-wronged wife, but she would miss Wychwood. Poor Claire. Rose realised she herself had no wish to be mistress of Wychwood, only, she thought wrily, of Edward. And no wish to take Claire's place as hostess at Edward's table, only her place in his bed ... but it was done now.

She looked up and saw her father's dead, sepia face gazing sadly at her from the polished and lace-covered top of her mother's dressing-table and was filled with overwhelming remorse. 'I am sorry,' she said aloud.

Her mother, halted in mid-flow, accepted the words as hers and continued after barely a pause, 'What is the good of being sorry now it is too late. Oh God,' she cried, with rare blasphemy, 'what am I to do?'

'You need not do anything, Mamma,' said Rose, pushing back the heavy quilt and swinging her legs over the side of the bed. 'Where are my shoes?'

'What are you doing?' cried Rebecca in alarm.

'Going home, of course. To my studio.' Rose knew that only in the impersonal company of paints and canvas could she hope for any semblance of peace or any calm in which to mourn dear Percy as he deserved to be mourned. She should never have spoken her secret – except that when she heard of Percy's death she had felt an overwhelming anger and guilt and need for self-abasement. She wanted to be scourged, abused, insulted, punished. Had there been such a thing she would gladly have knelt on a stool of repentance in front of the most censorious congregation, because Percy had loved her and had died when she was carrying another man's child. Perversely, by bringing the full force of her mother's fury down on her head she had felt that her guilt might be assuaged. But now, the torrent loosed, she wanted only to escape and be alone with her grief. 'We should be mourning *Percy*,' she cried in anguish. 'Not thinking of ourselves.'

Rebecca, however, thought otherwise. 'Stay where you are! Get back into bed at once! Don't dare to speak another word!' In her haste to keep her daughter's deadly secret from the rest of the world Rebecca did not know which command to give first. In the end she took Rose by the shoulders and forcibly pushed her back onto the pillows. 'You will go nowhere, do you understand, until I have decided what is to be done.'

'It is my child, Mamma,' said Rose, with something of her old spirit, 'and I am almost twenty-one. I shall decide for myself.'

'Nonsense. You will do exactly as I tell you.' But Rose's words had reminded Rebecca of her daughter's capacity for wayward and rebellious behaviour. It must, of course, be stopped. Instantly she knew what she must do. As soon as she thought of it, it was obvious. Family crises such as this must be laid before the head of the family, the male head.

'You will stay in this room, Rose, and you will speak to no one. I will give out that *you are prostrated by grief*. I shall order suitable clothing to be sent round from Millards, for you must, of course, wear mourning, and tomorrow you and I will go to Wychwood. Edward and Claire will know best what must be done.'

Rose made no protest. It was inevitable, after all. If she had taken a moment's thought she would have known it instead of singing her carefree way to destruction. *They are not long the days of wine and roses* ... and she had had her share. But as her mother so innocently said, Edward would know what must be done. He would take charge of everything.

Obediently, Rose lay back on the pillows and closed her eyes as the first tears of grief for Percy welled up and overflowed.

CHAPTER 4

Wychwood in January was not at its best, and nor was Claire. She was annoyed with the snow which, from being a sparkling pleasure had become a grey and inconvenient slush; annoyed with the fires which smoked; with the parlour maid who had a red-nosed and snuffling cold; with seven-month-old Fay who was teething and fractious; and, of course, with Edward, who, on the rare occasions when he was at home, spent far too much time doting on his daughter when he could have been doting on Claire instead.

Edward's absence from her bedroom was now habitual and accepted, though not without an occasional twinge of unease, especially as, following a discreet hint from Phoebe Burgess, Claire had made a private visit to a certain lady doctor in Ipswich, been equipped with an unlovely but useful device of an intimate nature, and been assured that she need no longer regard pregnancy as the inevitable result of wedded concourse. Her precautions had proved unnecessary, though as the nights passed undisturbed she was not entirely content. Something the doctor had said had given Claire the uneasy idea that such celibacy was unnatural, that other marriages were conducted otherwise. Why else had Phoebe given her the hint? Why else indeed should that embarrassing device be necessary? Moreover Edward's absences from Wychwood were becoming disconcertingly frequent.

It was one thing to tell her charitable morning gatherings of county friends, over delicate china cups of the best coffee and cream, that her husband was engaged in important war work. One thing to murmur modestly to the ladies, over afternoon tea in her drawing room, that her poor contribution of comforts 'for our brave soldiers far away' was nothing compared to dear Edward's. One thing to make subtly clear to anyone who called that Mr Rivers, if not himself responsible for the overall strategy of this unfortunate war, had the eager ears of those who were. It was quite another when her visitors left, the light faded, the sleet drove against the window panes with dreary persistence and she found herself alone, with only her infant daughter and the servants for company. Then it was both irritating and disquieting to think that Edward found so much to engage his attention elsewhere.

But today at least he had sufficient reason. As soon as they heard that dreadful news about Percy Woodstock Edward had ridden over to Woodstock Hall to see if he could be of any use to poor Mrs Woodstock, who now had not even Georgina to comfort her in her trouble.

'Such a tragedy,' Claire had said, but in spite of her genuine sympathy for poor Mrs Woodstock, she could not help a small whisper of relief that Rose had not actually been married to Percy. Rose a rich and tragic widow would have put Claire's nose very much out of joint, one way and another. Yet in spite of his extraordinary refusal to be Fay's godfather, Percy had been amiable enough in his way and an excellent dinner guest. She would miss him. So would Rose. Poor Rose ... she could be very emotional ... Percy had been right for her, of course. Stolid, stable, a steadying hand on her sister's wilder artistic propensities. Tolerant (an important point where Rose was concerned) and above all loyal. For Claire had decided long ago that it was only Percy's loyalty that had enabled him to resist Claire's overtures, and it had been that same loyalty, she realised, which had dictated his refusal to be godfather to Fay. The dear boy: one had to admire him. And mourn him.

But when a suitable time had passed, Claire would look around among her acquaintances and invite someone else to dinner with Rose; someone *compatible*. Idly, she wondered what degree of mourning might be expected of her as the elder sister of Percy's fiancée? But the engagement had not been publically announced, and there was no ring, at least not to Claire's knowledge, so perhaps it did not count?

She wished Edward would come home so she could discuss the finer points of mourning etiquette with him and the memorial arrangements usually made for military deaths abroad. Whatever they were, she wanted to be prepared, especially if they might be reported in the newspapers. She wondered if Queen Victoria would ask the family for a photograph, as she had done when that gallant Captain Vernon was killed at Mafeking? Edward would know, though to be sure Edward was disappointingly vague about such matters and the most irritating raconteur. He had told her little enough about Harry's embarkation last weekend and nothing at all of what she really wanted to hear. In fact, his account of Lady Clementina's party had been woefully brief – 'We all went down to Southampton, on one of the special trains, crowded and uncomfortable of course, but that was only to be expected. Then back to Stratton Street where we were required to sit up most of the night playing bezique. Hardly time to bath and change before catching the train home.'

When Claire asked about Lady Clementina's clothes, or what Phoebe was wearing, she got the expected answer: he hadn't noticed. Though he did say Phoebe had on a new hat. When she asked who else was there he merely said vaguely, 'Oh, the usual crowd.' Remembering Harry's jeering refusal to stand godfather to little Fay, Claire had thought devoted motherhood and the treachery of winter weather a sufficiently reproachful and dignified excuse, (there was also a particularly flattering invitation she did not want to miss), but now she almost wished she had gone with Edward after all. At least she could have discussed fashions with Phoebe.

If only Edward would come home....

She listened yet again for the sound of horse's hooves in the drive, heard nothing, and moved restlessly to the piano where she picked aimlessly at the keys for a few minutes before closing the lid with a frown of discontent. She took up her embroidery, but after half a dozen stitches discarded it; leafed through a magazine and finally, feeling decidedly peevish and misused, rang the bell for her afternoon tea. She was awaiting its arrival when the telephone rang in the hall.

The telephone was one of her newest acquisitions, installed with the electricity at Christmas and essential, she told Edward, for her war work, as she liked to call her charitable collections. So far she had hardly used it. Few of her neighbours had a similar luxury and those who did still preferred the traditional contact of a note. Her mother refused to install the machine in her house, as a needless expense, and though there was one in the shop of course, even Claire would not dare to telephone her mother at Millards. So it was a shock to her when the parlourmaid arrived to say that there was a message from Mrs Millard and that Mrs Rivers was wanted 'on that there speaking tube if you please, Mum.'

'It is *not* a speaking tube,' rebuked Claire, but with scant attention. For her mother to telephone was rare: it could only be bad news.

It was not her mother's voice, however, that crackled indistinctly in her ear when she picked up the receiver and said, in her special telephone voice, sharpened now by anxiety, 'Hello. Mrs Edward Rivers speaking.' It was the unwelcome voice of Mr Blunt, her mother's business partner.

Mrs Millard had asked him to telephone on her behalf to inform

Mrs Rivers that following the sudden, dreadful death of Captain Woodstock she would be bringing Miss Rose to Wychwood tomorrow to recover from the shock. He offered Mrs Rivers his sympathy and sincere condolences in this time of trouble and hung up.

Slowly Claire replaced the black and gold receiver on its hook and stood a moment in thought. She was actually smiling. At first an unguarded and excited smile, it changed quickly to a gentler one, of brave and sympathetic sadness. It was gratifying to be able to provide a haven for her stricken sister, to lend a supporting arm to her poor, grieving mother. She was more than happy for them to come to her for comfort in their hour of need and their company, sad though it must be, would enliven those dreary winter hours. It would be Claire's duty to see that those hours *were* enlivened, in order to sustain her guests' spirits and guard against despair; nothing unsuitable, of course, nothing frivolous. Perhaps a small musical evening of a quietly reverent kind? After the memorial service, of course, and then only when it was seemly. She would need to consult Cook about suitably discreet but sustaining menus for the days to come. A little steamed turbot, perhaps, or breast of chicken with a delicate mousseline sauce. Then Rose had better share a room with her mother, so that she need not be alone in her grief. Or would it be kinder to give them rooms with connecting doors so they could each enjoy privacy in which to mourn, yet be at the same time close? She must ask the gardener to send up hothouse lilies and hyacinths, white if possible. And a photograph of Percy, in a black frame on the piano, would be a delicate and sympathetic touch. She wondered if she had anything suitable? Or perhaps Rose would bring a picture with her?

Claire's spirits were quite restored as she hurried back to the drawing room and rang the bell to summon, in quick succession, Cook, the upper housemaid and Nanny. For it had occurred to Claire that perhaps the best therapy for poor Rose in her grief would be her beloved painting, so why not that portrait of dear little Fay?

Edward was weary when he reached Wychwood, weary in body and in spirit. Mrs Woodstock had been brave, almost agonisingly so, especially when she held out to him the black-edged letter from the War Office and asked him to read it aloud for her:

Dear Mrs Woodstock, Edward read, *It is with great sorrow and with heartfelt sympathy that I write to announce to you the death of your son Percival, killed in action on Spionkop hill on the morning of the 25th. Many brave and noble fellows fell that awful morning, but not one of them is more regretted than your son.*

Two companies of his battalion were detached to take part with other troops in the attack on a high ridge – nay a precipitous mountain. The ridge was carried by assault after a toilsome night's work – all except the spur of the hill, unfortunately strongly held. Your son led his troop repeatedly and with unfailing courage against this hill and though wounded in the first assault refused to relinquish command until, some three hours later, while leading his men in yet another attack against formidable odds, he was killed instantly by shell fire to the head. . . .

Edward paused, remembering with sudden vividness that scene in the billiard room of his club when Percy had woken, terrified, from 'a deuced uncomfortable dream' of unstoppable enemy attack and Harry had said, 'Lie down, old boy,' or some such meaningless panacea. Now Harry himself was caught up in this same war and Percy no longer had any choice. . . .

He had nobly encouraged his men throughout the morning, resumed Edward, with difficulty, *by both word and example, and is reported to have himself shot six of the enemy dead before his own noble death.*

Your dear son, all of him that is mortal, lies decently and reverently buried on that ill-fated ridge surrounded by comrades and friends. . . .

When Edward finished reading, Mrs Woodstock said only, 'His father would have been proud of him,' though she accepted Edward's arm to help her upstairs, 'to lie down for a little before tackling Nanny.'

It had taken their combined ministrations for most of the day to bring any semblance of comfort to poor old Nanny who had 'nursed poor Master Percy since he was a baby, bless him, and a sweeter-natured child you could not wish for, and as for poor Miss Georgina, always so devoted to her brother, her heart will break, that it will, and what a dreadful welcome for her in that nasty foreign land . . .' Finally Edward had left the two women to comfort each other and had occupied himself with what practical matters he could, sent telegrams (including one to Georgina forbidding her to come home on her mother's account), instructed lawyers, answered the telephone and taken messages of sympathy until the Price-Hills had arrived from London, with the first of the Wood-stock cousins, to take over. Then at last Edward was free to leave.

It was then, on the weary ride home through the gloomy winter countryside, that the full impact of the news had struck him hard, in the heart. Like Percy's old nanny, Edward had known Percy since childhood, had attended the same school, the same parties, moved in the same social circle; they had gone shooting and fishing together, to concerts and the theatre, even occasionally the races, and though never intimate had been easy and undemanding companions. Percy had no malice in him, Edward realised, and no vice. Because of that, he had been overlooked in many circles as a dull fellow, but he had been an honest man and a loyal friend. He had loved Rose Millard with devotion and utter trust, no doubt thinking every man as straightforward an English gentleman as he was himself. Edward's eyes were moist as he thought of Percy, dead across the sea, and he was glad of the darkness and the dank night air to hide his guilt and sorrow. So he had no more inkling than Claire of the real reason when Claire told him that Rose and Mrs Millard were arriving the next day to nurse their grief at Wychwood. With Woodstock Hall so close, it seemed only natural.

He drove to the station himself to meet them and though Rose gave him a swift look of startling entreaty, he thought only that she was asking for his discretion and understanding. Naturally they could not speak alone together and apart from his initial words of sympathy the journey to Wychwood passed in sombre silence.

Claire met them in the hall, in an atmosphere of hushed solicitude, with a bevy of hovering servants waiting in the shadows to be despatched on whatever errands might be required. But to Claire's anxious question of what she might provide for her mother's sustenance after such a harrowing journey, Mrs Millard said only, through thin lips, 'Tea, Claire. In *absolute* privacy.'

'Of course, Mummy darling,' fluttered Claire, endeavouring to aid her mother's faltering steps. 'Let me help you to the drawing room.' But Mrs Millard shook off her arm quite roughly and snapped, 'I am not yet decrepit!' Then, with a strange edge to her voice, she added, 'Though as circumstances are, it may not be long before I am.'

Claire, spurned, put her supporting arm round her sister's waist instead and said, 'I am so very sorry, Rose, dear. Poor, dear Percy ...'

Rose felt perilously near hysteria at this patent play-acting, and at her own duplicity. She wanted to laugh derisively at Claire, to weep tears of public remorse and tear her hair, to scream ... We are as bad as each other, she thought – the player sisters – Claire the sorrowing sister, me the sorrowing lover, and both of us a sham – a blatant, patent, hideous *sham*. She was tempted for a wild moment to stand defiantly in the panelled hall beside the polished Jacobean chest with its Chinese bowl of rose petal pot pourri, fling her arms wide in histrionic surrender and shout her treachery to

358

the rooftops. She might even have done it had not Mrs Millard, no doubt sensing rebellion, pushed her sharply between the shoulder blades in the direction of the drawing room.

There they sat, in silence: Rose, in the muted lavender garment heavily trimmed with crepe which Mrs Millard had provided and which Rose, in her sacrificial mood, had not resisted, Mrs Millard in her usual widow's black, side by rigid side on the cream-damasked sofa, no doubt so that Mrs Millard could restrain Rose by force, if necessary. Claire, in the plain, high-necked cream blouse and dark skirt which she had thought appropriate until circumstances dictated otherwise, sat opposite them on the other side of the simmering log fire, in the chair Lady Portia had used when Rose had sketched her an aeon ago, at that autumn house party at Wychwood. Already there was something of that lady's imperiousness about Claire herself – perhaps it was merely the high-backed chair against whose dark background Claire's profile when she turned her head had the clear-cut precision of a Roman coin. Behind her, the heavy velvet curtains at the french windows gave a touch of regal red, like theatre curtains, thought Rose, framing some mournful Chekhovian tragedy. Beyond the windows, in the fading afternoon light, the drab winter lawn glistened with lingering patches of moisture against the colourless, dripping mass of the woods where, in the vibrant colours of autumn, she and Percy had walked such a pitifully short time ago. She had never sent him the sketch of that little woodland glade, with the wood anemones and speckled toadstools.

Claire attempted words of comfort and was snubbed by Mrs Millard's sharp, 'Not now.' Rose said nothing. As they waited for tea to arrive Edward moved restlessly about the room, now kicking the logs in the grate into brighter life, now pacing the carpet by the french windows and frowning into the deepening winter gloom. There were ivory discs of honesty in an arrangement of dried flowers on Claire's writing desk, Rose noticed, and on the sofa table a wide bowl of early, sweet-scented hyacinths. Still no one spoke. Then at last they heard the faint tinkling sound of the tea tray in the hall and Mrs Millard said, rather too loudly, and for the obvious benefit of the servants, 'I see you are burning wood instead of coal, Claire dear.'

'The Home Woods need thinning,' explained Edward, turning towards them.

Mrs Millard waited in simmering silence, while Claire busied herself with the teapot and Edward handed the cups and saucers, positioned occasional tables, offered the bread and butter plate. The maid returned with hot water, asked if Madam required anything else. Claire asked for the lights to be turned on, then dismissed her with orders not to return until she was summoned.

There was a pause in which the maid's receding footsteps were clearly audible followed by the closing of a distant door. Then Mrs Millard placed her cup on the rosewood coffee table at her elbow and said, 'I had better tell you at once, Edward, and you, Claire, before this tea chokes me. Rose has disgraced us.'

Rose saw his face go rigid with shock, then change slowly from a healthy, outdoor red to the colour of Georgina's marble column. He was standing with his back to the fire, a cup of tea in one hand while with the other he stirred it slowly, round and round. Now with a hand that visibly trembled, he replaced the cup on the tray and when Claire stood up, moved quickly to his side, Rose saw his arm encircle her waist with a movement at once automatic and protective. Guiltily, she looked down at her hands, locked tight together in her lap, lest she see what she must not see....

'What can you mean, Mummy?' cried Claire, then, remembering the servants, toned down her alarm to a horrified whisper, 'What has she done?'

In spite of her resolve, Rose looked up, first at Claire, her expression wide-eyed and anxious, her hands clasped now in front of her breast, her husband's supporting arm still at her waist, then at Edward, grey-faced and old beside her, as if he had glimpsed his own grave. Both were staring, appalled, at Rebecca. In the stillness a smouldering log suddenly sputtered into crackling flame and the scent of pine hung sweet in the air. Somewhere in the darkness beyond the uncurtained windows a fox barked. Still Rose could not take her eyes from his face. Then her mother spoke.

'She is expecting his child.'

CHAPTER 5

In the horrified silence that followed Rose saw the shock she had expected in Edward's face, but she also saw alarm and naked, hunted fear. It was only momentary before the grey, expressionless mask took over, but it had been there just the same. Her mother's words hung, menacing, over the tiny triangles of bread and butter, the silver milk jug and delicate Sevres china as the silence stretched. Then, in an appalled whisper, Claire spoke a single, penetrating word.

'*What?*'

Edward's hand fell from her waist and moved instead to his collar, attempting to loosen it, before he took a hold on himself and clasped his hands, hard, behind his back. For one brief, accusing moment he looked straight at Rose, who lifted her chin a fraction and stared steadily back, waiting for him to speak. Now, she willed inside her head, *now*. Step forward, raise me up, acknowledge me. Claim me and our child before the world.

But he looked away and said nothing and Rose saw betrayal, like a black abyss, yawn at her feet. Her heart faltered, then began to thump uncomfortably fast. Surely he loved her? He had said so often enough, with a passion the memory of which drove knives of fire through her heart. Then why did he not speak?

If Rose had seen an abyss open at her feet, Edward Rivers was already at the bottom of his, trapped, appalled, beset on all sides by enemies, with no hope of escape. He loved Rose, there was no question of that. Loved her with every inch of his body, every drop of his passionate blood. She should have told him herself, of course, not left him to find out like this, in front of others, but if she had, would it have made any difference? Bleakly, hopelessly, he knew that it would not. All it would have done would have been to give him time to dissemble. He loved Rose. The thought of living without her was torment. But he was a married man. He had a charming, capable and blameless wife. He had made a solemn promise before God to love and care for that wife till death, and Edward was an honourable man. Yet he owed Rose just as much loyalty – more, for Rose had loved and trusted him and had given him as much and more than any wife – and now she was expecting his child. But his wife had already given him a child, a baby daughter whom he dearly loved. If he were to abandon Claire, then little Fay would grow up believing her father had cared nothing for her. It was a thought he could not bear. Oh God, why had he ever fallen from grace? Why had he not battered down Claire's door that fateful night of Fay's christening and stayed safely in their married bed?

Except that if he had, he and Rose would never have found that sweet, forbidden Paradise together ... And now he must choose between them and whichever choice he made would bring dishonour and pain.

Expressionless and apparently aloof, the impossible argument still raging in his head, Edward listened as Mrs Millard and Claire exchanged quick question and answer, plan and counter-plan, and the taut look gradually left his face as it became plain that Mrs Millard's ambiguous 'his' had meant only 'Percy's' and that Rose, after all, had not betrayed him. It was a small reprieve, though for how long? But when his mother-in-law and his wife both turned to him and said, in the same breath, 'What do you think, Edward?' he was able to reply, with measured thoughtfulness, 'As yet, I do not know what to advise for the best. The matter requires much careful, and private, consideration. Naturally, it has been a shock ...'

'A shock?' cried Claire. 'It is an outrage.' Then with concentrated venom she turned on Rose. 'How could you, Rose? When I think of the disgrace!'

Now? thought Rose, with a strangely detached interest. Shall I do it now? Shatter complacency and say what must be said? As she watched Edward's unnaturally impassive face she guessed at the thoughts which must be tormenting him, at the shame and guilt and divided loyalty. But surely not divided *love*? She had expected remorse, apology, shame, but had not dreamt of hesitation. Hesitation destroyed the foundation of her trust and put the whole outcome in doubt. As her faith in him died, pride rose defiantly to take its place.

'You must go away at once,' continued Claire, 'before it shows. You must have the thing in secret somewhere, where no one knows us.'

'*and when Joseph found that Mary was with child he was minded to put her away privily*' The words came bitter and unbidden to her lips.

'Rose!' cried her mother, 'How dare you blaspheme! If the good Lord sent a thunderbolt to strike you dead this minute it would be

362

no more than you deserve.' She was genuinely shocked and then, seeing Rose's expression, furious. 'Don't think to hide behind flippancy, young woman, or to escape your just punishment. You have sinned and must suffer.'

'She could perhaps pretend to be married, Mummy,' suggested Claire. 'A war widow? It does not need to be Percy.'

'Of course it does, fool. Otherwise she is no more than a whore.'

'She might miscarry?' said Claire with sudden hope. 'The shock. And then the travelling cannot be good for her. Those bumpy roads...'

'Do not rely on it,' said Rebecca bitterly. 'Rose would not be so accommodating.'

'I am in the room,' said Rose, 'in case you had forgotten. You may address your remarks to me. And before you go any further with your ridiculous speculations, I refuse to say I am married when I am not.'

'You refuse?' repeated her mother with concentrated fury. 'We will see about that. You will do as we think best in this matter, do you understand?'

'I understand,' said Rose with equal anger, for it was plain to her now that Edward would offer no support, 'that the child is mine, and ...' Now? She paused, looking directly at Edward, giving him one last chance. One word would do it, one small word from him. Or from her. But he said nothing and she found she could not do it to him. Instead, she finished, in a rush, 'and in the absence of a husband, *mine alone*. I shall do as I choose.'

'You will do no such thing. If you will not approach Mrs Woodstock, though with the estate and the entail there is no saying she would listen and who could blame her, then the child must be adopted, that is plain. I believe there are convents that see to such things.'

'What a splendid idea, Mummy!' said Claire, with the first touch of hope. 'In France, where no one knows us. Mademoiselle owes us a favour. She will arrange it, though we will not tell her the truth, of course. Rose made an unsuitable marriage, to a soldier who was killed. Something like that. We will work out the details later, Oh, Mummy, you are so clever. Perhaps after all everything can be hushed up without disgrace? You know we cannot afford even the teeniest whisper of scandal if Edward is to find the recognition he deserves.'

'So, in order that Edward may be given the Order of the Garter,' Rose said with heavy sarcasm and added, deliberately to hurt, 'or made a Gentleman of the Bedchamber, then I am to give birth to my child in some unknown foreign convent, is that it? And what then? Do tell me the second chapter of this fascinating serial.'

'The child is adopted,' said her mother before Claire could speak. 'Or brought up in an orphanage. The details need not concern us. The nuns will arrange all that, for a consideration.' Here Claire looked a question at Mrs Millard who nodded in grim acquiescence. The money would be found. 'As for you, Rose, you had better go on an extended art tour.'

'Of course, Mummy!' cried Claire and looked up at Edward with a quick smile of relief. 'In fact, we could say at this end that Rose was travelling abroad to assuage her grief and to paint, as Percy always wanted her to do. And afterwards she might even stay with Lady Portia,' went on Claire eagerly, 'I am sure Edward could arrange it, couldn't you, Edward dear?'

For the first time the Millard women all looked at Edward together, though with very different expressions. He avoided their eyes, clasped his hands tighter behind his back, rocked slightly on his heels as if deliberating, stared at the hearthrug and mumbled something about having to think things over, very carefully.

Rose, who had been sitting obediently on the sofa until this moment stood up. 'I have no objection to travelling abroad, Mamma, nor, Claire, to staying with Lady Portia. I would be happy to do both. I do, however, object to having my unborn child disposed of like a piece of unwanted furniture. So kindly *mind your own business*, all of you.' She made for the door, but Mrs Millard, with surprising agility, got there first and barred the exit.

'It is our business, you selfish, obstinate girl. The family honour is at stake.'

'Honour? What honour?' This, they both knew, was for Edward. And before her mother could answer, Edward spoke.

'I think, Mrs Millard,' he said slowly, 'that when I have had time to consider all the implications and possible courses of action, it would be best if I discussed the matter quietly with Rose, alone.'

There was a small silence, then Rose turned and with dignity resumed her seat on the sofa. 'Thank you, Edward,' she said. 'That is the first sensible suggestion I have heard today.'

'I think also,' continued Edward, whose colour was beginning to return, 'that in order to avoid undue gossip in the kitchens, we had better dispose of at least some of this bread and butter. The scones, too, are very good,' he continued, offering Rose the plate. 'You can rely on me.'

She glanced quickly up, caught his eye, and looked swiftly down again. 'Thank you,' she said, coldly. 'I hope I can.'

It was the strangest tea-party Rose had ever attended, even stranger than the Mad Hatter's in *Alice in Wonderland.* Silences alternated with, on Claire's part, frenetic social chatter and on Edward's, monosyllables. Mrs Millard glowered into her tea-cup and then, when Rose had the gall to ask Edward how Mrs Woodstock was bearing up under the grief, slammed it down so hard on the table that the tea splashed out onto the polished wood and had to be mopped up hastily lest it mark the surface. But at last, after a raised eyebrow from Claire and a nod from Edward, Claire rang the bell for the tea things to be removed. It was then, before Claire had resumed her seat and as if on cue (and indeed it was, though in the agitations of the moment Claire had forgotten) that Nanny appeared, with the infant Fay in her arms and, crossing the drawing room with a cheerful smile, offered the be-laced and be-ribboned marvel to her mother. Claire took the child, dandled her for a moment with sundry cooings, then handed her to Edward, saying 'Go to Daddy then, my little pet.' He took the child in his arms with a quick smile of pleasure and Claire leant against him, her hand tucked in his elbow, and smiled, in what Rose recognised instantly as a pre-planned Happy Family Group. She would have laughed had not the pain in her heart been too bitterly intense.

Yet Claire's whole fragile edifice of happy marriage could be shattered at one stroke if Rose chose. In spite of Claire's Rule, her extorted vows, and her lifetime of dominance Rose had absolute supremacy – and the fact that Claire was so smugly ignorant of it made Rose's power the greater. Claire had 'stolen' Edward and now Rose had stolen him triumphantly back. She even carried his child. One word and she would be absolute victor. For a long moment Rose hesitated, savouring the sweet fruit of triumph, while Claire, smiling and unsuspecting, posed with her husband and their baby daughter...

And Rose could not do it. It was not Edward – he, thought Rose with fleeting bitterness, can take care of himself. But Claire was her sister and unexpectedly vulnerable. Rose closed her eyes wearily on the self-knowledge that, whatever the provocation, whatever the private pain, she would keep her secret.

'I had thought, Rose,' said Claire, with unconscious irony, one eye on Nanny who hovered benignly in the background and to whom the plan had been confided, 'that you might lose yourself in painting. Just a small family group, nothing ambitious. But now ...'

'Out of the question,' said Mrs Millard, taking in the situation and dealing with it in the blink of an eye. 'Rose is emotionally exhausted. Later perhaps, in the spring.'

'As you think best, Mamma,' said Claire meekly and when the infant had pulled at Edward's moustache, poked an exploratory finger in his eye and laughed her delight when he tossed her in the air and caught her again before handing her back to Claire, Claire nodded to Nanny to remove her little charge.

Rose, watching, felt unutterably desolate and alone. Virtue might be its own reward, but it was a cold companion.

There followed ten minutes of comparative silence in which Rose, unseeing, turned the pages of an illustrated magazine, Rebecca and Claire exchanged confidential whispers or looked apprehensively at Edward, and Edward himself stood with his back to the room, staring out into the darkness. Firelight flickered in the uncurtained windowpanes where the room was reflected in ghostly mirrored duplicate. Rose saw Edward's frowning face, and beyond him her own seated figure, a stranger, insubstantial and vulnerable in those unfamiliar clothes. Her mother's black solidity loomed threatening beside her. Of Claire the only reflection was a chairback and a glimpse of profile, beautiful and sure. Then with a noise as swift and final as the guillotine, Edward drew the curtains and obliterated the scene.

'I suggest, Claire,' he said, turning to face them, 'that you take your mother to visit the nursery for half an hour, then return with her to the drawing room until I send for you. Meanwhile, I will see you, Rose, in the library.'

He held open the door for her and she stepped inside, as she had done once, long ago, when Lady Portia had sent her to fetch drawing materials from her room and Edward had waylaid and kissed her. But now when she turned to face him in that leather-scented, book-lined haven, he made no move to comfort her with kisses. Instead he said with an anger none the less bitter for being quietly controlled. 'Why didn't you warn me? It was unforgiveable to spring it on me, in public.'

'You took it very well. One might almost say you were – unmoved.'

'God, Rose, what did you expect me to do? Take you in my arms and congratulate you, in front of everybody?'

'Surely you mean in front of your wife?'

'It was an impossible position to put me in. You must see that.'

'And what about the position you have put me in?'

They stood confronting each other, each quivering with anger, and barely a foot apart. Fleetingly into Rose's mind came that scene in the studio when he had spoilt her painting: she fed on the memory, deliberately, to fuel her anger.

'Well?' she challenged. 'I seem to remember a small matter of honour was mentioned, though not, admittedly, by you.'

That hurt him, and she was glad.

'I said you could rely on me,' he said stiffly. 'I will support you, of course.' At the back of his mind he heard Harry's urbane voice saying, 'All you need do is pay if they're in trouble ... and wave them goodbye. It's all they expect, old boy', and was ashamed.

'Good,' said Rose. Then because she wanted to hurt and be hurt, she added, 'It could really work out very well. I could live in the old brewery, for I don't expect Claire would want me actually in the house. She is rather strait-laced, but then you know that. But it wouldn't matter. I could paint and you could visit me whenever you felt the need. Then our child will be only a year younger than Fay. They could share the same nanny and the same governess. Yes, it could work out very well.' She saw the colour ebb from his face, the gaunt, appalled expression that gripped it as for a moment he believed her – and she was duly punished.

'I am sorry,' she said quietly, 'I did not mean it.'

'No.' For a moment there was silence: he had had a ghastly shock. 'But I deserved it.'

Her legs felt suddenly weak and she was afraid she might crumple into abject, pleading misery. She turned away, found a chair and sat down.

'God, Rose, what are we to do?' He crossed the faded turkey carpet and stood beside her, looking down at her pale, uplifted face. With a small shake of the head, she said only, 'I did not plan it like this. I am sorry. But Percy died and I fainted and then Mamma ...'

'No matter. It is done now.'

'I suppose I could take Claire's advice, drive about over the bumpiest roads I can find and hope for the best.'

'Claire should not have said that. I apologise.'

'So do I. It is your child too.' After a small pause she said, 'I wonder what we would have done if Percy had not died. He said once,' she added sadly, 'that he would forgive me anything. But I think even Percy could not have been expected to forgive this.'

'No.'

'I wonder whose child he would have thought it was? In fact, all in all, you might say Percy has done us a favour by dying. And himself,' she added with returning bitterness. 'At least he never knew how I betrayed him.'

367

'It was my fault. My responsibility.'

'Oh? You gave no sign of it. There, in the drawing room, you did nothing, except blanch and gulp and pretend you were rectitude personified.'

There was silence in which either he heard her unspoken thoughts or his own conscience prompted him, for after a moment he said, 'Did you expect me to ask Claire for a divorce? Did you really want such a thing?'

Did she? She no longer knew what she wanted, except, she realised with blinding clarity, the absolute freedom to go on painting – and not to hurt Claire. Poor, predictable, bossy Claire with her social ambitions and her poses. As for the baby, his baby, she felt nothing as yet. Until yesterday she had denied its existence.

When she did not answer, he said quietly, 'You mentioned honour and you were right. It was dishonourable of me, as a married man, ever to love you. But I could not help myself. I loved ... I *love* you, Rose, with all my being. You were beautiful, talented, elusive, alluring, an unendurable torment, a passionate, consuming hunger, all of those things ...' But this time he did not correct the past tense and Rose knew what was coming before he spoke. 'Claire is not like you are. She has not your inner strength. She needs reassurance and stability. A divorce would shatter what little confidence she has and break her spirit.'

'You love her,' said Rose, in a dull, flat voice. It was half question, half statement.

He said only, 'She is my wife.'

Without warning and to Rose's fury, her tears spilled out and ran in glistening runnels down her cheeks. He made a move towards her, but she motioned him angrily away and felt in her pocket for a handkerchief. He watched her for a troubled moment, then crossed to the fireplace and rang the bell. Then he moved to his desk, sat down in the chair and, pulling a sheet of black-edged notepaper towards him, took up a pen. When the door opened, he looked up from what the maid took to be a letter of condolence and said, 'We are expecting a message from Woodstock Hall concerning the memorial service. Please ensure that I am informed the moment it arrives. There are arrangements to be made and naturally Miss Millard is most anxious to hear as soon as possible. One more thing,' he said as the maid turned to leave. 'Bring the decanter from the dining room, and glasses. Miss Millard is, naturally, a little overwrought. I think a glass of medicinal brandy is in order.'

Rose dabbed at her eyes, said lightly, 'The body's treachery, that is all. Take no notice. *Tears, idle tears, I know not what they mean,*' But she did, and so did he.

When the maid returned two minutes later it was to find, as she reported to the kitchen staff, 'that poor Miss Rose dabbing at her eyes with her handkerchief and babbling something about happy autumn fields and days that are no more. The poor thing. Such a tragedy. Quite touched in the head she is, and no wonder.'

When the door closed behind the parlourmaid, Edward poured Rose a large brandy and another, larger, for himself. 'Drink it,' he urged. 'It will help.'

Obediently she lifted her glass, said 'To our child,' and drained it in one joyless draught. Edward refilled her glass and said gravely, 'This is what I propose to do, if you agree ...'

As Rose listened the last shred of hope drained out of her, leaving her empty, scoured of all emotion and strangely free – but it was a cold freedom, devoid of joy.

'If our child is to be brought up as a child should be, it is the only way,' he finished. 'And you will have your art.'

'Yes.' It was a bleak word, bleak as her thoughts.

But the mention of art, here in his own library, had brought unwelcome memories. 'Does Sara suspect?'

'*Sara?*' She paused before shaking her head. 'I think not.'

'She must not.'

'No.' In the silence Rose heard the grandfather clock in the hall slowly ticking her life away. There was no more to be said. She stood up to go and he took the empty brandy glass from her hand, his fingers brushing hers. Slowly he put the glass down on the desk behind him. 'Rose,' he began, uncertainly. She moved towards him and suddenly his arms were around her and they were kissing as if the world was ending and this was the only moment left to them. Which, thought Rose bleakly when at last he let her go, is probably the truth. She walked to the door, opened it, and stepped out into the hall without a backward glance. He heard her footsteps mount the stairs then the distant closing of a bedroom door.

Edward poured himself another stiff brandy before ringing the bell for the maid. 'Find Mrs Rivers and send her to me.' At the maid's startled expression, he amended this to, 'Please ask my wife to spare me a moment. There are matters to discuss.'

When Claire emerged from the library a long time later, with barely time to dress for dinner, she looked baffled, angry, petulant and resentful, but also, under everything else, a little afraid.

For, as well as the appalling business of Rose's condition, certain

369

aspects of that private conversation had been disquieting. As she sat at her dressing table and unpinned her hair, prior to doing it up again for the evening in a more lavish concoction of combs and padded hoops, Claire turned over in her mind various things that had been said and the more she remembered, the less confident she became.

Claire could not put her finger on it, but she had had the impression of a certain evasion on her husband's part, of things he had not told her. She realised, of course, that he had had what was politely termed 'experience' before his marriage, and lately had wondered increasingly if he might not be reverting to his bachelor ways, even if there was someone in particular. When she had remarked that she could not understand how Rose could have been so 'wicked' Edward had told her, quite sharply, to have more compassion and understanding. When she had retorted that only servants and the lower classes behaved like that, he had muttered something that sounded very much like 'More's the pity!' though of course it couldn't have been. 'Some women,' he had told her with a very odd expression, 'actually believe in expressing their love in more intimate ways than a mere kiss on the forehead and a locked door. If the glorious strength and depth of that love lead them to indiscretion, then it is a sin of generosity – and the fault of nature and society if they are condemned for it.' He had actually said 'a sin of *generosity*'. It had given Claire a cold feeling inside and the mention of locked doors had not helped.

The idea of Edward siding with Rose, even, apparently, condoning her behaviour, had not been reassuring. Nor had the implied criticism of herself, unjust though it was. As to the solution he had finally proposed – Claire shuddered. But the more she thought of it, the more she realised it might be the only way. Especially if Edward persisted in his insistence on family responsibility and family loyalty. And she feared he would persist.

'You surely cannot tolerate the idea of your sister's child going to a stranger?' he had said, and when she had suggested that the child would know no better, and what did it matter anyway, and that 'Rose should have thought of that before she demeaned herself,' he had sworn, not quite under his breath and been really quite surprisingly angry. 'Would you like to see Fay reared in an orphanage, by strangers? God, woman, where is your heart?'

The whole affair had unsettled and disturbed her till she felt quite extraordinarily nervous and unsure of herself. She really should not have kept Edward at arm's length for so long; she realised that now. He had seemed like a stranger to her this evening, and as for that sin of generosity ... it was as if he actually approved ... and it was the opposite that was the sin. As if Rose was right and Claire was wrong. She shivered with something close to fear. Suppose Edward had ... were to ... but she dare not put that fear into words, even in her head. Suddenly she craved reassurance, of the most intimate and husbandly kind.

She dressed with care, choosing a dress she knew Edward liked, and arranging her hair in a particularly feminine way. Rose and her mother were taking dinner on a tray in their room, at Edward's suggestion, so she would have her husband entirely to herself. It might be her only chance. At the thought her apprehension returned. She realised she did not know what Edward was thinking, hoping for, planning ... she had let him become a stranger. Then all those absences in London ... A wild, impossible suspicion entered her mind and was instantly crushed. Rose was her sister. She had sworn the vow. Yet remembering that sin of generosity and her own shortcomings, a small worm of fear nibbled on, unchecked, and made her humble.

When the gong sounded for dinner, she descended the stairs with an expression of serenity and loving obedience, which took Edward by surprise. And she looked lovely. She made no reference to that disturbing conversation in the library, and as the meal progressed, let it be known, in a dozen little ways, that she bowed to his wishes in all things.

She lingered past her usual time in the drawing room and instead of saying, as she usually did, 'Well, goodnight, dear,' before bending over his chair and kissing him dismissively on the forehead, she held out her hand and said, 'Come to bed soon, Edward. It is getting late.'

He smoked one more cigar, then closed his book and put out the lights. Upstairs, he found the connecting door to her bedroom open, and Claire in a clinging crepe de chine nightdress, brushing her hair at the dressing table. 'Come in, Edward,' she said, smiling. Then she held out the hairbrush to him and said, 'Please?'

With a long, shuddering sigh he took it and began to brush her thick, chestnut-glinting hair while in his mind's eye he saw Rose naked in the studio and himself brushing her tangled hair which was as thick as Claire's, but redder. Then he had moved the brush downwards and gently brushed that curling triangle ... He closed his eyes. Oh God ... When Claire turned to him and said, 'What is it, darling?' he snatched her to him and kissed her with a need that left her gasping.

'Don't turn me out tonight, Claire,' he pleaded, 'Please.' Only in

Claire, in his wife, in the honour and respectability of married life, could he hope to find comfort and the strength to do what must be done. For the other course was unthinkable: he had known it, with blinding certainty, there in the drawing room this afternoon. As she had. But, dear God, how would he endure?

'Of course not, Edward dearest,' Claire was saying. 'Just give me a moment.' Then she took something out of her dressing table drawer and slipped behind the corner screen. He was still standing, desolate, where she had left him when she emerged, shyly, from behind the screen. She was naked.

'God, Claire, you should not have locked me out so long,' he said, a long time later.

'No. I am sorry.' Edward had been most gratifyingly passionate, yet at the same time considerate and gentle. In fact, she realised with faint surprise, it had been almost pleasant. Yes, decidedly pleasant, especially when she need not worry about an inconvenient pregnancy, and now that Edward was relaxed beside her, his head on her shoulder, and one arm across her breast, it was really very friendly.

The fire had almost died, but the ashes were still pinkly glowing in the grate, and where the curtains did not quite meet a sliver of moonlight crept into the room and lit it with pale and eerie light. Deep in the well of the sleeping house the grandfather clock whirred and struck the hour with a single, sonorous note. When the resonance died away, there was only the faint cry of an owl from distant woods and the creak of floorboards settling for the night. The door into Edward's dressing room stood open, for he had forgotten to close it, but she hoped he would stay. His body, warm against hers, gave her the reassurance she needed.

'Poor Rose,' she murmured. 'She must have loved him so much.' When Edward did not answer, she added, 'and poor, dear Percy. So young and brave. What a tragic loss.'

Edward stirred beside her, moved, repositioned himself and she felt sudden moisture cold on her skin. After a startled moment she realised that he was crying.

CHAPTER 6

The memorial service for Captain Woodstock was to be in three days' time, for close friends and family only. Rose spent the intervening days walking in the garden when weather permitted, sketching in the nursery, or reading alone in her room.

For since the events of that first day and Edward's decision, Rose had felt increasingly guilty. She felt a strange need to propitiate Claire for the secret harm she had done her and for what was to come. When Edward had proposed his solution, how had Claire reacted? Had she suspected? But such an admission would be to confess defeat and defeat, even if only of a temporary kind, was not something Claire could tolerate. Or even contemplate, especially at the hand of a younger sister. No, if Claire suspected she would, Rose was sure, instantly dismiss the suspicion as impossible – and set about shoring up her defences, consolidating her position, and making it doubly impregnable.

On the second day Rose had been coming downstairs on slippered feet when she saw Edward and Claire in the hall below her. They did not hear her. She saw Claire lay her hand on Edward's arm and he covered her hand with his. It was a small gesture, but at the same time intimate and easy. Rose knew then that Claire had reclaimed him and the jealousy, and memory, that it roused in her was a physical pain. She knew also that if she spoke out now it would make no difference: she could wipe that satisfied look from Claire's face with one word, but Edward would still be lost to her. She turned to go back upstairs. But only for a moment. After all, what did it matter? What did anything matter any more? It was over. She descended the stairs and crossed the hall to the drawing room without looking at them. She neither knew nor cared if they saw her.

After that she took up Claire's suggestion and sought refuge in her art. She offered to sketch the baby, though she refused absolutely to attempt a family group. It must be Fay on a cushion in her nursery or nothing. After the initial disappointment, Claire was gratified and even agreed to leave Rose and Fay alone in the nursery while the portrait progressed. Rose found Claire's company difficult enough as it was, and to have her cooing over 'Daddy's little precious' was more than she could take.

But, Claire away, Rose found the nursery strangely soothing, with its memories of untroubled childhood: nappies airing on the guard in front of the nursery fire and Nanny knitting in her chair. Fay was a good baby, placid and happy-natured. If she remained as equable there would be little danger of her dominating her siblings, as her mother had done, with an enforced and all-embracing rule of deference to the first-born. Rose remembered Sara's comment at little Fay's birth that it was not the eldest who suffered, but the others. Rose was not entirely convinced of this, but at least in Fay's case all seemed serene.

Fay was a pretty child and Rose enjoyed sketching her, though the sessions were necessarily short. In between times she wrote careful letters, vetted with majestic censure by her mother, to Georgina, to Harry and Guy Morton, to Sara, to anyone who wrote to her in sympathy. Charlotte and Maud both wrote hoping Rose would feel better soon and there was even a note in careful copperplate from Annie, saying how sorry she was about 'Miss Rose's poor young man'. The rest of the time was spent avoiding company, and particularly Edward's. She knew arrangements were being made, letters written, but wanted no part in them. All she wanted was the strength to bring to Percy's memorial service the dignity and honest grief he deserved. Above all, she wanted not to disgrace him.

Afterwards, she could not remember the details, only an impression of darkness and white flowers, of black veiled hats and black crepe, black ribbons and rustling black taffeta skirts, with candles on the altar and the clear voices of the choir boys singing 'Rock of ages cleft for me'. There was sherry at Woodstock Hall and so much brave dignity and kindness that Rose was humbled and ashamed.

Neither Edward's sister nor his mother had been expected to attend and neither did. But as the carriage turned into the drive of Wychwood Claire said suddenly, 'Lady Portia! Of course. Is it not the usual time for her to travel back to Venice? Then Rose can travel with her as far as Paris – as soon as we hear what her destination is to be.'

Rose said nothing. When she had agreed to Edward's proposal she had given up all right to protest. It was Claire's affair now. Claire was once more in the ascendant and would arrange everything – as she had arranged that first trip abroad for Rose, with Georgina – and for the same reason, thought Rose with wry amusement: to keep me conveniently out of the way.

'An excellent solution,' pronounced Mrs Millard, and added grimly, 'I had thought I might have to accompany the wretched girl myself. As soon as we hear from Mademoiselle Whatsername that her blessed convent will have you,' she continued, addressing Rose, 'and I trust she will have the courtesy to reply by return of post, you, madam, will be on your way to France.'

The further off from England the nearer is to France – Then turn not pale, beloved snail, but come and join the dance. The absurd lines danced in her mind, but Percy's memorial service was still too much with her and Rose had not the spirits for flippancy. Instead, she contented herself with an obedient, 'Yes, Mamma.'

It was a small party that gathered at Victoria station to see them off: Edward and Claire, Phoebe Burgess, Mrs Millard and, as a special concession, Sara. Had Mrs Millard had her way, Rose would have departed under the blackest cloud available, but if the public explanation of an art tour to heal her broken spirits was to be even half believed, then a solicitous family farewell was essential. Lady Portia's presence, fortunately, lent particular credence to the story, especially as she had announced loudly, to Phoebe's drawing room of gentlewomen, 'Best thing to do, work. No point in moping over what can't be helped. But then that particular Millard girl is both talented and sensible. Not like some.'

Later she sought out Rose alone and said, 'Now tell me the real reason, young lady, for I don't believe you are languishing for that poor young soldier. You are not the languishing kind.'

'I'm afraid I can't tell you, Lady Portia, much as I would like to. It is not my secret. But I did promise Percy, before he died, that I would paint enough for another exhibition.'

'Humph!' She glowered her annoyance for a brief moment before shaking it off. 'No matter. None of my business. But when your so-called languishing is over, come and see me in Venice. Keep a crochety old woman company.'

'Thank you, Lady Portia. I will.'

Rose was to travel with her as far as Paris, where she was to be met by 'a cousin', one of a distant branch of mythical French cousins which Mrs Millard and Claire had thought it prudent to acquire.

Doors banged, whistles blew, children cried, flags and handker-chiefs waved, the usual commotion of the railway station washed over and around them, augmented now by the ever-present reminders of the South African war, while Rose stood in her small

375

island of calm, impervious and unmoved. Her face was a little too white, her expression a little too carefully calm, her clenched hands in their black gloves hidden in the folds of her black travelling cape, but even her mother had to admit that she played the part of a brave, sad widow to perfection. Her trunk, with Lady Portia's bulkier luggage, was in the guard's van, her travelling bag and portfolios in the luggage rack, with Lady Portia's maid on guard, her sketchpad and drawing materials for the journey ready on her seat. All that remained was to say her farewells.

'Goodbye, Rose,' said Sara, hugging her with tearful affection. 'I am sorry about Percy. But I hope you will paint lots of beautiful pictures, and feel happy again, very soon. I will write to you as soon as I hear about Girton,' she added, with the air of suppressed excitement which so irritated her mother and which had been with her ever since she had sat her classics exam, two weeks before.

'Yes, do,' said Rose and added, teasing, 'but I know what the answer will be.'

'And promise you will tell me anything you hear of Harry?' said Sara, with sudden intensity. 'And if Georgina says anything in her letters to you ...'

'I promise,' said Rose.

Her mother kissed her, coldly, on the cheek and, under cover of their token embrace, whispered, 'Remember your instructions *to the letter*, and do not breathe a word to anyone, even to Lady Portia. Is that understood?'

'Of course.' Then, because she had not meant to cause her mother, or anyone, so much pain and trouble, added, 'I am sorry, Mamma. Forgive me?'

Her mother didn't answer, but with a humph of unspecified emotion, resorted to her handkerchief.

'Goodbye, Rose dear,' said Claire, and kissed her. Then she murmured with meaningful solicitude, 'I will pray that all goes well with you. Be brave, my dear,' before turning away to wish Lady Portia 'bon voyage'.

'Goodbye,' said Edward, offering his hand. 'And God bless you.' When she took his hand and held it, a little too tight, he looked deep into her eyes and she was back in the loft of the old brewery at Wychwood, bathed in the beauty of moonlight and love. Then he loosed her hand and turned away and it was once again a dreary February morning on Victoria station.

More whistles blew, they mounted the step into the carriage and closed the door. Flags waved, the engine shuddered, and in a final flurry of waving hands and handkerchiefs and a triumphant whistle of released steam, the train laboured into motion. As before, Rose saw Edward offer Claire his arm, as before Claire looked up at him and smiled, but this time when she took his arm they both turned and waved together in farewell.

CHAPTER 7

Miss Rose Millard, Poste Restante, Paris.

My dear Rose,
By now you will be somewhere beautiful, in the peaceful countryside of France, though I am taking your mother's advice and sending this to Paris in case you change your plans. Do you remember how cross you were in Siena when Claire's letter to you was delayed, in spite of your instructions? But it was sensible of you not to plan too rigidly ahead. Freedom is essential for a painter. You will be able to wander at will, finding solace in your painting and in the gentle landscape all about you. I am glad for you and I hope your sorrow eases with the coming of spring and the promise of new life and hope everywhere.

Here in South Africa this war is far more dreadful than any of us imagined – such illness and misery and pain. It may be glorious and patriotic and right to lay down one's life for one's country, but to die in anguish in a foreign land, whether of wounds or typhoid, for a cause that is not at all plain is something different. Of course we nurses must not question, only help the sick and wounded and comfort the dying, but there are so very many of them, Rose. Guy Morton is one of my patients – wounded in the same battle which took dear Percy's life. We talk about it sometimes, he and I. He is very understanding. His wound is not serious, thank God, a clean wound in the thigh which is healing well, but others are not so fortunate and enteric fever is a worse enemy by far than any Boer farmer. There is a typhoid epidemic at Bloemfontein, but with the water supply what it is and the heat and the poor troops having marched so far on inadequate food, it was no more than to be expected. They say as many as fifty men a day fall ill of the disease and too many of them die.

I put flowers for you on Percy's grave, as I promised. Harry came with me – he got special leave, bless him – and Guy, who can walk a little way now, with a stick, and the graveyard looked so peaceful. South Africa is a beautiful country – if only the killing and the disease and the terrible, disfiguring wounds would stop.

I am so glad you can still paint, Rose. I think of you surrounded by tranquillity and beauty, painting the pictures Percy loved, and

378

believe it is the best memorial he could have. I miss you, Rose dear. I wish I could be with you, not for any second rate attempts at art on my part but merely for your company. But there is work for me here, and until this wretched war is over, here is where I must stay. Think of me sometimes, and pray for me,

Your loving friend, Georgina Woodstock.

Miss Rose Millard, Poste Restante, Paris

Dear Rose,

I had to write the moment I heard to tell you that I have been accepted by Girton College. I am so excited I could sing aloud except that Mamma would complain – and probably the neighbours, too, though perhaps not, because last week, when the news arrived that Mafeking had been relieved, the whole city went mad, including Mamma, and sang and cheered with the rest of London. Crowds paraded the streets with placards and makeshift banners and when Annie ran out into the street to join them, shouting Hurray *and* Rule Brittania *Mamma made no attempt to stop her. She even stood on the doorstep herself and cheered. There now. Can you credit it? I cheered, too, though privately, in my heart, for perhaps now the war will soon be over and Harry will come home. I know now how you felt when that news vendor shouted his callous offerings and I dread to open the page at the casualty lists lest Harry's name is there. But I must put aside anxiety and work harder than ever so that when I go to Cambridge in the autumn I will not disgrace either myself or Miss Welsh who has chosen to allow me a place. Mamma will pay the fees. She said, 'At least it will keep you out of trouble' and that £100 a year was cheap at the price. I think she is angry with me for not encouraging that poor Fitzsimmons boy.*

Claire was dampening, of course, and said I was turning into a regular blue-stocking. She meant it as an insult. She has been very smug lately and tries to manage everybody for their own good. Or should that be for 'his' own good. Or perhaps even 'her'? I must take particular care with grammar, now that I am to be a university student. I am so happy and excited that I refuse to let Claire's attitude deflate me. Do you remember the Rule and how you told me to pretend to go along with whatever Claire said – and to take no notice? It is very sensible advice which I intend to follow.

Dear Rose, I hope you are growing happier. Everyone says that time heals (including Maud, who, be warned, is working you an improving sampler to that effect!) and perhaps it is true. I hope so, for your sake. As for me, I am so blissfully excited that I can scarcely pen the words and were it not for my daily anxiety about Harry I would be completely, absolutely happy. Your ever-loving sister, Sara. P. S. I saw Edward the other day and he asked me to send you his good wishes when next I wrote, and Claire's too, of course.

Mme Rose Millard Stanhope, Poste Restante, Tours.

Dear Rose,

I trust you are following instructions exactly and that our various arrangements for collection and re-direction of letters are still going smoothly. Claire is really an excellent organiser and you should be grateful to her for all her foresight and generosity of spirit. Not many sisters would have undertaken to do what she has undertaken to do and for no reward. I hope you appreciate it. I also hope that your health continues good. No doubt you will give us news if there should be anything of importance to tell us. You will remember the form of words that we discussed for the purpose.

Here things are much as usual. The war still dominates the news-papers, of course, and much of everyday conversation, but since General Buller's forces captured Pretoria there has been talk of an end to hostilities. Whether this is wishful thinking or informed conjecture remains to be seen. Claire is still caught up in her charitable war work and the setting up of some sort of convalescent home on the continent is a distinct possibility. Various ladies of her acquaintance, it seems, with properties abroad, have most generously put them at the disposal of any wounded officers who might benefit from time in a more clement climate than our own. The South of France is par-ticularly favoured and if necessary, Claire and possibly Edward too if he can be spared from the War Office, may well visit the continent, in late summer perhaps, to consider the idea at first hand. You will recognise the convenience of this, for all concerned.

I trust that you are working hard and that you will have much to show for your time abroad when you eventually return. As Claire rightly says, another Bond Street exhibition, in Percy's memory, would be entirely appropriate. Perhaps in the spring of next year?

Remember both Claire and I expect to hear from you at once, when you have any news to convey. Your affectionate mother, Rebecca Stanhope Millard.

Claire, always Claire, sighed Rose. But then Claire, the firstborn, had been there since before Rose was born, with her right of primogeniture and her Rule. It was the way things were.

A linnet sang in a nearby tree. The warm summer air was laced with the scent of lilac and sweet meadow grass. The river meandered slow and graceful under the convent walls and as far as the eye could see the sun-drenched, basking countryside breathed contentment under a shimmering azure sky.

Azure? Rose pondered. Cerulean? Or a porcelain whiteness tinted towards infinity with the palest lapis lazuli? She tipped her head back, under her wide straw hat, and studied her canvas with narrowed, critical eyes. A view of the river, with a bridge in the distance and the spire of the village church, and in the foreground a tree, its trunk dappled with a dozen shades of ochre and soft browns, its leaves canopying the grass with a lacework of dancing shadows. She was experimenting with a new technique involving thicker pigment and a palette knife and knew that the result was good. But she must remember to ask the nuns to buy her more burnt umber the next time someone went to town, and also cadmium red. It would not do to run out. But even the thought of that possible calamity could not long ruffle the calm surface of her peace.

For it was peaceful by the river. On her left, where the river curved into shimmering distance, a boat, flat-bottomed, lay motionless on the polished water, its occupant no more than a shapeless straw hat and a trailing fishing line. Reflections quivered in the green-tinted water-mirror, inverted and perfect. Underfoot were speedwell and clover flowers, daisies, buttercups, a profusion of wild flowers patterning the meadow grass and behind her, the cool verdure of summer trees. The sun was almost directly overhead. A bell in the clock-tower struck the half-hour and when the resonance faded, Rose heard birdsong suddenly loud in the trees behind her. To her right, further down the river, under the convent wall, ivy trailed slender fingers in the water and a clutch of willows dutifully wept.

A bee droned loud in a weighted clover-blossom at her feet and, leaning slightly sideways on her folding canvas stool in order that her eyes could negotiate her own bulk, Rose watched it as it systematically robbed each tiny floweret of its treasure. It was early July and she was very pregnant. If the child is not born soon, she thought, even my mother will suspect it is not Percy's. Who ever heard of a ten-month child? But her anxiety was no more than fleeting, of no real account.

For her months of seclusion in the guest wing of the convent – rooms set aside for gentlewomen seeking, for various reasons, a retreat from the eyes, or troubles, of the world – had bred in Rose a strange contentment. The unchanging ritual of the *religieuses*,

381

from dawn to Compline, the regular bells, the plainsong, the columns of silent, rosaried figures, heads dutifully bent in prayer, all soothed and steadied her in a way she would not have thought possible. And, because her child was not to be adopted, but to be collected, with herself, when the time came, by the same loving relatives who paid most generously every month for Madame Stanhope's care, she was not regarded as a sinner in need of rescue, as were some of her fellow guests in retreat, and as might otherwise have been the case.

For Rose, following her mother's instructions, had donned a wedding ring in Paris the moment the Blue Train carried Lady Portia safely on her way to Venice, and had added her mother's maiden name to her own. As the widowed Madame Stanhope, she had been met by a lay sister of the convent (not, as she had feared, by the dread Mademoiselle herself) and had been escorted, with gentleness and sympathy, to Mademoiselle's old convent, in the heart of Touraine.

From the first, the landscape had captivated Rose. She reflected that Mademoiselle must indeed be as hard-hearted and grasping as they had thought her to be to turn her back on such beauty for the pursuit of mere money. The great fields, the long rows of poplars, the dark roofs and creamy walls of the buildings enchanted her, with the woods and meadows and sleepy rivers, the fairy tale chateaux, and above all the glorious Loire sky, serene or turbulent, benign or lowering, but always breathtaking, like the canvas of a celestial artist divinely inspired. She had begun sketching on her very first day and had continued ever since, rising at dawn to walk in the dew-drenched gardens and watch the colours change under the strengthening sun, taking her easel and paints to the river bank or the stables, or to the glorious avenues of plane trees, their trunks like the delicate pillars of some sylvan nave. She hired a carrier, until the nuns forbade it for the infant's sake, to take her to the chateaux at Amboise and Azay-le-Rideau and the glorious elegance of Chenonceaux. Then, when her girth made such excursions unwise, she practised portraiture, using as her models her fellow *retraitées*, or those of the villagers who worked in the convent grounds. And, astonishingly, against all expectation, Rose was happy.

It was a strange happiness, a little rarified, a little too pure in that it encompassed nothing of human relationships – merely Rose, her canvasses, sketch pads and paints, and the endlessly beguiling subject-matter which surrounded and enclosed her wherever she looked. Sometimes it contented her merely to look. Then, she

382

strolled in the convent grounds, past the neat clipped hedges of the herb garden, the rows of bee-hives, the scented lilac trees and the tumbling profusion of wisteria, cascading like Brussels lace over the sun-warmed stone of the south wall. Or she walked at first light in the woods, sun-laced, dew-deep, and threaded with living shadows. At first, she had waited for memories of that other wood, at Wychwood, to crowd in and catch her throat with grief. But as the weeks passed, the grief faded and there was only the benison of memory, bitter-sweet perhaps, but sweet nonetheless. She learnt to absorb and transmute all emotion into the creative energy she brought to her painting, and gradually she lost her widow's look and thrived. And her painting grew better and better.

She had told Lady Portia that she must fulfil a promise to Percy and mount another exhibition. At the time, it was merely words, but now, as she saw her collection of canvasses grow and knew that they were good, the idea became a fixed ambition and a steady goal.

As for her child, she had decided at the beginning that her only safeguard against heartbreak was to think of it not as hers, but as Claire's. The child was for Claire and Edward. Her body was merely the means to that end. She had taken Claire's husband when she had no right, and it was only fair that she should do penance. Edward's child for Edward's wife. It was a just reparation. And when the child was born, her body would be her own again and she would be free to go wherever she chose. If, at the back of her mind, a small, despairing voice cried 'What if I love the child?' she ignored it and closed her ears. Love did not, *must* not, enter into it. She had agreed with Edward. And if, said a subversive whisper, if I change my mind, I can always keep it myself, love and care for it in my studio, strap it to my back like the peasants do and take it everywhere with me ... except that that was no life for Edward's child, and she had promised.

The bee lifted and lumbered off into the grasses, in search of further depredation and Rose resumed her tranquil contemplation of the river. Soon it would be time to return to the convent, for lunch and the afternoon siesta. Once, Rose would have ignored such a routine and painted on, impervious. But now, with her time so close, it would be unwise. Besides, bed in the somnolent, sun-drenched afternoons was increasingly welcome.

There were letters for her when she reached her room – a simple, high-ceilinged room with whitewashed walls, plain furniture, a crucifix of dark wood, and a faded blue counterpane on the narrow bed – where, when the time came, she would give birth to the child that she must give to Claire. The two, tall windows overlooked the river and the shimmering reflection of the water shone again from the whitewashed walls so that they seemed to quiver in the afternoon sunlight. Someone had put fresh flowers in the vase on her writing table. Tea-roses, sweet-smelling and luxuriant. With sudden vividness, Rose remembered that sun-baked garden in Dieppe – was it only six years ago? – when they had posed with Papa for a family photograph. There had been tea-roses then, with the same sweet perfume, heady on the summer air. And later, when they went inside, Edward Rivers had been on the hotel terrace. . . .

Rose stood motionless, lost in memory, while the stillness and solitude gathered around her. Then at last, with a small shake of the head, she moved. There were letters on the writing table, and, she noticed with surprise, a small parcel. One letter from her mother, another from Claire, and the packet . . . She studied the handwriting for a long moment before reaching for her paper-knife to ease open the seal. Inside there was a small book of poems by Ernest Dowson, in a soft leather binding. She did not need the ribbon marker, or the soft pencil mark in the margin, to guide her to the words. *They are not long, the days of wine and roses . . .*

A slip of paper fell from the leaves of the book and fluttered gently to her feet. She could read the words, in Edward's handwriting, from where she stood: *Be brave, my dearest. You are always in my thoughts.*

Dear Edward. He had counted the days and had risked a last indiscretion, for her sake. She bent to pick up the incriminating, precious note, and as she straightened, felt the first warning pang. . . .